THEIR FAVORITE HORROR STORIES

"I thought then and I think now that 'Sweets to the ~~~~~' has one of the most chilling sna~~~~~
—Stephen King on "Sw~~~

"Certainly no writer of f~~~ me more childhood nigh~~~
—Ramsey Campbell on ~~~~~~~~~ ~~~ous" by M.R. James

"Once you have tasted the best you are spoiled for life."
—Dennis Etchinson on "An Occurrence at Owl Creek Bridge" by Ambrose Bierce

"More than anyone else this century, Aickman was a genius of the uncanny, and in this story he exposed the mechanisms of the uncanny with subtle but remorseless imaginative precision."
—Peter Straub on "The Inner Room" by Robert Aickman

"It's scary, creepy, offbeat, and the horror is of a realistic nature—meaning no supernatural elements. Just plain old twisted meanness. And yet, it's funny."
—Joe R. Lansdale on "The Animal Fair" by Robert Bloch

"The last few paragraphs contain some of the most graphic, shocking imagery I'd ever encountered, yet the story is about more than blood and guts; it is about nothing less than the sheer inevitability of horror . . ."
—Poppy Z. Brite on "The Pattern" by Ramsey Campbell

"You are about to have that cathartic frisson of terror and awakening that once I knew on a cold night beneath the bonescraping branches. I envy you."
—Harlan Ellison on "The Human Chair" by Edogawa Rampo

More Masterful Anthologies
Brought to You by DAW:

MY FAVORITE SCIENCE FICTION STORY *Edited by Martin H. Greenberg*. Award-winning, career-changing, classic stories by such master as: Theodore Sturgeon, C. M. Kornbluth, Gordon R. Dickson, Robert Sheckley, Lester Del Rey, James Blish, and Roger Zelazny; personally selected by such modern-day greats as: Arthur C. Clarke, Anne McCaffrey, Frederik Pohl, Connie Willis, Lois McMaster Bujold, and Greg Bear. Each story is prefaced by the selector's explanation of his or her choice.

MY FAVORITE FANTASY STORY *Edited by Martin H. Greenberg*. Here are seventeen of the most memorable stores in the genre, each one personally selected by a well-known writer, and each prefaced by that writer's explanation of his or her choice. Includes stories by Charles de Lint, Jack Vance, Terry Pratchett, Poul Anderson, L. Sprague de Camp, Barbara Kingsolver, Robert Bloch, and Roger Zelazny; selected by Tanya Huff, Robert Silverberg, Morgan Llywelyn, Mickey Zucker Reichert, Katherine Kurtz, George R. R. Martin, and Stephen Donaldson.

CIVIL WAR FANTASTIC *Edited by Martin H. Greenberg*. Some of science fiction's finest take us back to this turbulent time with their own special visions of what might have been. So don your uniform, load your cap and ball rifles, raise the colors, and prepare to charge into *Civil War Fantastic* where: A mysterious old man shows a Confederate soldier how one well-placed shot can change the course of history. . . . Though he is only a horse used for children to ride on tours of Gettysburg, he can see things on the battlefield that no human was aware of. . . . General Lee is offered a guaranteed victory for the South, but can he bring himself to pay the price?

MY FAVORITE HORROR STORY

Edited by
Mike Baker
and
Martin H. Greenberg

DAW BOOKS, INC.
DONALD A. WOLLHEIM, FOUNDER
375 Hudson Street, New York, NY 10014
ELIZABETH R. WOLLHEIM
SHEILA E. GILBERT
PUBLISHERS

ACKNOWLEDGMENTS

"Sweets to the Sweet" by Robert Bloch. Copyright © 1947, renewed 1975 by Robert Bloch. Reprinted by permission of the agent for the author's Estate, Ralph Vicinanza, Ltd.

"The Father-Thing" by Phillip K. Dick. Copyright © 1954 by Phillip K. Dick. Reprinted by permission of the agent for the author's Estate, Scovil Chichak Galen Literary Agency, Inc.

"The Distributor" by Richard Matheson. Copyright © 1958 by Richard Matheson. Reprinted by permission of the agent for the author's Estate, Don Congdon Associates, Inc.

"The Colour Out of Space" by H. P. Lovecraft. Copyright © 1927 by Experimenter Publishing Company. Reprinted by permission of the agent for the author's Estate, JABberwocky Literary Agency, P.O. Box 4558, Sunnyside, NY 11104-0558.

"The Inner Room" by Robert Aickman. Copyright © 1966 by Robert Aickman. Reprinted by permission of the agent for the author's Estate, The Pimlico Agency, Inc.

"The Rats in the Walls" by H. P. Lovecraft. Copyright © 1924 by Popular Fiction Publishing Co. Reprinted by permission of the agent for the author's Estate, JABberwocky Literary Agency, P.O. Box 4558, Sunnyside, NY 11104-0558.

"The Dog Park" by Dennis Etchison. Copyright © 1993 by Dennis Etchison. Reprinted by permission of the author.

"The Animal Fair" by Robert Bloch. Copyright © 1971 by Robert Bloch. Reprinted by permission of the agent for the author's Estate, Ralph Vicinanza, Ltd.

"The Pattern" by Ramsey Campbell. Copyright © 1976 by Ramsey Campbell. First published in *Superhorror*, edited by Ramsey Campbell.

"The Human Chair" by Edogawa Rampo. Copyright © 1925 by the Charles E. Tuttle Company, Inc. of Boston, Massachusettes and Tokyo, Japan. Reprinted by permission of the Charles E. Tuttle Company, Inc.

CONTENTS

INTRODUCTION

Of the three main subgenres of popular fiction, horror is often considered the most recent to emerge as a viable literary form in its own right. Fantasy has roots stretching back thousands of years, to the cradle of civilization and beyond. Science fiction, with the aid of such luminaries as Jules Verne and H. G. Wells, was recognized in the late nineteenth century as a literature of ideas, perhaps fanciful at the time, yet still grounded in the ever-quickening advancement of technology. But until recently, horror was still viewed as an extrapolation of fantasy, just turned on its head to deal with mankind's fear.

If the tropes of the story are examined through the centuries, however, there is ample evidence that horror existed hundreds, even thousands of years ago. For example, in ancient times, cultures across the world each venerated a god of the dead or underworld. The Hindu god in particular, Nirrti, was a destructive goddess of darkness, and was associated with pain, misfortune, and death. Yum Cimil, the Mayan god of death, was often depicted with a skull head, bare ribs, and spiny projections from the vertebrae, or with bloated flesh marked with dark rings of decomposition. And what pantheon would be complete without Hades, whose attempts to woo Persephone mark him as more of a sympathetic god, but a god of the underworld nonetheless. The very beginnings of horror lie in the myths and legends mankind told itself to explain the unknown.

The Greeks in particular had their dark side. During Hercules' travels, he met Procrustes, an amiable sociopath whose only desire was to make sure travelers who rested in his home fit his bed. If they were too short, he stretched them on a rack. If they were too tall, he cut them down to size. Hercules made Procrustes' bed for him, then laid him in it, permanently. Other notables include the gorgon Medusa, a beautiful woman with snakes for hair and a gaze that turned men to stone, and the dreadful Scylla, whom Odysseus had to sail past on his way home to Greece, described as a monster with twelve feet and six heads, each with a mouth containing three rows of teeth, and a lower body composed of a pack of incessantly barking dogs. Even the creation myth of the gods themselves is rather morbid, with Chronos swallowing his children whole for fear that one of them would rise against him. His wife, Rhea, gave him a stone wrapped in cloth to gulp down instead of his seventh child, Zeus, and the rest is mythology.

The idea of horror continued into the Dark Ages. The classic Old English poem *Beowulf* had the Danish hero confronting a creature that could just as easily have sprung from the imagination of H. P. Lovecraft, the cannibalistic man-beast Grendel. And, knowing that audiences love one good scare after another, after Beowulf dispatched Grendel by tearing his arm off, the thing's mother came back for revenge. After these two, Beowulf's death at the claws of a dragon seems almost anticlimatic. The horror of the unknown is first given a tangible form, as the thing that is Grendel matches no known animal of the time.

The Middle Ages had its own real live horror to contend with: the Black Death. Responsible for wiping out approximately one-third of the European population, men and women were too busy trying to survive to think about stories of horror. Still, the notion persisted, often passed down in children's fairy tales. Rapunzel's prince leaping from the tower, only to lose his eyes to the thorns below. The Queen, jealous of Snow White's beauty, commanding her huntsman to take the girl to the forest, kill her, and deliver her heart to the Queen as proof of the deed. The tradition of scaring audiences, and the demand to be scared, was still alive and well.

This is about the time those two notorious creatures of darkness, the vampire and werewolf, first gained prominence. Both had been mentioned before, the shape-changers as early as Greek myth, but it was in Germanic and Romanian folktales that they gained immortality. However, in all legends there is a grain of truth, and nowhere was this more evident than in the conception of the vampire, which has been irrevocably linked with the Romanian count Vlad Dracul, whose habit of impaling his enemies and drinking their blood placed him in the realm of horror for eternity, and, combined with the prose of Bram Stoker, ensured that the vampire would haunt the dreams of a horrified populace for decades.

The English were the next to take up the gauntlet, with playwrights such as Christopher Marlowe writing about the pride of man and his downfall after making a deal with the devil in his famous play *Doctor Faustus*. But it was William Shakespeare who brought blood and death to the masses in his great tragedies. The twist of circumstance leading to death in *Romeo and Juliet*, and the bloodbaths that end *Hamlet* and *Macbeth* revealed the depths of evil and despair that can reside in the hearts of men and women alike. The English did not have to rely on the supernatural to cause fear, their fellow man was capable of causing enough on his own.

The seeds for modern horror were planted in the latter half of the eighteenth century, when authors such as Horace Walpole (*The Castle of Otranto*), William Beckford (*Vathek*), and Matthew Gregory Lewis (*The Monk*) created the Gothic novel, which gained prominence in the nineteenth century. The Gothic novel usually featured attractive heroines stuck in gloomy, forbidding mansions with handsomely brooding men, both of whom are menaced by some kind of evil, supernatural or otherwise. Henry James' short novel *The Turn of the Screw* and Charlotte Bronte's *Wuthering Heights* are both classic examples of the form.

In the nineteenth century, Mary Wollstonecraft Shelley (*Frankenstein*), Bram Stoker (*Dracula*), Algernon Blackwood (*Julius LeVallon*), and Edgar Allan Poe (almost any story he wrote) expanded on the traditional Gothic conventions by infusing their books with psychological insights into their characters, doing away with the simple, two-dimensional morality plays of the past by revealing their protagonists to be sometimes as flawed as the villains. Edgar Allan Poe deserves special mention for his expansion of the horror story, especially in short form, which is what he is primarily known for today. With such stories as "The Tell-Tale Heart," "The Cask of Amontillado," and "The Fall of the House of Usher," his adaptations of the Gothic romance form, he broke through the distance that previous authors had kept between the audience and their characters, making the emotions evoked by his fiction more personal and intimate. It is his fiction, more than any other, that set the foundation for modern horror.

Which brings us to the twentieth century. Compared to centuries past, when horror fiction was seen as an ugly stepchild of what society termed *real* fiction, there has been a veritable explosion of horror fiction that has endured over the decades.

As the world grew more industrialized, average people found themselves with more free time on their hands, and a wealth of new entertainment to amuse themselves with. One of these was the pulp magazine. With their often lurid covers and emphasis on hard-hitting action and fast-paced plots, the pulps flourished in the early part of the century, bringing with them a new breed of writers. Among them was a young man named Howard Phillips Lovecraft.

Lovecraft maintained that "the oldest and strongest emotion of mankind is fear, and the oldest and strongest kind of fear is that of the unknown. These facts few psychologists will dispute, and their admitted truth must establish for all time the genuineness and dignity of the weirdly horrible tales as a literary form." He has been attributed with taking the next step in horror fiction with the creation of his Cthulu mythos, the idea that supernatural events in the universe are all happening at the direction of the "Old Ones," ancient, incomprehensible monstrosities from other dimensions whose eventual plan is to enter this world and subjugate it. Practically all of his fiction dealt with this theme, and his evocative, finely-crafted stories elevated horror fiction to a new, more accessible and literary level. With the profusion of magazines such as *Amazing Stories*, *Weird Tales*, and later *The Magazine of Fantasy and Science Fiction* catering to the weird fantasy reader, writers were more than happy to give this audience what they wanted. August Derleth, Manly Wade Wellman, Robert Bloch, Henry Kuttner, Robert E. Howard, Fritz Leiber, and dozens of others rose to prominence in the first half of the twentieth century, producing stories that solidified horror's place in popular literature.

Horror fiction's fortunes rose and fell with other genre fiction, surviving the decline and eventual collapse of the slick magazine market, which was unable to survive with the advent of television and film. But there was still a core following of loyal fans who stuck by the genre, and eventually, they got their day. Or decade, as it were.

There is no doubt that horror fiction reached its highest point of acceptance and popularity in the 1970s. America, and the world in general, was living through the horrors of the war in Vietnam and the upheaval of society with the '60s counterculture revolution. The world was changing, and to many people, not for the better. The solidarity of the 1940s and '50s had been replaced by suspicion, distrust, and fragmentation. Of course, writers began to use the prevailing attitudes of the times in their own work. The publication of *Rosemary's Baby* by Ira Levin and *The Exorcist* by William Peter Blatty—both *New York Times* bestsellers—began the groundswell of what could be termed the domestic horror novel; the idea that no one is safe, no matter where you are. Evil was portrayed as so subtle and insidious that it could invade your neighborhood, your home, your bedroom, your children. All of which paved the way for the most successful horror writer of all time, Stephen King.

King's first novel, *Carrie*, wasn't a bestseller until the paperback release, which gained massive exposure and interest with the release of Brian De Palma's film version in 1976. But even then, King's gifts for storytelling were already apparent. Combining a malevolent sense of the macabre with realistic small-town settings containing everyday people that readers readily identified with, along with a healthy sense of optimism about man's ability to prevail against the forces of evil, no matter how powerful or pervasive, King's novels tapped into the growing sense of unease sweeping the nation at the time. His novels, including *Christine*, *The Shining*, *The Stand*, and *'Salem's Lot*, pitted ordinary people against evil in all of its various guises, and it was these normal people who won, although not without struggle or sacrifice. In King's work, good often has to pay a heavy price to ensure victory. His novels came along at just the right time, taking advantage of America's uncertainty about what was going on around us, tapping into that primal fear, again of the unknown, yet still letting us know it would be all right in the end.

With the increased interest in horror, authors also began reinventing the tropes of the genre. Anne Rice made it possible for her audience to sympathize with the vampire in her 1976 novel *Interview With the Vampire*. Whitley Strieber took the werewolf out of the forest and put him into the urban jungle of the city with his 1978 book *The Wolfen*.

Writers also found fertile new ground in which to stake their claims, such as Thomas Tessier's *The Nightwalker*, which dealt with the horrors of Vietnam.

With the beginnings of the 1980s, horror began suffering a severe backlash. With the rise in horror fiction came horror movies, including John Carpenter's classic *Halloween*. But as the genre grew, it degenerated from intelligently-made films into near parodies, with plot replaced by an ever-higher body count. As the movies devolved, so did the rest of the genre. There was a brief resurgence of horror in the early half of the decade, where stories filled with lengthy descriptions of gore and deviant behavior were written. They even had a name for themselves: splatterpunk. Horror had gone from the classic novels of the 1960s and 1970s, including *Psycho*, *Hell House*, *Something Wicked This Way Comes*, and many others, to pale imitations where violence and savagery were heaped on by the shovelful instead of in calculated doses. Horror audiences, weaned on the over-the-top excesses of film, wanted the same visceral thrills in their fiction, and, when they didn't get it, many abandoned the form altogether.

However dim the light of horror grows, it never fades out altogether. In the latter years of the 1990s, horror made a small comeback, at least on film. Movies which used the classic ideas of horror appeared, such as *Scream*, which reinvented horror by taking an ironic look at the entire genre, and *The Sixth Sense*, which did more for the simple ghost story using suspense, suggestion, and mere glimpses of horror than the previous two dozen ghost films before it. Stephen King combined the ghost story with the mainstream novel in his bestseller *Bag of Bones*. The fire is still there, burning, ever burning.

As we plunge into the twenty-first century, it is all too easy to look forward to what the future may hold. But, as always, we must remember who and what has come before us, laying out the framework upon which successive generations will build their own achievements. The past masters reveal their secrets upon revisiting their bodies of work, secrets which are still as effective today as they were decades ago. Especially today, in a world where there are so many choices vying for an admittedly fickle audience's attention, writers have to make their work stand out even more, and one way is to take those lessons of days past and make them work for the modern audience.

With that in mind, we gathered some of the best authors working in horror today, and asked them to choose the story that impacted them, the one piece of fiction that left an indelible imprint on them, and explain why they chose this particular story. As always, the fiction chosen varies as widely as the authors themselves. The classic master, Edgar Allan Poe, is represented here, along with modern masters such as Robert Bloch and Richard Matheson, and authors like Dennis Etchison, part of the next generation taking the genre into new territory. The stories gathered here are by no means a complete retrospective of the horror genre, but can be considered a collection of the evolution of horror, as chosen by those who know it best, the authors themselves. So keep the lights on, turn the page, and prepare to be unnerved by some of the best horror fiction doing what it does best—playing on the fears of mankind.

Bloch was the first horror writer whose work was easily available to me in paperback editions while I was growing up. Consequently, he was the first horror writer whose works I owned. Belmont Books issued his two classic Arkham House collections, *Pleasant Dreams* and *The Opener of the Way*, in about four paperback editions. Many of those stories stand out clearly in my memory, but I thought then and think now that "Sweets to the Sweet" had one of the most chilling snap endings I had ever read.

—Stephen King

SWEETS TO THE SWEET
by Robert Bloch

Irma didn't look like a witch. She had small, regular features, a peaches-and-cream complexion, blue eyes, and fair, almost ash-blonde hair. Besides, she was only eight years old.

"Why does he tease her so?" sobbed Miss Pall. "That's where she got the idea in the first place—because he calls her a little witch."

Sam Steever bulked his paunch back into the squeaky swivel chair and folded his heavy hands on his lap. His fat lawyer's mask was immobile, but he was really quite distressed.

Women like Miss Pall should never sob. The glasses wiggle, their thin noses twitch, the creasy eyelids redden, and their stringy hair becomes disarrayed.

"Please, control yourself," coaxed Sam Steever. "Perhaps if we could just talk this whole thing over sensibly—"

"I don't care!" Miss Pall sniffled. "I'm not going back there again. I can't stand it. There's nothing I can do, anyway. The man is your brother and she's your brother's child. It's not my responsibility. I've tried—"

"Of course you've tried." Sam Steever smiled benignly, as if Miss Pall were foreman of a jury. "I quite understand. But I still don't see why you are so upset, dear lady."

Miss Pall removed her spectacles and dabbed at her eyes with a floral-print handkerchief. Then she deposited the soggy ball in her purse, snapped the catch, replaced her spectacles, and sat up straight.

"Very well, Mr. Steever," she said. "I shall do my best to acquaint you with my reasons for quitting your brother's employ."

She suppressed a tardy sniff.

"I came to John Steever two years ago in response to an advertisement for a housekeeper, as you know. When I found that I was to be governess to a motherless six-year-old child, I was at first distressed. I know nothing of the care of children."

"John had a nurse the first six years," Sam Steever nodded. "You know Irma's mother died in childbirth."

"I am aware of that," said Miss Pall, primly. "Naturally, one's heart goes out to a lonely, neglected little girl. And she was so terribly lonely, Mr. Steever—if you could have seen her, moping around in the corners of that big, ugly old house—"

"I have seen her," said Sam Steever, hastily, hoping to forestall another outburst. "And I know what you've done for Irma. My brother is inclined to be thoughtless, even a bit selfish at times. He doesn't understand."

"He's cruel," declared Miss Pall, suddenly vehement. "Cruel and wicked. Even if he is your brother, I say he's no fit father for any child. When I came there, her little arms were black and blue from beatings. He used to take a belt—"

"I know. Sometimes, I think John never recovered from the shock of Mrs. Steever's death. That's why I was so pleased when you came, dear lady. I thought you might help the situation."

"I tried," Miss Pall whimpered. "You know I tried. I never raised a hand to that child in two years, though many's the time your brother has told me to punish her. 'Give the little witch a beating' he used to say. 'That's all she needs—a good thrashing.' And then she'd hide behind my back and whisper to me to protect her. But she wouldn't cry, Mr. Steever. Do you know, I've never seen her cry."

Sam Steever felt vaguely irritated and a bit bored. He wished the old hen would get on with it. So he smiled and oozed treacle. "But just what is your problem, dear lady?"

"Everything was all right when I came there. We got along just splendidly. I started to teach Irma to read—and was surprised to find that she had already mastered reading. Your brother disclaimed having taught her, but she spent hours curled up on the sofa with a book. 'Just like her,' he used to say. 'Unnatural little witch. Doesn't play with the other children. Little witch.' That's the way he kept talking. Mr. Steever. As if she were some sort of—I don't know what. And she's so sweet and quiet and pretty!

"Is it any wonder she read? I used to be that way myself when I was a girl, because—but never mind.

"Still, it was a shock that day I found her looking through the Encyclopedia Britannica. 'What are you reading, Irma?' I asked. She showed me. It was the article on Witchcraft.

"You see what morbid thoughts your brother has inculcated in her poor little head?

"I did my best. I went out and bought her some toys—she had absolutely nothing, you know; not even a doll. She didn't even know how to *play!* I tried to get her interested in some of the other little girls in the neighborhood, but it was no use. They didn't understand her and she didn't understand them. There were scenes. Children can be cruel, thoughtless. And her father wouldn't let her go to public school. I was to teach her—

"Then I brought her the modeling clay. She liked that.

She would spend hours just making faces with clay. For a child of six Irma displayed real talent.

"We made little dolls together, and I sewed clothes for them. That first year was a happy one, Mr. Steever. Particularly during those months when your brother was away in South America. But this year, when he came back—oh, I can't bear to talk about it!"

"Please," said Sam Steever. "You must understand. John is not a happy man. The loss of his wife, the decline of his import trade, and his drinking—but you know all that."

"All I know is that he hates Irma," snapped Miss Pall, suddenly. "He hates her. He wants her to be bad, so he can whip her. 'If you don't discipline the little witch, I shall,' he always says. And then he takes her upstairs and thrashes her with his belt—you must do something, Mr. Steever, or I'll go to the authorities myself."

The crazy old biddy would at that, Sam Steever thought. Remedy—more treacle. "But about Irma," he persisted.

"She's changed, too. Ever since her father returned this year. She won't play with me any more, hardly looks at me. It is as though I failed her, Mr. Steever, in not protecting her from that man. Besides—she thinks she's a witch."

Crazy. Stark, staring crazy. Sam Steever creaked upright in his chair.

"Oh, you needn't look at me like that, Mr. Steever. She'll tell you so herself—if your ever visited the house!"

He caught the reproach in her voice and assuaged it with a deprecating nod.

"She told me all right, if her father wants her to be a witch she'll be a witch. And she won't play with me, or anyone else, because witches don't play. Last Halloween she wanted me to give her a broomstick. Oh, it would be funny if it weren't so tragic. That child is losing her sanity.

"Just a few weeks ago I thought she'd changed. That's when she asked me to take her to church one Sunday. 'I want to see the baptism,' she said. Imagine that—an eight-year-old interested in baptism! Reading too much, that's what does it.

"Well, we went to church and she was as sweet as can be, wearing her new blue dress and holding my hand. I was proud of her, Mr. Steever, really proud.

"But after that, she went right back into her shell. Reading around the house, running through the yard at twilight and talking to herself.

"Perhaps it's because your brother wouldn't bring her a kitten. She was pestering him for a black cat, and he asked why, and she said, 'Because witches always have black cats.' Then he took her upstairs.

"I can't stop him, you know. He beat her again the night the power failed and we couldn't find the candles. He said she'd stolen them. Imagine that—accusing an eight-year-old child of stealing candles!

"That was the beginning of the end. Then today, when he found his hairbrush missing—"

"You say he beat her with his hairbrush?"

"Yes. She admitted having stolen it. Said she wanted it for her doll."

"But didn't you say she has no dolls?"

"She made one. At least I think she did. I've never seen it—she won't show us anything any more; won't talk to us at table, just impossible to handle her.

"But this doll she made—it's a small one, I know, because at times she carries it tucked under her arm. She talks to it and pets it, but she won't show it to me or to him. He asked her about the hairbrush and she'd said she took it for the doll.

"Your brother flew into a terrible rage—he'd been drinking in his room again all morning, oh don't think I don't know it!—and she just smiled and said he could have it now. She went over to her bureau and handed it to him.

She hadn't harmed it in the least; his hair was still in it, I noticed.

"But he snatched it up, and then he started to strike her about the shoulders with it, and he twisted her arm and then he—"

Miss Pall huddled in her chair and summoned great racking sobs from her thin chest.

Sam Steever patted her shoulder, fussing about her like an elephant over a wounded canary.

"That's all, Mr. Steever. I came right to you. I'm not even going back to that house to get my things. I can't stand any more—the way he beat her—and the way she didn't cry, just giggled and giggled and giggled—sometimes I think she is a witch—that he made her into a witch—"

Sam Steever picked up the phone. The ringing had broken the relief of silence after Miss Pall's hasty departure.

"Hello—that you, Sam?"

He recognized his brother's voice, somewhat the worse for drink.

"Yes, John."

"I suppose the old bat came running straight to you to shoot her mouth off."

"If you mean Miss Pall, I've seen her, yes."

"Pay no attention. I can explain everything."

"Do you want me to stop in? I haven't paid you a visit in months."

"Well—not right now. Got an appointment with the doctor this evening."

"Something wrong?"

"Pain in my arm. Rheumatism or something. Getting a little diathermy. But I'll call you tomorrow and we'll straighten this whole mess out."

"Right."

But John Steever did not call the next day. Along about supper time, Sam called him.

Surprisingly enough, Irma answered the phone. Her thin, squeaky little voice sounded faintly in Sam's ears.

"Daddy's upstairs sleeping. He's been sick."

"Well don't disturb him. What is it—his arm?"

"His back, now. He has to go to the doctor again in a little while."

"Tell him I'll call tomorrow, then. Uh—everything all right, Irma? I mean, don't you miss Miss Pall?"

"No. I'm glad she went away. She's stupid."

"Oh. Yes. I see. But you phone me if you want anything. And I hope your Daddy's better."

"Yes. So do I," said Irma, and then she began to giggle, and then she hung up.

There was no giggling the following afternoon when John Steeler called Sam at the office. His voice was sober—with the sharp sobriety of pain.

"Sam—for God's sake, get over here. Something's happening to me!"

"What's the trouble?"

"The pain—it's killing me! I've got to see you, quickly."

"There's a client in the office, but I'll get rid of him. Say, wait a minute. Why don't you call the doctor?"

"That quack can't help me. He gave me diathermy for my arm and yesterday he did the same thing for my back."

"Didn't it help?"

"The pain went away, yes. But it's back now. I feel— like I was being crushed. Squeezed, here in the chest. I can't breathe."

"Sounds like pleurisy. Why don't you call him?"

"It isn't pleurisy. He examined me. Said I was sound as a dollar. No, there's nothing organically wrong. And I couldn't tell him the real cause."

"Real cause?"

"Yes. The pins. The pin that little fiend is sticking into the doll she made. Into the arm, the back. And now heaven only knows how she's causing *this*."

"John, you mustn't—"

"Oh, what's the use of talking? I can't move off the bed here. She has me now. I can't go down and stop her, get hold of the doll. And nobody else would believe it. But it's the doll all right, the one she made with the candle-wax and the hair from my brush. Oh—it hurts to talk—that cursed little witch! Hurry, Sam. Promise me you'll do something—anything—get that doll from her—get that doll—"

Half an hour later, at four-thirty, Sam Steever entered his brother's house.

Irma opened the door.

It gave Sam a shock to see her standing there, smiling and unperturbed, pale blonde hair brushed immaculately back from the rosy oval of her face. She looked just like a little doll. A little doll—

"Hello, Uncle Sam."

"Hello, Irma. Your Daddy called me, did he tell you? He said he wasn't feeling well—"

"I know. But he's all right now. He's sleeping."

Something happened to Sam Steever; a drop of ice-water trickled down his spine.

"Sleeping?" he croaked. "Upstairs?"

Before she opened her mouth to answer he was bounding up the steps to the second floor, striding down the hall to John's bedroom.

John lay on the bed. He was asleep, and only asleep. Sam Steever noted the regular rise and fall of his chest as he breathed. His face was calm, relaxed.

Then the drop of ice-water evaporated, and Sam could afford to smile and murmur "Nonsense" under his breath as he turned away.

As he went downstairs he hastily improvised plans. A six-month vacation for his brother; avoid calling it a "cure." An orphanage for Irma; give her a chance to get away from this morbid old house, all those books . . .

He paused halfway down the stairs. Peering over the banister through the twilight he saw Irma on the sofa, cuddled up like a little white ball. She was talking to something she cradled in her arms, rocking it to and fro.

Then there was a doll, after all.

Sam Steever tiptoed quietly down the stairs and walked over to Irma.

"Hello," he said.

She jumped. Both arms rose to cover completely whatever it was she had been fondling. She squeezed it tightly.

Sam Steever thought of a doll being squeezed across the chest—

Irma stared up at him, her face a mask of innocence. In the half-light her face did resemble a mask. The mask of a little girl, covering—what?

"Daddy's better now, isn't he?" lisped Irma.

"Yes, much better."

"I knew he would be."

"But I'm afraid he's going to have to go away for a rest. A long rest."

A smile filtered through the mask. "Good," said Irma.

"Of course," Sam went on, "you couldn't stay here all alone. I was wondering—maybe we could send you off to school, or to some kind of a home—"

Irma giggled. "Oh, you needn't worry about me," she said. She shifted about on the sofa as Sam sat down, then sprang up quickly as he came close to her.

Her arms shifted with the movement, and Sam Steever saw a pair of tiny legs dangling down below her elbow. There were trousers on the legs, and little bits of leather for shoes.

"What's that you have, Irma?" he asked. "Is it a doll?" Slowly, he extended his pudgy hand.

She pulled back.

"You can't see it," she said.

"But I want to. Miss Pall said you made such lovely ones."

"Miss Pall is stupid. So are you. Go away."

"Please, Irma. Let me see it."

But even as he spoke, Sam Steever was staring at the top of the doll, momentarily revealed when she backed away. It was a head all right, with wisps of hair over a white face. Dusk dimmed the features, but Sam recognized the eyes, the nose, the chin—

He could keep up the pretense no longer.

"Give me that doll, Irma!" he snapped. "I know what it is. I know *who* it is—"

For an instant, the mask slipped from Irma's face, and Sam Steever stared into naked fear.

She knew. She knew he knew.

Then, just as quickly, the mask was replaced.

Irma was only a sweet, spoiled, stubborn little girl as she shook her head merrily and smiled with impish mischief in her eyes.

"Oh, Uncle Sam," she giggled. "You're so silly! Why, this isn't a *real* doll."

"What is it, then?" he muttered.

Irma giggled once more, raising the figure as she spoke. "Why, it's only—candy!" Irma said.

"Candy?"

Irma nodded. Then, very swiftly, she slipped the tiny head of the image into her mouth.

And bit it off.

There was a single piercing scream from upstairs.

As Sam Steever turned and ran up the steps, little Irma, still gravely munching, skipped out of the front door and into the night beyond.

"The Father-Thing" is so far and away my favorite horror story, I don't know how to praise it without sounding foolish. I've read it at least twenty times over the course of my life and it gets richer—and more frightening—with each reading. Philip K. Dick is my favorite SF writer not because of his concepts or his social satire but because of his characters. He's never praised enough for his people. And his people have never been more vivid than here. Dick conveys the mystery of adulthood as perceived by adolescents. These kids sense that beneath the surface of suburban tranquillity all sorts of dark activities are going on. They also sense that their parents aren't Parents at all but an individual man and woman capable of deceit and terrible secrets and sad denial of certain facts that are right in their faces. I've often wondered if the genesis for this story was Henry Kuttner's "Call Him Demon," my second favorite horror story, wherein only very young children know that there is a monster living in the house with them—disguised as their friendly uncle. A few critics have noted the similarities between "The Father Thing" and "The Invasion of The Body Snatchers" but to me they're very different pieces of work. The latter, as I read it, is a parable about smug conformity. Dick's piece is about the darkness at the top of the stairs— the real nature of our parents and ourselves.

—Ed Gorman

THE FATHER-THING
by Philip K. Dick

"Dinner's ready," commanded Mrs. Walton. "Go get your father and tell him to wash his hands. The same applies to you, young man." She carried a steaming casserole to the neatly set table. "You'll find him out in the garage."

Charles hesitated. He was only eight years old, and the problem bothering him would have confounded Hillel. "I . . ." he began uncertainly.

"What's wrong?" June Walton caught the uneasy tone in her son's voice and her matronly bosom fluttered with sudden alarm. "Isn't Ted out in the garage? For heaven's sake, he was sharpening the hedge shears a minute ago. He didn't go over to the Andersons', did he? I told him dinner was practically on the table."

"He's in the garage," Charles said. "But he's . . . talking to himself."

"Talking to himself!" Mrs. Walton removed her bright plastic apron and hung it over the doorknob. "Ted? Why, he never talks to himself. Go tell him to come in here." She poured boiling black coffee in the little blue-and-white china cups and began ladling out creamed corn. "What's wrong with you? Go tell him!"

"I don't know which of them to tell," Charles blurted out desperately. "They both look alike."

June Walton's fingers lost their hold on the aluminum pan; for a moment the creamed corn slushed dangerously. "Young man—" she began angrily, but at that moment Ted Walton came striding into the kitchen, inhaling and sniffing and rubbing his hands together.

"Ah," he cried happily. "Lamb stew."

"Beef stew," June murmured. "Ted, what were you doing out there?"

Ted threw himself down at his place and unfolded his napkin. "I got the shears sharpened like a razor. Oiled and sharpened. Better not touch them—they'll cut your hand off." He was a good-looking man in his early thirties; thick blond hair, strong arms, competent hands, square face, and flashing brown eyes. "Man, this stew looks good. Hard day at the office—Friday, you know. Stuff piles up and we have to get all the accounts out by five. Al McKinley claims the department could handle twenty percent more stuff if we organized our lunch hours; staggered them so somebody was there all the time." He beckoned Charles over. "Sit down and let's go."

Mrs. Walton served the frozen peas. "Ted," she said, as she slowly took her seat, "is there anything on your mind?"

"On my mind?" He blinked. "No, nothing unusual. Just the regular stuff. Why?"

Uneasily June Walton glanced over at her son. Charles was sitting bolt-upright at his place, face expressionless, white as chalk. He hadn't moved, hadn't unfolded his napkin or even touched his milk. A tension was in the air; she could feel it. Charles had pulled his chair away from his father's; he was huddled in a tense little bundle as far from his father as possible. His lips were moving, but she couldn't catch what he was saying.

"What is it?" she demanded, leaning toward him.

"*The other one*," Charles was muttering under his breath. "The other one came in."

"What do you mean, dear?" June Walton asked out loud. "What other one?"

Ted jerked. A strange expression flitted across his face. It vanished at once; but in the brief instant Ted Walton's face lost all familiarity. Something alien and cold gleamed out, a twisting, wriggling mass. The eyes blurred and receded, as an archaic sheen filmed over them. The ordinary look of a tired, middle-aged husband was gone.

And then it was back—or nearly back. Ted grinned and began to wolf down his stew and frozen peas and creamed corn. He laughed, stirred his coffee, kidded, and ate. But something terrible was wrong.

"The other one," Charles muttered, face white, hands beginning to tremble. Suddenly he leaped up and backed away from the table. "Get away!" he shouted. "Get out of here!"

"Hey," Ted rumbled ominously. "What's got into you?" He pointed sternly at the boy's chair. "You sit down there and eat your dinner, young man. Your mother didn't fix it for nothing."

Charles turned and ran out of the kitchen, upstairs to his

room. June Walton gasped and fluttered in dismay. "What in the world—"

Ted went on eating. His face was grim; his eyes were hard and dark. "That kid," he grated, "is going to have to learn a few things. Maybe he and I need to have a little private conference together."

Charles crouched and listened.

The father-thing was coming up the stairs, nearer and nearer. "Charles!" it shouted angrily. "Are you up there?"

He didn't answer. Soundlessly he moved back into his room and pulled the door shut. His heart was pounding heavily. The father-thing had reached the landing; in a moment it would come in his room.

He hurried to the window. He was terrified; it was already fumbling in the dark hall for the knob. He lifted the window and climbed out on the roof. With a grunt he dropped into the flower garden that ran by the front door, staggered and gasped, then leaped to his feet and ran from the light that streamed out the window, a patch of yellow in the evening darkness.

He found the garage; it loomed up ahead, a black square against the skyline. Breathing quickly, he fumbled in his pocket for his flashlight, then cautiously slid the door up and entered.

The garage was empty. The car was parked out front. To the left was his father's workbench. Hammers and saws on the wooden walls. In the back were the lawnmower, rake, shovel, hoe. A drum of kerosene. License plates nailed up everywhere. Floor was concrete and dirt; a great oil slick stained the center, tufts of weeds greasy and black in the flickering beam of the flashlight.

Just inside the door was a big trash barrel. On top of the barrel were stacks of soggy newspapers and magazines, moldy and damp. A thick stench of decay issued from them as Charles began to move them around. Spiders dropped to the cement and scampered off; he crushed them with his foot and went on looking.

The sight made him shriek. He dropped the flashlight and leaped wildly back. The garage was plunged into instant gloom. He forced himself to kneel down, and for an ageless moment, he groped in the darkness for the light, among the spiders and greasy weeds. Finally he had it again. He managed to turn the beam down into the barrel, down the well he had made by pushing back the piles of magazines.

The father-thing had stuffed it down in the very bottom of the barrel. Among the old leaves and torn-up cardboard, the rotting remains of magazines and curtains, rubbish from the attic his mother had lugged down here with the idea of burning someday. It still looked a little like his father, enough for him to recognize. He had found it—and the sight made him sick at his stomach. He hung onto the barrel and shut his eyes until finally he was able to look again. In the barrel were the remains of his father, his real father. Bits the father-thing had no use for. Bits it had discarded.

He got the rake and pushed it down to stir the remains. They were dry. They cracked and broke at the touch of the rake. They were like a discarded snake skin, flaky and crumbling, rustling at the touch. *An empty skin.* The insides were gone. The important part. This was all that remained, just the brittle, cracking skin, wadded down at the bottom of the trash barrel in a little heap. This was all the father-thing had left; it had eaten the rest. Taken the insides—and his father's place.

A sound.

He dropped the rake and hurried to the door. The father-thing was coming down the path, toward the garage. Its shoes crushed the gravel; it felt its way along uncertainly. "Charles!" it called angrily. "Are you in there? Wait'll I get my hands on you, young man!"

His mother's ample, nervous shape was outlined in the

bright doorway of the house. "Ted, please don't hurt him. He's all upset about something."

"I'm not going to hurt him," the father-thing rasped; it halted to strike a match. "I'm just going to have a little talk with him. He needs to learn better manners. Leaving the table like that and running out at night, climbing down the roof—"

Charles slipped from the garage; the glare of the match caught his moving shape, and with a bellow the father-thing lunged forward.

"Come here!"

Charles ran. He knew the ground better than the father-thing, it knew a lot, had taken a lot when it got his father's insides, but nobody knew the way like *he* did. He reached the fence, climbed it, leaped into the Andersons' yard, raced past their clothesline, down the path around the side of their house, and out on Maple Street.

He listened, crouched down and not breathing. The father-thing hadn't come after him. It had gone back. Or it was coming around the sidewalk.

He took a deep, shuddering breath. He had to keep moving. Sooner or later it would find him. He glanced right and left, made sure it wasn't watching, and then started off at a rapid dog-trot.

"What do you want?" Tony Peretti demanded belligerently. Tony was fourteen. He was sitting at the table in the oak-paneled Peretti dining room, books and pencils scattered around him, half a ham-and-peanut-butter sandwich and a Coke beside him. "You're Walton, aren't you?"

Tony Peretti had a job uncrating stoves and refrigerators after school at Johnson's Appliance Shop, downtown. He was big and blunt-faced. Black hair, olive skin, white teeth. A couple of times he had beaten up Charles; he had beaten up every kid in the neighborhood.

Charles twisted. "Say, Peretti. Do me a favor?"

"What do you want?" Peretti was annoyed. "You looking for a bruise?"

Gazing unhappily down, his fists clenched, Charles explained what had happened in short, mumbled words.

When he had finished, Peretti let out a low whistle. "No kidding."

"It's true." He nodded quickly. "I'll show you. Come on and I'll show you."

Peretti got slowly to his feet. "Yeah, show me. I want to see."

He got his b.b. gun from his room, and the two of them walked silently up the dark street, toward Charles's house. Neither of them said much. Peretti was deep in thought, serious and solemn-faced. Charles was still dazed; his mind was completely blank.

They turned down the Anderson driveway, cut through the backyard, climbed the fence, and lowered themselves cautiously into Charles's backyard. There was no movement. The yard was silent. The front door of the house was closed.

They peered through the living room window. The shades were down, but a narrow crack of yellow streamed out. Sitting on the couch was Mrs. Walton, sewing a cotton T-shirt. There was a sad, troubled look on her large face. She worked listlessly, without interest. Opposite her was the father-thing. Leaning back in his father's easy chair, its shoes off, reading the evening newspaper. The TV was on, playing to itself in the corner. A can of beer rested on the arm of the easy chair. The father-thing sat exactly as his own father had sat; it had learned a lot.

"Looks just like him," Peretti whispered suspiciously. "You sure you're not bulling me?"

Charles led him to the garage and showed him the trash barrel. Peretti reached his long tanned arms down and carefully pulled up the dry, flaking remains. They spread out, unfolded, until the whole figure of his father was outlined.

Peretti laid the remains on the floor and pieced broken parts back into place. The remains were colorless. Almost transparent. An amber yellow, thin as paper. Dry and utterly lifeless.

"That's all," Charles said. Tears welled up in his eyes. "That's all that's left of him. The thing has the insides."

Peretti had turned pale. Shakily he crammed the remains back in the trash barrel. "This is really something," he muttered. "You say you saw the two of them together?"

"Talking. They looked exactly alike. I ran inside." Charles wiped the tears away and sniveled; he couldn't hold it back any longer. "It ate him while I was inside. Then it came in the house. It pretended it was him. But it isn't. It killed him and ate his insides."

For a moment Peretti was silent. "I'll tell you something," he said suddenly. "I've heard about this sort of thing. It's a bad business. You have to use your head and not get scared. You're not scared, are you?"

"No," Charles managed to mutter.

"The first thing we have to do is figure out how to kill it." He rattled his b.b. gun. "I don't know if this'll work. It must be plenty tough to get hold of your father. He was a big man." Peretti considered. "Let's get out of here. It might come back. They say that's what a murderer does."

They left the garage. Peretti crouched down and peeked through the window again. Mrs. Walton had got to her feet. She was talking anxiously. Vague sounds filtered out. The father-thing threw down its newspaper. They were arguing.

"For God's sake!" the father-thing shouted. "Don't do anything stupid like that."

"Something's wrong," Mrs. Walton moaned. "Something terrible. Just let me call the hospital and see."

"Don't call anybody. He's all right. Probably up the street playing."

"He's never out this late. He never disobeys. He was terribly upset—afraid of you! I don't blame him." Her voice broke with misery. "What's wrong with you? You're so strange." She moved out of the room, into the hall. "I'm going to call some of the neighbors."

The father-thing glared after her until she had disappeared. Then a terrifying thing happened. Charles gasped; even Peretti grunted under his breath.

"Look," Charles muttered. "What—"

"Golly," Peretti said, black eyes wide.

As soon as Mrs. Walton was gone from the room, the father-thing sagged in its chair. It became limp. Its mouth fell open. Its eyes peered vacantly. Its head fell forward, like a discarded rag doll.

Peretti moved away from the window. "That's it," he whispered. "That's the whole thing."

"What is it?" Charles demanded. He was shocked and bewildered. "It looked like somebody turned off its power."

"Exactly." Peretti nodded slowly, grim and shaken. "It's controlled from outside."

Horror settled over Charles. "You mean, something outside our world?"

Peretti shook his head with disgust. "Outside the house! In the yard. You know how to find?"

"Not very well." Charles pulled his mind together. "But I know somebody who's good at finding." He forced his mind to summon the name. "Bobby Daniels."

"That little colored kid? Is he good at finding?"

"The best."

"All right," Peretti said. "Let's go get him. We have to find the thing that's outside. That made *it* in there, and keeps it going . . ."

"It's near the garage," Peretti said to the small, thin-faced Negro boy who crouched beside them in the darkness. "When it got him, he was in the garage. So look there."

"In the garage?" Daniels asked.

"*Around* the garage. Walton's already gone over the garage, inside. Look around outside. Nearby."

There was a small bed of flowers growing by the garage, and a great tangle of bamboo and discarded debris between the garage and the back of the house. The moon had come out; a cold, misty light filtered down over everything. "If we don't find it pretty soon," Daniels said, "I got to go back home. I can't stay up much later." He wasn't any older than Charles. Perhaps nine.

"All right," Peretti agreed. "Then get looking."

The three of them spread out and began to go over the ground with care. Daniels worked with incredible speed; his thin little body moved in a blur of motion as he crawled among the flowers, turned over rocks, peered under the house, separated stalks of plants, ran his expert hands over leaves and stems, in tangles of compost and weeds. No inch was missed.

Peretti halted after a short time. "I'll guard. It might be dangerous. The father-thing might come and try to stop us." He posted himself on the back step with his b.b. gun while Charles and Bobby Daniels searched. Charles worked slowly. He was tired, and his body was cold and numb. It seemed impossible, the father-thing and what had happened to his own father, his real father. But terror spurred him on; what if it happened to his mother, or to him? Or to everyone? Maybe the whole world.

"I found it!" Daniels called in a thin, high voice. "You all come around here quick!"

Peretti raised his gun and got up cautiously. Charles hurried over; he turned the flickering yellow beam of his flashlight where Daniels stood.

The Negro boy had raised a concrete stone. In the moist, rotting soil the light gleamed on a metallic body. A thin, jointed thing with endless crooked legs was digging frantically. Plated, like an ant; a red-brown bug that rapidly disappeared before their eyes. Its rows of legs scrabbled and clutched. The ground gave rapidly under it. Its wicked-looking tail twisted furiously as it struggled down the tunnel it had made.

Peretti ran into the garage and grabbed up the rake. He pinned down the tail of the bug with it. "Quick! Shoot it with the b.b. gun!"

Daniels snatched the gun and took aim. The first shot tore the tail of the bug loose. It writhed and twisted frantically; its tail dragged uselessly and some of its legs broke off. It was a foot long, like a great millipede. It struggled desperately to escape down its hole.

"Shoot again," Peretti ordered.

Daniels fumbled with the gun. The bug slithered and hissed. Its head jerked back and forth; it twisted and bit at the rake holding it down. Its wicked specks of eyes gleamed with hatred. For a moment it struck futilely at the rake; then abruptly, without warning, it thrashed in a frantic convulsion that made them all draw away in fear.

Something buzzed through Charles's brain. A loud humming, metallic and harsh, a billion metal wires dancing and vibrating at once. He was tossed about violently by the force; the banging crash of metal made him deaf and confused. He stumbled to his feet and backed off; the others were doing the same, white-faced and shaken.

"If we can't kill it with the gun," Peretti gasped, "we can drown it. Or burn it. Or stick a pin through its brain." He fought to hold onto the rake, to keep the bug pinned down.

"I have a jar of formaldehyde," Daniels muttered. His fingers fumbled nervously with the b.b. gun. "How do this thing work? I can't seem to—"

Charles grabbed the gun from him. "I'll kill it." He squatted down, one eye to the sight, and gripped the trigger. The bug lashed and struggled. Its force-field hammered in his ears, but he hung onto the gun. His finger tightened . . .

"All right, Charles," the father-thing said. Powerful fin-

gers gripped him, a paralyzing pressure around his wrists.
The gun fell to the ground as he struggled futilely. The
father-thing shoved against Peretti. The boy leaped away
and the bug, free of the rake, slithered triumphantly down
its tunnel.

"You have a spanking coming, Charles," the father-thing
droned on. "What got into you? Your poor mother's out of
her mind with worry."

It had been there, hiding in the shadows. Crouched in
the darkness watching them. Its calm, emotionless voice, a
dreadful parody of his father's, rumbled close to his ear as
it pulled him relentlessly toward the garage. Its cold breath
blew in his face, an icy-sweet odor, like decaying soil. Its
strength was immense; there was nothing he could do.

"Don't fight me," it said calmly. "Come along, into the
garage. This is for your own good. I know best, Charles."

"Did you find him?" his mother called anxiously, opening the back door.

"Yes, I found him."

"What are you going to do?"

"A little spanking." The father-thing pushed up the garage
door. "In the garage." In the half-light a faint smile, humorless and utterly without emotion, touched its lips. "You
go back in the living room, June. I'll take care of this. It's
more in my line. You never did like punishing him."

The back door reluctantly closed. As the light cut off,
Peretti bent down and groped for the b.b. gun. The father-
thing instantly froze.

"Go on home, boys," it rasped.

Peretti stood undecided, gripping the b.b. gun.

"Get going," the father-thing repeated. "Put down that
toy and get out of here." It moved slowly toward Peretti,
gripping Charles with one hand, reaching toward Peretti
with the other. "No b.b. guns allowed in town, sonny. Your
father know you have that? There's a city ordinance. I think
you better give me that before—"

Peretti shot it in the eye.

The father-thing grunted and pawed at its ruined eye. Abruptly it slashed out at Peretti. Peretti moved down the driveway, trying to cock the gun. The father-thing lunged. Its powerful fingers snatched the gun from Peretti's hands. Silently the father-thing mashed the gun against the wall of the house.

Charles broke away and ran numbly off. Where could he hide? It was between him and the house. Already, it was coming back toward him, a black shape creeping carefully, peering into the darkness, trying to make him out. Charles retreated. If there were only some place he could hide . . .

The bamboo.

He crept quickly into the bamboo. The stalks were huge and old. They closed after him with a faint rustle. The father-thing was fumbling in its pocket; it lit a match, then the whole pack flared up. "Charles," it said, "I know you're here, someplace. There's no use hiding. You're only making it more difficult."

His heart hammering, Charles crouched among the bamboo. Here, debris and filth rotted. Weeds, garbage, papers, boxes, old clothing, boards, tin cans, bottles. Spiders and salamanders squirmed around him. The bamboo swayed with the night wind. Insects and filth.

And something else.

A shape, a silent, unmoving shape that grew up from the mound of filth like some nocturnal mushroom. A white column, a pulpy mass that glistened moistly in the moonlight. Webs covered it, a moldy cocoon. It had vague arms and legs. An indistinct half-shaped head. As yet, the features hadn't formed. But he could tell what it was.

A mother-thing. Growing here in the filth and dampness, between the garage and the house. Behind the towering bamboo.

It was almost ready. Another few days and it would reach maturity. It was a larva, white and soft and pulpy. But the sun would dry and warm it. Harden its shell. Turn it dark and strong. It would emerge from its cocoon, and one day when his mother came by the garage . . .

Behind the mother-thing were other pulpy white larvae, recently laid by the bug. Small. Just coming into existence. He could see where the father-thing had broken off; the place where it had grown. It had matured here. And in the garage, his father had met it.

Charles began to move numbly away, past the rotting boards, the filth and debris, the pulpy mushroom larvae. Weakly he reached out to take hold of the fence—and scrambled back.

Another one. Another larva. He hadn't seen this one, at first. It wasn't white. It had already turned dark. The web, the pulpy softness, the moistness, were gone. It was ready. It stirred a little, moved its arm feebly.

The Charles-thing.

The bamboo separated, and the father-thing's hand clamped firmly around the boy's wrist. "You stay right here," it said. "This is exactly the place for you. Don't move." With its other hand it tore at the remains of the cocoon binding the Charles-thing. "I'll help it out—it's still a little weak."

The last shred of moist gray was stripped back, and the Charles-thing tottered out. It floundered uncertainly, as the father-thing cleared a path for it toward Charles.

"This way," the father-thing grunted. "I'll hold him for you. When you're fed you'll be stronger."

The Charles-thing's mouth opened and closed. It reached greedily toward Charles. The boy struggled wildly, but the father-thing's immense hand held him down.

"Stop that, young man," the father-thing commanded. "It'll be a lot easier for you if you—"

It screamed and convulsed. It let go of Charles and staggered back. Its body twitched violently. It crashed against the garage, limbs jerking. For a time it rolled and flopped in a dance of agony. It whimpered, moaned, tried to crawl away. Gradually it became quiet. The Charles-thing settled down in a silent heap. It lay stupidly among the bamboo and rotting debris, body slack, face empty and blank.

At last the father-thing ceased to stir. There was only the faint rustle of the bamboo in the night wind.

Charles got up awkwardly. He stepped down onto the cement driveway. Peretti and Daniels approached, wide-eyed and cautious. "Don't go near it," Daniels ordered sharply. "It ain't dead yet. Takes a little while."

"What did you do?" Charles muttered.

Daniels set down the drum of kerosene with a gasp of relief. "Found this in the garage. We Daniels always used kerosene on our mosquitoes, back in Virginia."

"Daniels poured kerosene down the bug's tunnel," Peretti explained, still awed. "It was his idea."

Daniels kicked cautiously at the contorted body of the father-thing. "It's dead, now. Died as soon as the bug died."

"I guess the others'll die too," Peretti said. He pushed aside the bamboo to examine the larvae growing here and there among the debris. The Charles-thing didn't move at all, as Peretti jabbed the end of a stick into its chest. "This one's dead."

"We better make sure," Daniels said grimly. He picked up the heavy drum of kerosene and lugged it to the edge of the bamboo. "It dropped some matches in the driveway. You get them, Peretti."

They looked at each other.

"Sure," Peretti said softly.

"We better turn on the hose," Charles said. "To make sure it doesn't spread."

"Let's get going," Peretti said impatiently. He was already moving off. Charles quickly followed him and they began searching for the matches, in the moonlit darkness.

It's a rare story that won't go away. Most are forgotten as soon as you turn the page; some linger for a while, then join their brethren in the void. But every so often you encounter one with a special, mysterious quality that encodes it into you synapses, making it a part of you. We all have our own set of special stories. Here's one of mine.

But first, a little background. I was thirteen when I decided to write horror fiction. That was in 1959—a banner year for me. I discovered Lovecraft in Donald A. Wollheim's *The Macabre Reader*, and then went out and bought everything good ol' H. P. had in print. When I exhausted him, I started in on the rest of the old masters: Bloch, Howard, Derleth, Long, Hodgson, Leiber, and whoever else I could find. The reading exacerbated a lifelong writing itch, one I'd started scratching in second grade. Now I began to believe I could write this stuff. Not at age thirteen, but later on. I could do it. I *would* do it. But for now, I'd keep reading.

When I ran through everything overtly horrific in print, I started on the Alfred Hitchcock collections. And so in that same year, in *13 More Stories They Wouldn't Let Me Do on TV*, I came across Ray Bradbury's "The October Game," which left me gasping and convinced me I had to write horror fiction. I *had* to do to other people what Ray Bradbury had just done to me.

Here's the point to all this me-focused stuff: All along I wanted to write horror fiction; all along I was convinced I could do it. No question about it: "Someday I'll do this."

Then, two years later I picked up a paperback called *Shock* by Richard Matheson. I'd read Matheson's work before, had been deeply touched by "Born of Man and Woman," and suitably impressed by many of his other stories. Here was a guy who delivered. And *Shock* was okay. Lots of interesting stories—sf, social commentary, suspense—but not much horror.

Then I came to the last story. "The Distributor" stopped me dead. All along I'd been telling myself, "I can do this."

Now I was muttering and mumbling, "No way I can do *that.*"

I don't know how it is with other writers, but most of the time when I finish a story or novel, I may be pleased, I may even be impressed, but somewhere in the back of my mind I'm thinking, *I can do that.*

Every so often, though, you come across a piece of fiction that blows you away, not just because you've been hanging onto every word, but because when you're done you have to admit, *I couldn't do that.*

That's what makes certain stories special to me; those are the ones I admire most: the ones I lack the talent or insight or command of the language to write myself.

"The Distributor" is one of those. And now it's your turn to read it. What I have to say on the other side of the story will make a lot more sense once you've experienced "The Distributor."

—F. Paul Wilson

THE DISTRIBUTOR
by Richard Matheson

July 20

Time to move.

He'd found a small, furnished house on Sylmar Street. The Saturday morning he moved in, he went around the neighborhood introducing himself.

"Good morning," he said to the old man pruning ivy next door. "My name is Theodore Gordon. I just moved in."

The old man straightened up and shook Theodore's hand. "How do," he said. His name was Joseph Alston.

A dog came shuffling from the porch to sniff Theodore's cuffs. "He's making up his mind about you," said the old man.

"Isn't that cute?" said Theodore.

Across the street lived Inez Ferrel. She answered the door in a housecoat, a thin woman in her late thirties. Theodore apologized for disturbing her.

"Oh, that's all right," she said. She had lots of time to herself when her husband was selling on the road.

"I hope we'll be good neighbors," said Theodore.

"I'm sure we will," said Inez Ferrel. She watched him through the window as he left.

Next door, directly across from his own house, he knocked quietly because there was a *Nightworker Sleeping* sign. Dorothy Backus opened the door—a tiny, withdrawn woman in her middle thirties.

"I'm so glad to meet you," said Theodore.

Next door lived the Walter Mortons. As Theodore came up the walk, he heard Bianca Morton talking loudly to her son, Walter, Jr.

"You are not old enough to stay out till three o'clock in the morning!" she was saying. "Especially with a girl as young as Katherine McCann!"

Theodore knocked and Mr. Morton, fifty-two and bald, opened the door.

"I just moved in across the street," said Theodore, smiling at them.

Patty Jefferson let him in next door. As he talked to her Theodore could see, through the back window, her husband Arthur filling a rubber pool for their son and daughter.

"They just love that pool," said Patty, smiling.

"I bet they do," said Theodore. As he left, he noticed the vacant house next door.

Across the street from the Jeffersons lived the McCanns and their fourteen-year-old daughter Katherine. As Theodore approached the door, he heard the voice of James McCann saying, "Aah, he's nuts. Why should I take his lawn edger? Just because I borrowed his lousy mower a couple of times."

"Darling, *please*," said Faye McCann. "I've got to finish these notes in time for the Council's next meeting."

"Just because Kathy goes out with his lousy son . . ." grumbled her husband.

Theodore knocked on the door and introduced himself.

He chatted briefly with them, informing Mrs. McCann that he certainly would like to join the National Council For Christians and Jews. It was a worthy organization.

"What's your business, Gordon?" asked McCann.

"I'm in distribution," said Theodore.

Next door, two boys mowed and raked while their dog gamboled around them.

"Hello there," said Theodore. They grunted and watched him as he headed for the porch. The dog ignored him.

"I just *told* him." Henry Putnam's voice came through the living room window. "Put a coon in my department and I'm through. That's all."

"Yes, dear," said Mrs. Irma Putnam.

Theodore's knock was answered by the undershirted Mr. Putnam. His wife was lying on the sofa. Her heart, explained Mr. Putnam.

"Oh, I'm sorry," Theodore said.

In the last house lived the Gorses.

"I just moved in next door," said Theodore. He shook Eleanor Gorse's lean hand and she told him that her father was at work.

"Is that him?" asked Theodore, pointing at the portrait of a stony-faced old man that hung above a mantel crowded with religious objects.

"Yes," said Eleanor, thirty-four and ugly.

"Well, I hope we'll be good neighbors," Theodore said.

That afternoon, he went to his new office and set up the darkroom.

July 23

That morning, before he left for the office, he checked the telephone directory and jotted down four numbers. He dialed the first.

"Would you please send a cab to 12057 Sylmar Street?" he said. "Thank you."

He dialed the second number. "Would you please send
a repairman to my house," he said. "I don't get any picture. I live at 12070 Sylmar Street."

He dialed the third number. "I'd like to run this ad in
Sunday's edition," he said. "1957 Ford. Perfect Condition.
789 dollars. That's right, 789. The number is DA-4-7408."

He made the fourth call and set up an afternoon appointment with Mr. Jeremiah Osborne. Then he stood by
the living room window until the taxicab stopped in front
of the Backus house.

As he was driving off, a television repair truck passed
him. He looked back and saw it stop in front of Henry Putnam's house.

Dear Sirs, he typed in the office later, *Please send me
ten booklets for which I enclose twenty dollars in payment.*
He put down the name and address.

The envelope dropped into the OUT box.

July 27

When Inez Ferrel left her house that evening, Theodore
followed in his car. Downtown, Mrs. Ferrel got off the bus
and went into a bar called the Irish Lantern. Parking, Theodore
entered the bar cautiously and slipped into a shadowy booth.

Inez Ferrel was at the back of the room perched on a
bar stool. She'd taken off her jacket to reveal a clinging
yellow sweater. Theodore ran his gaze across the studied
exposition of her bust.

At length, a man accosted her and spoke and laughed
and spent a modicum of time with her. Theodore watched
them exit, arm in arm. Paying for his coffee, he followed.
It was a short walk; Mrs. Ferrel and the man entered a hotel
on the next block.

Theodore drove home, whistling.

The next morning, when Eleanor Gorse and her father
had left with Mrs. Backus, Theodore followed.

He met them in the church lobby when the service was over. Wasn't it a wonderful coincidence, he said, that he, too, was a Baptist? And he shook the indurate hand of Donald Gorse.

As they walked into the sunshine, Theodore asked them if they wouldn't share his Sunday dinner with him. Mrs. Backus smiled faintly and murmured something about her husband. Donald Gorse looked doubtful.

"Oh, please," begged Theodore. "Make a lonely widower happy."

"Widower," tasted Mr. Gorse.

Theodore hung his head. "These many years," he said. "Pneumonia."

"Been a Baptist long?" asked Mr. Gorse.

"Since birth," said Theodore with fervor. "It's been my only solace."

For dinner he served lamb chops, peas and baked potatoes. For dessert, apple cobbler and coffee.

"I'm so pleased you'd share my humble food," he said. "This is, truly, loving thy neighbor as thyself." He smiled at Eleanor who returned it stiffly.

That evening, as darkness fell, Theodore took a stroll. As he passed the McCann house, he heard the telephone ringing, then James McCann shouting, "It's a *mistake*, damn it! Why in the lousy hell should I sell a '57 Ford for 789 bucks!"

The phone slammed down. "God *damn!*" howled James McCann.

"Darling, please be *tolerant!*" begged his wife.

The telephone rang again.

Theodore moved on.

August 1

At exactly two-fifteen A.M. Theodore slipped outside, pulled up one of Joseph Alston's longest ivy plants and left it on the sidewalk.

In the morning, as he left the house, he saw Walter Morton, Jr., heading for the McCann house with a blanket, a towel and a portable radio. The old man was picking up his ivy.

"Was it pulled up?" asked Theodore.

Joseph Alston grunted.

"So *that* was it," said Theodore.

"*What?*" the old man looked up.

"Last night," said Theodore, "I heard some noise out here. I looked out and saw a couple of boys."

"You seen their faces?" asked Alston, his face hardening.

"No, it was too dark," said Theodore. "But I'd say they were—oh, about the age of the Putnam boys. Not that it was them, of course."

Joe Alston nodded slowly, looking up the street.

Theodore drove up to the boulevard and parked. Twenty minutes later, Walter Morton, Jr., and Katherine McCann boarded a bus.

At the beach, Theodore sat a few yards behind them.

"That Mack is a character," he heard Walter Morton say. "He gets the urge, he drives to Tijuana; just for kicks."

In a while Morton and the girl ran into the ocean, laughing. Theodore stood and walked to a telephone booth.

"I'd like to have a swimming pool installed in my back yard next week," he said. He gave the details.

Back on the beach he sat patiently until Walter Morton and the girl were lying in each other's arms. Then, at specific moments, he pressed a shutter hidden in his palm. This done, he returned to his car, buttoning his shirt front over the tiny lens. On his way to the office, he stopped at a hardware store to buy a brush and a can of black paint.

He spent the afternoon printing the pictures. He made them appear as if they had been taken at night and as if the young couple had been engaged in something else.

The envelope dropped softly into the OUT box.

August 5

The street was silent and deserted. Tennis shoes soundless on the paving, Theodore moved across the street.

He found the Morton's lawn mower in the backyard. Lifting it quietly, he carried it back across the street to the McCann garage. After carefully raising the door, he slid the mower behind the work bench. The envelope of photographs he put in a drawer behind a box of nails.

Returning to his house then, he phoned James McCann and, muffledly, asked if the Ford was still for sale.

In the morning, the mailman placed a bulky envelope on the Gorses' porch. Eleanor Gorse emerged and opened it, sliding out one of the booklets. Theodore watched the furtive look she cast about, the rising of dark color in her cheeks.

As he was mowing the lawn that evening he saw Walter Morton, Sr., march across the street to where James McCann was trimming bushes. He heard them talking loudly. Finally, they went into McCann's garage from which Morton emerged pushing his lawn mower and making no reply to McCann's angry protests.

Across the street from McCann, Arthur Jefferson was just getting home from work. The two Putnam boys were riding their bicycles, their dog racing around them.

Now, across from where Theodore stood, a door slammed. He turned his head and watched Mr. Backus, in work clothes, storming to his car, muttering disgustedly, "A *swimming pool!*" Theodore looked to the next house and saw Inez Ferrel moving in her living room.

He smiled and mowed along the side of his house, glancing into Eleanor Gorse's bedroom. She was sitting with her back to him, reading something. When she heard the clatter of his mower she stood and left the bedroom, pushing the bulky envelope into a bureau drawer.

August 15

Henry Putnam answered the door.

"Good evening," said Theodore. "I hope I'm not intruding."

"Just chatting in the den with Irma's folks," said Putnam. "They're drivin' to New York in the mornin'."

"Oh? Well, I'll only be a moment." Theodore held out a pair of BB guns. "A plant I distribute for was getting rid of these," he said. "I thought your boys might like them."

"Well, *sure*," said Putnam. He started for the den to get his sons.

While the older man was gone, Theodore picked up a couple of matchbooks whose covers read *Putnam's Wines and Liquors*. He slipped them into his pocket before the boys were led in to thank him.

"Mighty nice of you, Gordon," said Putnam at the door. "Sure appreciate it."

"My pleasure," said Theodore.

Walking home, he set the clock-radio for three-fifteen and lay down. When the music began, he moved outside on silent feet and tore up forty-seven ivy plants, strewing them over Alston's sidewalk.

"Oh, *no*," he said to Alston in the morning. He shook his head, appalled.

Joseph Alston didn't speak. He glanced down the block with hating eyes.

"Here, let me help you," Theodore said. The old man shook his head but Theodore insisted. Driving to the nearest nursery he brought back two sacks of peat moss, then squatted by Alston's side to help him replant.

"You hear anything last night?" the old man asked.

"You think it was those boys again?" asked Theodore, open-mouthed.

"Ain't sayin'," Alston said.

Later, Theodore drove downtown and bought a dozen postcard photographs. He took them to the office.

Dear Walt, he printed crudely on the back of one, *Got these here in Tijuana. Hot enough for you?* In addressing the envelope, he failed to add *Jr.* to *Mr. Walter Morton.*

Into the OUT box.

August 23

"Mrs. Ferrel!"

She shuddered on the bar stool. "Why, Mister—"

"Gordon," he provided, smiling. "How nice to see you again."

"Yes." She pressed together lips that trembled.

"You come here often?" Theodore asked.

"Oh, no, *never*," Inez Ferrel blurted. "I'm—just supposed to meet a friend here tonight. A *girl* friend."

"Oh, I see," said Theodore. "Well, may a lonely widower keep you company until she comes?"

"Why . . ." Mrs. Ferrel shrugged. "I guess." Her lips were painted brightly red against the alabaster of her skin. The sweater clung adhesively to the hoisted jut of her breasts.

After a while, when Mrs. Ferrel's friend didn't show up, they slid into a darkened booth. There, Theodore used Mrs. Ferrel's powder room retreat to slip a pale and tasteless powder in her drink. On her return she swallowed this and, in minutes, grew stupefied. She smiled at Theodore.

"I like you, Misser Gor'n," she confessed. The words crawled viscidly across her lolling tongue.

Shortly thereafter, he led her, stumbling and giggling, to his car and drove her to a motel. Inside the room, he helped her strip to stockings, garter belt and shoes and, while she posed with drugged complacency, Theodore took flashbulb pictures.

After she collapsed at two A.M. Theodore dressed her and drove her home. He stretched her fully dressed across her bed. After that he went outside and poured concentrated weed killer on Alston's replanted ivy.

Back in the house he dialed the Jeffersons' number.

"Yes?" said Arthur Jefferson irritably.

"*Get out of this neighborhood or you'll be sorry,*" whispered Theodore, then hung up.

In the morning he walked to Mrs. Ferrel's house and rang the bell.

"Hello," he said politely. "Are you feeling better?"

She stared at him blankly while he explained how she'd gotten violently ill the night before and he'd taken her home from the bar. "I do hope you're feeling better," he concluded.

"Yes," she said, confusedly, "I'm—all right."

As he left her house he saw a red-faced James McCann approaching the Morton house, an envelope in his hand. Beside him walked a distraught Mrs. McCann.

"We must be *tolerant,* Jim," Theodore heard her say.

August 31

At two-fifteen A.M. Theodore took the brush and the can of paint and went outside.

Walking to the Jefferson house, he set the can down and painted, jaggedly, across the door—NIGGER!

Then he moved across the street allowing an occasional drip of paint. He left the can under Henry Putnam's back porch, accidentally upsetting the dog's plate. Fortunately, the Putnams' dog slept indoors.

Later, he put more weed killer on Joseph Alston's ivy.

In the morning, when Donald Gorse had gone to work, he took a heavy envelope and went to see Eleanor Gorse. "Look at this," he said, sliding a pornographic booklet from the envelope. "I received this in the mail today. *Look* at it." He thrust it into her hands.

She held the booklet as if it were a spider.

"Isn't it hideous?" he said.

She made a face. "*Revolting*," she said.

"I thought I'd check with you and several others before I phoned the police," said Theodore. "Have you received any of this filth?"

Eleanor Gorse bristled. "Why should I receive them?" she demanded.

Outside, Theodore found the old man squatting by his ivy. "How are they coming?" he asked.

"They're dyin'."

Theodore looked stricken. "How can this be?" he asked.

Alston shook his head.

"Oh, this is *horrible*." Theodore turned away, clucking. As he walked to his house he saw, up the street, Arthur Jefferson cleaning off his door and, across the way, Henry Putnam watching carefully.

She was waiting on his porch.

"Mrs. McCann," said Theodore, surprised, "I'm so glad to see you."

"What I came to say may not make you so glad," she said unhappily.

"Oh?" said Theodore. They went into his house.

"There have been a lot of . . . *things* happening in this neighborhood since you moved in," said Mrs. McCann after they were seated in the living room.

"Things?" asked Theodore.

"I think you know what I mean," said Mrs. McCann. "However, this—this *bigotry* on Mr. Jefferson's door is too much, Mr. Gordon, too much."

Theodore gestured helplessly. "I don't understand."

"Please don't make it difficult," she said. "I may have to call the authorities if these things don't stop, Mr. Gordon. I hate to think of doing such a thing but—"

"*Authorities?*" Theodore looked terrified.

"None of these things happened until you moved in, Mr. Gordon," she said. "Believe me, I hate what I'm saying but I simply have no choice. The fact that none of these things has happened to you—"

She broke off startledly as a sob wracked Theodore's chest. She stared at him. "Mr. Gordon—" she began uncertainly.

"I don't know what these things are you speak of," said Theodore in a shaking voice, "but I'd *kill* myself before I harmed another, Mrs. McCann."

He looked around as if to make sure they were alone.

"I'm going to tell you something I've never told a single soul," he said. He wiped away a tear. "My name isn't Gordon," he said. "It's Gottlieb. I'm a Jew. I spent a year at Dachau."

Mrs. McCann's lips moved but she said nothing. Her face was getting red.

"I came from there a broken man,'" said Theodore. "I haven't long to live, Mrs. McCann. My wife is dead, my three children are dead. I'm all alone. I only want to live in peace—in a little place like this—among people like you. To be a neighbor, a friend . . ."

"Mr.—*Gottlieb*," she said brokenly.

After she was gone, Theodore stood silent in the living room, hands clenched whitely at his sides. Then he went into the kitchen to discipline himself.

"Good morning, Mrs. Backus," he said an hour later when the little woman answered the door, "I wonder if I might ask you some questions about our church?"

"Oh. Oh, yes." She stepped back feebly. "Won't you—come in?"

"I'll be very still so as not to wake your husband," Theodore whispered. He saw her looking at this bandaged hand. "I burned myself," he said. "Now, about the church. Oh, there's someone knocking at your back door."

"There is?"

When she'd gone into the kitchen, Theodore pulled open the hall closet door and dropped some photographs behind a pile of overshoes and garden tools. The door was shut when she returned.

"There wasn't anyone," she said.

"I could have sworn . . ." He smiled deprecatingly. He looked down at a circular bag on the floor. "Oh, does Mr. Backus bowl?"

"Wednesdays and Fridays when his shift is over," she said. "There's an all-night alley over on Western Avenue."

"I love to bowl," said Theodore.

He asked his questions about the church, then left. As he started down the path he heard loud voices from the Morton house.

"It wasn't bad enough about Katherine McCann and *those* awful pictures," shrieked Mrs. Morton. "Now this . . . *filth!*"

"But, Mom!" cried Walter, Jr.

September 14

Theodore awoke and turned the radio off. Standing, he put a small bottle of grayish powder in his pocket and slipped from the house. Reaching his destination, he sprinkled powder into the water bowl and stirred it with a finger until it dissolved.

Back in the house he scrawled four letters reading: *Arthur Jefferson is trying to pass the color line. He is my cousin and should admit he is a Negro like the rest of us. I am doing this for his own good.*

He signed the letter *John Thomas Jefferson* and addressed three of the envelopes to Donald Gorse, the Mortons and Mr. Henry Putnam.

This completed, he saw Mrs. Backus walking toward the boulevard and followed. "May I walk you?" he asked.

"Oh," she said. "All right."

"I missed your husband last night," he told her.

She glanced at him.

"I thought I'd join him bowling," Theodore said, "but I guess he was sick again."

"Sick?"

"I asked the man behind the counter at the alley and he said that Mr. Backus hadn't been coming in because he was sick."

"Oh." Mrs. Backus's voice was thinly stricken.

"Well, maybe next Friday," said Theodore.

Later, when he came back, he saw a panel truck in front of Henry Putnam's house. A man came out of the alley carrying a blanket-wrapped body which he laid in the truck. The Putnam boys were crying as they watched.

Arthur Jefferson answered the door. Theodore showed the letter to Jefferson and his wife. "It came this morning," he said.

"This is *monstrous!*" said Jefferson, reading it.

"Of *course* it is," said Theodore.

While they were talking, Jefferson looked through the window at the Putnam house across the street

September 15

Pale morning mist engulfed Sylmar Street. Theodore moved through it silently. Under the back porch of the Jeffersons' house he set fire to a box of damp papers. As it began to smolder he walked across the yard and, with a single knife stroke, slashed apart the rubber pool. He heard it pulsing water on the grass as he left. In the alley, he dropped a book of matches that read *Putnam's Wines and Liquors*.

A little after six that morning he woke to the howl of sirens and felt the small house tremble at the heavy trucks passing by. Turning on his side, he yawned, and mumbled, "Goody."

September 17

It was a paste-complexioned Dorothy Backus who answered Theodore's knock.

"May I drive you to church?" asked Theodore.

"I—I don't believe I—I'm not . . . feeling too well," stumbled Mrs. Backus.

"Oh, I'm sorry," Theodore said. He saw the edges of some photographs protruding from her apron pocket.

As he left he saw the Mortons getting in their car, Bianca wordless, both Walters ill at ease. Up the street, a police car was parked in front of Arthur Jefferson's house.

Theodore went to church with Donald Gorse who said that Eleanor was feeling ill.

"I'm so sorry," Theodore said.

That afternoon, he spent a while at the Jefferson house helping clear away the charred debris of their back porch. When he saw the slashed rubber pool he drove immediately to a drug store and bought another one.

"But they love that pool," said Theodore, when Patty Jefferson protested. "You told me so yourself."

He winked at Arthur Jefferson but Jefferson was not communicative that afternoon.

September 23

Early in the evening Theodore saw Alston's dog walking in the street. He got his BB gun and, from the bedroom window, soundlessly, fired. The dog nipped fiercely at its side and spun around. Then, whimpering, it started home.

Several minutes later, Theodore went outside and started pulling up the door to the garage. He saw the old man hurrying down his alley, the dog in his arms.

"What's wrong?" asked Theodore.

"Don't know," said Alston in a breathless, frightened voice. "He's hurt."

"Quickly!" said Theodore. "Into my car!"

He rushed Alston and the dog to the nearest veterinary, passing three stop signs and groaning when the old man held his hand up, palsiedly, and whimpered, "*Blood!*"

For three hours Theodore sat in the veterinary's waiting

room until the old man staggered forth, his face a grayish white.

"*No*," said Theodore, jumping to his feet.

He led the old man, weeping, to the car and drove him home. There, Alston said he'd rather be alone so Theodore left. Shortly afterward, the black and white police car rolled to a stop in front of Alston's house and the old man led the two officers past Theodore's house.

In a while, Theodore heard angry shouting up the street. It lasted quite a long time.

September 27

"Good evening," said Theodore. He bowed.

Eleanor Gorse nodded stiffly.

"I've brought you and your father a casserole," said Theodore, smiling, holding up a towel-wrapped dish. When she told him that her father was gone for the night, Theodore clucked and sighed as if he hadn't seen the old man drive away that afternoon.

"Well then," he said, proffering the dish, "for *you*. With my sincerest compliments."

Stepping off the porch he saw Arthur Jefferson and Henry Putnam standing under a street lamp down the block. While he watched, Arthur Jefferson struck the other man and, suddenly, they were brawling in the gutter. Theodore broke into a hurried run.

"But this is *terrible!*" he gasped, pulling the men apart.

"Stay out of this!" warned Jefferson, then, to Putnam, challenged, "You better tell me how that paint can got under your porch! The police may believe it was an accident I found that matchbook in my alley but I don't!"

"I'll tell you nothing," Putnam said, contemptuously. "*Coon.*"

"Coon! Oh, of course! You'd be the first to believe that, you stupid—!"

Five times Theodore stood between them. It wasn't until Jefferson had, accidentally, struck him on the nose that tension faded. Curtly, Jefferson apologized; then, with a murderous look at Putnam, left.

"Sorry he hit you," Putnam sympathized. "Damned boogie."

"Oh, surely you're mistaken," Theodore said, daubing at his nostrils. "Mr. Jefferson told me how afraid he was of people believing this talk. Because of the value of his two houses, you know."

"Two?" asked Putnam.

"Yes, he owns the vacant house next door to his," said Theodore. "I assumed you knew."

"*No*," said Putnam warily.

"Well, you see," said Theodore, "if people think Mr. Jefferson is a Negro, the value of his houses will go down."

"So will the values of all of them," said Putnam, glaring across the street. "That dirty, son-of-a—"

Theodore patted his shoulder. "How are your wife's parents enjoying their stay in New York?" he asked as if changing the subject.

"They're on their way back," said Putnam.

"Good," said Theodore.

He went home and read the funny papers for an hour. Then he went out.

it was a florid-faced Eleanor Gorse who opened to his knock. Her bathrobe was disarrayed, her dark eyes feverish.

"May I get my dish?" asked Theodore politely.

She grunted, stepping back jerkily. His hand, in passing, brushed on hers. She twitched away as if he'd stabbed her.

"Ah, you've eaten it all," said Theodore, noticing the tiny residue of powder on the bottom of the dish. He turned. "When will your father return?" he asked.

Her body seemed to tense. "After midnight," she muttered.

Theodore stepped to the wall switch and cut off the light. He heard her gasp in the darkness. "No," she muttered.

"Is this what you want, Eleanor?" he asked, grabbing harshly.

Her embrace was a mindless, fiery swallow. There was nothing but ovening flesh beneath her robe.

Later, when she lay snoring satedly on the kitchen floor, Theodore retrieved the camera he'd left outside the door. Drawing down the shades, he arranged Eleanor's limbs and took twelve exposures. Then he went home and washed the dish.

Before retiring, he dialed the phone.

"Western Union," he said. "I have a message for Mrs. Irma Putnam of 12070 Sylmar Street."

"That's me," she said.

"Both parents killed in auto collision this afternoon," said Theodore. "Await word regarding disposition of bodies. Chief of Police, Tulsa, Okla—"

At the other end of the line there was a strangled gasp, a thud; then Henry Putnam's cry of "Irma!" Theodore hung up.

After the ambulance had come and gone, he went outside and tore up thirty-five of Joseph Alston's ivy plants. He left, in the debris, another matchbook reading *Putnam's Wines and Liquors.*

September 28

In the morning, when Donald Gorse had gone to work, Theodore went over. Eleanor tried to shut the door on him but he pushed in.

"I want money," he said. "These are my collateral." He threw down copies of the photographs and Eleanor recoiled, gagging. "Your father will receive a set of these tonight," he said, "unless I get two hundred dollars."

"But I—!"

"*Tonight.*"

He left and drove downtown to the Jeremiah Osborne Realty office where he signed over, to Mr. George Jackson, the vacant house at 12069 Sylmar Street. He shook Mr. Jackson's hand.

"Don't you worry now," he comforted. "The people next door are Negroes too."

When he returned home, there was a police car in front of the Backus house.

"What happened?" he asked Joseph Alston who was sitting quietly on his porch.

"Mrs. Backus," said the old man lifelessly. "She tried to kill Mrs. Ferrel."

"Is that right?" said Theodore.

That night, in his office, he made his entries on page 700 of the book.

> *Mrs. Ferrel dying of knife wounds in local hospital. Mrs. Backus in jail; suspects husband of adultery. J. Alston accused of dog poisoning, probably more. Putnam boys accused of shooting Alston's dog, ruining his lawn. Mrs. Putnam dead of heart attack. Mr. Putnam being sued for property destruction. Jeffersons thought to be Negroes. McCanns and Mortons deadly enemies. Katherine McCann believed to have had relations with Walter Morton, Jr. Morton, Jr. being sent to school in Washington. Eleanor Gorse has hanged herself. Job completed.*

Time to move.

Yeah, I know. Pretty damn unsettling. First published in *Playboy* in 1957 and look what's happened to the country since. "Mr. Gordon" (or whatever his real name is) and his fellow distributors have been busy, busy, busy.

Maybe it's a little dated. What used to be scandalous is now daily fodder for today's talk shows (more evidence of Mr. Gordon's handiwork?), but change maybe fifty words, substituting incest and pedophilia—not too many people anxious to wave those flags yet—for a couple of passé taboos, and the story is right up to date.

Why did I say *I can't do that* after reading "The Distributor"? Not because I couldn't sit down and imitate it—I couldn't have *originated* it.

Did you notice the utterly flat affect? "The Distributor" is an epiphany in that sense. All horror fiction I'd read until then pulsed with vibrant emotion—rage, hate, fear, lust for revenge. "The Distributor" has none of that. And that's what makes it so horrifying.

Note Matheson's perfect pitch. The story is a parade of simple declarative sentences (hell, he uses fewer adverbs than Elmore Leonard) with only an occasional off-the-wall adjective to let us know "Mr. Gordon" is well educated. We spend the entire story in Mr. Gordon's point of view but experience no emotion; we witness only the surfaces of events. This is one of the most effective uses of minimalist technique you will ever see.

Mr. Gordon doesn't hate the residents of Sylmar Street. Nothing personal here. They're just people and this is just another town along his distribution route. It's just a job, folks.

Just a job.

But who does he work for?

That's Matheson's final coup. If he'd revealed that Mr. Gordon worked for the CIA or the KGB, or even some invented secret organization or cult, "The Distributor" would have migrated to short story limbo long ago. But he didn't. Who is behind this? Where is their home office? What is their agenda? *Why are they doing this?*

I wanted to know in 1961.

I still want to know.

—F. Paul Wilson

I'm delighted to introduce M. R. James to this anthology, but first let me mention some other tales I might have picked. I might have selected "The Colour Out of Space" or "The White People" until I discovered that Lovecraft and Machen were already represented. Still, I'm here to praise James, and I shall, because he is one of the absolute masters of the British tale of terror.

His influence alone would ensure him a place in the pantheon. As with all influential writers, his superficial traces can be found in the work of some bad ones—M. P. Dare was surely his most ludicrous literary offspring, and hardly one he would have been pleased to acknowledge—but such excellent and different contributors to the genre as L. P. Hartley, Fritz Leiber, Kingsley Amis, T. E. D. Klein, and Terry Lamsley learned from him. So did I, and in a tale called "The Guide" attempted to acknowledge my debt in full. He even appears as a character (Dr. Matthews) and tells a new story in Penelope Fitzgerald's superb novel, *The Gate of Angels*. For me, his achievement is twofold, or more accurately, his two strongest qualities are united in it. No writer better demonstrates how, at its best, the ghost story or supernatural horror story (either term fits his work) achieves its effects through the eloquence and skill of its prose style—and, I think, no writer in the field has shown greater willingness to make his tales as frightening as possible. He can convey more spectral terror in a single glancing phrase than most authors manage in a paragraph or a book.

Certainly no writer of fiction aimed mainly at adults gave me more childhood nightmares and night fears. It quickly became apparent to the shrinking short-trousered Campbell that James habitually described just enough to suggest far worse. If only there were more like him today to nourish the dark side of the imagination with a little haute cuisine! I often wonder if he acquired some of his technique from George MacDonald's *The Princess and the Goblin*, which he might well have read. Among his many memorable horrors are the sheeted spectre of "Oh, Whistle, and I'll Come to You, My Lad," the thing that crawls out of the well in "The Treasure of Abbot Thomas," the various dismaying manifestations of the powers of Count Magnus (one example of which later appeared, lit too brightly, in the film, *The Brides of Dracula*), and the unwelcome visitor mistaken for a dog in "The Diary of Mr. Poynter" (an encounter reworked with less style by Paul Suter in an early *Weird Tales* story, "Beyond the Door"). I could have chosen any of these tales, or quite a few others, by James for this book.

"A Warning to the Curious," however, continues to impress me as offering the most sustained sense of relentless menace of any of his stories. In some ways it resembles "The Familiar," his favorite ghost story by J. Sheridan Le Fanu, whose work he championed; but it is very much its own tale, particularly in its lightness of style. I hope readers new to either author will be impelled to seek out their work. A revival of their influence can do our field nothing but good. It was James who said of the *Not at Night* anthologies that they were "merely nauseating, and it is very easy to be nauseating"—a criticism many of our current writers might usefully consider, along with the following tale.

—Ramsey Campbell.

A WARNING TO THE CURIOUS
M. R. JAMES

The place on the east coast which the reader is asked to consider is Seaburgh. It is not very different now from what I remember it to have been when I was a child. Marshes intersected by dykes to the south, recalling the early chapters of *Great Expectations*; flat fields to the north, merging into heath; heath, fir woods, and, above all, gorse, inland. A long sea-front and a street: behind that a spacious church of flint, with a broad, solid western tower and a peal of six bells. How well I remember their sound on a hot Sunday in August, as our party went slowly up the white, dusty slope of road towards them, for the church stands at the top of a short, steep incline. They rang with a flat clacking sort of sound on those hot days, but when the air was softer they were mellower too. The railway ran down to its little terminus farther along the same road. There was a gay white windmill just before you came to the station, and another down near the shingle at the south end of the town, and yet others on higher ground to the north. There were cottages of bright red brick with slate roofs . . . but why do I encumber you with these commonplace details? The fact is that they come crowding to the point of the pencil when it begins to write of Seaburgh. I should like to be sure that I had allowed the right ones to get on to the paper. But I forgot. I have not quite done with the word-painting business yet.

Walk away from the sea and the town, pass the station, and turn up the road on the right. It is a sandy road, parallel with the railway, and if you follow it, it climbs to somewhat higher ground. On your left (you are now going northward) is heath, on your right (the side towards the sea) is a belt of old firs, wind-beaten, thick at the top, with the slope that old seaside trees have; seen on the sky-line from the train they would tell you in an instant, if you did not know it, that you were approaching a windy coast. Well, at the top of my little hill, a line of these firs strikes out and runs towards the sea, for there is a ridge that goes that way; and the ridge ends in a rather well-defined mound commanding the level fields of rough grass, and a little knot of fir trees crowns it. And here you may sit on a hot spring day, very well content to look at blue sea, white windmills, red cottages, bright green grass, church tower, and distant martello tower on the south.

As I have said, I began to know Seaburgh as a child; but a gap of a good many years separates my early knowledge from that which is more recent. Still it keeps its place in my affections, and any tales of it that I pick up have an interest for me. One such tale is this: it came to me in a place very remote from Seaburgh, and quite accidentally, from a man whom I had been able to oblige—enough in his opinion to justify his making me his confidant to this extent.

I know all that country more or less (he said). I used to go to Seaburgh pretty regularly for golf in the spring. I generally put up at the "Bear," with a friend—Henry Long it was, you knew him perhaps—("Slightly," I said) and we used to take a sitting-room and be very happy there. Since he died I haven't cared to go there. And I don't know that I should anyhow after the particular thing that happened on our last visit.

It was in April, 19— , we were there, and by some chance we were almost the only people in the hotel. So the ordinary public rooms were practically empty, and we were the more surprised when, after dinner, our sitting-room door opened, and a young man put his head in. We were aware of this young man. He was rather a rabbity anæmic subject—light hair and light eyes—but not unpleasing. So when he said: "I beg your pardon, is this a private room?" we did not growl and say: "Yes, it is," but Long said, or I did— no matter which: "Please come in." "Oh, may I?" he said, and seemed relieved. Of course it was obvious that he wanted company; and as he was a reasonable kind of person—not the sort to bestow his whole family history on you—we urged him to make himself at home. "I dare say you find the other rooms rather bleak," I said. Yes, he did: but it was really too good of us, and so on. That being got over, he made some pretence of reading a book. Long was playing Patience, I was writing. It became plain to me after a few minutes that this visitor of ours was in rather a state of fidgets or nerves, which communicated itself to me, and so I put away my writing and turned to at engaging him in talk.

After some remarks, which I forget, he became rather confidential. "You'll think it very odd of me" (this was the sort of way he began), "but the fact is I've had something of a shock." Well, I recommended a drink of some cheering kind, and we had it. The waiter coming in made an interruption (and I thought our young man seemed very jumpy when the door opened), but after a while he got back to his woes again. There was nobody he knew in the place, and he did happen to know who we both were (it turned out there was some common acquaintance in town), and really he did want a word of advice, if we didn't mind. Of course we both said: "By all means," or "Not at all," and Long put away his cards. And we settled down to hear what his difficulty was.

"It began," he said, "more than a week ago, when I bicycled over to Froston, only about five or six miles, to see the church; I'm very much interested in architecture, and it's got one of those pretty porches with niches and shields. I took a photograph of it, and then an old man who was tidying up in the churchyard came and asked if I'd care to look into the church. I said yes, and he produced a key and let me in. There wasn't much inside, but I told him it was a nice little church, and he kept it very clean, 'but,' I said, 'the porch is the best part of it.' We were just outside the porch then, and he said, 'Ah, yes, that is a nice porch; and do you know, sir, what's the meanin' of that coat of arms there?'

"It was the one with the three crowns, and though I'm not much of a herald, I was able to say yes, I thought it was the old arms of the kingdom of East Anglia.

" 'That's right, sir,' he said, 'and do you know the meanin' of them three crowns that's on it?'

"I said I'd no doubt it was known, but I couldn't recollect to have heard it myself.

" 'Well, then,' he said, 'for all you're a scholard, I can tell you something you don't know. Them's the three 'oly crowns what was buried in the ground near by the coast to keep the Germans from landing—ah, I can see you don't believe that. But I tell you, if it hadn't have been for one of them 'oly crowns bein' there still, them Germans would a landed here time and again, they would. Landed with their ships, and killed man, woman and child in their beds. Now then, that's the truth what I'm telling you, that is; and if you don't believe me, you ast the rector. There he comes: you ast him, I says.'

"I looked round, and there was the rector, a nice-looking old man, coming up the path; and before I could begin assuring my old man, who was getting quite excited, that I didn't disbelieve him, the rector struck in, and said: 'What's all this about, John? Good day to you, sir. Have you been looking at our little church?'

"So then there was a little talk which allowed the old man to calm down, and then the rector asked him again what was the matter.

" 'Oh,' he said, 'it warn't nothink, only I was telling this gentleman he'd ought to ast you about them 'oly crowns.'

" 'Ah, yes, to be sure,' said the rector, 'that's a very curious matter, isn't it? But I don't know whether the gentleman is interested in our old stories, eh?'

" 'Oh, he'll be interested fast enough,' says the old man, 'he'll put his confidence in what you tells him, sir; why, you known William Ager yourself, father and son too.'

"Then I put in a word to say how much I should like to hear all about it, and before many minutes I was walking up the village street with the rector, who had one or two words to say to parishioners, and then to the rectory, where he took me into his study. He had made out, on the way, that I really was capable of taking an intelligent interest in a piece of folk-lore, and not quite the ordinary tripper. So he was very willing to talk, and it is rather surprising to me that the particular legend he told me has not made its way into print before. His account of it was this: 'There has always been a belief in these parts in the three holy crowns. The old people say they were buried in different places near the coast to keep off the Danes or the French or the Germans. And they say that one of the three was dug up a long time ago, and another has disappeared by the encroaching of the sea, and one's still left doing its work, keeping off invaders. Well, now, if you have read the ordinary guides and histories of this county, you will remember perhaps that in 1687 a crown, which was said to be the crown of Redwald, King of the East Angles, was dug up at Rendlesham, and alas! alas! melted down before it was even properly described or drawn. Well, Rendlesham isn't on the coast, but it isn't so very far inland, and it's on a very important line of access. And I believe that is the crown which the people mean when they say that one has been dug up. Then on the south you don't want me to tell you where there was a Saxon royal palace which is now under the sea, eh? Well, there was the second crown, I take it. And up beyond these two, they say, lies the third.'

" 'Do they say where it is?' of course I asked.

"He said, 'Yes, indeed, they do, but they don't tell,' and his manner did not encourage me to put the obvious question. Instead of that I waited a moment, and said: 'What did the old man mean when he said you knew William Ager, as if that had something to do with the crowns?'

" 'To be sure,' he said, 'now that's another curious story. These Agers—it's a very old name in these parts, but I can't find that they were ever people of quality or big owners— these Agers say, or said, that their branch of the family were the guardians of the last crown. A certain old Nathaniel Ager was the first one I knew—I was born and brought up quite near here—and he, I believe, camped out at the place during the whole of the war of 1870. William, his son, did the same, I know, during the South African War. And young William, *his* son, who has only died fairly recently, took lodgings at the cottage nearest the spot, and I've no doubt hastened his end, for he was a consumptive, by exposure and night watching. And he was the last of that branch. It was a dreadful grief to him to think that he was the last, but he could do nothing, the only relations at all near to him were in the colonies. I wrote letters for him to them imploring them to come over on business very important to their family, but there has been no answer. So the last of the holy crowns, if it's there, has no guardian now.'

"That was what the rector told me, and you can fancy how interesting I found it. The only thing I could think of when I left him was how to hit upon the spot where the crown was supposed to be. I wish I'd left it alone.

"But there was a sort of fate in it, for as I bicycled back past the churchyard wall my eye caught a fairly new grave-stone, and on it was the name of William Ager. Of course I got off and read it. It said 'of this parish, died at Seaburgh, 19—, aged 28.' There it was, you see. A little judicious questioning in the right place, and I should at least find the cottage nearest the spot. Only I didn't quite know what was the right place to begin my questioning at. Again there was fate: it took me to the curiosity-shop down that way—you know—and I turned over some old books, and, if you please, one was a prayerbook of 1740 odd, in a rather handsome binding—I'll just go and get it, it's in my room."

He left us in a state of some surprise, but we had hardly time to exchange any remarks when he was back, panting, and handed us the book opened at the fly-leaf, on which was, in a straggly hand:

Nathaniel Ager is my name and England is my nation,
Seaburgh is my dwelling-place and Christ is my Salvation,
When I am dead and in my Grave, and all my bones are
    rotton,
I hope the Lord will think on me when I am quite forgotton.

This poem was dated 1754, and there were many more entries of Agers, Nathaniel, Frederick, William, and so on, ending with William, 19—.

"You see," he said, "anybody would call it the greatest bit of luck. *I* did, but I don't now. Of course I asked the shopman about William Ager, and of course he happened to remember that he lodged in a cottage in the North Field and died there. This was just chalking the road for me. I knew which the cottage must be: there is only one sizeable one about there. The next thing was to scrape some sort of acquaintance with the people, and I took a walk that way at once. A dog did the business for me: he made at me so fiercely that they had to run out and beat him off, and then naturally begged my pardon, and we got into talk. I had only to bring up Ager's name, and pretend I knew, or thought I knew something of him, and then the woman said how sad it was him dying so young, and she was sure it came of him spending the night out of doors in the cold weather. Then I had to say: "Did he go out on the sea at night?" and she said: "Oh, no, it was on the hillock yonder with the trees on it." And there I was.

"I know something about digging in these barrows: I've opened many of them in the down country. But that was with owner's leave, and in broad daylight and with men to help. I had to prospect very carefully here before I put a spade in: I couldn't trench across the mound, and with those old firs growing there I knew there would be awkward tree roots. Still the soil was very light and sandy and easy, and there was a rabbit hole or so that might be developed into a sort of tunnel. The going out and coming back at odd hours to the hotel was going to be the awkward part. When I made up my mind about the way to excavate I told the people that I was called away for a night, and I spent it out there. I made my tunnel: I won't bore you with the details of how I supported it and filled it in when I'd done, but the main thing is that I got the crown."

Naturally we both broke out into exclamations of surprise and interest. I for one had long known about the find of the crown at Rendlesham and had often lamented its fate.

No one has ever seen an Anglo-Saxon crown—at least no one had. But our man gazed at us with a rueful eye. "Yes," he said, "and the worst of it is I don't know how to put it back."

"Put it back?" we cried out. "Why, my dear sir, you've made one of the most exciting finds ever heard of in this country. Of course, it ought to go to the Jewel House at the Tower. What's your difficulty? If you're thinking about the owner of the land, and treasure-trove, and all that, we can certainly help you through. Nobody's going to make a fuss about technicalities in a case of this kind."

Probably more was said, but all he did was to put his face in his hands, and mutter: "I don't know how to put it back."

At last Long said: "You'll forgive me, I hope, if I seem impertinent, but are you *quite* sure you've got it?" I was wanting to ask much the same question myself, for of course the story did seem a lunatic's dream when one thought over it. But I hadn't quite dared to say what might hurt the poor young man's feelings. However, he took it quite calmly—really, with the calm of despair, you might say. He sat up and said: "Oh, yes, there's no doubt of that: I have it here, in my room, locked up in my bag. You can come and look at it if you like: I won't offer to bring it here."

We were not likely to let the chance slip. We went with him; his room was only a few doors off. The boots was just collecting shoes in the passage: or so we thought: afterwards we were not sure. Our visitor—his name was Paxton—was in a worse state of shivers than before, and went hurriedly into the room, and beckoned us after him, turned on the light, and shut the door carefully. Then he unlocked his kit-bag, and produced a bundle of clean pocket-handkerchiefs in which something was wrapped, laid it on the bed, and undid it. I can now say I *have* seen an actual Anglo-Saxon crown. It was of silver—as the Rendlesham one is always said to have been—it was set with some gems, mostly antique intaglios and cameos, and was of rather plain, almost rough workmanship. In fact, it was like those you see on the coins and in the manuscripts. I found no reason to think it was later than the ninth century. I was intensely interested, of course, and I wanted to turn it over in my hands, but Paxton prevented me. "Don't *you* touch it," he said, "I'll do that." And with a sigh that was, I declare to you, dreadful to hear, he took it up and turned it about so that we could see every part of it. "Seen enough?" he said at last, and we nodded. He wrapped it up and locked it in his bag, and stood looking at us dumbly. "Come back to our room," Long said, "and tell us what the trouble is." He thanked us, and said: "Will you go first and see if—if the coast is clear?" That wasn't very intelligible, for our proceedings hadn't been, after all, very suspicious, and the hotel, as I said, was practically empty. However, we were beginning to have inklings of—we didn't know what, and anyhow nerves are infectious. So we did go, first peering out as we opened the door, and fancying (I found we both had the fancy) that a shadow, or more than a shadow—but it made no sound—passed from before us to one side as we came out into the passage. "It's all right," we whispered to Paxton—whispering seemed the proper tone—and we went, with him between us, back to our sitting-room. I was preparing, when we got there, to be ecstatic about the unique interest of what we had seen, but when I looked at Paxton I saw that would be terribly out of place, and I left it to him to begin.

"What *is* to be done?" was his opening. Long thought it right (as he explained to me afterwards) to be obtuse, and said: "Why not find out who the owner of the land is, and inform—" "Oh, no, no!" Paxton broke in impatiently, "I beg your pardon: you've been very kind, but don't you see it's *got* to go back, and I daren't be there at night, and day-time's impossible. Perhaps, though, you don't see: well, then, the truth is that I've never been alone since I touched it." I was beginning some fairly stupid comment, but Long caught my eye, and I stopped. Long said: "I think I do see, perhaps: but wouldn't it be—a relief—to tell us a little more clearly what the situation is?"

Then it all came out: Paxton looked over his shoulder and beckoned to us to come nearer to him, and began speaking in a low voice: we listened most intently, of course, and compared notes afterwards, and I wrote down our version, so I am confident I have what he told us almost word for word. He said: "It began when I was first prospecting, and put me off again and again. There was always somebody— a man—standing by one of the firs. This was in daylight, you know. He was never in front of me. I always saw him with the tail of my eye on the left or the right, and he was never there when I looked straight for him. I would lie down for quite a long time and take careful observations, and make sure there was no one, and then when I got up and began prospecting again, there he was. And he began to give me hints, besides; for wherever I put that prayer-book— short of locking it up, which I did at last—when I came back to my room it was always out on my table open at the fly-leaf where the names are, and one of my razors across it to keep it open. I'm sure he just can't open my bag, or something more would have happened. You see, he's light and weak, but all the same I daren't face him. Well, then, when I was making the tunnel, of course it was worse, and if I hadn't been so keen I should have dropped the whole thing and run. It was like someone scraping at my back all the time: I thought for a long time it was only soil dropping on me, but as I got nearer the—the crown, it was unmistakable. And when I actually laid it bare and got my fingers into the ring of it and pulled it out, there came a sort of cry behind me—oh, I can't tell you how desolate it was! And horribly threatening too. It spoilt all my pleasure in my find—cut it off that moment. And if I hadn't been the wretched fool I am, I should have put the thing back

and left it. But I didn't. The rest of the time was just awful.
I had hours to get through before I could decently come
back to the hotel. First I spent time filling up my tunnel
and covering my tracks, and all the while he was there trying to thwart me. Sometimes, you know, you see him, and
sometimes you don't, just as he pleases, I think: he's there,
but he has some power over your eyes. Well, I wasn't off
the spot very long before sunrise, and then I had to get to
the junction for Seaburgh, and take a train back. And though
it was daylight fairly soon, I don't know if that made it
much better. There were always hedges, or gorsebushes, or
park fences along the road—some sort of cover, I mean—
and I was never easy for a second. And then when I began
to meet people going to work, they always looked behind
me very strangely: it might have been that they were surprised at seeing anyone so early; but I didn't think it was
only that, and I don't now: they didn't look exactly at *me*.
And the porter at the train was like that too. And the guard
held open the door after I'd got into the carriage—just as
he would if there was somebody else coming, you know.
Oh, you may be very sure it isn't my fancy," he said with
a dull sort of laugh. Then he went on: "And even if I do
get it put back, he won't forgive me: I can tell that. And I
was so happy a fortnight ago." He dropped into a chair, and
I believe he began to cry.

We didn't know what to say, but we felt we must come
to the rescue somehow, and so—it really seemed the only
thing—we said if he was so set on putting the crown back
in its place, we would help him. And I must say that after
what we had heard it did seem the right thing. If these horrid consequences had come on this poor man, might there
not really be something in the original idea of the crown
having some curious power bound up with it, to guard the
coast? At least, that was my feeling, and I think it was
Long's too. Our offer was very welcome to Paxton, anyhow. When could we do it? It was nearing half-past ten.

Could we contrive to make a late walk plausible to the hotel people that very night? We looked out of the window: there was a brilliant full moon—the Paschal moon. Long undertook to tackle the boots and propitiate him. He was to say that we should not be much over the hour, and if we did find it so pleasant that we stopped out a bit longer we would see that he didn't lose by sitting up. Well, we were pretty regular customers of the hotel, and did not give much trouble, and were considered by the servants to be not under the mark in the way of tips; and so the boots *was* propitiated, and let us out on to the sea-front, and remained, as we heard later, looking after us. Paxton had a large coat over his arm, under which was the wrapped-up crown.

So we were off on this strange errand before we had time to think how very much out of the way it was. I have told this part quite shortly on purpose, for it really does represent the haste with which we settled our plan and took action. "The shortest way is up the hill and through the churchyard," Paxton said, as we stood a moment before the hotel looking up and down the front. There was nobody about—nobody at all. Seaburgh out of the season is an early, quiet place. "We can't go along the dyke by the cottage, because of the dog," Paxton also said, when I pointed to what I thought a shorter way along the front and across two fields. The reason he gave was good enough. We went up the road to the church, and turned in at the churchyard gate. I confess to having thought that there might be some lying there who might be conscious of our business: but if it was so, they were also conscious that one who was on their side, so to say, had us under surveillance, and we saw no sign of them. But under observation we felt we were, as I have never felt it at another time. Specially was it so when we passed out of the churchyard into a narrow path with close high hedges, through which we hurried as Christian did through that Valley; and so got out into open fields. Then along hedges, though I would sooner have been in the open, where I could see if anyone was visible behind me; over a gate or two, and then a swerve to the left, taking us up on to the ridge which ended in that mound.

As we neared it, Henry Long felt, and I felt too, that there were what I can only call dim presences waiting for us, as well as a far more actual one attending us. Of Paxton's agitation all this time I can give you no adequate picture: he breathed like a hunted beast, and we could not either of us look at his face. How he would manage when we got to the very place we had not troubled to think: he had seemed so sure that that would not be difficult. Nor was it. I never saw anything like the dash with which he flung himself at a particular spot in the side of the mound, and tore at it, so that in a very few minutes the greater part of his body was out of sight. We stood holding the coat and that bundle of handkerchiefs, and looking, very fearfully, I must admit, about us. There was nothing to be seen: a line of dark firs behind us made one skyline, more trees and the church tower half a mile off on the right, cottages and a windmill on the horizon on the left, calm sea dead in front, faint barking of a dog at a cottage on a gleaming dyke between us and it: full moon making that path we know across the sea: the eternal whisper of the Scotch firs just above us, and of the sea in front. Yet, in all this quiet, an acute, an acrid consciousness of a restrained hostility very near us, like a dog on a leash that might be let go at any moment.

Paxton pulled himself out of the hole, and stretched a hand back to us. "Give it to me," he whispered, "unwrapped." We pulled off the handkerchiefs, and he took the crown. The moonlight just fell on it as he snatched it. We had not ourselves touched that bit of metal, and I have thought since that it was just as well. In another moment Paxton was out of the hole again and busy shoveling back the soil with hands that were already bleeding. He would have none of our help, though. It was much the longest part of the job to get the place to look undisturbed: yet—I don't know how—he made a wonderful success of it. At last he was satisfied, and we turned back.

We were a couple of hundred yards from the hill when Long suddenly said to him: "I say, you've left your coat there. That won't do. See?" And I certainly did see—the long dark overcoat lying where the tunnel had been. Paxton had not stopped, however: he only shook his head, and held up the coat on his arm. And when we joined him, he said, without any excitement, but as if nothing mattered any more: "That wasn't my coat." And, indeed, when we looked back gain, that dark thing was not to be seen.

Well, we got out on to the road, and came rapidly back that way. It was well before twelve when we got in, trying to put a good face on it, and saying—Long and I—what a lovely night it was for a walk. The boots was on the lookout for us, and we made remarks like that for his edification as we entered the hotel. He gave another look up and down the sea-front before he locked the front door, and said: "You didn't meet many people about, I s'pose, sir" "No, indeed, not a soul," I said; at which I remember Paxton looked oddly at me. "Only I thought I see someone turn up the station road after you gentlemen," said the boots. "Still, you was three together, and I don't suppose he meant mischief." I didn't know what to say; Long merely said "Good night," and we went off upstairs, promising to turn out all the lights, and to go to bed in a few minutes.

Back in our room, we did our very best to make Paxton take a cheerful view. "There's the crown safe back," we said; "very likely you'd have done better not to touch it" (and he heavily assented to that), "but no real harm has been done, and we shall never give this away to anyone who would be so mad as to go near it. Besides, don't you feel better yourself? I don't mind confessing," I said, "that on the way there I was very much inclined to take your view about—well, about being followed; but going back, it wasn't at all the same thing, was it?" No, it wouldn't do: "*You've* nothing to trouble yourselves about," he said, "but I'm not forgiven. I've got to pay for that miserable sacrilege still. I know what you are going to say. The Church might help. Yes, but it's the body that has to suffer. It's true I'm not feeling that he's waiting outside for me just now. But—" Then he stopped. Then he turned to thanking us, and we put him off as soon as we could. And naturally we pressed him to use our sitting-room next day, and said we should be glad to go out with him. Or did he play golf, perhaps? Yes, he did, but he didn't think he should care about that to-morrow. Well, we recommended him to get up late and sit in our room in the morning while we were playing, and we would have a walk later in the day. He was very submissive and *piano* about it all: ready to do just what we thought best, but clearly quite certain in his own mind that what was coming could not be averted or palliated. You'll wonder why we didn't insist on accompanying him to his home and seeing him safe into the care of brothers or someone. The fact was he had nobody. He had had a flat in town, but lately he had made up his mind to settle for a time in Sweden, and he had dismantled his flat and shipped off his belongings, and was whiling away a fortnight or three weeks before he made a start. Anyhow, we didn't see what we could do better than sleep on it— or not sleep very much, as was my case—and see what we felt like to-morrow morning.

We felt very different, Long and I, on as beautiful an April morning as you could desire; and Paxton also looked very different when we saw him at breakfast. "The first approach to a decent night I seem ever to have had," was what he said. But he was going to do as we had settled: stay in probably all the morning, and come out with us later. We went to the links; we met some other men and played with them in the morning, and had lunch there rather early, so as not to be late back. All the same, the snares of death overtook him.

Whether it could have been prevented, I don't know. I think he would have been got at somehow, do what we might. Anyhow, this is what happened.

We went straight up to our room. Paxton was there, reading quite peaceably. "Ready to come out shortly?" said Long, "say in half an hour's time?" "Certainly," he said: and I said we would change first, and perhaps have baths, and call for him in half an hour. I had my bath first, and went and lay down on my bed, and slept for about ten minutes. We came out of our rooms at the same time, and went together to the sitting-room. Paxton wasn't there—only his book. Nor was he in his room, nor in the downstair rooms. We shouted for him. A servant came out and said: "Why, I thought you gentlemen was gone to already, and so did the other gentleman. He heard you a-calling from the path there, and run out in a hurry, and I looked out of the coffee-room window, but I didn't see you. 'Owever, he run off down the beach that way."

Without a word we ran that way too—it was the opposite direction to that of last night's expedition. It wasn't quite four o'clock, and the day was fair, though not so fair as it had been, so there was really no reason, you'd say, for anxiety: with people about, surely a man couldn't come to much harm.

But something in our look as we ran out must have struck the servant, for she came out on the steps, and pointed, and said, "Yes, that's the way he went." We ran on as far as the top of the shingle bank, and there pulled up. There was a choice of ways: past the houses on the sea-front, or along the sand at the bottom of the beach, which, the tide being now out, was fairly broad. Or of course we might keep along the shingle between these two tracks and have some view of both of them; only that was heavy going. We chose the sand, for that was the loneliest, and someone *might* come to harm there without being seen from the public path.

Long said he saw Paxton some distance ahead, running and waving his stick, as if he wanted to signal to people who were on ahead of him. I couldn't be sure: one of these sea-mists was coming up very quickly from the south. There was someone, that's all I could say. And there were tracks on the sand as of someone running who wore shoes; and there were other tracks made before those—for the shoes sometimes trod in them and interfered with them—of someone not in shoes. Oh, of course, it's only my word you've got to take for all this: Long's dead, we'd no time or means to make sketches or take casts, and the next tide washed everything away. All we could do was to notice these marks as we hurried on. But there they were over and over again, and we had no doubt whatever that what we saw was the track of a bare foot, and one that showed more bones than flesh.

The notion of Paxton running after—after anything like this, and supposing it to be the friends he was looking for, was very dreadful to us. You can guess what we fancied: how the thing he was following might stop suddenly and turn round on him, and what sort of face it would show, half-seen at first in the mist—which all the while was getting thicker and thicker. And as I ran on wondering how the poor wretch could have been lured into mistaking that other thing for us, I remembered his saying, "He has some power over your eyes." And then I wondered what the end would be, for I had no hope now that the end could be averted, and—well, there is no need to tell all the dismal and horrid thoughts that flitted through my head as we ran on into the mist. It was uncanny, too, that the sun should still be bright in the sky and we could see nothing. We could only tell that we were now past the houses and had reached that gap there is between them and the old martello tower. When you are past the tower, you know, there is nothing but shingle for a long way—not a house, not a human creature, just that spit of land, or rather shingle, with the river on your right and the sea on your left.

But just before that, just by the martello tower, you remember there is the old battery, close to the sea. I believe there are only a few blocks of concrete left now: the rest has all been washed away, but at this time there was a lot more, though the place was a ruin. Well, when we got there, we clambered to the top as quick as we could to take breath and look over the shingle in front if by chance the mist would let us see anything. But a moment's rest we must have. We had run a mile at least. Nothing whatever was visible ahead of us, and we were just turning by common consent to get down and run hopelessly on, when we heard what I can only call a laugh: and if you can understand what I mean by a breathless, a lungless laugh, you have it: but I don't suppose you can. It came from below, and swerved away into the mist. That was enough. We bent over the wall. Paxton was there at the bottom.

You don't need to be told that he was dead. His tracks showed that he had run along the side of the battery, had turned sharp round the corner of it, and, small doubt of it, must have dashed straight into the open arms of someone who was waiting there. His mouth was full of sand and stones, and his teeth and jaws were broken to bits. I only glanced once at his face.

At the same moment, just as we were scrambling down from the battery to get to the body, we heard a shout, and saw a man running down the bank of the martello tower. He was the caretaker stationed there, and his keen old eyes had managed to descry through the mist that something was wrong. He had seen Paxton fall, and had seen us a moment after, running up—fortunate this, for otherwise we could hardly have escaped suspicion of being concerned in the dreadful business. Had he, we asked, caught sight of anybody attacking our friend? He could not be sure.

We sent him off for help, and stayed by the dead man till they came with the stretcher. It was then that we traced out how he had come, on the narrow fringe of sand under the battery wall. The rest was shingle, and it was hopelessly impossible to tell whither the other had gone.

What were we to say at the inquest? It was a duty, we felt, not to give up, there and then, the secret of the crown, to be published in every paper. I don't know how much you would have told; but what we did agree upon was this: to say that we had only made acquaintance with Paxton the day before, and that he had told us he was under some apprehension of danger at the hands of a man called William Ager. Also that we had seen some other tracks besides Paxton's when we followed him along the beach. But of course by that time everything was gone from the sands.

No one had any knowledge, fortunately, of any William Ager living in the district. The evidence of the man at the martello tower freed us from all suspicion. All that could be done was to return a verdict of wilful murder by some person or persons unknown.

Paxton was so totally without connections that all the inquiries that were subsequently made ended in a No Thoroughfare. And I have never been at Seaburgh, or even near it, since.

Though his reputation remains solid among the more serious practitioners and enthusiasts in the horror field, the visionary Welsh writer Arthur Machen (1863–1947) undoubtedly suffers that peculiar kind of fame in which his name is dropped more often than his books are read. This is perhaps not altogether surprising because Machen, like the fine wines and good ales of which he was so fond, has always been something of an acquired taste—though he lived long enough to enjoy more than one brief period of voguish adulation, he lived and worked for the most part in obscure poverty. Near the end of his eighty-four years he once did some foolish arithmetic and calculated that six decades worth of devotion to his muse had earned him approximately six hundred pounds. This is roughly equivalent to twenty dollars a year. The fact that he greeted this revelation with a mix of stoicism and amusement is a tribute to his character and seems, from all published accounts by friends and colleagues, to have been typical of a man profoundly blessed with warmth, wit, wisdom, and a healthy cynicism as regards the world and its rewards.

One reason why Machen will probably always count his core audience in the hundreds rather than the hundreds of thousands is that quite frankly he's not an easy read. His prose, of course, is always beautiful, fluent, and masterly—whether it be the Stevensonian pastiche of "The Three Imposters," the hallucinogenic child-speak of "The White People," or the measured and elegant simplicity of his later tales—but he has little patience with the undereducated. He assumes of his readership the same classical learning that he himself possessed and thus his writings abound with Latin and Greek quotations which he rarely bothers to translate or explain and references to philosophical theorems with which the modern reader, unschooled in classical logic and renaissance theology, might be far from familiar. The other problem is that in order to experience the full Machenian magic you really need to read a lot of his stuff—essays, autobiographies, and articles as well as novels and stories. The effect he has on you is cumulative—and consciously so because Machen, like the medieval alchemists whom he admired and to whom he made constant metaphorical reference throughout his writings, knew that each individual experiment (or story) was but one aspect of the Great Work, one facet only of the inexpressible mystery at the heart of the universe.

Mystery—and a reverence for it rather than a desire to solve—is the essential key to any understanding of Machen. His favorite Latin quotation was *Omnia Exeunt In Mysterium* (all things end in mystery) and his method in most of his storytelling is to maneuver the reader into a place where he or she feels that they have glanced tangentially at some aspect of the unknowable. The first chapter of *The Great Return*, his 1915 novella about the Grail, is called "Rumours of the Marvellous" and I can think of no better nor more poetically elegant a description of his work than that. This sense of a proximity to the Transcendent is one of the things H. P. Lovecraft admired so much about Machen and one of the things he appropriated from him for his own fiction (appropriated as narrative technique at least; philosophically they couldn't have been more different—Machen a Catholic mystic and Lovecraft an agnostic rationalist). Whether the Transcendence that is glimpsed is horrifying or spiritually uplifting can vary from story to story and in his best work is usually both. Like his contemporary, Algernon Blackwood, Machen's concern was to inculcate *awe* in his readers and it mattered little to him whether that awe was achieved by terror or by wonder. He was wonderfully dismissive of oc-cultist mumbo-jumbo—though a member of the Order of the Golden Dawn at the same time as the notorious Aleister Crowley, he considered Crowley a buffoon at best and a dangerous charlatan at worst. The way to the Great Secret for Machen was not via obscurantist rituals but via a Wordsworthian communion with nature in which one can glimpse the miraculous in the everyday. In an essay enti-tled *With the Gods in Spring* Machen describes how on a walk with friends he saw beneath a black thornbush a sin-gle daffodil. "Forgotten then," he writes, "but remembered always: the shining apparition of the god."

"Opening the Door," the story I have selected for this volume, dates from 1931. It is not, I tell you honestly, Machen's masterpiece, but it is a fine example of his art of suggestiveness, of his ability to demonstrate the intercon-nection of the mundane and the marvelous, and the reason I chose it is that when so little of Machen's work is currently in print it seems pointless to republish yet again "The White People" or "The Great God Pan," which are (deservedly) the most anthologized of his stories. My choice was also determined, I have to admit, by the desire to offer a small rejoinder to S. T. Joshi. In his otherwise excellent volume, *The Weird Tale* (a critical study of Machen and five other classic horror writers), Mr. Joshi declares that all the Machen fiction worth reading dates from his first decade of work. This, in my opinion, is far too dismissive of Machen's later period—a period that not only produced such tales as "N" or "Out of the Earth" or "The Exalted Omega" or, indeed, "Opening the Door," but one in which Machen's prose, always breathtakingly good, actually got better.

So here is "Opening the Door." I commend it to you with the suggestion that you read it slowly. Don't look for sudden shocks or punchline endings. It offers no quick thrills, no instant frissions of horror. It will, however, leave the careful reader with a lingering sense of something beyond this world, a feeling that, however briefly, the veil that separates the natural from the supernatural (or, in Machen's phrase, the Actual from the Real) has been lifted, that a door has indeed been opened.

—Peter Atkins

OPENING THE DOOR
by Arthur Machen

The newspaper reporter, from the nature of the case, has generally to deal with the commonplaces of life. He does his best to find something singular and arresting in the spectacle of the day's doings; but in spite of himself, he is generally forced to confess that whatever there may be beneath the surface, the surface itself is dull enough.

I must allow, however, that during my ten years or so in Fleet Street, I came across some tracks that were not devoid of oddity. There was that business of Campo Tosto, for example. That never got into the papers. Campo Tosto, I must explain, was a Belgian, settled for many years in England, who had left all his property to the man who looked after him.

My news editor was struck by something odd in the brief story that appeared in the morning paper, and sent me down to make enquiries. I left the train at Reigate; and there I found that Mr. Campo Tosto had lived at a place called Burnt Green—which is a translation of his name into English—and that he shot at trespassers with a bow and arrows. I was driven to his house, and saw through a glass door some of the property which he had bequeathed to his servant: fifteenth-century triptychs, dim and rich and golden; carved statues of the saints; great spiked altar candlesticks; storied censers in tarnished silver; and much more of old church treasure. The legatee, whose name was Lurk, would not let me enter; but, as a treat, he took my newspaper from my pocket and read it upside down with great accuracy and facility. I wrote this very queer story, but Fleet Street would not suffer it. I believe it struck them as too strange a thing for their sober columns.

And then there was the affair of the J.H.V.S. Syndicate, which dealt with a Cabalistic cipher, and the phenomenon called in the Old Testament, "the Glory of the Lord," and the discovery of certain objects buried under the site of the Temple at Jerusalem: that story was left half told, and I never heard the ending of it. And I never understood the affair of the hoard of coins that a storm disclosed on the Suffolk coast near Aldborough. From the talk of the longshoremen, who were on the look-out amongst the dunes, it appeared that a great wave came in and washed away a slice of the sand cliff just beneath them. They saw glittering objects as the sea washed back, and retrieved what they could. I viewed the treasure—it was a collection of coins; the earliest of the twelfth century, the latest, pennies, three

or four of them, of Edward VII, and a bronze medal of
Charles Spurgeon. There are, of course, explanations of the
puzzle, but there are difficulties in the way of accepting
any one of them. It is very clear, for example, that the
hoard was not gathered by a collector of coins: neither the
twentieth-century pennies nor the medal of the great Baptist preacher would appeal to a numismatologist.

But, perhaps, the queerest story to which my newspaper
connections introduced me, was the affair of the Reverend
Secretan Jones, the "Canonbury Clergyman," as the head-
lines called him.

To begin with, it was a matter of sudden disappearance.
I believe people of all sorts disappear by dozens in the
course of every year, and nobody hears of them or their
vanishing. Perhaps they turn again, or perhaps they don't;
anyhow, they never get so much as a line in the papers, and
there is an end of it. Take, for example, that unknown man
in the burning car, who cost the amorous commercial trav-
eller his life. In a certain sense, we all heard of him; but
he must have disappeared from somewhere in space, and
nobody knew that he had gone from his world. So it is
often; but now and then there is some circumstance that
draws attention to the fact that A. or B. was in his place
on Monday and missing from it on Tuesday and Wednes-
day; and then enquiries are made and usually the lost man
is found, alive or dead, and the explanation is often simple
enough.

But as to the case of Secretan Jones. This gentleman, a
cleric as I have said, but seldom, it appeared, exercising his
sacred office, lived retired in a misty, 1830–40 square in
the recesses of Canonbury. He was understood to be engaged in some kind of scholarly research, was a well-known
figure in the Reading Room of the British Museum, and
looked anything between fifty and sixty. It seems probable
that if he had been content with that achievement, he might
have disappeared as often as he pleased and nobody would

have troubled; but one night as he sat late over his books in the stillness of the retired quarter, a motor lorry passed along a road not far from Tollit Square, breaking the silence with a heavy rumble and causing a tremor of the ground that penetrated into Secretan Jones's study. A teacup and saucer on a side-table trembled slightly, and Secretan Jones's attention was taken from his authorities and notebooks.

This was in February or March of 1907, and the motor industry was still in its early stages. If you preferred a horse bus, there were plenty left in the streets. Motor coaches were nonexistent, hansom cabs still jogged and jingled on their cheerful way; and there were very few heavy motor vans in use. But to Secretan Jones, disturbed by the rattle of his cup and saucer, a vision of the future, highly coloured, was vouchsafed, and he began to write to the papers. He saw the London streets almost as we know them today; streets where a horsed vehicle would be almost a matter to show one's children for them to remember in their old age; streets in which a great procession of huge omnibuses carrying fifty, seventy, a hundred people was continually passing; streets in which vans and trailers loaded far beyond the capacity of any manageable team of horses would make the ground tremble without ceasing.

The retired scholar, with the happy activity which does sometimes, oddly enough, distinguish the fish out of water, went on and spared nothing. Newton saw the apple fall, and built up a mathematical universe; Jones heard the teacup rattle, and laid the universe of London in ruins. He pointed out that neither the roadways nor the houses beside them, were constructed to withstand the weight and vibration of the coming traffic. He crumbled all the shops in Oxford Street and Piccadilly into dust, he cracked the dome of St. Paul's, brought down Westminster Abbey, reduced the Law Courts to a fine powder. What was left was dealt with by fire, flood, and pestilence. The prophetic Jones demonstrated that the roads must collapse, involving the various services

beneath them. Here, the water-mains and the main drainage
would flood the streets; there, huge volumes of gas would
escape, and electric wires fuse; the earth would be rent with
explosions, and the myriad streets of London would go up
in a great flame of fire. Nobody really believed that it would
happen, but it made good reading, and Secretan Jones gave
interviews, started discussions and enjoyed himself thoroughly. Thus he became the "Canonbury Clergyman."
"Canonbury Clergyman says that Catastrophe is Inevitable";
"Doom of London pronounced by Canonbury Cleryman";
"Canonbury Clergyman's Forecast; London a Carnival of
Flood, Fire, and Earthquake"—that sort of thing.

And thus Secretan Jones, though his main interests were
liturgical, was able to secure a few newspaper paragraphs
when he disappeared—rather more than a year after his great
campaign in the Press, which was not quite forgotten, but
not very clearly remembered.

A few paragraphs, I said, and stowed away, most of them,
in out-of-the-way corners of the papers. It seemed that Mrs.
Sedger, the woman who shared with her husband the business of looking after Secretan Jones, brought in tea on a
tray to his study at four o'clock as usual, and came, again
as usual, to take it away at five. And a good deal to her astonishment, the study was empty. She concluded that her
master had gone out for a stroll, though he never went out
for strolls between tea and dinner. He didn't come back for
dinner; and Sedger, inspecting the hall, pointed out that the
master's hats and coats and sticks and umbrellas were all
on their pegs and in their places. The Sedgers conjectured
this, that, and the other, waited a week, and then went to
the police, and the story came out and perturbed a few
learned friends and correspondents: Prebendary Lincoln, author of *The Roman Canon in the Third Century*; Dr. Bright-
well, the authority on the Rite of Malabar; and Stokes, the
Mozarabic man. The rest of the populace did not take very
much interest in the affair, and when, at the end of six

weeks, there was a line or two stating that "the Rev. Secretan Jones, whose disappearance at the beginning of last
month from his house in Tollit Square, Canonbury, caused
some anxiety to his friends, returned yesterday," there was
neither enthusiasm nor curiosity. The last line of the paragraph said that the incident was supposed to be the result
of a misunderstanding; and nobody even asked what the
statement meant.

And there would have been the end of it—if Sedger had
not gossiped to the circle in the private bar of "The King
of Prussia." Some mysterious and unofficial person, in touch
with this circle, insinuated himself into the presence of my
news editor and told him Sedger's tale. Mrs. Sedger, a careful woman, had kept all the rooms tidy and well dusted.
On the Tuesday afternoon, she had opened the study door
and saw, to her amazement and delight, her master sitting
at his table with a great book open beside him and a pencil in his hand. She exclaimed:

"Oh sir, I *am* glad to see you back again!"

"Back again?" said the clergyman. "What do you mean?
I think I should like some more tea."

"I don't know in the least what it's all about," said the
news editor, "but you might go and see Secretan Jones and
have a chat with him. There may be a story in it." There
was a story in it but not for my paper, or any other paper.

I got into the house in Tollit Square on some unhand-
some pretext connected with Secretan Jones's traffic scare
of the year before. He looked at me in a dim, abstracted
way at first—the "great book" of his servant's story, and
other books, and many black quarto notebooks were about
him—but my introduction of the proposed design for a
"mammoth carrier" clarified him and he began to talk eagerly, and as it seemed to me lucidly, of the grave menace
of the new mechanical transport.

"But what's the use of talking?" he ended. 'I tried to
wake people up to the certain dangers ahead. I seemed to

succeed for a few weeks; and then they forgot all about it. You would really say that the great majority are like dreamers, like sleepwalkers. Yes; like men walking in a dream; shutting out all the actualities, all the facts of life. They know that they are, in fact, walking on the edge of a precipice; and yet they are able to believe, it seems, that the precipice is a garden path; and they behave as if it were a garden path, as safe as that path you see down there, going to the door at the bottom of my garden.'

The study was at the back of the house, and looked on the long garden, heavily overgrown with shrubs run wild, mingling with one another and happily obscuring and confounding the rigid grey walls that, doubtless, separated each garden from its neighbours. Above the tall shrubs, taller elms and planes and ash trees grew unlopped and handsomely neglected; and under this deep concealment of green boughs, the path went down to a green door, just visible under a cloud of white roses.

"As safe as that path you see there," Secretan Jones repeated, and looking at him, I thought his expression changed a little; very slightly, indeed, but to a certain questioning, one might say to a meditative doubt. He suggested to me a man engaged in an argument, who puts his case strongly, decisively; and then hesitates for the fraction of a second as a point occurs to him of which he had never thought before; a point as yet unweighed, unestimated; dimly present, but more as a shadow than a shape.

The newspaper reporter needs the gestures of the serpent as well as its wisdom. I forget how I glided from the safe topic of the traffic peril to the dubious territory which I had been sent to explore. At all events, my contortions were the most graceful that I could devise; but they were altogether vain. Secretan Jones's kind, clean-shaven face took on an expression of distress. He looked at me as one in perplexity; he seemed to search his mind not for the an-

swer that he should give me, but rather for some answer
due to himself.

"I am extremely sorry that I cannot give you the information you want," he said, after a considerable pause. "But
I really can't go any farther into the matter. In fact, it is
quite out of the question to do so. You must tell your editor—or sub-editor; which is it?—that the whole business is
due to a misunderstanding, a misconception, which I am
not at liberty to explain. But I am really sorry that you have
come all this way for nothing."

There was real apology and regret, not only in his words,
but in his tones, and in his aspect. I could not clutch my
hat and get on my way with a short word in the character
of a disappointed and somewhat disgusted emissary; so we
fell on general talk, and it came out that we both came from
the Welsh borderland, and had long ago walked over the
same hills and drank of the same wells. Indeed, I believe
we proved cousinship, in the seventh degree or so, and tea
came in, and before long Secretan Jones was deep in liturgical problems, of which I knew just enough to play the
listener's part. Indeed, when I had told him that the *hwyl*,
or chanted eloquence, of the Welsh Methodists was, in fact,
the Preface Tone of the Roman Missal, he overflowed with
grateful interest, and made a note in one of his books, and
said the point was most curious and important. It was a
pleasant evening, and we strolled through the french windows into the green-shadowed, blossoming garden, and went
on with our talk, till it was time—and high time—for me
to go. I had taken up my hat as we left the study, and as
we stood by the green door in the wall at the end of the
garden, I suggested that I might use it.

"I'm so sorry," said Secretan Jones, looking, I thought,
a little worried, "but I am afraid it's jammed, or something
of that kind. It has always been an awkward door, and I
hardly ever use it."

So we went through the house, and on the doorstep he

pressed me to come again, and was so cordial that I agreed
to his suggestion of the Saturday sennight. And so at last
I got an answer to the question with which my newspaper
had originally entrusted me; but an answer by no means for
newspaper use. The tale, or experience, or the impression,
or whatever it may be called, was delivered to me by very
slow degrees, with hesitations, and in a manner of tenta-
tive suggestion that often reminded me of our first talk together. It was as if Jones were, again and again, questioning
himself as to the matter of his utterances, as if he doubted
whether they should not rather be treated as dreams, and
dismissed as trifles without consequence.

He said once to me: "People do tell their dreams, I know;
but isn't it usually felt that they are telling nothing? That's
what I am afraid of."

I told him that I thought we might throw a great deal of
light on very dark places if more dreams were told.

"But there," I said, "is the difficulty. I doubt whether the
dreams that I am thinking of *can* be told. There are dreams
that are perfectly lucid from beginning to end, and also perfectly insignificant. There are others which are blurred by
a failure of memory, perhaps only on one point: you dream
of a dead man as if he were alive. Then there are dreams
which are prophetic: there seems, on the whole, no doubt
of that. Then you may have sheer, clotted nonsense; I once
chased Julius Cæsar all over London to get his recipe for
curried eggs. But, besides these, there is a certain dream of
another order: utter lucidity up to the moment of waking,
and then perceived to be beyond the power of words to ex-
press. It is neither sense nor nonsense; it has, perhaps, a
notation of its own, but . . . well, you can't play Euclid on
the violin."

Secretan Jones shook his head. "I am afraid my experiences are rather like that," he said. It was clear, indeed, that
he found great difficulty in finding a verbal formula which
should convey some hint of his adventures.

But that was later. To start with, things were fairly easy; but, characteristically enough, he began his story before I realized that the story was begun. I had been talking of the queer tricks a man's memory sometimes plays him. I was saying that a few days before, I was suddenly interrupted in some work I was doing. It was necessary that I should clear my desk in a hurry. I shuffled a lot of loose papers together and put them away, and awaited my caller with a fresh writing-pad before me. The man came, I attended to the business with which he was concerned, and went back to my former affair when he had gone. But I could not find the sheaf of papers. I thought I had put them in a drawer. They were not in the drawer; they were not in any drawer, or in the blotting-book, or in any place where one might reasonably expect to find them. They were found next morning by the servant who dusted the room, stuffed hard down into the crevice between the seat and the back of an armchair, and carefully hidden under a cushion.

"And," I finished, "I hadn't the faintest recollecton of doing it. My mind was blank on the matter."

"Yes," said Secretan Jones, "I suppose we all suffer from that sort of thing at times. About a year ago I had a very odd experience of the same kind. It was soon after I had taken up that question of the new traffic and its probable— its certain—results. As you may have gathered, I have been absorbed for most of my life in my own special studies, which are remote enough from the activities and interests of the day. It hasn't been at all my way to write to the papers to say there are too many dogs in London, or to denounce street musicians. But I must say that the extraordinary dangers of using our present road system for a traffic for which is was not designed did impress themselves very deeply upon me; and I daresay I allowed myself to be over-interested and over-excited.

"There is a great deal to be said for the Apostolic maxim: 'Study to be quiet and to mind your own business.' I am afraid I got the whole thing on the brain, and neglected my own business, which at that particular time, if I remember, was the investigation of a very curious question—the validity or non-validity of the Consecration Formula of the *Grand Saint Graal: Car chou est li sanc di ma nouviele loy, li miens meismes.* Instead of attending to my proper work I allowed myself to be drawn into the discussion I had started, and for a week or two I thought of very little else: even when I was looking up authorities at the British Museum, I couldn't get the rumble of the motor van out of my head. So you see I allowed myself to get harried and worried and distracted, and I put down what followed to all the bother and excitement I was going through. The other day, when you had to leave your work in the middle and start on something else, I daresay you felt annoyed and put out, and shoved those papers of yours away without really thinking of what you were doing, and I suppose something of the same kind happened to me. Though it was still queerer, I think."

He paused, and seemed to meditate doubtfully, and then broke out with an apologetic laugh, and: "It really sounds quite crazy!" And then: "I forgot where I lived."

"Loss of memory, in fact, through overwork and nervous excitement?"

"Yes, but not quite in the usual way. I was quite clear about my name, and my identity. And I knew my address perfectly well: 39, Tollit Square, Canonbury."

"But you said you forgot where you lived."

"I know; but there's the difficulty of expression we were talking about the other day. I am looking for the notation, as you called it. But it was like this. I had been working all the morning in the Reading Room with the motor danger at the back of my mind, and as I left the Museum, feeling a sort of heaviness and confusion, I made up my mind to walk home. I thought the air might freshen me a little. I set out at a good pace. I knew every foot of the way, as

I had often done the walk before, and I went ahead mechanically, with my mind wrapt up in a very important matter relating to my proper studies. As a matter of fact, I had
found in a most unexpected quarter a statement that threw
an entirely new light on the Rite of the Celtic Church, and
I felt that I might be on the verge of an important discovery. I was lost in a maze of conjectures, and when I looked
up I found myself standing on the pavement by the 'Angel,'
Islington, totally unaware of where I was to go next.

"Yes, quite so: I knew the 'Angel' when I saw it, and I
knew I lived in Tollit Square; but the relation between the
two had entirely vanished from my consciousness. For me,
there were on longer any points of the compass; there was
no such thing as direction, neither north nor south, nor left
nor right, an extraordinary sensation, which I don't feel I
have made plain to you at all. I was a good deal disturbed,
and felt that I must move somewhere, so I set off—and
found myself at King's Cross railway station. Then I did
the only thing there was to be done: took a hansom and got
home, feeling shaky enough."

I gathered that this was the first incident of significance
in a series of odd experiences that befell this learned and
amiable clergyman. His memory became thoroughly unre-
liable, or so he thought at first.

He began to miss important papers from his table in the
study. A series of notes, on three sheets lettered A, B, and
C were placed by him on the table under a paperweight one
night, just before he went up to bed. They were missing
when he went into his study the next morning. He was certain that he had put them in that particular place, under the
bulbous glass weight with the pink roses embedded in its
depths: but they were not there. Then Mrs. Sedger knocked
at the door and entered with the papers in her hand. She
said she had found them between the bed and the mattress
in the master's bedroom, and thought they might be wanted.

Secretan Jones could not make it out at all. He supposed

he must have put the papers where they were found and
then forgotten all about it, and he was uneasy, feeling afraid
that he was on the brink of a nervous breakdown. Then
there were difficulties about his books, as to which he was
very precise, every book having its own place. One morning he wanted to consult the *Missale de Arbuthnot*, a big
red quarto, which lived at the end of a bottom shelf near
the window. It was not there. The unfortunate man went up
to his bedroom, and felt the bed all over and looked under
his shirts in the chest of drawers, and searched all the room
in vain. However, determined to get what he wanted, he
went to the Reading Room, verified his reference, and returned to Canonbury: and there was the red quarto in its
place. Now here, it seemed certain, there was no room for
loss of memory; and Secretan Jones began to suspect his
servants of playing tricks with his possessions, and tried to
find a reason for their imbecility or villainy—he did not
know what to call it. But it would not do at all. Papers and
books disappeared and reappeared, or, now and then, vanished without return. One afternoon, struggling, as he told
me, against a growing sense of confusion and bewilderment, he had with considerable difficulty filled two quarto
sheets of ruled paper with a number of extracts necessary
to the subject he had in hand. When this was done, he felt
his bewilderment thickening like a cloud about him: "It was,
physically and mentally, as if the objects in the room became indistinct, were presented in a shimmering mist or
darkness." He felt afraid, and rose, and went out into the
garden. The two sheets of paper he had left on his table
were lying on the path by the garden door.

I remember he stopped dead at this point. To tell the
truth, I was thinking that all these instances were rather matter for the ear of a mental specialist than for my hearing.
There was evidence enough of a bad nervous breakdown,
and, it seemed to me, of delusions. I wondered whether it

was my duty to advise the man to go to the best doctor he knew, and without delay. Then Secretan Jones began again:

"I won't tell you any more of these absurdities. I know they are drivel, pantomime tricks and traps, children's conjuring; contemptible, all of it.

"But it made me afraid. I felt like a man walking in the dark, beset with uncertain sounds and faint echoes of his footstep that seem to come from a vast depth, till he begins to fear that he is treading by the edge of some awful precipice. There was something unknown about me; and I was holding on hard to what I knew, and wondering whether I should be kept up.

"One afternoon I was in a very miserable and distracted state. I could not attend to my work. I went out into the garden, and walked up and down trying to calm myself. I opened the garden door and looked into the narrow passage which runs at the end of all the gardens on this side of the square. There was nobody there—except three children playing some game or other. They were horrible, stunted little creatures, and I turned back into the garden and walked into the study. I had just sat down, and had turned to my work hoping to find relief in it, when Mrs. Sedger, my servant, came into the room and cried out, in an excited sort of way, that she was glad to see me back again.

"I made up some story. I don't know whether she believes it. I suppose she thinks I have been mixed up in something disreputable."

"And what had happened?"

"I haven't the remotest notion."

We sat looking at each other for some time.

"I suppose what happened was just this," I said at last. "Your nervous system had been in a very bad way for some time. It broke down utterly: you lost your memory, your sense of identity—everything. You may have spent the six weeks addressing envelopes in the City Road."

He turned to one of the books on the table and opened

it. Between the leaves there were the dimmed red and white petals of some flower that looked like an anemone.

"I picked this flower," he said, "as I was walking down the path that afternoon. It was the first of its kind to be in bloom—very early. It was still in my hand when I walked back into this room, six weeks later, as everybody declares. But it was quite fresh."

There was nothing to be said. I kept silent for five minutes, I suppose, before I asked him whether his mind was an utter blank as to the six weeks during which no known person had set eyes on him; whether he had no sort of recollection, however vague.

"At first, nothing at all. I could not believe that more than a few seconds came between my opening the garden door and shutting it. Then in a day or two there was a vague impression that I had been somewhere where everything was absolutely right. I can't say more than that. No fairyland joys, or bowers of bliss, or anything of that kind; no sense of anything strange or unaccustomed. But there was no care there at all. *Est enim magnum chaos*."

But that means "For there is a great void," or "A great gulf."

We never spoke of the matter again. Two months later he told me that his nerves had been troubling him, and that he was going to spend a month or six weeks at a farm near Llanthony, in the Black Mountains, a few miles from his old home. In three weeks I got a letter, addressed in Secretan Jones's hand. Inside was a slip of paper on which he had written the words:

Est enim magnum chaos.

The day on which the letter was posted he had gone out in wild autumn weather, late one afternoon, and never come back. No trace of him has ever been found.

Last night I had the strangest dream . . .

Not last night, exactly. This morning. The dream woke me up at around 6:15 AM and I couldn't get back to sleep.

It had frightened me, disturbed me.

Let's call it what it was—a nightmare.

In which I was being pursued by a bunny.

This was no *Night of the Lepus* giant rabbit. If my reaction to that film is any indication, pursuit by a giant, twitchy-nosed rabbit probably would've awakened me laughing.

This was a normal-sized bunny rabbit and it freaked me out.

In my dream, I was walking alone. Whether on a concrete sidewalk in a residential area or on a dirt path through a wilderness, I don't know. I only know that I was alone, and nobody else was around to help.

I seemed to be on my way home, walking cheerfully along, not a care in the world, when a rabbit suddenly hopped past me from behind, narrowly missed my knee and landed slightly in front of me.

Landed a bit crooked, and looked back at me.

A cute little brown rabbit—almost.

Something was not quite right about it. Though I saw no blood or other signs of injury, the rabbit seemed slightly off-kilter. Slightly deformed?

I sensed its deformity, but couldn't quite *detect* what was out of place.

It stared up at me with a certain expectancy or eagerness or hope similar to looks I've sometimes received from stray dogs. It seemed to *want* something.

Did it want me to help it, somehow?

Did it want to follow me home?

Maybe it wanted to *bite* me.

Is it rabid?

Something was obviously wrong with it.

Suddenly eager to get away, I began walking fast. I hadn't taken more than a few steps, however, before it came bounding past the side of my leg . . . off-kilter in the air, and landed just ahead of me and stumbled and turned toward me and stared up at me.

This time, the eyes didn't look quite so expectant. They seemed to say, *Try that again, and you'll be sorry.*

I did try again . . . strode past the rabbit and hurried on my way. Again, it easily caught up, leaped past my side and flopped to the ground a short distance in front of me.

Hunkered down, ears drooping, it glared up at me and bared its teeth.

I got goosebumps.

It isn't gonna let me go.

I stood over it, stared down at it, wondered what was *wrong* with it, felt sorry for it, wanted to help it but didn't know how, feared it . . . and above all wanted it *gone*.

I could probably outrun it. After all, the rabbit was somehow deformed, crippled, unhealthy. If I put on a real burst of speed . . .

It'll bite me if I try.

In my imagination, I saw it take a short hop and sink its teeth into my ankle.

It *will* bite me, I thought, if I don't take care of it first.

I needed to kill it.

But I had no weapon.

I've got my feet, I thought. And good, substantial leather shoes.

I'll give it a good punt.

Or stomp it to death.

As if reading my mind, the bunny rabbit glared into my eyes and snarled.

And I woke up, thank God.

Only a nightmare!

Lying in bed, upset by my confrontation with the oddly monstrous rabbit—I wondered what on earth had caused me to have such a disturbing dream.

Would've made a lot more sense if my tormentor had been a squirrel. In recent years, my life has "gone to the squirrels." My wife has been feeding them, so our house has become the neighborhood diner for at least half a dozen squirrels. They're wonderful creatures. Very smart, frisky, full of antics . . . and *they want nuts*.

They'll do *anything* to get a nut.

A couple of years ago, an overeager squirrel went for a nut and got my finger by mistake. In shock, I twirled the squirrel around my head a couple of times before it let go.

Don't worry, the squirrel didn't get hurt. I, however, was bleeding all over the place and went to the emergency room. Afraid of rabies. Thing is, according to the doctor, squirrels don't carry rabies. I did, however, get a tetanus booster.

In other words, it seemed that this morning's nightmare should've been about a squirrel, not a rabbit.

So what the heck was a *bunny* doing in my dream?

Then I remembered.

The Colour Out of Space.

Last night, I had reread the story in order to prepare for writing this introduction. In H. P. Lovecraft's story, something like a meteorite strikes a wild, wooded area near Arkham. Early on, animals in the region begin to undergo strange changes.

Last night, I read the following:

Nahum . . . was disturbed about certain footprints in the snow. They were the usual winter prints of red squirrels, white rabbits, and foxes, but the brooding farmer professed to see something not quite right about their nature and arrangement. He was never specific, but appeared to think that they were not as characteristic of the anatomy and habits of squirrels and rabbits and foxes as they ought to be.

And this:

There had been a moon, and a rabbit had run across the road, and the leaps of that rabbit were longer than either Ammi or his horse liked. The latter, indeed, had almost run away when brought up by a firm rein.

Apparently, Lovecraft's images of the "not quite right" rabbits had triggered a certain unease in me . . . a disquiet that had prompted me to dream of being taunted by a subtly monstrous bunny.

I rarely experience nightmares. My dreams are usually pleasant . . . which may come as a surprise to those who know the sort of fiction I write. Perhaps dealing with imaginary mayhem on a daily basis provides me with a conscious outlet for my various fears and frustrations and anxieties, so that I have little need for nightmares.

But "The Colour Out of Space" gave me one.

"The Colour Out of Space" was first published in *Amazing Stories* in 1927. When I read the story in 1968, I was an aspiring writer in my junior year as an English major at Willamette University.

Lovecraft wasn't assigned reading. He wasn't even "optional" reading.

As far as I recall, I never heard his name uttered within the hallowed halls of academia. Though H. P. Lovecraft is certainly one of America's most important writers, has written several classics, and has influenced countless other authors, his name (at least in the 1950s and 1960s) never came up in any literature class that I'm aware of.

It should have.

How did I discover H. P. Lovecraft?

I was a big fan of Robert Bloch. Mostly through Bloch's writings, I became aware of the existence of H. P. Lovecraft and several other major horror writers who were flourishing near the end of the nineteen century and early decades of the twentieth.

After becoming aware of Lovecraft, however, I was unable to find any of his stories until I happened upon the Lancer paperback, *The Colour Out of Space and Others*, published in 1967.

The first story in the collection happened to be "The Colour Out of Space," so it was the first Lovecraft story I ever read.

I was hooked from then on.

I'm delighted that the story which introduced me to H. P. Lovecraft so many years ago is within the covers of the book you now hold in your hands. If you've already read it, you're sure to discover new treasures when you read it again.

If you've never read it before, have fun.

To quote from the story itself, "The place is not good for imagination, and does not bring restful dreams at night."

I definitely found that to be true.
Read on.
Sweet dreams.

—Richard Laymon

THE COLOUR OUT OF SPACE
by H. P. Lovecraft

West of Arkham the hills rise wild, and there are valleys with deep woods that no axe has ever cut. There are dark narrow glens where the trees slope fantastically, and where thin brooklets trickle without ever having caught the glint of sunlight. On the gentler slopes there are farms, ancient and rocky, with squat, moss-coated cottages brooding eternally over old New England secrets in the lee of great ledges; but these are all vacant now, the wide chimneys crumbling and the shingled sides bulging perilously beneath low gambrel roofs.

The old folk have gone away, and foreigners do not like to live there. French-Canadians have tried it, Italians have tried it, and the Poles have come and departed. It is not because of anything that can be seen or heard or handled, but because of something that is imagined. The place is not good for imagination, and does not bring restful dreams at night. It must be this which keeps the foreigners away, for old Ammi Pierce has never told them of anything he recalls from the strange days. Ammi, whose head has been a little queer for years, is the only one who still remains, or who ever talks of the strange days; and he dares to do this because his house is so near the open fields and the traveled roads around Arkham.

There was once a road over the hills and through the valleys, that ran straight where the blasted heath is now;

but people ceased to use it and a new road was laid curving far toward the south. Traces of the old one can still be found amidst the weeds of a returning wilderness, and some of them will doubtless linger even when half the hollows are flooded for the new reservoir. Then the dark woods will be cut down and the blasted heath will slumber far below blue waters whose surface will mirror the sky and ripple in the sun. And the secrets of the strange days will be one with the deep's secrets; one with the hidden lore of old ocean, and all the mystery of primal earth.

When I went into the hills and vales to survey for the new reservoir they told me the place was evil. They told me this in Arkham, and because that is a very old town full of witch legends I thought the evil must be something which grandmas had whispered to children through centuries. The name "blasted heath" seemed to me very odd and theatrical, and I wondered how it had come into the folklore of a Puritan people. Then I saw that dark westward tangle of glens and slopes for myself, and ceased to wonder at anything besides its own elder mystery. It was morning when I saw it, but shadow lurked always there. The trees grew too thickly, and their trunks were too big for any healthy New England wood. There was too much silence in the dim alleys between them, and the floor was too soft with the dank moss and mattings of infinite years of decay.

In the open spaces, mostly along the line of the old road, there were little hillside farms; sometimes with all the buildings standing, sometimes with only one or two, and sometimes with only a lone chimney or fast-filling cellar. Weeds and briers reigned, and furtive wild things rustled in the undergrowth. Upon everything was a haze or restlessness and oppression; a touch of the unreal and the grotesque, as if some vital element of perspective or chiaroscuro were awry. I did not wonder that the foreigners would not stay, for this was no region to sleep in. It was too much like a landscape of Salvator Rosa; too much like some forbidden woodcut in a tale of terror.

But even all this was not so bad as the blasted heath. I knew it the moment I came upon it at the bottom of a spacious valley; for no other name could fit such a thing, or any other thing fit such a name. It was as if the poet had coined the phrase from having seen this one particular region. It must, I thought as I viewed it, be the outcome of a fire; but why had nothing new ever grown over those five acres of gray desolation that sprawled open to the sky like a great spot eaten by acid in the woods and fields? It lay largely to the north of the ancient road line, but encroached a little on the other side. I felt an odd reluctance about approaching, and did so at last only because my business took me through and past it. There was no vegetation of any kind on that broad expanse, but only a fine gray dust or ash which no wind seemed ever to blow about. The trees near it were sickly and stunted, and as many dead trunks stood or lay rotting at the rim. As I walked hurriedly by I saw the tumbled bricks and stones of an old chimney and cellar on my right, and the yawning black maw of an abandoned well whose stagnant vapours played strange tricks with the hues of the sunlight. Even the long, dark woodland climb beyond seemed welcome in contrast, and I marveled no more at the frightened whispers of the Arkham people. There had been no house or ruin near; even in the old days the place must have been lonely and remote. And at twilight, dreading to repass that ominous spot, I walked circuitously back to the town by the curving road on the south. I vaguely wished some clouds would gather, for an odd timidity about the deep skyey voids above had crept into my soul.

In the evening I asked old people in Arkham about the blasted heath, and what was meant by that phrase "strange days" which so many evasively muttered. I could not, however, get any good answers, except that all the mystery was much more recent than I had dreamed. It was not a matter of old legendry at all, but something within the lifetime of those who spoke. It had happened in the 'eighties, and a family had disappeared or was killed. Speakers would not be exact; and because they all told me to pay no attention to old Ammi Pierce's crazy tales, I sought him out the next morning, having heard that he lived alone in the ancient tottering cottage where the trees first begin to get very thick. It was a fearsomely ancient place, and had begun to exude the faint miasmal odour which clings about houses that have stood too long. Only with persistent knocking could I rouse the aged man, and when he shuffled timidly to the door I could tell he was not glad to see me. He was not so feeble as I had expected; but his eyes dropped in a curious way, and his unkempt clothing and white beard made him seem very worn and dismal.

Not knowing just how he could best be launched on his tales, I feigned a matter of business; told him of my surveying, and asked vague questions about the district. He was far brighter and more educated than I had been led to think, and before I knew it had grasped quite as much of the subject as any man I had talked with in Arkham. He was not like other rustics I had known in the sections where reservoirs were to be. From him there were no protests at the miles of old wood and farmland to be blotted out, though perhaps there would have been had not his home lain outside the bounds of the future lake. Relief was all that he showed; relief at the doom of the dark ancient valleys through which he had roamed all his life. They were better under water now—better under water since the strange days. And with this opening his husky voice sank low, while his body leaned forward and his right forefinger began to point shakily and impressively.

It was then that I heard the story, and as the rambling voice scraped and whispered on I shivered again and again despite the summer day. Often I had to recall the speaker from ramblings, piece out scientific points which he knew only by a fading parrot memory of professors' talk, or bridge over gaps, where his sense of logic and continuity broke down. When he was done I did not wonder that his mind had snapped a trifle, or that the folk of Arkham would not speak much of the blasted heath. I hurried back before sunset to my hotel, unwilling to have the stars come out above me in the open; and the next day returned to Boston to give up my position. I could not go into that dim chaos of old forest and slope again, or face another time that gray blasted heath where the black well yawned deep beside the tumbled bricks and stones. The reservoir will soon be built now, and all those elder secrets will lie safe under watery fathoms. But even then I do not believe I would like to visit that country by night—at least not when the sinister stars are out; and nothing could bribe me to drink the new city water of Arkham.

It all began, old Ammi said, with the meteorite. Before that time there had bee no wild legends at all since the witch trials, and even then these western woods were not feared half so much as the small island in the Miskatonic where the devil held court beside a curious stone altar older than the Indians. These were not haunted woods, and their fantastic dusk was never terrible till the strange days. Then there had come that white noontide cloud, that string of explosions in the air, and that pillar of smoke from the valley far in the wood. And by night all Arkham had heard of the great rock that fell out of the sky and bedded itself in the ground beside the well at the Nahum Gardner place. That was the house which had stood where the blasted heath was to come—the trim white Nahum Gardner house amidst its fertile gardens and orchards.

Nahum had come to town to tell people about the stone, and had dropped in at Ammi Pierce's on the way. Ammi was forty then, and all the queer things were fixed very strongly in his mind. He and his wife had gone with the

three professors from Miskatonic University who hastened
out the next morning to see the weird visitor from unknown
stellar space, and had wondered why Nahum had called it
so large the day before. It had shrunk, Nahum said as he
pointed out the big brownish mound above the ripped earth
and charred grass near the archaic well-sweep in his front
yard; but the wise men answered that stones do not shrink.
Its heat lingered persistently, and Nahum declared it had
glowed faintly in the night. The professors tried it with a
geologist's hammer and found it was oddly soft. It was, in
truth, so soft as to be almost plastic; and they gouged rather
than chipped a specimen to take back to the college for testing. They took it in an old pail borrowed from Nahum's
kitchen, for even the small piece refused to grow cool. On
the trip back they stopped at Ammi's to rest, and seemed
thoughtful when Mrs. Pierce remarked that the fragment
was growing smaller and burning the bottom of the pail.
Truly, it was not large, but perhaps they had taken less than
they thought.

The day after that—all this was in June of '82—the professors had trooped out again in a great excitement. As they
passed Ammi's they told him what queer things the specimen had done, and how it faded wholly away when they
put it in a glass beaker. The beaker had gone, too, and the
wise men talked of the strange stone's affinity for silicon.
It had acted quite unbelievably in that well-ordered laboratory; doing nothing at all and showing no occluded gases
when heated on charcoal, being wholly negative in the borax
bead, and soon proving itself absolutely non-volatile at any
producible temperature, including that of the oxy-hydrogen
blowpipe. On an anvil it appeared highly malleable, and in
the dark its luminosity was very marked. Stubbornly refus-
ing to grow cool, it soon had the college in a state of real
excitement; and when upon heating before the spectroscope
it displayed shining bands unlike any known colours of the
normal spectrum there was much breathless talk of new el-

ements, bizarre optical properties, and other things which puzzled men of science are wont to say when faced by the unknown.

Hot as it was, they tested it in a crucible with all the proper reagents. Water did nothing. Hydrochloric acid was the same. Nitric acid and even aqua regia merely hissed and spattered against its torrid invulnerability. Ammi had difficulty in recalling all these things, but recognized some solvents as I mentioned them in the usual order of use. There were ammonia and caustic soda, alcohol and ether, nauseous carbon disulphide and a dozen others; but although the weight grew steadily less as time passed, and the fragment seemed to be slightly cooling, there was no change in the solvents to show that they had attacked the substance at all. It was a metal, though, beyond a doubt. It was magnetic, for one thing; and after its immersion in the acid solvents there seemed to be faint traces of the Widmänstätten figures found on meteoric iron. When the cooling had grown very considerable, the testing was carried on in glass; and it was in a glass beaker that they left all the chips made of the original fragment during the work. The next morning both chips and beaker were gone without a trace, and only a charred spot marked the place on the wooden shelf where they had been.

All this the professors told Ammi as they paused at his door, and once more he went with them to see the stony messenger from the stars, though this time his wife did not accompany him. It had now most certainly shrunk, and even the sober professors could not doubt the truth of what they saw. All around the dwindling brown lump near the well was a vacant space, except where the earth had caved in; and whereas it had been a good seven feet across the day before, it was now scarcely five. It was still hot, and the sages studied its surface curiously as they detached another and larger piece with hammer and chisel. They gouged deeply this time, and as they pried

away the smaller mass they saw that the core of the thing
was not quite homogeneous.

They had uncovered what seemed to be the side of a
large coloured globule embedded in the substance. The
colour, which resembled some of the bands in the meteor's
strange spectrum, was almost impossible to describe; and it
was only by analogy that they called it colour at all. Its texture was glossy, and upon tapping it appeared to promise
both brittleness and hollowness. One of the professors gave
it a smart blow with a hammer, and it burst with a nervous
little pop. Nothing was emitted, and all trace of the thing
vanished with the puncturing. It left behind a hollow spher-
ical space about three inches across, and all thought it probable that others would be discovered as the enclosing
substance wasted away.

Conjecture was vain; so after a futile attempt to find
additional globules by drilling, the seekers left again with
their new specimen—which proved, however, as baffling
in the laboratory as its predecessor. Aside from being almost plastic, having heat, magnetism, and slight luminosity, cooling slightly in powerful acids, possessing an
unknown spectrum, wasting away in air, and attacking silicon compounds with mutual destruction as a result, it presented no identifying features whatsoever; and at the end
of the tests the college scientists were forced to own that
they could not place it. It was nothing of this earth, but
a piece of the great outside; and as such dowered with
outside properties and obedient to outside laws.

That night there was a thunderstorm, and when the professors went out to Nahum's the next day they met with a
bitter disappointment. The stone, magnetic as it had been,
must have had some peculiar electrical property; for it had
"drawn lightning," as Nahum said, with a singular persistence. Six times within an hour the farmer saw the lightning strike the furrow in the front yard, and when the storm
was over nothing remained but a ragged pit by the ancient

well-sweep, half-choked with caved-in earth. Digging had
borne no fruit, and the scientists verified the fact of the
utter vanishment. The failure was total; so that nothing was
left to do but go back to the laboratory and test again the
disappearing fragment left carefully cased in lead. That
fragment lasted a week, at the end of which nothing of
value had been learned of it. When it was gone, no residue
was left behind, and in time the professors felt scarcely
sure they had indeed seen with waking eyes that cryptic
vestige of the fathomless gulfs outside; that lone, weird
message from other universes and other realms of matter,
force, and entity.

As was natural, the Arkham papers made much of the
incident with its collegiate sponsoring, and sent reporters to
talk with Nahum Gardner and his family. At least one Boston
daily also sent a scribe, and Nahum quickly became a kind
of local celebrity. He was a lean, genial person of about
fifty, living with his wife and three sons on the pleasant
farmstead in the valley. He and Ammi exchanged visits fre-
quently, as did their wives; and Ammi had nothing but praise
for him after all these years. He seemed slightly proud of
the notice his place had attracted, and talked often of the
meteorite in the succeeding weeks. That July and August
were hot; and Nahum worked hard at his haying in the ten-
acre pasture across Chapman's Brook; his rattling wain
wearing deep ruts in the shadowy lanes between. The labour
tired him more than it had in other years, and he felt that
age was beginning to tell on him.

Then fell the time of fruit and harvest. The pears and
apples slowly ripened, and Nahum vowed that his orchards
were prospering as never before. The fruit was growing to
phenomenal size and unwonted gloss, and in such abundance that extra barrels were ordered to handle the future
crop. But with the ripening came sore disappointment, for
of all that gorgeous array of specious lusciousness not one
single jot was fit to eat. Into the fine flavour of the pears

and apples had crept a stealthy bitterness and sickishness, so that even the smallest of bites introduced a lasting disgust. It was the same with the melons and tomatoes, and Nahum sadly saw that his entire crop was lost. Quick to connect events, he declared that the meteorite had poisoned the soil, and thanked Heaven that most of the other crops were in the upland lot along the road.

Winter came early, and was very cold. Ammi saw Nahum less often than usual, and observed that he had begun to look worried. The rest of his family, too, seemed to have grown taciturn; and were far from steady in their church-going or their attendance at the various social events of the countryside. For this reserve or melancholy no cause could be found, though all the household confessed now and then to poorer health and a feeling of vague disquiet. Nahum himself gave the most definite statement of anyone when he said he was disturbed about certain footprints in the snow. They were the usual winter prints of red squirrels, white rabbits, and foxes, but the brooding farmer professed to see something not quite right about their nature and arrangement. He was never specific, but appeared to think that they were not as characteristic of the anatomy and habits of squirrels and rabbits and foxes as they ought to be. Ammi listened without interest to this talk until one night when he drove past Nahum's house in his sleigh on the way back from Clark's Corners. There had been a moon, and a rabbit had run across the road; and the leaps of that rabbit were longer than either Ammi or his horse liked. The latter, indeed, had almost run away when brought up by a firm rein. Thereafter Ammi gave Nahum's tales more respect, and wondered why the Gardner dogs seemed so cowed and quivering every morning. They had, it developed, nearly lost the spirit to bark.

In February the McGregor boys from Meadow Hill were out shooting woodchucks, and not far away from the Gardner place bagged a very peculiar specimen. The proportions of its body seemed slightly altered in a queer way impossible to describe, while its face had taken on an expression which no one had ever seen in a woodchuck before. The boys were genuinely frightened, and threw the thing away at once, so that only their grotesque tales of it ever reached the people of the countryside. But the shying of horses near Nahum's house had now become an acknowledged thing, and all the basis for a cycle of whispered legend was fast taking form.

People vowed that the snow melted faster around Nahum's than it did anywhere else, and early in March there was an awed discussion in Potter's general store at Clark's Corners. Stephen Rice had driven past Gardner's in the morning, and had noticed the skunk-cabbages coming up through the mud by the woods across the road. Never were things of such size seen before, and they held strange colours that could not be put into any words. Their shapes were monstrous, and the horse had snorted at an odour which struck Stephen as wholly unprecedented. That afternoon several persons drove past to see the abnormal growth, and all agreed that plants of that kind ought never to sprout in a healthy world. The bad fruit of the fall before was freely mentioned, and it went from mouth to mouth that there was a poison in Nahum's ground. Of course it was the meteorite; and remembering how strange the men from the college had found that stone to be, several farmers spoke about the matter to them.

One day they paid Nahum a visit; but having no love of wild tales and folklore were very conservative in what they inferred. The plants were certainly odd, but all skunk-cabbages are more or less odd in shape and hue. Perhaps some mineral element from the stone had entered the soil, but it would soon be washed away. And as for the footprints and frightened horses—of course this was mere country talk which such a phenomenon as the aerolite would be certain to start. There was really nothing for serious men to do in cases of wild gossip, for superstitous rustics will say and believe anything. And so all through the strange days the professors stayed away in contempt. Only one of them, when given two phials of dust for analysis in a police job over a year and a half later, recalled that the queer colour of that skunk-cabbage had been very like one of the anomalous bands of light shown by the meteor fragment in the college spectroscope, and like the brittle globule found imbedded in the stone from the abyss. The samples in this analysis case gave the same odd bands at first, though later they lost the property.

The trees budded prematurely around Nahum's, and at night they swayed ominously in the wind. Nahum's second son Thaddeus, a lad of fifteen, swore that they swayed also when there was no wind; but even the gossips would not credit this. Certainly, however, restlessness was in the air. The entire Gardner family developed the habit of stealthy listening, though not for any sound which they could consciously name. The listening was, indeed, rather a product of moments when consciousness seemed half to slip away. Unfortunately such moments increased week by week, till it became common speech that "something was wrong with all Nahum's folks." When the early saxifrage came out it had another strange colour; not quite like that of the skunk-cabbage, but plainly related and equally unknown to anyone who saw it. Nahum took some blossoms to Arkham and showed them to the editor of the *Gazette*, but that dignitary did no more than write a humorous article about them, in which the dark fears of rustics were held up to polite ridicule. It was a mistake of Nahum's to tell a stolid city man about the way the great, overgrown mourning-cloak butterflies behaved in connection with these saxifrages.

April brought a kind of madness to the country folk, and began that disuse of the road past Nahum's which led to its ultimate abandonment. It was next the vegetation. All the orchard trees blossomed forth in strange colours, and through the stony soil of the yard and adjacent pasturage there sprang up a bizarre growth which only a botanist could connect with the proper flora of the region. No sane wholesome colours were anywhere to be seen except in the green grass and leafage; but everywhere were those hectic and prismatic variants of some diseased, underlying primary tone without a place among the known tints of earth. The "Dutchman's breeches" became a thing of sinister menace, and the bloodroots grew insolent in the chromatic perversion. Ammi and the Gardners thought that most of the colours had a sort of haunting familiarity, and decided that they reminded one of the brittle globule in the meteor. Nahum ploughed and sowed the ten-acre pasture and the upland lot, but did nothing with the land around the house. He knew it would be of no use, and hoped that the summer's strange growths would draw all the poison from the soil. He was prepared for almost anything now, and had grown used to the sense of something near him waiting to be heard. The shunning of his house by neighbours told on him, of course; but it told on his wife more. The boys were better off, being at school each day; but they could not help being frightened by the gossip. Thaddeus, an especially sensitive youth, suffered the most.

In May the insects came, and Nahum's place became a nightmare of buzzing and crawling. Most of the creatures seemed not quite usual in their aspects and motions, and their nocturnal habits contradicted all former experience. The Gardners took to watching at night—watching in all directions at random for something they could not tell what. It was then that they all owned that Thaddeus had been right about the trees. Mrs. Gardner was the next to see it from the window as she watched the swollen boughs of a maple against a moonlit sky. The boughs surely moved, and there was no wind. It must be the sap. Strangeness had come into everything growing now. Yet it was none of Nahum's family at all who made the next discovery. Fa-

miliarity had dulled them, and what they could not see was
glimpsed by a timid windmill salesman from Bolton who
drove by one night in ignorance of the country legends.
What he told in Arkham was given a short paragraph in the
Gazette; and it was there that all the farmers, Nahum included, saw it first. The night had been dark and the buggy-
lamps faint, but around a farm in the valley which everyone
knew from the account must be Nahum's, the darkness had
been less thick. A dim though distinct luminosity seemed
to inhere in all the vegetation, grass, leaves and blossoms
alike, while at one moment a detached piece of the phosphorescence appeared to stir furtively in the yard near the
barn.

The grass had so far seemed untouched, and the cows
were freely pastured in the lot near the house, but toward
the end of May the milk began to be bad. Then Nahum had
the cows driven to the uplands, after which this trouble
ceased. Not long after this the change in grass and leaves
became apparent to the eye. All the verdure was going gray,
and was developing a highly singular quality of brittleness.
Ammi was now the only person who ever visited the place,
and his visits were becoming fewer and fewer. When school
closed the Gardners were virtually cut off from the world,
and sometimes let Ammi do their errands in town. They
were failing curiously both physically and mentally, and no
one was surprised when the news of Mrs. Gardner's madness stole around.

It happened in June, about the anniversary of the meteor's fall, and the poor woman screamed about things in
the air which she could not describe. In her raving there
was not a single specific noun, but only verbs and pronouns.
Things moved and changed and fluttered, and ears tingled
to impulses which were not wholly sounds. Something was
taken away—she was being drained of something—something was fastening itself on her that ought not to be—
someone must make it keep off—nothing was ever still in

the night—the walls and windows shifted. Nahum did not send her to the county asylum, but let her wander about the house as long as she was harmless to herself and others. Even when her expression changed he did nothing. But when the boys grew afraid of her, and Thaddeus nearly fainted at the way she made faces at him, he decided to keep her locked in the attic. By July she had ceased to speak and crawled on all fours, and before that month was over, Nahum got the mad notion that she was slightly luminous in the dark, as he now clearly saw was the case with the nearby vegetation.

It was a little before this that the horses had stampeded. Something had aroused them in the night, and their neighing and kicking in their stalls had been terrible. There seemed virtually nothing to do to calm them, and when Nahum opened the stable door they all bolted out like frightened woodland deer. It took a week to track all four, and when found they were seen to be quite useless and unmanageable. Something had snapped in their brains, and each one had to be shot for its own good. Nahum borrowed a horse from Ammi for his haying, but found it would not approach the barn. It shied, balked, and whinnied, and in the end he could do nothing but drive it into the yard while the men used their own strength to get the heavy wagon near enough the hayloft for convenient pitching. And all the while the vegetation was turning gray and brittle. Even the flowers whose hues had been so strange were graying now, and the fruit was coming out gray and dwarfed and tasteless. The asters and goldenrod bloomed gray and distorted, and the roses and zinnias and hollyhocks in the front yard were such blasphemous-looking things that Nahum's oldest boy, Zenas, cut them down. The strangely puffed insects died about that time, even the bees that had left their hives and taken to the woods.

By September all the vegetation was fast crumbling to a grayish powder, and Nahum feared that the trees would die before the poison was out of the soil. His wife now had spells of terrific screaming, and he and the boys were in a constant state of nervous tension. They shunned people now, and when school opened the boys did not go. But it was Ammi, on one of his rare visits, who first realized that the well water was no longer good. It had an evil taste that was not exactly fetid nor exactly salty, and Ammi advised his friend to dig another well on higher ground to use till the soil was good again. Nahum, however, ignored the warning, for he had by that time become calloused to strange and unpleasant things. He and the boys continued to use the tainted supply, drinking it as listlessly and mechanically as they ate their meager and ill-cooked meals and did their thankless and monotonous chores through the aimless days. There was something of a stolid resignation about them all, as if they walked half in another world between lines of nameless guards to a certain and familiar doom.

Thaddeus went mad in September after a visit to the well. He had gone with a pail and had come back empty-handed, shrieking and waving his arms, and sometimes lapsing into an inane titter or a whisper about "the moving colours down there." Two in one family was pretty bad, but Nahum was very brave about it. He let the boy run about for a week until he began stumbling and hurting himself, and then he shut him in an attic room across the hall from his mother's. The way they screamed at each other from behind their locked doors was very terrible, especially to little Merwin, who fancied they talked in some terrible language that was not of earth. Merwin was getting frightfully imaginative, and his restlessness was worse after the shutting away of the brother who had been his greatest playmate.

Almost at the same time the mortality among the livestock commenced. Poultry turned grayish and died very quickly, their meat being found dry and noisome upon cutting. Hogs grew inordinately fat, then suddenly began to undergo loathsome changes which no one could explain. Their meat was of course useless, and Nahum was at his wit's end. No rural veterinary could approach his place, and the city veterinary from Arkham was openly baffled. The swine began growing gray and brittle and falling to pieces before they died, and their eyes and muzzles developed singular alterations. It was very inexplicable, for they had never been fed from tainted vegetation. Then something struck the cows. Certain areas or sometimes the whole body would be uncannily shriveled or compressed, and atrocious collapses or disintegrations were common. In the last stages—and death was always the result—there would be a graying and turning brittle like that which beset the hogs. There could be no question of poison, for all the cases occurred in a locked and undisturbed barn. No bites of prowling things could have brought the virus, for what live beast of earth can pass through solid obstacles? It must be only natural disease—yet what disease could wreak such results was beyond any mind's guessing. When the harvest came there was not an animal surviving on the place, for the stock and poultry were dead and the dogs had run away. These dogs, three in number, had all vanished one night and were never heard of again. The five cats had left some time before, but their going was scarcely noticed since there now seemed to be no mice, and only Mrs. Gardner had made pets of the graceful felines.

On the nineteenth of October Nahum staggered into Ammi's house with hideous news. The death had come to poor Thaddeus in his attic room, and it had come in a way which could not be told. Nahum had dug a grave in the railed family plot behind the farm, and had put therein what he found. There could have been nothing from outside, for the small barred window and locked door were intact; but it was much as it had been in the barn. Ammi and his wife consoled the stricken man as best they could, but shuddered

as they did so. Stark terror seemed to cling round the Gardners and all they touched, and the very presence of one in
the house was a breath from regions unnamed and unnam-
able. Ammi accompanied Nahum home with the greatest
reluctance, and did what he might to calm the hysterical
sobbing of little Merwin. Zenas needed no calming. He had
come of late do to nothing but stare into space and obey
what his father told him; and Ammi thought that his fate
was very merciful. Now and then Merwin's screams were
answered faintly from the attic, and in response to an inquiring look Nahum said that his wife was getting very feeble. When night approached, Ammi managed to get away;
for not even friendship could make him stay in that spot
when the faint glow of the vegetation began and the trees
may or may not have swayed without wind. It was really
lucky for Ammi that he was not more imaginative. Even as
things were, his mind was bent ever so slightly; but had he
been able to connect and reflect upon all the portents around
him he must inevitably have turned a total maniac. In the
twilight he hastened home, the screams of the mad woman
and the nervous child ringing horribly in his ears.

Three days later Nahum burst into Ammi's kitchen in
the early morning, and in the absence of his host stammered
out a desperate tale once more, while Mrs. Pierce listened
in a clutching fright. It was little Merwin this time. He was
gone. He had gone out late at night with a lantern and pail
for water, and had never come back. He'd been going to
pieces for days, and hardly knew what he was about.
Screamed at everything. There had been a frantic shriek
from the yard then, but before the father could get to the
door the boy was gone. There was no glow from the lantern
he had taken, and of the child himself no trace. At the time
Nahum thought the lantern and pail were gone too; but when
dawn came, and the man had plodded back from his all-
night search of the woods and fields, he had found some
very curious things near the well. There was a crushed and

apparently somewhat melted mass of iron which had certainly been the lantern; while a bent pail and twisted iron hoops beside it, both half-fused, seemed to hint at the remnants of the pail. That was all. Nahum was past imagining, Mrs. Pierce was blank, and Ammi, when he had reached home and heard the tale, could give no guess. Merwin was gone, and there would be no use in telling the people around, who shunned all Gardners now. No use, either, in telling the city people at Arkham who laughed at everything. Thad was gone, and now Merwin was gone. Something was creeping and creeping and waiting to be seen and heard. Nahum would go soon, and he wanted Ammi to look after his wife and Zenas if they survived him. It must be a judgment of some sort; though he could not fancy what for, since he had always walked uprightly in the Lord's ways so far as he knew.

For over two weeks Ammi saw nothing of Nahum; and then, worried about what might have happened, he overcame his fears and paid the Gardner place a visit. There was no smoke from the great chimney, and for a moment the visitor was apprehensive of the worst. The aspect of the whole farm was shocking—graying withered grass and leaves on the ground, vines falling in brittle wreckage from archaic walls and gables, and great bare trees clawing up at the gray November sky with a studied malevolence which Ammi could not but feel had come from some subtle change in the tilt of the branches. But Nahum was alive, after all. He was weak, and lying in a couch in the low-ceiled kitchen, but perfectly conscious and able to give simple orders to Zenas. The room was deadly cold; and as Ammi visibly shivered, the host shouted huskily to Zenas for more wood. Wood, indeed, was sorely needed; since the cavernous fireplace was unlit and empty, with a cloud of soot blowing about in the chill wind that came down the chimney. Presently Nahum asked him if the extra wood had made him any more comfortable, and then Ammi saw what had happened. The stoutest cord had broken at last, and the hapless farmer's mind was proof against more sorrow.

Questioning tactfully, Ammi could get no clear data at all about the missing Zenas. "In the well—he lives in the well—" was all that the clouded father would say. Then there flashed across the visitor's mind a sudden thought of the mad wife, and he changed his line of inquiry. "Nabby? Why, here she is!" was the surprised response of poor Nahum, and Ammi soon saw that he must search for himself. Leaving the harmless babbler on the couch, he took the keys from their nail beside the door and climbed the creaking stairs to the attic. It was very close and noisome up there, and no sound could be heard from any direction. Of the four doors in sight, only one was locked, and on this he tried various keys on the ring he had taken. The third key proved the right one, and after some fumbling Ammi threw open the white door.

It was quite dark inside, for the window was small and half-obscured by the crude wooden bars; and Ammi could see nothing at all on the wide-planked floor. The stench was beyond enduring, and before proceeding further he had to retreat to another room and return with his lungs filled with breathable air. When he did enter he saw something dark in the corner, and upon seeing it more clearly he screamed outright. While he screamed he thought a momentary cloud eclipsed the window, and a second later he felt himself brushed as if by some hateful current of vapour. Strange colours danced before his eyes; and had not a present horror numbed him he would have thought of the globule in the meteor that the geologist's hammer had shattered, and of the morbid vegetation that had sprouted in the spring. As it was he thought only of the blasphemous monstrosity which confronted him, and which all too clearly had shared the nameless fate of young Thaddeus and the livestock. But the terrible thing about the horror was that it very slowly and perceptibly moved as it continued to crumble.

Ammi would give me no added particulars of this scene, but the shape in the corner does not reappear in his tale as a moving object. There are things which cannot be mentioned, and what is done in common humanity is sometimes cruelly judged by the law. I gathered that no moving thing was left in that attic room, and that to leave anything capable of motion there would have been a deed too monstrous as to damn any accountable being to eternal torment. Anyone but a stolid farmer would have fainted or gone mad, but Ammi walked conscious through that low doorway and locked the accursed secret behind him. There would be Nahum to deal with now; he must be fed and tended, and removed to some place where he could be cared for.

Commencing his descent of the dark stairs, Ammi heard a thud below him. He even thought a scream had been suddenly choked off, and recalled nervously the clammy vapour which had brushed by him in that frightful room above. What presence had his cry and entry started up? Halted by some vague fear, he heard still further sounds below. Indubitably there was a sort of heavy dragging, and a most detestably sticky noise as of some fiendish and unclean species of suction. With an associative sense goaded to feverish heights, he thought unaccountably of what he had seen upstairs. Good God! What eldritch dreamworld was this into which he had blundered? He dared moved neither backward nor forward, but stood there trembling at the black curve of the boxed-in staircase. Every trifle of the scene burned itself into his brain. The sounds, the sense of dread expectancy, the darkness, the steepness of the narrow steps—and merciful Heaven!—the faint but unmistakable luminosity of all the woodwork in sight; steps, sides, exposed laths, and beams alike.

Then there burst forth a frantic whinny from Ammi's horse outside, followed at once by a clatter which told of a frenzied runaway. In another moment horse and buggy had gone beyond earshot, leaving the frightened man on the dark stairs to guess what had sent them. But that was not all. There had been another sound out there. A sort of liquid splash—water—it must have been the well. He had left Hero untied near it, and a buggy-wheel must have brushed the coping and knocked in a stone. And still the pale phosphorescence glowed in that detestably ancient woodwork. God! How old the house was! Most of it built before 1700.

A feeble scratching on the floor downstairs now sounded distinctly, and Ammi's grip tightened on a heavy stick he had picked up in the attic for some purpose. Slowly nerving himself, he finished his descent and walked boldly toward the kitchen. But he did not complete the walk, because what he sought was no longer there. It had come to meet him, and it was still alive after a fashion. Whether it had crawled or whether it had been dragged by any external forces, Ammi could not say; but the death had been at it. Everything had happened in the last half-hour, but collapse, graying, and disintegration were already far advanced. There was a horrible brittleness, and dry fragments were scaling off. Ammi could not touch it, but looked horrifiedly into the distorted parody that had been a face. "What was it, Nahum—what was it?" He whispered, and the cleft, bulging lips were just able to crackle out a final answer.

"Nothin' . . . nothin' . . . the colour . . . it burns . . . it lived in the well . . . I seen it . . . a kind o' smoke . . . jest like the flowers last spring . . . the well shone at night . . . Thad an' Merwin an' Zenas . . . everything alive . . . suckin' the life out of everything . . . in that stone . . . it must o' come in that stone . . . pizened the whole place . . . don't know what it wants . . . that round thing them men from the college dug outen the stone . . . they smashed . . . it was that same colour . . . jest the same, like the flowers an' plants . . . must a' ben more of 'em . . . seeds . . . seeds . . . they growed . . . I seen it the fust time this week . . . must a' got strong on Zenas . . . he was a big boy, full o' life . . . it beats down your mind an' then gits ye . . . burns ye up . . . in the well water . . . you was right about that . . . evil water . . . Zenas never come back from the well . . . can't git away . . . draws ye . . . ye know summ'at's comin', but tain't no use . . . I seen it time an' agin Zenas was took . . . whar's Nabby, Ammi? . . . my head's no good . . . dun't know how long sence I fed her . . . it'll get her ef we ain't keerful . . . jest a colour . . . her face is gittin' to hev that colour some-times towards night . . . an' it burns an' sucks . . . it come from some place whar things ain't as they is here . . . one o' them professors said so . . . he was right . . . look out, Ammi, it'll do suthin' more . . . sucks the life out . . ."

But that was all. That which spoke could speak no more because it had completely caved in. Ammi laid a red checked tablecloth over what was left and reeled out the back door into the fields. He climbed the slope to the ten-acre pasture and stumbled home by the north road and the woods. He could not pass that well from which his horses had run away. He had looked at it through the window, and had seen that no stone was missing from the rim. Then the lurch-ing buggy had not dislodged anything after all—the splash had been something else—something which went in the well after it had done with poor Nahum. . . .

When Ammi reached his house the horses and buggy had arrived before him and thrown his wife into fits of anx-iety. Reassuring her without explanations, he set out at once for Arkham and notified the authorities that the Gardner family was no more. He indulged in no details, but merely told of the deaths of Nahum and Nabby, that of Thaddeus being already known, and mentioned that the cause seemed to be the same strange ailment which had killed the live-stock. He also stated that Merwin and Zenas had disappeared. There was considerable questioning at the police station, and in the end Ammi was compelled to take three officers to the Gardner farm, together with the coroner, the medical

examiner, and the veterinary who had treated the diseased
animals. He went much against his will, for the afternoon
was advancing and he feared the fall of night over that accursed place, but it was some comfort to have so many people with him.

The six men drove out in a democrat-wagon, following
Ammi's buggy, arrived at the pest-ridden farmhouse about
four o'clock. Used as the officers were to gruesome experiences, not one remained unmoved at what was found in
the attic, and under the red checked tablecloth on the floor
below. The whole aspect of the farm with its gray desolation was terrible enough, but those two crumbling objects
were beyond all bounds. No one could look long at them,
and even the medical examiner admitted that there was very
little to examine. Specimens could be analyzed, of course,
so he busied himself in obtaining them—and here it de-
velops that a very puzzling aftermath occurred at the college laboratory where the two phials of dust were finally
taken. Under the spectroscope both samples gave off an unknown spectrum, in which many of the baffling bands were
precisely like those which the strange meteor had yielded
in the previous year. The property of emitting this spectrum
vanished in a month, the dust thereafter consisting mainly
of alkaline phosphates and carbonates.

Ammi would not have told the men about the well if he
had thought they meant to do anything then and there. It
was getting toward sunset, and he was anxious to be away.
But he could not help glancing nervously at the stony curb
by the great sweep, and when a detective questioned him
he admitted that Nahum had feared something down there—
so much so that he had never even thought of searching it
for Merwin or Zenas. After that nothing would do but that
they empty and explore the well immediately, so Ammi had
to wait trembling while pail after pail of rank water was
hauled up and splashed on the soaking ground outside. The

men sniffed in disgust at the fluid, and toward the last held their noses against the foetor they were uncovering. It was not so long a job as they had feared it would be, since the water was phenomenally low. There is no need to speak too exactly of what they found. Merwin and Zenas were both there, in part, though the vestiges were mainly skeletal. There were also a small deer and a large dog in about the same state, and a number of bones of smaller animals. The ooze and slime at the bottom seemed inexplicably porous and bubbling, and a man who descended on hand-holds with a long pole found that he could sink the wooden shaft to any depth in the mud of the floor without meeting any solid obstruction.

Twilight had now fallen, and lanterns were brought from the house. Then, when it was seen that nothing further could be gained from the well, everyone went indoors and conferred in the ancient sitting-room while the intermittent light of a spectral half-moon played wanly on the gray desolation outside. The men were frankly nonplused by the entire case, and could find no convincing common element to link the strange vegetable conditions, the unknown disease of livestock and humans, and the unaccountable deaths of Merwin and Zenas in the tainted well. They had heard the common country talk, it is true; but could not believe that anything contrary to natural law had occurred. No doubt the meteor had poisoned the soil, but the illness of person and animals who had eaten nothing grown in that soil was another matter. Was it the well water? Very possibly. It might be a good idea to analyze it. But what peculiar madness could have made both boys jump into the well? Their deeds were so similar—and the fragments showed that they had both suffered from the gray brittle death. Why was everything so gray and brittle?

It was the coroner, seated near a window overlooking the yard, who first noticed the glow about the well. Night had fully set in, and all the abhorrent grounds seemed faintly luminous with more than the fitful moonbeams; but this new glow was something definite and distinct, and appeared to shoot up from the black pit like a softened ray from a searchlight, giving dull reflections in the little ground pools where the water had been emptied. It had a very queer colour, and as all the men clustered round the window Ammi gave a violent start. For this strange beam of ghastly miasma was to him of no unfamiliar hue. He had seen that colour before, and feared to think what it might mean. He had seen it in the nasty brittle globule in that aerolite two summers ago, had seen it in the crazy vegetation of the springtime, and had thought he had seen it for an instant that very morning against the small barred window of that terrible attic room where nameless things had happened. It had flashed there a second, and a clammy and hateful current of vapour had brushed past him—and then poor Nahum had been taken by something of that colour. He had said so at the last—said it was like the globule and the plants. After that had come the runaway in the yard and the splash in the well—now that well was belching forth to the night a pale insidious beam of the same demoniac tint.

It does credit to the alertness of Ammi's mind that he puzzled even at that tense moment over a point which was essentially scientific. He could not but wonder at his gleaning of the same impression from a vapour glimpsed in the daytime, against window opening in the morning sky, and from a nocturnal exhalation seen as a phosphorescent mist against the black and blasted landscape. It wasn't right— it was against Nature—and he thought of those terrible last words of his stricken friend, "It come from some place whar things ain't as they is here . . . one o' them professors said so. . . ."

All three horses outside, tied to a pair of shriveled saplings by the road, were now neighing and pawing frantically. The wagon driver started for the door to do something, but Ammi laid a shaky hand on his shoulder. "Dun't go out thar," he whispered. "They's more to this nor what we know. Nahum said somthin' lived in the well that sucks your life out. He said it must be some'at growed from a round ball like one we all seen in the meteor stone that fell a year ago June. Sucks an' burns, he said, an' is jest a cloud of colour like that light out thar now, that ye can hardly see an' can't tell what it is. Nahum thought it feeds on everything livin' an gits stronger all the time. He said he seen it this last week. It must be somethin' from away off in the sky like the men from the college last year says the meteor stone was. The way it's made an' the way it works ain't like no way o' God's world. It's some'at from beyond."

So the men paused indecisively as the light from the well grew stronger and the hitched horses pawed and whinnied in increasing frenzy. It was truly an awful moment; with terror in that ancient and accursed house itself, four monstrous sets of fragments—two from the house and two from the well—in the woodshed behind, and that shaft of unknown and unholy iridescence from the slimy depths in front. Ammi had restrained the driver on impulse, forgetting how uninjured he himself was after the clammy brushing of that coloured vapour in the attic room, but perhaps it is just as well that he acted as he did. No one will ever know what was abroad that night; and though the blasphemy from beyond had not so far hurt any human of unweakened mind, there is no telling what it might have done at that last moment, and with its seemingly increased strength and the special signs of purpose it was soon to display beneath the half-clouded moonlit sky.

All at once one of the detectives at the window gave a short, sharp gasp. The others looked at him, and then quickly followed his own gaze upward to the point at which its idle straying had been suddenly arrested. There was no need for words. What had been disputed in country gossip was disputable no longer, and it is because of the thing which every man of that party agreed in whispering later on, that strange days are never talked about in Arkham. It is necessary to premise that there was no wind at that hour of the evening. One did arise not long afterward, but there was absolutely none then. Even the dry tips of the lingering hedge-mustard, gray and blighted, and the fringe of the roof of the standing democrat-wagon were unstirred. And yet amid that tense, godless calm the high bare boughs of all the trees in the yard were moving. They were twitching morbidly and spasmodically, clawing in convulsive and epileptic madness at the moonlit clouds; scratching impotently in the noxious air as if jerked by some allied and bodiless line of linkage with subterrene horrors writhing and struggling below the black roots.

Not a man breathed for several seconds. Then a cloud of darker depth passed over the moon, and the silhouette of clutching branches faded out momentarily. At this there was a general cry; muffled with awe, but husky and almost identical from every throat. For the terror had not faded with the silhouette, and in a fearsome instant of deeper darkness the watchers saw wriggling at the treetop height a thousand tiny points of faint and unhaloed radiance, tipping each bough like the fire of St. Elmo or the flames that came down on the apostles' heads at Pentecost. It was a monstrous constellation of unnatural light, like a glutted swarm of corpse-fed fireflies dancing hellish sarabands over an accursed marsh; and its colour was that same nameless intrusion which Ammi had come to recognize and dread. All the while the shaft of phosphorescence from the well was getting brighter and brighter, bringing to the minds of the huddled men, a sense of doom and abnormality which far outraced any image their conscious minds could form. It was no longer *shining* out; it was *pouring* out; and as the shapeless stream of unpeaceable colour left the well it seemed to flow directly into the sky.

The veterinary shivered, and walked to the front door to drop the heavy extra bar across it. Ammi shook no less, and had to tug and point for lack of a controllable voice when he wished to draw notice to the growing luminosity of the trees. The neighing and stamping of the horses had become utterly frightful, but not a soul of that group in the old house would have ventured forth for any earthly reward. With the moments the shining of the trees increased, while their restless branches seemed to strain more and more toward verticality. The wood of the well-sweep was shining now, and presently a policeman dumbly pointed to some wooden sheds and beehives near the stone wall on the west. They were commencing to shine, too, though the tethered vehicles of the visitors seemed so far unaffected. Then there was a wild commotion and clopping in the road, and as Ammi quenched the lamp for better seeing they realized that the span of frantic grays had broken their sapling and run off with the democrat-wagon.

The shock served to loosen several tongues, and embarrassed whispers were exchanged. "It spreads on everything organic that's been around here," muttered the medical examiner. No one replied, but the man who had been in the well gave a hint that his long pole must have stirred up something intangible. "It was awful," he added. "There was no bottom at all. Just ooze and bubbles and the feeling of something lurking under there." Ammi's horse still pawed and screamed deafeningly in the road outside, and nearly drowned its owner's faint quaver as he mumbled his formless reflections. "It come from that stone—it growed down thar—it got everything livin'—it fed itself on 'em, mind and body—Thad an' Merwin, Zenas an' Nabby—Nahum was the last—they all drunk the water—it got strong on 'em—it come from beyond, whar things ain't like they be here—now it's goin' home—"

At this point, as the column of unknown colour flared suddenly stronger and began to weave itself into fantastic suggestions of shape which each spectator later described differently, there came from poor tethered Hero such a sound as no man before or since ever heard from a horse. Every person in that low-pitched sitting room stopped his ears, and Ammi turned away from the window in horror and nausea. Words could not convey it—when Ammi looked out again the hapless beast lay huddled inert on the moonlit ground between the splintered shafts of the buggy. That was the last of Hero till they buried him next day. But the present was no time to mourn, for almost at this instant a detective silently called attention to something terrible in the very room with them. In the absence of the lamplight it was clear that a faint phosphorescence had begun to pervade the entire apartment. It glowed on the broad-planked floor where the rag carpet left it bare, and shimmered over the sashes of the small-paned windows. It ran up and down the exposed corner-posts, coruscated about the shelf and mantel, and infected the very doors and furniture. Every minute saw it strengthen, and at last it was very plain that healthy living things must leave that house.

Ammi showed them the back door and the path up through the fields to the ten-acre pasture. They walked and stumbled as in a dream, and did not dare look back till they were far away on the high ground. They were glad of the path, for they could not have gone the front way, by that well. It was bad enough passing the glowing barn and sheds, and those shining orchard trees with their gnarled, fiendish contours; but thank Heaven the branches did their worst twisting high up. The moon went under some very black clouds as they crossed the rustic bridge over Chapman's Brook, and it was blind groping from there to the open meadows.

When they looked back toward the valley and the distant Gardner place at the bottom they saw a fearsome sight. All the farm was shining with the hideous unknown blend of colour; trees, buildings, and even such grass and herbage as had not been wholly changed to lethal gray brittleness. The boughs were all straining skyward, tipped with tongues of foul flame, and lambent tricklings of the same monstrous fire were creeping about the ridgepoles of the house, barn and sheds. It was a scene from a vision of Fuseli, and over all the rest reigned that riot of luminous amorphousness, that alien and undimensioned rainbow of cryptic poison from the well—seething, feeling, lapping, reaching, scintillating, straining and malignly bubbling in its cosmic and unrecognizable chromaticism.

Then without warning the hideous thing shot vertically up toward the sky like a rocket or meteor, leaving behind no trail and disappearing through a round and curiously regular hole in the clouds before any man could gasp or cry out. No watcher can ever forget that sight, and Ammi stared blankly at the stars of Cygnus, Deneb twinkling above the others, where the unknown colour had melted into the Milky Way. But his gaze was the next moment called swiftly to earth by the crackling in the valley. It was just that. Only a wooden ripping and crackling, and not an explosion, as so many others of the party vowed. Yet the outcome was the same, for in one feverish kaleidoscopic instant there burst up from that doomed and accursed farm a gleamingly eruptive cataclysm of unnatural sparks and substance; blurring the glance of the few who saw it, and sending forth to the zenith a bombarding cloudburst of such coloured and fantastic fragments as our universe must needs disown. Through quickly re-closing vapours they followed the great morbidity that had vanished, and in another second they had vanished too. Behind and below was only a darkness to which the men dared not return, and all about was a mounting wind which seemed to sweep down in black, frore gusts from interstellar space. It shrieked and howled, and lashed the fields and distorted woods in a mad cosmic frenzy, till soon the trembling party realized it would be of no use waiting for the moon to show what was left down there at Nahum's.

Too awed even to hint theories, the seven shaking men trudged back toward Arkham by the north road. Ammi was worse than his fellows, and begged them to see him inside his own kitchen, instead of keeping straight on to town. He did not wish to cross the blighted, wind-whipped woods alone to his home on the main road. For he had an added shock that the others were spared, and was crushed forever with a brooding fear he dared not even mention for many years to come. As the rest of the watchers on that tempestuous hill had stolidly set their faces toward the road, Ammi had looked back an instant at the shadowed valley of desolation so lately sheltering his ill-starred friend. And from that stricken, faraway spot, he had seen something feebly rise, only to sink down again upon the place from which the great shapeless horror had shot into the sky. It was just a colour—but not any colour of our earth or heavens. And because Ammi recognized that colour, and knew that this last faint remnant must still lurk down there in the well, he has never been quite right since.

Ammi would never go near the place again. It is forty-four years now since the horror happened, but he has never been there, and will be glad when the new reservoir blots it out. I shall be glad, too, for I do not like the way the sunlight changed colour around the mouth of that abandoned well I passed. I hope the water will always be very deep—but even so, I shall never drink it. I do not think I shall visit the Arkham county hereafter. Three of the men who had been with Ammi returned the next morning to see the ruins by daylight, but there were not any real ruins. Only the bricks of the chimney, the stones of the cellar, some mineral and metallic litter here and there, and the rim of that nefandous well. Save for Ammi's dead horse, which they towed away and buried, and the buggy, which they shortly returned to him, everything that had ever been living had gone. Five eldritch acres of dusty gray desert remained, nor has anything ever grown there since. To this day it sprawls open to the sky like a great spot eaten by acid in the woods and fields, and the few who have ever dared glimpse it in spite of the rural tales have named it "the blasted heath."

The rural tales are queer. They might be even queerer if city men and college chemists could be interested enough to analyze the water from that disused well, or the gray dust that no wind seems ever to disperse. Botanists, too, ought to study the stunted flora on the borders of that spot, for they might shed light on the country notion that the blight is spreading—little by little, perhaps an inch a year. People say the colour of the neighboring herbage is not quite right in the spring, and that wild things leave queer prints in the light winter snow. Snow never seems quite so heavy on the blasted heath as it is elsewhere. Horses—the few that are left in this motor age—grow skittish in the silent valley; and hunters cannot depend on their dogs too near the splotch of grayish dust.

They say the mental influences are very bad, too; numbers went queer in the years after Nahum's taking, and always they lacked the power to get away. Then the stronger-minded folk all left the region, and only the foreigners tried to live in crumbling old homesteads. They could not stay, though; and one sometimes wonders what insight beyond ours their wild, weird stories of whispered magic have given them. Their dreams at night, they protest, are very horrible in that grotesque country; and surely the very look of the dark realm is enough to stir a morbid fancy. No traveler has ever escaped a sense of strangeness in those deep ravines, and artists shiver as they paint thick woods whose mystery is as much of the spirit as of the eye. I myself am curious about the sensation I derived from my one lone walk before Ammi told me his tale. When twilight came I had vaguely wished some clouds would gather, for odd timidity about the deep skyey voids above had crept into my soul.

Do not ask me for my opinion. I do not know—that is all. There was no one but Ammi to question; for Arkham people will not talk about the strange days, and all three professors who saw the aerolite and its coloured globule are dead. There were other globules—depend upon that. One must have fed itself and escaped, and probably there was another which was too late. No doubt it is still down the well—I know there was something wrong with the sunlight I saw above that miasmal brink. The rustics say the blight creeps an inch a year, so perhaps there is a kind of growth or nourishment even now. But whatever demon hatchling is there, it must be tethered to something or else it would quickly spread. Is it fastened to the roots of those trees that claw the air? One of the current Arkham tales is about fat oaks that shine and move as they ought not to do at night.

What it is, only God knows. In terms of matter I suppose the thing Ammi described would be called a gas, but this gas obeyed laws that are not of our cosmos. This was no fruit of such worlds and suns as shine on the telescopes and photographic plates of our observatories. This was no breath from the skies whose motions and dimensions our astronomers measure or deem too vast to measure. It was just a colour out of space—a frightful messenger from unformed realms of infinity beyond all Nature as we know it; from realms whose mere existence stuns the brain and numbs us with the black extra-cosmic gulfs it throws open before our unfettered eyes.

I doubt very much if Ammi consciously lied to me, and I do not think his tale was all a freak of madness as the townsfolk had forewarned. Something terrible came to the hills and valleys on that meteor, and something terrible—though I know not in what proportion—still remains. I shall be glad to see the water come. Meanwhile I hope nothing

will happen to Ammi. He saw so much of the thing—and
its influence was so insidious. Why has he never been able
to move away? How clearly he recalled those dying words
of Nahum's—"can't git away—draws ye—know summ'at's
comin', but 'tain't no use—" Ammi is such a good old
man—when the reservoir gang gets to work I must write
the chief engineer to keep a sharp watch on him. I would
hate to think of him as the gray, twisted, brittle monstrosity which persists more and more in troubling my sleep.

It is with an entirely appropriate touch of uneasiness that I select as my "favorite" this one lonely tale out of the many great horror stories I have cherished ever since the eleven-year-old me happened to buy the Modern Library's *Great Tales of Terror and the Supernatural*, the book from which I learned that imagination could twist the suggestiveness of daily reality into forms which seemed mysteriously to enlarge that reality even as they gleefully undermined it. One of the stories in that anthology demands a moment's fanfare. Nothing I had read before had gone into me as deeply as Arthur Machen's "The Great God Pan," nothing had seemed so to open out as a conscious act of *telling*, of narration dividing itself into abrupt, enigmatic fragments which needed only the reader's attention to unite into a powerful whole. At the time, I possessed none of the vocabulary to explain what I found so powerful, but that's what it was—a narrative manner perfectly matched to the secretive, horrified shame of Machen's hypothetical narrator.

By the time I first encountered Robert Aickman's stories, I had read a great deal more and begun to publish my own forays into the psychic landscape mapped by Machen, M. R. James, Lovecraft, and the other writers included in the Modern Library anthology. Aickman's literary agent was also mine, and she suggested that I read his work. Dutifully, I looked up Aickman in a Pan anthology, read "The Inner Room," and wound up blinking and shaking my head, not at all sure of what had just happened either in the story or to me. Few writers offer a genuinely original and unique experience, and those that do often baffle, even irritate, the readers coming to them for the first time. Some of those readers will never come back, and Aickman's reputation has suffered from the daunting facade he presents to anyone who expects a straightforward *frisson*. The reason I decided, years later, to give Aickman a second chance was that, unlike a hundred other, more immediately satisfying stories (but exactly like "The Great God Pan"), "The Inner Room" had obstinately refused to leave *my* inner room, the chamber where selected fictional details, characters, and situations are warehoused by an internal auditor with a mind of his own. So I tried a second time to read some of his "strange stories" (Aickman's own designation), and almost immediately experienced the awed gratitude one feels when coming on the work of a master.

In all of Aickman's greatest stories, "The Trains," "Into the Wood," "Ravissante," "Ringing the Changes," "The View," this one, and a few others, the reader's conventional expectations are frustrated at every turn. It is as if each story is taking dictation from its own unconscious; as in a dream, the world has become unstable, threatening, illogical; but because Aickman was the Freud of the horror story, what at first seems illogical is always in fact profoundly resonant because it is thoroughly embedded in the stream of details which precede it. Here is a father with a dubious past, an idealized and foreign mother, a childhood immersed in currents so submerged that the adult who emerges from it can say, "I doubt whether there is much to be desired but death; or whether there is endurance in anything but suffering." A dollhouse hideous as a prison appears, disappears, reappears again and again like the effects of a repressed and denied comprehension, charged like them with fatality. More than anyone else in this century, Aickman was a genius of the uncanny, and in this story—as in half a dozen others— he exposed the mechanisms of the uncanny with subtle but remorseless imaginative precision.

—Peter Straub

THE INNER ROOM
by Robert Aickman

It was never less than half an hour after the engine stopped running that my father deigned to signal for succour. If in the process of breaking down, we had climbed, or descended, a bank, then first we must all exhaust ourselves pushing. If we had collided, there was, of course, a row. If, as had happened that day, it was simply that, while we coasted along, the machinery had ceased to churn and rattle, then my father tried his hand as a mechanic. That was the worst contingency of all; at least, it was the worst one connected with motoring.

I had learned by experience that neither rain nor snow made much difference, and certainly not fog; but that afternoon it was hotter than any day I could remember. I realized later that it was the famous Long Summer of 1921, when the water at the bottom of cottage wells turned salt, and when eels were found baked and edible in their mud. But to know this at the time, I should have had to read the papers, and though, through my mother's devotion, I had the trick of reading before my third birthday, I mostly left the practice to my younger brother, Constantin. He was reading now from a pudgy volume, as thick as it was broad, and resembling his own head in size and proportion. As always, he had resumed his studies immediately the bumping of our almost springless car permitted, and even before motion had ceased. My mother sat in the front seat inevitably correcting pupils' exercises. By teaching her native German in five schools at once, three of them distant, one of them fashionable, she surprisingly managed to maintain the four of us, and even our car. The front offside door of the car leaned dangerously open into the seething highway.

"I say," cried my father.

The young man in the big yellow racer shook his head as he tore by. My father had addressed the least appropriate car on the road.

"I say."

I cannot recall what the next car looked like, but it did not stop.

My father was facing the direction from which we had come, and sawing the air with his left arm, like a very inexperienced policeman. Perhaps no one stopped because all thought him eccentric. Then a car going in the opposite direction came to a standstill behind my father's back. My father perceived nothing. The motorist sounded his horn, In those days, horns squealed, and I covered my ears with my hands. Between my hands and my head my long fair hair was like brittle flax in the sun.

My father darted through the traffic. I think it was the Portsmouth Road. The man in the other car got out and came to us. I noticed his companion, much younger and in a cherry-colored cloche, begin to deal with her nails.

"Broken down?" asked the man. To me it seemed obvious, as the road was strewn with bits of the engine and oozy blobs of oil. Moreover, surely my father had explained?

"I can't quite locate the seat of the trouble," said my father.

The man took off one of his driving gauntlets, big and dirty.

"Catch hold for a moment." My father caught hold.

The man put his hand into the engine and made a casual movement. Something snapped loudly.

"Done right in. If you ask me, I'm not sure she'll ever go again."

"Then I don't think I'll ask you," said my father affably. "Hot, isn't it?" My father began to mop his tall corrugated brow, and front-to-back ridges of grey hair.

"Want a tow?"

"Just to the nearest garage." My father always spoke the word in perfect French.

"Where to?"

"To the nearest car repair workshop. If it would not be troubling you too much."

"Can't help myself now, can I?"

From under the backseat in the other car, the owner got out a thick, frayed rope, black and greasy as the hangman's. The owner's friend simply said, "Pleased to meet you," and began to replace her scalpels and enamels in their cabinet. We jolted towards the town we had traversed an hour or two before; and were then untied outside a garage on the outskirts.

"Surely it is closed for the holiday?" said my mother. Hers is a voice I can always recall upon an instant: guttural, of course, but beautiful, truly golden.

"'Spect he'll be back," said our benefactor, drawing in his rope like a fisherman. "Give him a bang." He kicked three times very loudly upon the dropped iron shutter. Then without another word he drove away.

It was my birthday, I had been promised the sea, and I began to weep. Constantin, with a fretful little wriggle, closed further into himself and his book; but my mother leaned over the front seat of the car and opened her arms to me. I went to her and sobbed on the shoulder of her bright red dress.

"Kleine Lene, wir stecken schön in der Tinte."

My father, who could pronounce six languages perfectly but speak only one of them, never liked my mother to use her native tongue within the family. He rapped more sharply on the shutter. My mother knew his ways, but, where our welfare was at stake, ignored them.

"Edgar," said my mother, "let us give the children presents. Especially my little Lene." My tears, though childish, and less viscous than those shed in later life, had turned the scarlet shoulder of her dress to purple. She squinted smilingly sideways at the damage.

My father was delighted to defer the decision about what next to do with the car. But, as pillage was possible, my mother took with her the exercises, and Constantin his fat little book.

We straggled along the main road, torrid, raucous, adequate only for a gentler period of history. The grit and dust stung my face and arms and knees, like granulated glass. My mother and I went first, she holding my hand. My father struggled to walk at her other side, but for most of the way, the path was too narrow. Constantin mused along in the rear, abstracted as usual.

"It is true what the papers say," exclaimed my father.

"British roads were never built for motor traffic. Beyond the odd car, of course."

My mother nodded and slightly smiled. Even in the line-less hopsacks of the twenties, she could not ever but look magnificent, with her rolling, turbulent, honey hair, and Hellenic proportions. Ultimately we reached the High Street. The very first shop had one of its windows stuffed with toys; the other being stacked with groceries and draperies and coal-hods, all dingy. The name POPULAR BAZAAR, in wooden relief as if glued on in building blocks, stretched across the whole front, not quite centre.

It was not merely an out-of-fashion shop, but a shop that at the best sold too much of what no one wanted. My father comprehended the contents of the Toy Department window with a single, anxious glance, and said, "Choose whatever you like. Both of you. But look very carefully first. Don't hurry." Then he turned away and began to hum a fragment from "The Lady of the Rose."

But Constantin spoke at once. "I choose those telegraph wires." They ranged beside a line of tin railway that stretched right across the window, long undusted and tending to buckle. There were seven or eight posts, with six wires on each side of the post. Though I could not think why Constantin wanted them, and though in the event he did not get them, the appearance of them, and of the rusty track beneath them, is all that remains clear in my memory of that window.

"I doubt whether they're for sale," said my father. "Look again. There's a good boy. No hurry."

"They're all I want," said Constantin, and turned his back on the uninspiring display.

"Well, we'll see," said my father. "I'll make a special point of it with the man . . ." He turned to me. "And what about you? Very few dolls, I'm afraid."

"I don't like dolls any more." As a matter of fact, I had never owned a proper one, although I suffered from this fact only when competing with other girls, which meant very seldom, for our friends were few and occasional. The dolls in the window were flyblown and detestable.

"I think we could find a better shop from which to give Lene a birthday present," said my mother, in her correct, dignified English.

"We must not be unjust," said my father, "when we have not even looked inside."

The inferiority of the goods implied cheapness, which unfortunately always mattered; although, as it happened, none of the articles seemed actually to be priced.

"I do not like this shop," said my mother. "It is a shop that has died."

Her regal manner when she said such things was, I think, too Germanic for my father's Englishness. That, and the prospect of unexpected economy, perhaps led him to be firm.

"We have Constantin's present to consider as well as Lene's. Let us go in."

By contrast with the blazing highway, the main impression of the interior was darkness. After a few moments, I also became aware of a smell. Everything in the shop smelt of that smell, and, one felt, always would do so, the mixed odour of any general store, but at once enhanced and passé. I can smell it now.

"We do not necessarily want to buy anything," said my father, "but if we may, should like to look around?"

Since the days of Mr. Selfridge the proposition is supposed to be taken for granted, but at that time the message had yet to spread. The bazaar keeper seemed hardly to welcome it. He was younger than I had expected (an unusual thing for a child, but I had probably been awaiting a white-bearded gnome); though pale, nearly bald, and perceptibly grimy. He wore an untidy grey suit and bedroom slippers.

"Look about you, children," said my father. "Take your time. We can't buy presents every day."

I noticed that my mother still stood in the doorway.

"I want those wires," said Constantin.

"Make quite sure by looking at the other things first."

Constantin turned aside bored, his book held behind his back. He began to scrape his feet. It was up to me to uphold my father's position. Rather timidly, I began to peer about, not going far from him. The bazaar keeper silently watched me with eyes colourless in the twilight.

"Those toy telegraph poles in your window," said my father after a pause, fraught for me with anxiety and responsibility. "How much would you take for them?"

"They are not for sale," said the bazaar keeper, and said no more.

"Then why do you display them in the window?"

"They are a kind of decoration, I suppose." Did he not know? I wondered.

"Even if they're not normally for sale, perhaps you'll sell them to me," said my vagabond father, smiling like Rothschild. "My son, you see, has taken a special fancy to them."

"Sorry," said the man in the shop.

"Are you the principal here?"

"I am."

"Then surely as a reasonable man," said my father, switching from superiority to ingratiation—

"They are to dress the window," said the bazaar man. "They are not for sale."

This dialogue entered through the back of my head as, diligently and unobtrudingly, I conned the musty stock. At the back of the shop was a window, curtained all over in grey lace: to judge by the weak light it offered, it gave on to the living quarters. Through this much filtered illumination glimmered the façade of an enormous dolls' house. I wanted it at once. Dolls had never been central to my happiness, but this abode of theirs was the most grown-up thing in the shop.

It had battlements, and long straight walls, and a variety of pointed windows. A gothic revival house, no doubt; or even mansion. It was painted the colour of stone; a grey stone darker than the grey light, which flickered round it. There was a two-leaved front door, with a small classical portico. It was impossible to see the whole house at once, as it stood grimed and neglected on the corner of the wide trestle-shelf. Very slowly I walked along two of the sides; the other two being dark against the walls of the shop. From a first-floor window in the side not immediately visible as one approached, leaned a doll, droopy and unkempt. It was unlike any real house I had seen, and, as for dolls' houses, they were always after the style of the villa near Gerrard's Cross belonging to my father's successful brother. My uncle's house itself looked much more like a toy than this austere structure before me.

"Wake up," said my mother's voice. She was standing just behind me.

"What about some light on the subject?" enquired my father.

A switch clicked.

The house really was magnificent. Obviously, beyond all financial reach.

"Looks like a model for Pentonville Gaol," observed my father.

"It is beautiful," I said. "It's what I want."

"It's the most depressing-looking plaything I ever saw."

"I want to pretend I live in it," I said, "and give masked balls." My social history was eager but indiscriminate.

"How much is it?" asked my mother. The bazaar keeper stood resentfully in the background, sliding each hand between the thumb and fingers of the other.

"It's only second-hand," he said. "Tenth-hand, more like. A lady brought it in and said she needed to get rid of it. I don't want to sell you something you don't want."

"But suppose we *do* want it?" said my father truculently. "Is nothing in this shop for sale?"

"You can take it away for a quid," said the bazaar keeper. "And glad to have the space."

"There's someone looking out," said Constantin. He seemed to be assessing the house, like a surveyor or valuer.

"It's full of dolls," said the bazaar keeper. "They're thrown in. Sure you can transport it?"

"Not at the moment," said my father, "but I'll send someone down." This, I knew, would be Moon the seedman, who owned·a large canvas-topped lorry, and with whom my father used to fraternize on the putting green.

"Are you quite sure?" my mother asked me.

"Will it take up too much room?"

My mother shook her head. Indeed, our home, though out of date and out at elbows, was considerably too large for us.

"Then, please."

Poor Constantin got nothing.

Mercifully, all our rooms had wide doors, so that Moon's driver, assisted by the youth out of the shop, lent specially for the purpose, could ease my birthday present to its new resting place without tilting it or inflicting a wound upon my mother's new and self-applied paint. I noticed that the doll at the first-floor side window had prudently withdrawn.

For my house, my parents had allotted me the principal spare room, because in the centre of it stood a very large dinner table, once to be found in the servants' hall of my father's childhood home in Lincolnshire, but now the sole furniture our principal spare room contained. (The two lesser spare rooms were filled with cardboard boxes, which every now and then toppled in heart-arresting avalanches on still summer nights.) On the big table the driver and the shop boy set my house. It reached almost to the sides, so that those passing along the narrow walks would be in peril of tumbling into a gulf; but, the table being much longer than it was wide, the house was provided at front and back with splendid parterres of deal, embrocated with caustic until they glinted like fluorspar.

When I had settled upon the exact site for the house, so that the garden front would receive the sun from the two windows, and a longer parterre stretched at the front than at the back, where the columned entry faced the door of the room, I withdrew to a distant corner while the two males eased the edifice into exact alignment.

"Snug as a bug in a rug," said Moon's driver when the perilous walks at the sides of the house had been made straight and equal.

"Snugger," said Moon's boy.

I waited for their boots, mailed with crescent silvers of steel, to reach the bottom of our creaking, coconut-matted stair, then I tiptoed to the landing, looked, and listened. The sun had gone in just before the lorry arrived, and down the passage the motes had ceased to dance. It was three o'clock, my mother was still at one of her schools, my father was at the rifle range. I heard the men shut the back door. The principal spare room had never before been occupied, so that the key was outside. In a second, I transferred it to the inside, and shut and locked myself in.

As before in the shop, I walked slowly round my house, but this time round all four sides of it. Then, with the knuckles of my thin white forefinger, I tapped gently at the front door. It seemed not to have been secured, because it opened, both leaves of it, as I touched it. I pried in, first with one eye, then with the other. The lights from various of the pointed windows blotched the walls and floor of the miniature Entrance Hall. None of the dolls was visible.

It was not one of those dolls' houses of commerce from which sides can be lifted in their entirety. To learn about my house, it would be necessary, albeit impolite, to stare through the windows, one at a time. I decided first to take the ground floor. I started in a clockwise direction from the front portico. The front door was still open, but I could not see how to shut it from the outside.

There was a room to the right of the hall, leading into two other rooms along the right side of the house, of which, again, one led into the other. All the rooms were decorated and furnished in a Mrs. Fitzherbert-ish style; with handsomely striped wallpapers, botanical carpets, and chairs with legs like sticks of brittle golden sweetmeat. There were a number of pictures. I knew just what they were: family portraits. I named the room next the Hall, the Occasional Room, and the room beyond it, the Morning Room. The third room was very small: striking out confidently, I named it the Canton Cabinet, although it contained neither porcelain nor fans. I knew what the rooms in a great house should be called, because my mother used to show me the pictures in large, once-fashionable volumes on the subject which my father had bought for their bulk at junk shops.

Then came the Long Drawing Room, which stretched across the entire garden front of the house, and contained the principal concourse of dolls. It had four pointed French windows, all made to open, though now sealed with dust and rust; above which were bulbous triangles of coloured glass, in tiny snowflake panes. The apartment itself played at being a cloister in a Horace Walpole convent; lierne vaulting ramified across the arched ceiling, and the spidery gothic pilasters were tricked out in mediaeval patchwork, as in a Puseyite church. On the stout golden wallpaper were decent Swiss pastels of indeterminate subjects. There was a grand piano, very black, scrolly, and, no doubt, resounding; four shapely chandeliers; a baronial fireplace with a mythical blazon above the mantel; and eight dolls, all of them female, dotted about on chairs and ottomans with their backs to me. I hardly dared to breathe as I regarded their wooly heads, and noted the colors of their hair: two black, two nondescript, one grey, one a discolored silver beneath the dust, one blonde, and one a dyed-looking red. They wore woolen Victorian clothes, of a period later, I should say, than that when the house was built, and certainly too warm for the present season; in varied colours, all of them dull. Happy people, I felt even then, would not wear these variants of rust, indigo, and greenwood.

I crept onwards; to the Dining Room. It occupied half its side of the house, and was dark and oppressive. Perhaps it might look more inviting when the chandelier blazed, and the table candles, each with a tiny purple shade, were lighted. There was no cloth on the table, and no food or drink. Over the fireplace was a big portrait of a furious old man: his white hair was a spiky aureole round his distorted face, beetroot-red with rage; the mouth was open, and even the heavy lips were drawn back to show the savage, strong teeth; he was brandishing a very thick walking stick, which seemed to leap from the picture and stun the beholder. He was dressed neutrally, and the painter had not provided him with a background: there was only the aggressive figure menacing the room. I was frightened.

Two rooms on the ground floor remained before I once more reached the front door. In the first of them a lady was writing with her back to the light and therefore to me. She frightened me also; because her gray hair was disordered and of uneven length, and descended in matted plaits, like snakes escaping from a basket, to the shoulder of her coarse grey dress. Of course, being a doll, she did not move, but the back of her head looked mad. Her presence prevented me from regarding at all closely the furnishings of the Writing Room.

Back at the north front, as I resolved to call it, perhaps superseding the compass rather than leading it, there was a cold-looking room, with a carpetless stone floor and white walls, upon which were the mounted heads and horns of many animals. They were all the room contained, but they covered the walls from floor to ceiling. I felt sure that the ferocious old man in the Dining Room had killed all these creatures, and I hated him for it. But I knew what the room would be called: it would be the Trophy Room.

Then I realized that there was no kitchen. It could hardly be upstairs. I had never heard of such a thing. But I looked.

It wasn't there. All the rooms on the first floor were bedrooms. There were six of them, and they so resembled one another, all with dark ochreous wallpaper and narrow brass bedsteads corroded with neglect, that I found it impracticable to distinguish them other than by numbers, at least for the present. Ultimately I might know the house better. Bedrooms 2, 3, and 6 contained two beds each. I recalled that at least nine people lived in the house. In one room the dark walls, the dark floor, the bed linen, and even the glass in the window were splashed, smeared, and further darkened with ink: it seemed apparent who slept there.

I sat on an orange box and looked. My house needed painting and dusting and scrubbing and polishing and renewing; but on the whole I was relieved that things were not worse. I had felt that the house had stood in the dark corner of the shop for no one knew how long, but this, I now saw, could hardly have been true. I wondered about the lady who had needed to get rid of it. Despite that need, she must have kept things up pretty thoroughly. How did she do it? How did she get in? I resolved to ask my mother's advice. I determined to be a good landlord, although, like most who so resolve, my resources were nil. We simply lacked the money to regild my Long Drawing Room in proper gold leaf. But I would bring life to the nine dolls now drooping with boredom and neglect . . .

Then I recalled something. What had become of the doll who had been sagging from the window? I thought she must have been jolted out, and felt myself a murderess. But none of the windows was open. The sash might easily have descended with the shaking; but more probably the poor doll lay inside on the floor of her room. I again went round from room to room, this time on tiptoe, but it was impossible to see the areas of floor just below the dark windows. . . . It was not merely sunless outside, but heavily overcast. I unlocked the door of our principal spare room and descended pensively to await my mother's return and tea.

Wormwood Grange, my father called my house, with penological associations still on his mind. (After he was run over, I realized for the first time that there might be a reason for this, and for his inability to find work worthy of him.) My mother had made the most careful inspection on my behalf, but had been unable to suggest any way of making an entry, or at least of passing beyond the Hall, to which the front doors still lay open. There seemed no question of whole walls lifting off, of the roof being removable, or even of a window being opened, including, mysteriously, on the first floor.

"I don't think it's meant for children, Liebchen," said my mother, smiling her lovely smile. "We shall have to consult the Victoria and Albert Museum."

"Of course it's not meant for children," I replied. "That's why I wanted it. I'm going to receive, like La Belle Otero."

Next morning, after my mother had gone to work, my father came up, and wrenched and prodded with his unskilful hands.

"I'll get a chisel," he said. "We'll prise it open at each corner, and when we've got the fronts off, I'll go over to Woolworths and buy some hinges and screws. I expect they'll have some."

At that I struck my father in the chest with my fist. He seized my wrists, and I screamed that he was not to lay a finger on my beautiful house, that he would be sure to spoil it, that force never got anyone anywhere. I knew my father: when he took an idea for using tools into his head, the only

hope for one's property lay in a scene, and in the implication of tears without end in the future, if the idea were not
dropped.

While I was screaming and raving, Constantin appeared
from the room below, where he worked at his books.

"Give us a chance, Sis," he said. "How can I keep it all
in my head about the Thirty Years War when you haven't
learnt to control your tantrums?"

Although two years younger than I, Constantin should
have known that I was past the age for screaming except
of set purpose.

"You wait until he tries to rebind all your books, you
silly sneak," I yelled at him.

My father released my wrists.

"Wormwood Grange can keep," he said. "I'll think of
something else to go over to Woolworths for." He saun-
tered off.

Constantin nodded gravely. "I understand," he said. "I
understand what you mean. I'll go back to my work. Here,
try this." He gave me a small, chipped nail file.

I spent most of the morning fiddling very cautiously with
the imperfect jemmy, and trying to make up my mind about
the doll at the window.

I failed to get into my house, and I refused to let my
parents give me any effective aid. Perhaps by now I did not
really want to get in, although the dirt and disrepair, and
the apathy of the dolls, who so badly needed plumping up
and dispersing, continued to cause me distress. Certainly I
spent as long trying to shut the front door as trying to open
a window or find a concealed spring (that idea was Constantin's). In the end I wedged the two halves of the front
door with two halves of match; but I felt that the arrangement was makeshift and undignified. I refused everyone access to the principal spare room until something more
appropriate could be evolved. My plans for routs and or-

gies had to be deferred: one could hardly riot among dust and cobwebs.

Then I began to have dreams about my house, and about its occupants.

One of the oddest dreams was the first. It was three or four days after I entered into possession. During that time it had remained cloudy and oppressive, so that my father took to leaving off his knitted waistcoat; then suddenly it thundered. It was long, slow, distant, intermittent thunder; and it continued all the evening, until, when it was quite dark, my bedtime and Constantin's could no longer be deferred.

"Your ears will get accustomed to the noise," said my father. "Just try to take no notice of it."

Constantin looked dubious; but I was tired of the slow, rumbling hours, and ready for the different dimension of dreams.

I slept almost immediately, although the thunder was rolling round my big, rather empty bedroom, round the four walls, across the floor, and under the ceiling, weighting the black air as with a smoky vapour. Occasionally, the lightning glinted, pink and green. It was still the long-drawn-out preliminary to a storm; the tedious, imperfect dispersal of the accumulated energy of the summer. The rollings and rumblings entered my dreams, which flickered, changed, were gone as soon as come, failed, like the lightning, to concentrate or strike home, were as difficult to profit by as the events of an average day.

After exhausting hours of phantasmagoria, anticipating so many later nights in my life, I found myself in a black wood, with huge, dense trees. I was following a path, but reeled from tree to tree, bruising and cutting myself on their hardness and roughness. There seemed no end to the wood or to the night; but suddenly, in the thick of both, I came upon my house. It stood solid, immense, hemmed in, with a single light, little more, it seemed, than a night-light, burning in every upstairs window (as often in dreams, I could see all four sides of the house at once), and illuminating two wooden wedges, jagged and swollen, which held tight the front doors. The vast trees dipped and swayed their elephantine boughs over the roof; the wind peeked and creaked through the black battlements. Then there was a blaze of whitest lightning, proclaiming the storm itself. In the second it endured, I saw my two wedges fly through the air and the double front door burst open.

For the hundredth time, the scene changed, and now I was back in my room, though still asleep or half-asleep, still dragged from vision to vision. Now the thunder was coming in immense, calculated bombardments; the lightning ceaseless and searing the face of the earth. From being a weariness the storm had become an ecstasy. It seemed as if the whole world would be in dissolution before the thunder had spent its impersonal, unregarding strength. But, as I say, I must still have been at least half asleep, because between the fortissimi and the lustre I still from time to time saw scenes, meaningless or nightmarish, which could not be found in the wakeful world; still, between and through the volleys, heard impossible sounds.

I do not know whether I was asleep or awake when the storm rippled into tranquillity. I certainly did not feel that the air had been cleared; but this may have been because, surprisingly, I heard a quick soft step passing along the passage outside my room, a passage uncarpeted through our poverty. I well knew all the footsteps in the house, and this was none of them.

Always one to meet trouble half-way, I dashed in my nightgown to open the door. I looked out. The dawn was seeping, without effort or momentum, through every cranny, and showed shadowy the back of a retreating figure, the size of my mother but with woolly red hair and long rust-coloured dress. The padding feet seemed actually to start soft echoes amid all that naked woodwork. I had no need

to consider who she was or whither she was bound. I burst
into the purposeless tears I so despised.

In the morning, and before deciding upon what to im-
part, I took Constantin with me to look at the house. I more
than half-expected big changes; but none was to be seen.
The sections of match-stick were still in position, and the
dolls as inactive and diminutive as ever, sitting with their
backs to me on chairs and sofas in the Long Drawing Room;
their hair dusty, possibly even mothy. Constantin looked at
me curiously, but I imparted nothing.

Other dreams followed; though at considerable intervals.
Many children have recurring nightmares of oppressive realism and terrifying content; and I realized from past experience that I must outgrow the habit or lose my house—my
house at least. It is true that my house now frightened me,
but I felt that I must not be foolish and should strive to
take a grown-up view of painted woodwork and nine un-
derstuffed dolls. Still it was bad when I began to hear them
in the darkness; some tapping, some stumping, some creeping, and therefore not one, but many, or all; and worse when
I began not to sleep for fear of the mad doll (as I was sure
she was) doing something mad, although I refused to think
what. I never dared again to look; but when something happened, which, as I say, was only at intervals (and to me,
being young, they seemed long intervals), I lay taut and
straining among the forgotten sheets. Moreover, the steps
themselves were never quite constant, certainly too incon-
stant to report to others; and I am not sure that I should
have heard anything significant if I had not once seen. But
now I locked the door of our principal spare room on the
outside, and altogether ceased to visit my beautiful, im-
pregnable mansion.

I noticed that my mother made no comment. But one
day my father complained of my ingratitude in never playing with my handsome birthday present. I said I was oc-

cupied with my holiday task: *Moby Dick*. This was an approved answer, and even, as far as it went, a true one, though I found the book pointless in the extreme, and horribly cruel.

"I told you the Grange was the wrong thing to buy," said my father. "Morbid sort of object for a toy."

"None of us can learn except by experience," said my mother.

My father said, "Not at all," and bristled.

All this, naturally, was in the holidays. I was going at the time to one of my mother's schools, where I should stay until I could begin to train as a dancer, upon which I was conventionally but entirely resolved. Constantin went to another, a highly cerebral co-educational place, where he would remain until, inevitably, he won a scholarship to a University, perhaps a foreign one. Despite our years, we went our different ways dangerously on small dingy bicycles. We reached home at assorted hours, mine being the longer journey.

One day I returned to a find our dining-room table littered with peculiarly uninteresting printed drawings. I could make nothing of them whatever (they did not seem even to belong to the kind of geometry I was—regretfully—used to); and they curled up on themselves when one tried to examine them, and bit one's finger. My father had a week or two before taking one of his infrequent jobs; night work of some kind a long way off, to which he had now departed in our car. Obviously the drawings were connected with Constantin, but he was not there.

I went upstairs, and saw that the principal spare room door was open. Constantin was inside. There had, of course, been no question of the key to the room being removed. It was only necessary to turn it.

"Hallo, Lene," Constantin said in his matter-of-fact way. "We've been doing axonometric projection, and I'm projecting your house." He was making one of the drawings;

on a sheet of thick white paper. "It's for home-work. It'll knock out all the others. They've got to do their real houses."

It must not be supposed that I did not like Constantin, although often he annoyed me with his placidity and precision. It was weeks since I had seen my house, and it looked unexpectedly interesting. A curious thing happened: nor was it the last a time in my life that I experienced it. Temporarily I became a different person; confident, practical, simple. The clear evening sun of autumn may have contributed.

"I'll help," I said. "Tell me what to do."

"It's a bore I can't get in to take measurements. Although we haven't *got* to. In fact, the Clot told us not. Just a general impression, he said. It's to give us the *concept* of axonometry. But a, golly, it would be simpler with feet and inches."

To judge by the amount of white paper he had covered in what could only have been a short time, Constantin seemed to me to be doing very well, but he was one never to be content with less than perfection.

"Tell me," I said, "what to do, and I'll do it."

"Thanks," he replied, sharpening his pencil with a special instrument. "But it's a one-man job this. In the nature of the case. Later I'll show you how to do it, and you can do some other building if you like."

I remained, looking at my house and fingering it, until Constantin made it clearer that I was a distraction. I went away, changed my shoes, and put on the kettle against my mother's arrival, and our High Tea.

When Constantin came down (my mother had called for him three times, but that was not unusual), he said, "I say, Sis, here's a rum thing."

My mother said, "Don't use slang, and don't call your sister Sis."

He said, as he always did when reproved by her, "I'm sorry, Mother." Then he thrust the drawing paper at me.

"Look, there's a bit missing. See what I mean?" He was showing me with his stub of emerald pencil, pocked with toothmarks.

Of course, I didn't see. I didn't understand a thing about it.

"After Tea," said my mother. She gave to such familiar words not a maternal but an imperial decisiveness.

"But Mum—" pleaded Constantin.

"Mother," said my mother

Constantin started dipping for sauerkraut.

Silently we ate ourselves into tranquillity; or, for me, into the appearance of it. My alternative personality, though it had survived Constantin's refusal of my assistance, was now beginning to ebb.

"What is all this that you are doing?" enquired my mother in the end. "It resembles the Stone of Rosetta."

"I'm taking an axonometric cast of Lene's birthday house."

"And so?"

But Constantin was not now going to expound immediately. He put in his mouth a finger of rye bread smeared with homemade cheese. Then he said quietly, "I got down a rough idea of the house, but the rooms don't fit. At least, they don't on the bottom floor. It's all right, I think, on the top floor. In fact that's the rummest thing of all. Sorry, Mother." He had been speaking with his mouth full, and now filled it fuller.

"What nonsense is this?" To me it seemed that my mother was glaring at him in a way most unlike her.

"It's not nonsense, Mother. Of course, I haven't measured the place, because you can't. But I haven't done axonometry for nothing. There's a part of the bottom floor I can't get at. A secret room or something."

"Show me."

"Very well, Mother." Constantin put down his remnant

of bread and cheese. He rose, looking a little pale. He took the drawing round the table to my mother.

"Not that thing. I can't understand it, and I don't believe you can understand it either." Only sometimes to my father did my mother speak like that. "Show me in the house."

I rose too.

"You stay here, Lene. Put some more water in the kettle and boil it."

"But it's my house. I have a right to know."

My mother's expression changed to one more familiar. "Yes, Lene," she said, "you have a right. But please not now. I ask you."

I smiled at her and picked up the kettle.

"Come, Constantin."

I lingered by the kettle in the kitchen, not wishing to give an impression of eavesdropping or even undue eagerness, which I knew would distress my mother. I never wished to learn things that my mother wished to keep from me; and I never questioned her implication of "All in good time."

But they were not gone long, for well before the kettle had begun even to grunt, my mother's beautiful voice was summoning me back.

"Constantin is quite right," she said, when I had presented myself at the dining room table, "and it was wrong of me to doubt it. The house is built in a funny sort of way. But what does it matter?"

Constantin was not eating.

"I am glad that you are studying well, and learning such useful things," said my mother.

She wished the subject to be dropped, and we dropped it.

Indeed, it was difficult to think what more could be said. But I waited for a moment in which I was alone with Constantin. My father's unhabitual absence made this difficult, and it was completely dark before the moment came.

And when, as was only to be expected, Constantin had nothing to add, I felt, most unreasonably, that he was joined with my mother in keeping something from me.

"But what *happened?*" I pressed him. "What happened when you were in the room with her?"

"What do you think happened?" replied Constantin, wishing, I thought, that my mother would re-enter. "Mother realized that I was right. Nothing more. What does it matter anyway?"

That final query confirmed my doubts.

"Constantin," I said. "Is there anything I ought to do?"

"Better hack the place open," he answered, almost irritably.

But a most unexpected thing happened, that, had I even considered adopting Constantin's idea, would have saved me the trouble. When next day I returned from school, my house was gone.

Constantin was sitting in his usual corner, this time absorbing Greek paradigms. Without speaking to him (nothing unusual in that when he was working), I went straight to the principal spare room. The vast deal table, less scrubbed than once, was bare. The place where my house had stood was very visible, as if indeed a palace had been swept off by a djinn. But I could see no other sign of its passing: no scratched woodwork, or marks of boots, or disjoined fragments.

Constantin seemed genuinely astonished at the news. But I doubted him.

"You knew," I said.

"Of course I didn't know."

Still, he understood what I was thinking.

He said again, "I didn't know."

Unlike me on occasion, he always spoke the truth.

I gathered myself together and blurted out, "Have they

done it themselves?" Inevitably I was frightened, but in a way I was also relieved.

"Who do you mean?"

"They."

I was inviting ridicule, but Constantin was kind.

He said, "I know who I think has done it, but you mustn't let on. I think Mother's done it."

I did not again enquire uselessly into how much more he knew than I. I said, "But *how?*"

Constantin shrugged. It was a habit he had assimilated with so much else.

"Mother left the house with us this morning and she isn't back yet."

"She must have put Father up to it."

"But there are no marks."

"Father might have got help." There was a pause. Then Constantin said, "Are you sorry?"

"In a way," I replied. Constantin with precocious wisdom left it at that.

When my mother returned, she simply said that my father had already lost his new job, so that we had had to sell things.

"I hope you will forgive your father and me," she said. "We've had to sell one of my watches also. Father will soon be back to Tea."

She too was one I had never known to lie; but now I began to perceive how relative and instrumental truth could be.

I need not say: not in those terms. Such clear concepts, with all they offer of gain and loss, come later, if they come at all. In fact, I need not say that the whole of what goes before is so heavily filtered through later experience as to be of little evidential value. But I am scarcely putting forward evidence. There is so little. All I can do is to tell something of what happened, as it now seems to me to have been.

I remember sulking at my mother's news, and her explaining to me that really I no longer liked the house and that something better would be bought for me in replacement when our funds permitted.

I did ask my father when he returned to our evening meal, whistling and falsely jaunty about the lost job, how much he had been paid for my house.

"A trifle more than I gave for it. That's only business."

"Where is it now?"

"Never you mind."

"Tell her," said Constantin. "She wants to know."

"Eat your herring," said my father very sharply. "And mind your own business."

And, thus, before long my house was forgotten, my occasional nightmares returned to earlier themes.

It was, as I say, for two or three months in 1921 that I owned the house and from time to time dreamed that creatures I supposed to be its occupants had somehow invaded my home. The next thirty years, more or less, can be disposed of quickly: It was the period when I tried conclusions with the outer world.

I really became a dancer; and, although the upper reaches alike of the art and of the profession notably eluded me, yet I managed to maintain myself for several years, no small achievement. I retired, as they say, upon marriage. My husband aroused physical passion in me for the first time, but diminished and deadened much else. He was reported missing in the late misguided war. Certainly he did not return to me. I at least still miss him, though often I despise myself for doing so.

My father died in a street accident when I was fifteen: It happened on the day I received a special commendation from the sallow Frenchwoman who taught me to dance.

After his death my beloved mother always wanted to return to Germany. Before long I was spiritually self-sufficient enough, or said I was, to make that possible. Unfailingly, she wrote to me twice a week, although to find words in which to reply was often difficult for me. Sometimes I visited her, while the conditions in her country became more and more uncongenial to me. She had a fair position teaching English Language and Literature at a small university; and she seemed increasingly to be infected by the new notions and emotions raging around her. I must acknowledge that sometimes their tumult and intoxication unsteadied my own mental gait, although I was a foreigner and by no means of sanguine temperament. It is a mistake to think that all professional dancers are gay.

Despite what appeared to be increasing sympathies with the new régime, my mother disappeared. She was the first of the two people who mattered to me in such very different ways, and who so unreasonably vanished. For a time I was ill, and of course I love her still more than anybody. If she had remained with me, I am sure I should never have married. Without involving myself in psychology, which I detest, I shall simply say that the thought and recollection of my mother lay, I believe, behind the self-absorption my husband complained of so bitterly and so justly. It was not really myself in which I was absorbed but the memory of perfection. It is the plain truth that such beauty, and goodness, and depth, and capacity· for love were my mother's alone.

Constantin abandoned all his versatile reading and became a priest, in fact a member of the Society of Jesus. He seems exalted (possibly too much so for his colleagues and superiors), but I can no longer speak to him or bear his presence. He frightens me. Poor Constantin!

On the other hand, I, always dubious, have become a complete unbeliever. I cannot see that Constantin is doing anything but listening to his own inner voice (which has changed its tone since we were children); and mine speaks a different language. In the long run, I doubt whether there is much to be desired but death; or whether there is endurance in anything but suffering. I no longer see myself feasting crowned heads on quails.

So much for biographical intermission. I proceed to the circumstances of my second and recent experience of landlordism.

In the first place, I did something thoroughly stupid. Instead of following the road marked on the map, I took a short cut. It is true that the short cut was shown on the map also, but the region was much too unfrequented for a wandering footpath to be in any way dependable, especially in this generation which has ceased to walk beyond the garage or the bus stop. It was one of the least populated districts in the whole country, and, moreover, the slow autumn dusk was already perceptible when I pushed at the first, dilapidated gate.

To begin with, the path trickled and flickered across a sequence of small damp meadows, bearing neither cattle nor crop. When it came to the third or fourth of these meadows, the way had all but vanished in the increasing sogginess, and could be continued only by looking for the stile or gate in the unkempt hedge ahead. This was not especially difficult as long as the fields remained small; but after a time I reached a depressing expanse which could hardly be termed a field at all, but was rather a large marsh. It was at this point that I should have returned and set about tramping the winding road.

But a path of some kind again continued before me, and I perceived that the escapade had already consumed twenty minutes. So I risked it, although soon I was striding laboriously from tussock to brown tussock in order not to sink above my shoes into the surrounding quagmire. It is quite extraordinary how far one can stray from a straight or de-

termined course when thus preoccupied with elementary
comfort. The hedge on the far side of the marsh was still
a long way ahead, and the tussocks themselves were becoming both less frequent and less dense, so that too often
I was sinking through them into the mire. I realized that
the marsh sloped slightly downwards in the direction I was
following, so that before I reached the hedge, I might have
to cross a river. In the event, it was not so much a river as
an indeterminately bounded augmentation of the softness,
and moistness, and ooziness: I struggled across, jerking from
false foothold to palpable pitfall, and before long despairing even of the attempt to step securely. Both my feet were
now soaked to well above the ankles, and the visibility had
become less than was entirely convenient.

When I reached what I had taken for a hedge, it proved
to be the boundary of an extensive thicket. Autumn had infected much of the greenery with blotched and dropping
senility; so that bare brown briars arched and tousled, and
purple thorns tilted at all possible angles for blood. To go
further would demand an axe. Either I must retraverse the
dreary bog in the perceptibly waning light, or I must skirt
the edge and seek an opening in the thicket. Undecided, I
looked back. I realized that I had lost the gate through which
I had entered upon the marsh on the other side. There was
nothing to do but creep as best I could upon the still treach-
erous ground along the barrier of dead dogroses, mildewed
blackberries, and rampant nettles.

But it was not long before I reached a considerable gap,
from which through the tangled vegetation seemed to lead
a substantial track, although by no means a straight one.
The track wound on unimpeded for a considerable distance,
even becoming firmer underfoot; until I realized that the
thicket had become an entirely indisputable wood. The bram-
bles clutching maliciously from the sides had become watching branches above my head. I could not recall that the map
had showed a wood. If, indeed, it had done so, I should not

have entered upon the footpath, because the only previous occasion in my life when I had been truly lost, in the sense of being unable to find the way back as well as being unable to go on, had been when my father had once so effectively lost us in a wood that I have never again felt the same about woods. The fear I had felt for perhaps an hour and a half on that occasion, though told to no one, and swiftly evaporating from consciousness upon our emergence, had been the veritable fear of death. Now I drew the map from where it lay against my thigh in the big pocket of my dress. It was not until I tried to read it that I realized how near I was to night. Until it came to print, the problems of the route had given me cat's eyes.

I peered, and there was no wood, no green patch on the map, but only the wavering line of dots advancing across contoured whiteness to the neck of yellow road where the shortcut ended. But I did not reach any foolish conclusion. I simply guessed that I had strayed very badly: the map was spattered with green marks in places where I had no wish to be; and the only question was in which of those many thickets I now was. I could think of no way to find out. I was nearly lost, and this time I could not blame my father.

The track I had been following still stretched ahead, as yet not too indistinct; and I continued to follow it. As the trees around me became yet bigger and thicker, fear came upon me, though not the death fear of that previous occasion, I felt, now that I knew what was going to happen next; or, rather, I felt I knew one thing that was going to happen next, a thing which was but a small and far from central part of an obscure, inapprehensible totality. As one does on such occasions, I felt more than half outside my body. If I continued much further, I might change into somebody else.

But what happened was not what I expected. Suddenly I saw a flicker of light. It seemed to emerge from the left, to weave momentarily among the trees, and to disappear to the right. It was not what I expected, but it was scarcely reassuring. I wondered if it could be a will-o'-the-wisp, a thing I had never seen, but which I understood to be connected with marshes. Next a still more prosaic possibility occurred to me, one positively hopeful: the headlights of a motor car turning a corner. It seemed the likely answer, but my uneasiness did not perceptibly diminish.

I struggled on, and the light came again: a little stronger, and twisting through the trees around me. Of course another car at the same corner of the road was not an impossibility, even though it was an unpeopled area. Then, after a period of soft but not comforting dusk, it came a third time; and, soon, a fourth. There was no sound of an engine: and it seemed to me that the transit of the light was too swift and fleeting for any car.

And then what I had been awaiting happened. I came suddenly upon a huge square house. I had known it was coming, but still it struck at my heart.

It is not every day that one finds a dream come true; and, scared though I was, I noticed details: for example, that there did not seem to be those single lights burning in every upstairs window. Doubtless dreams, like poems, demand a certain licence; and, for the matter of that, I could not see all four sides of the house at once, as I had dreamed I had. But that perhaps was the worst of it: I was plainly not dreaming now.

A sudden greeny-pink radiance illuminated around me a morass of weed and neglect; and then seemed to hide itself among the trees on my right. The explanation of the darting lights was that a storm approached. But it was unlike other lightning I had encountered: being slower, more silent, more regular.

There seemed nothing to do but run away, though even then it seemed sensible not to run back into the wood. In the last memories of daylight, I began to wade through the dead knee-high grass of the lost lawn. It was still possible to see that the wood continued, opaque as ever, in a long line to my left; I felt my way along it, in order to keep as far as possible from the house. I noticed, as I passed, the great portico, facing the direction from which I had emerged. Then, keeping my distance, I crept along the grey east front with its two tiers of pointed windows, all shut and one or two broken; and reached the southern parterre, visibly vaster, even in the storm-charged gloom, than the northern, but no less ravaged. Ahead, and at the side of the parterre far off to my right, ranged the encircling woodland. If no path manifested, my state would be hazardous indeed; and there seemed little reason for a path, as the approach to the house was provided by that along which I had come from the marsh.

As I struggled onwards, the whole scene was transformed: in a moment the sky became charged with roaring thunder, the earth with tumultuous rain. I tried to shelter in the adjacent wood, but instantly found myself enmeshed in vines and suckers, lacerated by invisible spears. In a minute I should be drenched. I plunged through the wet weeds towards the spreading portico.

Before the big doors I waited for several minutes, watching the lightning, and listening. The rain leapt up where it fell, as if the earth hurt it. A rising chill made the old grass shiver. It seemed unlikely that anyone could live in a house so dark; but suddenly I heard one of the doors behind me scrape open. I turned. A dark head protruded between the portals, like Punch from the side of his booth.

"Oh." The shrill voice was of course surprised to see me. I turned. "May I please wait until the rain stops?"

"You can't come inside."

I drew back; so far back that a heavy drip fell on the back of my neck from the edge of the portico. With absurd melodrama, there was a loud roll of thunder.

"I shouldn't think of it," I said. "I must be on my way the moment the rain lets me." I could still see only the round head sticking out between the leaves of the door.

"In the old days we often had visitors." This statement was made in the tone of a Cheltenham lady remarking that when a child she often spoke to gypsies. "I only peeped out to see the thunder."

Now, within the house, I heard another, lower voice, although I could not hear what it said. Through the long crack between the doors, a light slid out across the flagstones of the porch and down the darkening steps.

"She's waiting for the rain to stop," said the shrill voice.

"Tell her to come in," said the deep voice. "Really, Emerald, you forget your manners after all this time."

"I *have* told her," said Emerald very petulantly, and withdrawing her head. "She won't do it."

"Nonsense," said the other. "You're just telling lies." I got the idea that thus she always spoke to Emerald.

Then the door opened, and I could see the two of them silhouetted in the light of a lamp which stood on a table behind them; one much the taller, but both with round heads, and both wearing long, unshapely garments. I wanted very much to escape, and failed to do so only because there seemed nowhere to go.

"Please come in at once," said the taller figure, "and let us take off your wet clothes."

"Yes, yes," squeaked Emerald, unreasonably jubilant.

"Thank you. But my clothes are not at all wet."

"None the less, please come in. We shall take it as a discourtesy if you refuse."

Another roar of thunder emphasized the impracticability of continuing to refuse much longer. If this was a dream, doubtless, and to judge by experience, I should awake.

And a dream it must be, because there at the front door were two big wooden wedges; and there to the right of the Hall, shadowed in the lamplight, was the Trophy Room; although now the animal heads on the walls were shoddy, fungoid ruins, their sawdust spilled and clotted on the cracked and uneven flagstones of the floor.

"You must forgive us," said my tall hostess. "Our land-lord neglects us sadly, and we are far gone in wrack and ruin. In fact, I do not know what we should do were it not for our own resources." At this Emerald cackled. Then she came up to me, and began fingering my clothes.

The tall one shut the door.

"Don't touch," she shouted at Emerald, in her deep, rather grinding voice. "Keep your fingers off."

She picked up the large oil lamp. Her hair was a dis-coloured white in its beams.

"I apologize for my sister," she said. "We have all been so neglected that some of us have quite forgotten how to behave. Come, Emerald."

Pushing Emerald before her, she led the way.

In the Occasional Room and the Morning Room, the gilt had flaked from the gingerbread furniture, the family por-traits stared from their heavy frames, and the striped wall-paper drooped in the lamplight like an assembly of sodden, half-inflated balloons.

At the door of the Canton Cabinet, my hostess turned. "I am taking you to meet my sisters," she said.

"I look forward to doing so," I replied, regardless of truth, as in childhood.

She nodded slightly, and proceeded. "Take care," she said. "The floor has weak places."

In the little Canton Cabinet, the floor had, in fact, largely given way, and been plainly converted into a hospice for rats.

And then, there they all were, the remaining six of them, thinly illumined by what must surely be rushlights in the four shapely chandeliers. But now, of course, I could see their faces.

"We are all named after our birthstones," said my host-ess. "Emerald you know. I am Opal. Here are Diamond and Garnet, Cornelian and Chrysolite. The one with the grey hair is Sardonyx, and the beautiful one is Turquoise."

They all stood up. During the ceremony of introduction, they made odd little noises.

"Emerald and I are the eldest, and Turquoise of course is the youngest."

Emerald stood in the corner before me, rolling her dyed-red head. The Long Drawing Room was raddled with decay. The cobwebs gleamed like steel filigree in the beam of the lamp, and the sisters seemed to have been seated in cocoons of them, like cushions of gossamer.

"There is one other sister, Topaz. But she is busy writing."

"Writing all our diaries," said Emerald.

"Keeping the record," said my hostess.

A silence followed.

"Let us sit down," said my hostess. "Let us make our visitor welcome."

The six of them gently creaked and subsided into their former places. Emerald and my hostess remained standing.

"Sit down, Emerald. Our visitor shall have *my* chair as it is the best." I realized that inevitably there was no extra seat.

"Of course not," I said. "I can only stay for a minute. I am waiting for the rain to stop," I explained feebly to the rest of them.

"I insist," said my hostess.

I looked at the chair to which she was pointing. The padding was burst and rotten, the woodwork bleached and crumbling to collapse. All of them were watching me with round, vague eyes in their flat faces.

"Really," I said, "no, thank you. It's kind of you, but I must go." All the same, the surrounding wood and the dark marsh beyond it loomed scarcely less appalling than the house itself and its inmates.

"We should have more to offer, more and better in every way, were it not for our landlord." She spoke with bitterness, and it seemed to me that on all the faces the expression changed. Emerald came towards me out of her corner, and again began to finger my clothes. But this time her sister did not correct her; and when I stepped away, she stepped after me and went on as before.

"She has failed in the barest duty of sustentation."

I could not prevent myself starting at the pronoun. At once, Emerald caught hold of my dress, and held it tightly.

"But there is one place she cannot spoil for us. One place where we can entertain in our own way."

"Please," I cried. "Nothing more. I am going now."

Emerald's pygmy grip tautened.

"It is the room where we eat."

All the watching eyes lighted up, and became something they had not been before.

"I may almost say where we feast."

The six of them began again to rise from their spidery bowers.

"Because *she* cannot go there."

The sisters clapped their hands, like a rustle of leaves.

"There we can be what we really are."

The eight of them were now grouped round me. I noticed that the one pointed out as the youngest was passing her dry, pointed tongue over her lower lip.

"Nothing unladylike, of course."

"Of course not," I agreed.

"But firm," broke in Emerald, dragging at my dress as she spoke. "Father said that must always come first."

"Our father was a man of measureless wrath against a slight," said my hostess. "It is his continuing presence about the house which largely upholds us."

"Shall I show her?" asked Emerald.

"Since you wish to," said her sister disdainfully.

From somewhere in her musty garments Emerald produced a scrap of card, which she held out to me.

"Take it in your hand. I'll allow you to hold it."

It was a photograph, obscurely damaged.

"Hold up the lamp," squealed Emerald. With an aloof gesture her sister raised it.

It was a photograph of myself when a child, bobbed and waistless. And through my heart was a tiny brown needle.

"We've all got things like it," said Emerald jubilantly. "Wouldn't you think her heart would have rusted away by now?"

"She never had a heart," said the elder sister scornfully, putting down the light.

"She might not have been able to help what she did," I cried.

I could hear the sisters catch their fragile breath.

"It's what you do that counts," said my hostess, regarding the discoloured floor, "not what you feel about it afterwards. Our father always insisted on that. It's obvious."

"Give it back to me," said Emerald, staring into my eyes. For moment I hesitated.

"Give it back to her," said my hostess in her contemptuous way. "It makes no difference now. Everyone but Emerald can see that the work is done."

I returned the card, and Emerald let go of me as she stuffed it away.

"And now will you join us?" asked my hostess. "In the inner room?" As far as was possible, her manner was almost casual.

"I am sure the rain has stopped," I replied. "I must be on my way."

"Our father would never have let you go so easily, but I think we have done what we can with you."

I inclined my head.

"Do not trouble with adieux," she said. "My sisters no longer expect them." She picked up the lamp. "Follow me. And take care. The floor has weak places."

"Goodbye," squealed Emerald.

"Take no notice, unless you wish," said my hostess.

I followed her through the mouldering rooms and across

the rotten floors in silence. She opened both the outer doors and stood waiting for me to pass through. Beyond, the moon was shining, and she stood dark and shapeless in the silver flood.

On the threshold, or somewhere on the far side of it, I spoke.

"I did nothing," I said. "Nothing."

So far from replying, she dissolved into the darkness and silently shut the door.

I took up my painful, lost, and forgotten way through the wood, across the dreary marsh, and back to the little yellow road.

Somebody named Stephen King started college the same year I did at the University of Maine at Orono. We were both English majors, and we both lived in Gannett Hall our freshman year. It goes without saying that it was one hell of a revelation to me when, a few years later, Steve sold *Carrie* to Doubleday.

Unlike the famous, "great" authors my professors had me read—all of whom were dead and cold—here was a *real* writer, a flesh and blood person I *knew* who had actually *done* it . . . had written and sold a novel!

Before Steve, though, there was another famous author whom I had encountered. Although he most certainly was dead by the time I read him, he'd been born and raised in Salem, Massachusetts, only a couple of towns over from where I grew up in Rockport. So for me, at least, that made him a "local" author.

His name was Nathaniel Hawthorne, and the story he wrote that frightened me the most is "Young Goodman Brown." It still gives me chills, and rereading it recently, I was amazed to realize how much this story has influenced my own writing as well as my world view. I have never read more truthful words than these. "The fiend in his own shape is less hideous than when he rages in the breast of a man."

It's surprising that a story first published in 1835 can seem so contemporary, but that was part of Hawthorne's genius. Within a very few pages, he masterfully lays bare the dark side of the human heart and soul, and deftly shows us the torment of a man who desperately wants to live a Godly, decent life but sees hypocrisy and evil everywhere he looks. (Better make that *Evil* with a capital *E*, because "Old Scratch" is a major character in the story.)

The poignancy of the end, where Young Goodman Brown—against his hope that "virtue were not a dream"—comes to believe that Evil permeates the world and is the true legacy of humanity (because he has lost his "Faith") is as true today as it was two hundred—or two thousand—years ago. Even though this is probably a story you were forced to read at one time or another in English class, reread it now and see if it still rings true for you.

—Rick Hautala

YOUNG GOODMAN BROWN
by Nathaniel Hawthorne

Young Goodman Brown came forth at sunset into the street at Salem village; but put his head back, after crossing the threshold, to exchange a parting kiss with his young wife. And Faith, as the wife was aptly named, thrust her own pretty head into the street, letting the wind play with the pink ribbons of her cap while she called to Goodman Brown.

"Dearest heart," whispered she, softly and rather sadly, when her lips were close to his ear, "prithee put off your journey until sunrise and sleep in your own bed tonight. A lone woman is troubled with such dreams and such thoughts that she's afeard of herself sometimes. Pray tarry with me this night, dear husband, of all nights in the year."

"My love and my Faith," replied young Goodman Brown, "of all nights in the year, this one night must I tarry away from thee. My journey, as thou callest it, forth and back again, must needs be done 'twixt now and sunrise. What, my sweet, pretty wife, dost thou doubt me already, and we but three months married?"

"Then God bless you!" said Faith, with the pink ribbons, "and may you find all well when you come back."

"Amen!" cried Goodman Brown. "Say thy prayers, dear Faith, and go to bed at dusk, and no harm will come to thee."

So they parted; and the young man pursued his way until, being about to turn the corner by the meetinghouse, he looked back and saw the head of Faith still peeping after him with a melancholy air, in spite of her pink ribbons.

"Poor little Faith!" thought he, for his heart smote him. "What a wretch am I to leave her on such an errand! She talks of dreams, too. Methought as she spoke there was trouble in her face, as if a dream had warned her what work is to be done tonight. But no, no; 'twould kill her to think it. Well, she's a blessed angel on earth; and after this one night I'll cling to her skirts and follow her to heaven."

With this excellent resolve for the future, Goodman Brown felt himself justified in making more haste on his present evil purpose. He had taken a dreary road, darkened by all the gloomiest trees of the forest, which barely stood aside to let the narrow path creep through, and closed immediately behind. It was all as lonely as could be; and there is this peculiarity in such a solitude, that the traveler knows not who may be concealed by the innumerable trunks and the thick boughs overhead; so that with lonely footsteps he may yet be passing through an unseen multitude.

"There may be a devilish Indian behind every tree," said Goodman Brown to himself; and he glanced fearfully behind him as he added, "What if the devil himself should be at my very elbow!"

His head being turned back, he passed a crook of the road, and, looking forward again, beheld the figure of a man, in grave and decent attire, seated at the foot of an old tree. He arose at Goodman Brown's approach and walked onward side by side with him.

"You are late, Goodman Brown," said he. "The clock of the Old South was striking as I came through Boston, and that is full fifteen minutes agone."

"Faith kept me back awhile," replied the young man, with a tremor in his voice, caused by the sudden appearance of his companion, though not wholly unexpected.

It was now deep dusk in the forest, and deepest in that part of it where these two were journeying. As nearly as could be discerned, the second traveler was about fifty years old, apparently in the same rank of life as Goodman Brown, and bearing a considerable resemblance to him, though perhaps more in expression than features. Still they might have been taken for father and son. And yet, though the elder person was as simply clad as the younger, and as simple in manner, too, he had an indescribable air of one who knew the world, and who would not have felt abashed at the Governor's dinner table or in King William's court, were it possible that his affairs should call him thither. But the only thing about him that could be fixed upon as remarkable was his staff, which bore the likeness of a great black snake, so curiously wrought that it might almost be seen to twist and wriggle itself like a living serpent. This, of course, must have been an ocular deception, assisted by the uncertain light.

"Come, Goodman Brown," cried his fellow traveler, "this is a dull pace for the beginning of a journey. Take my staff, if you are so soon weary."

"Friend," said the other, exchanging his slow pace for a full stop, "having kept covenant by meeting thee here, it is my purpose now to return whence I came. I have scruples touching the matter thou wot'st of."

"Sayest thou so?" replied he of the serpent, smiling apart. "Let us walk on, nevertheless, reasoning as we go; and if I convince thee not, thou shalt turn back. We are but a little way in the forest yet."

"Too far! too far!" exclaimed the goodman, unconsciously resuming his walk. "My father never went into the woods on such an errand, nor his father before him. We have been a race of honest men and good Christians since the days of the martyrs; and shall I be the first of the name of Brown that ever took this path and kept—"

"Such company, thou wouldst say," observed the elder person, interpreting his pause. "Well said, Goodman Brown! I have been as well acquainted with your family as with ever a one among the Puritans; and that's no trifle to say. I helped your grandfather, the constable, when he lashed the Quaker woman so smartly through the streets of Salem; and it was I that brought your father a pitch-pine knot, kindled at my own hearth, to set fire to an Indian village, in

King Philip's war. They were my good friends, both; and many a pleasant walk have we had along this path, and returned merrily after midnight. I would fain be friends with you for their sake."

"If it be as thou sayest," replied Goodman Brown, "I marvel they never spoke of these matters; or, verily, I marvel not, seeing that the least rumor of the sort would have driven them from New England. We are a people of prayer, and good works to boot, and abide no such wickedness."

"Wickedness or not," said the traveler with the twisted staff, "I have a very general acquaintance here in New England. The deacons of many a church have drunk the communion wine with me; the selectmen of divers town make me their chairman; and a majority of the Great and General Court are firm supporters of my interest. The Governor and I, too— But these are state secrets."

"Can this be so?" cried Goodman Brown, with a stare of amazement at his undisturbed companion. "Howbeit, I have nothing to do with the Governor and council; they have their own ways and are no rule for a simple husbandman like me. But, were I to go on with thee, how should I meet the eye of that good old man, our minister, at Salem village? Oh, his voice would make me tremble both Sabbath day and lecture day."

Thus far the elder traveler had listened with due gravity; but now burst into a fit of irrepressible mirth, shaking himself so violently that his snakelike staff actually seemed to wriggle in sympathy.

"Ha! ha! ha!" shouted he again and again; then composing himself, "Well, go, on, Goodman Brown, go on; but, prithee, don't kill me with laughing."

"Well, then, to end the matter at once," said Goodman Brown, considerably nettled, "there is my wife, Faith. It would break her dear little heart; and I'd rather break my own."

"Nay, if that be the case," answered the other, "e'en go

thy ways, Goodman Brown. I would not for twenty old women like the one hobbling before us that Faith should come to any harm."

As he spoke, he pointed his staff at a female figure on the path, in whom Goodman Brown recognized a very pious and exemplary dame, who had taught him his catechism in youth, and was still his moral and spiritual adviser, jointly with the minister and Deacon Gookin.

"A marvel, truly, that Goody Cloyse should be so far in the wilderness at nightfall," said he. "But with your leave, friend, I shall take a cut through the woods until we have left this Christian woman behind. Being a stranger to you, she might ask whom I was consorting with and whither I was going."

"Be it so," said his fellow traveler. "Betake you to the woods, and let me keep the path."

Accordingly the young man turned aside, but took care to watch his companion, who advanced softly along the road until he had come within a staff's length of the old dame. She, meanwhile, was making the best of her way, with singular speed for so aged a woman, and mumbling some indistinct words—a prayer, doubtless—as she went. The traveler put forth his staff and touched her withered neck with what seemed the serpent's tail.

"The devil!" screamed the pious old lady.

"Then Goody Cloyse knows her old friend?" observed the traveler, confronting her and leaning on his writhing stick.

"Ah, forsooth, and is it your worship indeed?" cried the good dame. "Yea, truly is it, and in the very image of my old gossip Goodman Brown, the grandfather of the silly fellow that now is. But—would your worship believe it?—my broomstick hat strangely disappeared, stolen, as I suspect, by that unhanged witch, Goody Cory, and that, too, when I was all anointed with the juice of smallage, and cinquefoil, and wolfsbane—"

"Mingled with fine wheat and the fat of a newborn babe," said the shape of old Goodman Brown.

"Ah, your worship knows the recipe," cried the old lady, cackling aloud. "So, as I was saying, being all ready for the meeting, and no horse to ride on, I made up my mind to foot it; for they tell me there is a nice young man to be taken into communion tonight. But now your good worship will lend me your arm, and we shall be there in a twinkling."

"That can hardly be," answered her friend. "I may not spare you my arm, Goody Cloyse; but here is my staff, if you will."

So saying, he threw it down at her feet, where, perhaps, it assumed life, being one of the rods which its owner had formerly lent to the Egyptian magi. Of this fact, however, Goodman Brown could not take cognizance. He had cast up his eyes in astonishment, and looking down again, beheld neither Goody Cloyse nor the serpentine staff, but his fellow traveler alone, who waited for him as calmly as if nothing had happened.

"That old woman taught me my catechism," said the young man; and there was a world of meaning in this simple comment.

They continued to walk onward, while the elder traveler exhorted his companion to make good speed and persevere in the path, discoursing so aptly that his arguments seemed rather to spring up in the bosom of his auditor than to be suggested by himself. As they went, he plucked a branch of maple to serve for a walking stick, and began to strip it of the twigs and little boughs, which were wet with evening dew. The moment his fingers touched them, they became strangely withered and dried up as with a week's sunshine. Thus the pair proceeded, at a good free pace, until suddenly, in a gloomy hollow of the road, Goodman Brown sat himself down on the stump of a tree and refused to go any farther.

"Friend," said he, stubbornly, "my mind is made up. Not another step will I budge on this errand. What if a wretched old woman do choose to go to the devil when I thought she was going to heaven: is that any reason why I should quit my dear Faith and go after her?"

"You will think better of this by and by," said his acquaintance, composedly. "Sit here and rest yourself awhile; and when you feel like moving again, there is my staff to help you along."

Without more words, he threw his companion the maple stick, and was as speedily out of sight as if he had vanished into the deepening gloom. The young man sat a few moments by the roadside, applauding himself greatly, and thinking with how clear a conscience he should meet the minister in his morning walk, nor shrink from the eye of good old Deacon Gookin. And what calm sleep would be his that very night, which was to have been spent so wickedly, but so purely and sweetly now, in the arms of Faith! Amidst these pleasant and praiseworthy meditations, Goodman Brown heard the tramp of horses along the road, and deemed it advisable to conceal himself within the verge of the forest, conscious of the guilty purpose that brought him thither, though now so happily turned from it.

On came the hoof tramps and the voices of the riders, two grave old voices, conversing soberly as they drew near. These mingled sounds appeared to pass along the road, within a few yards of the young man's hiding place; but, owing doubtless to the depth of the gloom at that particular spot, neither the travelers nor their steeds were visible. Though their figures brushed the small boughs by the wayside, it could not be seen that they intercepted, even for a moment, the faint gleam from the strip of bright sky athwart which they must have passed. Goodman Brown alternately crouched and stood on tiptoe, pulling aside the branches and thrusting forth his head as far as he durst without discerning so much as a shadow. It vexed him the more, be-

cause he could have sworn, were such a thing possible, that
he recognized the voices of the minister and Deacon Gookin,
jogging along quietly, as they were wont to do, when bound
to some ordination or ecclesiastical council. While yet within
hearing, one of the riders stopped to pluck a switch.

"Of the two, reverend sir," said the voice like the deacon's, "I had rather miss an ordination dinner than tonight's
meeting. They tell me that some of our community are to
be here from Falmouth and beyond, and others from Con-
necticut and Rhode Island, besides several of the Indian
powwows, who, after their fashion, know almost as much
deviltry as the best of us. Moreover, there is a goodly young
woman to be taken into communion."

"Mighty well, Deacon Gookin!" replied the solemn old
tones of the minister. "Spur up, or we shall be late. Nothing can be done, you know, until I get on the ground."

The hoofs clattered again; and the voices, talking so
strangely in the empty air, passed on through the forest,
where no church had ever been gathered or solitary Christian prayed. Whither, then, could these holy men be journeying so deep into the heathen wilderness? Young
Goodman Brown caught hold of a tree for support, being
ready to sink down on the ground, faint and overburdened
with the heavy sickness of his heart. He looked up to the
sky, doubting whether there really was a heaven above him.
Yet there was the blue arch, and the stars brightening in it.

"With heaven above and Faith below, I will yet stand
firm against the devil!" cried Goodman Brown.

While he still gazed upward into the deep arch of the
firmament and had lifted his hands to pray, a cloud, though
no wind was stirring, hurried across the zenith and hid the
brightening stars. The blue sky was still visible, except directly overhead, where this black mass of cloud was sweeping swiftly northward. Aloft in the air, as if from the depths
of the cloud, came a confused and doubtful sound of voices.
Once the listener fancied that he could distinguish the ac-

cents of townspeople of his own, men and women, both
pious and ungodly, many of whom he had met at the communion table, and had seen others rioting at the tavern. The
next moment, so indistinct were the sounds, he doubted
whether he had heard aught but the murmur of the old forest, whispering without a wind. Then came a stronger swell
of those familiar tones, heard daily in the sunshine at Salem
village, but never until now from a cloud of night. There
was one voice, of a young woman, uttering lamentations,
yet with an uncertain sorrow, and entreating for some favor,
which, perhaps, it would grieve her to obtain; and all the
unseen multitude, both saints and sinners, seemed to encourage her onward.

"Faith!" shouted Goodman Brown, in a voice of agony
and desperation; and the echoes of the forest mocked him,
crying "Faith! Faith!" as if bewildered wretches were seeking her all through the wilderness.

The cry of grief, rage, and terror was yet piercing the
night, when the unhappy husband held his breath for a response. There was a scream, drowned immediately in a
louder murmur of voices, fading into far-off laughter, as
the dark cloud swept away, leaving the clear and silent sky
above Goodman Brown. But something fluttered lightly
down through the air and caught on the branch of a tree.
The young man seized it, and beheld a pink ribbon.

"My Faith is gone!" cried he, after one stupefied moment. "There is no good on earth; and sin is but a name.
Come, devil; for to thee is this world given."

And, maddened with despair, so that he laughed loud
and long, did Goodman Brown grasp his staff and set forth
again, at such a rate that he seemed to fly along the forest
path rather than to walk or run. The road grew wilder and
drearier and more faintly traced, and vanished at length,
leaving him in the heart of the dark wilderness, still rushing onward with the instinct that guides mortal man to evil.
The whole forest was peopled with frightful sounds—the

creaking of the trees, the howling of wild beasts, and the yell of Indians; while sometimes the wind tolled like a distant church bell, and sometimes gave a broad roar around the traveler, as if all Nature were laughing him to scorn. But he was himself the chief horror of the scene, and shrank not from its other horrors.

"Ha! ha! ha!" roared Goodman Brown when the wind laughed at him. "Let us hear which will laugh loudest. Think not to frighten me with your deviltry. Come witch, come wizard, come Indian powwow, come devil himself, and here comes Goodman Brown. You may as well fear him as he fear you."

In truth, all through the haunted forest there could be nothing more frightful than the figure of Goodman Brown. On he flew among the black pines, brandishing his staff with frenzied gestures, now giving vent to an inspiration of horrid blasphemy, and now shouting forth such laughter as set all the echoes of the forest laughing like demons around him. The fiend in his own shape is less hideous than when he rages in the breast of man. Thus sped the demoniac on his course, until, quivering among the trees, he saw a red light before him, as when the felled trunks and branches of a clearing have been set on fire, and thrown up their lurid blaze against the sky, at the hour of midnight. He paused, in a lull of the tempest that had driven him onward, and heard the swell of what seemed a hymn, rolling solemnly from a distance with the weight of many voices. He knew the tune; it was a familiar one in the choir of the village meetinghouse. The verse died heavily away, and was lengthened by a chorus, not of human voices, but of all the sounds of the benighted wilderness pealing in awful harmony together. Goodman Brown cried too, and his cry was lost to his own ear by its unison with the cry of the desert.

In the interval of silence, he stole forward until the light glared full upon his eyes. At one extremity of an open space, hemmed in by the dark wall of the forest, arose a rock, bearing some rude, natural resemblance either to an altar or a pulpit, and surrounded by four blazing pines, their tops aflame, their stems untouched, like candles at an evening meeting. The mass of foliage that had overgrown the summit of the rock was all on fire, blazing high into the night and fitfully illuminating the whole field. Each pendent twig and leafy festoon was in a blaze. As the red light arose and fell, a numbrous congregation alternately shone forth, then disappeared in shadow, and again grew, as it were, out of the darkness, peopling the heart of the solitary woods at once.

"A grave and dark-clad company," quoth Goodman Brown.

In truth they were such. Among them, quivering to and fro between gloom and splendor, appeared faces that would be seen next day at the council board of the province, and others which, Sabbath after Sabbath, looked devoutly heavenward, and benignantly over the crowded pews, from the holiest pulpits in the land. Some affirm that the lady of the Governor was there. At least, there were high dames well known to her, and wives of honored husbands, and widows, a great multitude, and ancient maidens, all of excellent repute, and fair young girls, who trembled lest their mothers should espy them. Either the sudden gleams of light flashing over the obscure field bedazzled Goodman Brown, or he recognized a score of the church members of Salem village famous for their especial sanctity. Good old Deacon Gookin had arrived, and waited at the skirts of that venerable saint, his revered pastor. But, irreverently consorting with these grave, reputable, and pious people, these elders of the church, these chaste dames and dewy virgins, there were men of dissolute lives and women of spotted fame, wretches given over to all mean and filthy vice, and suspected even of horrid crimes. It was strange to see that the good shrank not from the wicked, nor were the sinners abashed by the saints. Scattered also among their pale-faced enemies were the Indian priests, or powwows, who had often scared their native forest with more hideous incantations than any known to English witchcraft.

"But wherc is Faith?" thought Goodman Brown, and, as hope came into his heart, he trembled.

Another verse of the hymn arose, a slow and mournful strain, such as the pious love, but joined to words which expressed all that our nature can conceive of sin, and darkly hinted at far more. Unfathomable to mere mortals is the lore of fiends. Verse after verse was sung; and still the chorus of the desert swelled between like the deepest tone of a mighty organ; and with the final peal of that dreadful anthem there came a sound, as if the roaring wind, the rushing streams, the howling beasts, and every other voice of the unconcerted wilderness were mingling and according with the voice of guilty man in homage to the prince of all. The four blazing pines threw up a loftier flame, and obscurely discovered shapes and visages of horror on the smoke wreaths above the impious assembly. At the same moment, the fire on the rock shot redly forth and formed a glowing arch above its base, where now appeared a figure. With reverence be it spoken, the figure bore no slight similitude, both in garb and manner, to some grave divine of the New England churches.

"Bring forth the converts!" cried a voice that echoed through the field and rolled into the forest.

At the word, Goodman Brown stepped forth from the shadow of the trees and approached the congregation, with whom he felt a loathful brotherhood by the sympathy of all that was wicked in his heart. He could have well-nigh sworn that the shape of his own dead father beckoned him to advance, looking downward from a smoke wreath, while a woman, with dim features of despair, threw out her hand to warn him back. Was it his mother? But he had no power to retreat one step, nor to resist, even in thought, when the minister and good old Deacon Gookin seized his arms and led him to the blazing rock. Thither came also the slender form of a veiled female, led between Goody Cloyse, that pious teacher of the catechism, and Martha Carrier, who had received the devil's promise to be queen of hell. A rampant hag was she. And there stood the proselytes beneath the canopy of fire.

"Welcome, my children," said the dark figure, "to the communion of your race. Ye have found thus young your nature and your destiny. My children, look behind you!"

They turned; and flashing forth, as it were, in a sheet of flame, the fiend-worshipers were seen; the smile of welcome gleamed darkly on every visage.

"There," resumed the sable form, "are all whom ye have reverenced from youth. Ye deemed them holier than yourselves, and shrank from your own sin, contrasting it with their lives of righteousness and prayerful aspirations heavenward. Yet here are they all in my worshiping assembly. This night it shall be granted you to know their secret deeds: how hoary-bearded elders of the church have whispered wanton words to the young maids of their household; how many a woman, eager for widows' weeds, has given her husband a drink at bedtime and let him sleep his last sleep in her bosom; how beardless youths have made haste to inherit their fathers' wealth; and how fair damsels—blush not, sweet ones—have dug little graves in the garden, and bidden me, the sole guest, to an infant's funeral. By the sympathy of your human hearts for sin ye shall scent out all the places—whether in church, bedchamber, street, field, or forest—where crime has been committed, and shall exult to behold the whole earth one stain of guilt, one mighty blood spot. Far more than this. It shall be yours to penetrate, in every bosom, the deep mystery of sin, the fountain of all wicked arts, and which inexhaustibly supplies more evil impulses than human power—than my power at its utmost—can make manifest in deeds. And now, my children, look upon each other."

They did so; and, by the blaze of the hell-kindled torches, the wretched man beheld his Faith, and the wife her husband, trembling before that unhallowed altar.

"Lo, there ye stand, my children," said the figure, in a deep and solemn tone, almost sad with its despairing awfulness, as if his once angelic nature could yet mourn for our miserable race. "Depending upon one another's hearts, ye had still hoped that virtue were not all a dream. Now are ye undeceived. Evil is the nature of mankind. Evil must be your only happiness. Welcome again, my children, to the communion of your race."

"Welcome," repeated the fiend-worshipers, in one cry of despair and triumph.

And there they stood, the only pair, as it seemed, who were yet hesitating on the verge of wickedness in this dark world. A basin was hollowed, naturally, in the rock. Did it contain water, reddened by the lurid light? or was it blood? or, perchance a liquid flame? Herein did the shape of evil dip his hand and prepare to lay the mark of baptism upon their foreheads, that they might be partakers of the mystery of sin, more conscious of the secret guilt of others, both in deed and thought, than they could now be of their own. The husband cast one look at his pale wife, and Faith at him. What polluted wretches would the next glance show them to each other, shuddering alike at what they disclosed and what they saw!

"Faith! Faith!" cried the husband, "look up to heaven, and resist the wicked one."

Whether Faith obeyed he knew not. Hardly had he spoken when he found himself amid calm night and solitude, listening to a roar of the wind which died heavily away through the forest. He staggered against the rock, and felt it chill and damp; while a hanging twig, that had been all on fire, besprinkled his cheek with the coldest dew.

The next morning, young Goodman Brown came slowly into the street of Salem village, staring around him like a bewildered man. The good old minister was taking a walk along the graveyard to get an appetite for breakfast and meditate his sermon, and bestowed a blessing, as he passed, on Goodman Brown. He shrank from the venerable saint as if to avoid an anathema. Old Deacon Gookin was at domestic worship, and the holy words of his prayer were heard through the open window. "What God doth the wizard pray to?" quoth Goodman Brown. Goody Cloyse, that excellent old Christian, stood in the early sunshine at her own lattice, catechizing a little girl who had brought her a pint of morning's milk. Goodman Brown snatched away the child as from the grasp of the fiend himself. Turning the corner by the meetinghouse, he spied the head of Faith, with the pink ribbons, gazing anxiously forth, and bursting into such joy at sight of him that she skipped along the street and almost kissed her husband before the whole village. But Goodman Brown looked sternly and sadly into her face, and passed on without a greeting.

Had Goodman Brown fallen asleep in the forest and only dreamed a wild dream of a witch meeting?

Be it so if you will; but, alas! it was a dream of evil omen for young Goodman Brown. A stern, a sad, a darkly meditative, a distrustful, if not a desperate man did he become from the night of that fearful dream. On the Sabbath day, when the congregation were singing a holy psalm, he could not listen because an anthem of sin rushed loudly upon his ear and drowned all the blessed strain. When the minister spoke from the pulpit with power and fervid eloquence, and, with his hand on the open Bible, of the sacred truths of our religion, and of saintlike lives and triumphant deaths, and of future bliss or misery unutterable, then did Goodman Brown turn pale, dreading lest the roof should thunder down upon the gray blasphemer and his hearers. Often, awakening suddenly at midnight, he shrank from the bosom of Faith; and at morning or eventide, when the family knelt down at prayer, he scowled and muttered to himself, and gazed sternly at his wife, and turned away. And when he had lived long, and was borne to his grave a hoary corpse, followed by Faith, an aged woman, and children and grandchildren, a goodly procession, besides neighbors not a few, they carved no hopeful verse upon his tombstone, for his dying hour was gloom.

Formication, n., a tactile hallucination involving the belief something is crawling on the body or under the skin.

What I ask of a horror story is that it gets under my skin. Like "The Rats in the Walls."

Flea season was upon us and the cat was to blame. I searched the Yellow Pages under "Exterminating" and made a call. I'm sure the man who rapped on my door had an inbred cousin in the hills with whom he played dueling banjos. "You call this a flea problem?" he scoffed, standing in the room where I write. "The dump I did ten minutes ago, *that* was a flea problem." I knew that was true since the fleas jumping *off* him were the size of rats. "Damn," he said. "Spray pump's broken. I'll have to come back."

Formication.

That time for real.

Researching the chapter "Bugs" in *Ripper* produced this passage: *The reek of rotting beef liver hung heavy in the air of the narrow corridor linking a dozen closet-sized labs. Inside each environmentally controlled room, wooden shelves were lined with jars full of maggots writhing in sawdust, cockroaches clambering over wads of paper towel, and minuscule flies savoring the leaves of potted plants. Each red door of the Insectary had a wire-mesh window for monitoring bug activity within. Craven waited outside the murder lab, the only door with a padlock and blacked-out window . . . Forensic entomology is the study of insects that invade a rotting corpse . . . Wearing a face mask to protect her from the bugs and sickening-sweet smell, Dr. Sandra Wong exited from the blacked-out lab and locked its door . . . Her hands and that part of her face not covered by the mask were welted red from myriad insect bites. While she and Nick conversed in the hall she scratched them constantly, and soon the Mountie was scratching too.*

And so was I.

When I returned with a sheaf of notes to the room where I write, a stowaway from the Insectary leapt from between two of the sheets and scurried into the carpet. Was it female? Was it pregnant? Where'd it go? My notes informed me: *Different species of insects are lured by different stages*

*of decomposition. By knowing the succession of bugs that
colonize a corpse—metallic green blowflies and house flies
land first, followed by flesh flies, larder beetles, cheese skip-
pers, etc.—and the life-span of each carnivorous wave, en-
tomologists calculate back to when the person died.*

Carnivorous?

I'm scratching now.

I never found that bug.

Slade is the pen name of two criminal lawyers who spe-
cialize in the defense of insanity. Psychotics and psy-
chopaths make up the clientele. Cocaine psychosis is
spooky to behold, like the wretch who grabbed a pen and
repeatedly stabbed his arm, crying "Gotcha! Gotcha!
Gotcha!" with each phantom bug impaled. Lab mice, wired
to coke, will gnaw their limbs to the bone to end formication. Organic psychosis is spookier to behold, like the client
who grew his nails to claw flesh from his skull. It has been
said we all reside in the houses of our minds, so pity claus-
trophobic brains walled in by skull and scalp.

Formication.

Big time.

Like "The Rats in the Walls."

—Michael Slade

THE RATS IN THE WALLS
by H. P. Lovecraft

On July 16, 1923, I moved into Exham Priory after the
last workman had finished his labors. The restoration
had been a stupendous task, for little had remained of the
deserted pile but a shell-like ruin; yet because it had been
the seat of my ancestors, I let no expense deter me. The
place had not been inhabited since the reign of James the
First, when a tragedy of intensely hideous, though largely
unexplained, nature had struck down the master, five of his
children, and several servants; and driven forth under a cloud

of suspicion and terror the third son, my lineal progenitor and the only survivor of the abhorred line.

With this sole heir denounced as a murderer, the estate had reverted to the crown, nor had the accused man made any attempt to exculpate himself or regain his property. Shaken by some horror greater than that of conscience or the law, and expressing only a frantic wish to exclude the ancient edifice from his sight and memory, Walter de la Poer, eleventh Baron Exham, fled to Virginia and there founded the family which by the next century had become known as Delapore.

Exham Priory had remained untenanted, though later allotted to the estates of the Norrys family and much studied because of its peculiarly composite architecture; an architecture involving Gothic towers resting on a Saxon or Romanesque substructure, whose foundation in turn was of a still earlier order or blend of orders—Roman, and even Druidic or native Cymric, if legends speak truly. This foundation was a very singular thing, being merged on one side with the solid limestone of the precipice from whose brink the priory overlooked a desolate valley three miles west of the village of Anchester.

Architects and antiquarians loved to examine this strange relic of forgotten centuries, but the country folk hated it. They had hated it hundreds of years before, when my ancestors lived there, and they hated it now with the moss and mould of abandonment on it. I had not been a day in Anchester before I knew I came of an accursed house. And this week workmen have blown up Exham Priory, and are busy obliterating the traces of its foundations. The bare statistics of my ancestry I had always known, together with the fact that my first American forebear had come to the colonies under a strange cloud. Of details, however, I had been kept wholly ignorant through the policy of reticence always maintained by the Delapores. Unlike our planter neighbors, we seldom boasted of crusading ancestors or

other mediaeval and Renaissance heroes; nor was any kind
of tradition handed down except what may have been
recorded in the sealed envelope left before the Civil War
by every squire to his eldest son for posthumous opening.
The glories we cherished were those achieved since the migration; the glories of a proud and honorable, if somewhat
reserved and unsocial Virginia line.

During the war our fortunes were extinguished and our
whole existence changed by the burning of Carfax, our home
on the banks of the James. My grandfather, advanced in
years, had perished in that incendiary outrage, and with him
the envelope that had bound us all to the past. I can recall
that fire today as I saw it then at the age of seven, with the
Federal soldiers shouting, the women screaming, and the
Negroes howling and praying. My father was in the army,
defending Richmond, and after many formalities my mother
and I were passed through the lines to join him.

When the war ended we all moved north, whence my
mother had come; and I grew to manhood, middle age, and
ultimate wealth as a stolid Yankee. Neither my father nor I
ever knew what our hereditary envelope had contained as
I merged into the greyness of Massachusetts business life.
I lost all interest in the mysteries which evidently lurked
far back in my family tree. Had I suspected their nature,
how gladly I would have left Exham Priory to its moss,
bats, and cobwebs!

My father died in 1904, but without any message to leave
to me, or to my only child, Alfred, a motherless boy of ten.
It was this boy who reversed the order of family information, for although I could give him only jesting conjectures
about the past, he wrote me of some very interesting ancestral legends when the late war took him to England in
1917 as an aviation officer. Apparently the Delapores had
a colorful and perhaps sinister history, for a friend of my
son's, Capt. Edward Norrys of the Royal Flying Corps,
dwelt near the family seat at Anchester and related some

peasant superstitions which few novelists could equal for wildness and incredibility. Norrys himself, of course, did not take them so seriously; but they amused my son and made good material for his letters to me. It was this legendry which definitely turned my attention to my transatlantic heritage, and made me resolve to purchase and restore the family seat which Norrys showed to Alfred in its picturesque desertion, and offered to get for him at a surprisingly reasonable figure, since his own uncle was the present owner.

I bought Exham Priory in 1918, but was almost immediately distracted from my plans of restoration by the return of my son as a maimed invalid. During the two years that he lived I thought of nothing but his care, having even placed my business under the direction of partners.

In 1921, as I found myself bereaved and aimless, a retired manufacturer no longer young, I resolved to divert my remaining years with my new possession. Visiting Anchester in December, I was entertained by Capt. Norrys, a plump, amiable young man who had thought much of my son, and secured his assistance in gathering plans and anecdotes to guide in the coming restoration. Exham Priory itself I saw without emotion, a jumble of tottering mediaeval ruins covered with lichens and honeycombed with rooks' nests, perched perilously upon a precipice, and denuded of floors or other interior features save the stone walls of the separate towers.

As I gradually recovered the image of the edifice as it had been when my ancestors left it over three centuries before, I began to hire workmen for the reconstruction. In every case I was forced to go outside the immediate locality, for the Anchester villagers had an almost unbelievable fear and hatred of the place. This sentiment was so great that it was sometimes communicated to the outside laborers, causing numerous desertions; whilst its scope appeared to include both the priory and its ancient family.

My son had told me that he was somewhat avoided during
his visits because he was a de la Poer, and I now found myself subtly ostracised for a like reason until I convinced the
peasants how little I knew of my heritage. Even then they
sullenly disliked me, so that I had to collect most of the
village traditions through the mediation of Norrys. What the
people could not forgive perhaps, was that I had come to
restore a symbol so abhorrent to them; for, rationally or not,
they viewed Exham Priory as nothing less than a haunt of
fiends and werewolves.

Piercing together the tales which Norrys collected for
me, and supplementing them with the accounts of several
savants who had studied the ruins, I deduced the Exham
Priory stood on the site of a prehistoric temple; a Druidi-
cal or ante-Druidical thing which must have been contemporary with Stonehenge. That indescribable rites had been
celebrated there, few doubted, and there were unpleasant
tales of the transference of these rites into the Cybele-
worship which the Romans had introduced.

Inscriptions still visible in the sub-cellar bore such unmistakable letters as "DIV . . . OPS . . . MAGNA. MAT . . ." sign
of the Magna Mater whose dark worship was once vainly
forbidden to Roman citizens. Anchester had been the camp
of the third Augustan legion, as many remains attest, and
it was said that the temple of Cybele was splendid and
thronged with worshippers who performed nameless cere-
monies at the bidding of a Phrygian priest. Tales added that
the fall of the old religion did not end the orgies at the temple, but that the priests lived on in the new faith without
real change. Likewise was it said that the rites did not van-
ish with the Roman power, and that certain among the Saxons added to what remained of the temple, and gave it the
essential outline it subsequently preserved, making it the
center of a cult feared through half the heptarchy. About
1000 A.D. the place is mentioned in a chronicle as being a
substantial stone priory housing a strange and powerful

monastic order and surrounded by extensive gardens which needed no walls to exclude a frightened populace. It was never destroyed by the Danes, though after the Norman Conquest it must have declined tremendously; since there was no impediment when Henry the Third granted the site to my ancestor, Gilbert de la Poer, first Baron Exham, in 1261.

Of my family before this date there is no evil report, but something strange must have happened then. In one chronicle there is a reference to a de la Poer as "cursed of God" in 1307, whilst village legendry had nothing but evil and frantic fear to tell of the castle that went up on the foundations of the old temple and priory. The fireside tales were of the most grisly reticence and cloudy evasiveness. They represented my ancestors as a race of hereditary daemons beside whom Gilles de Retz and the Marquis de Sade would seem the veriest tyros, and hinted whisperingly at their responsibility for the occasional disappearances of villagers through several generations.

The worst characters, apparently, were the barons and their direct heirs; at least, most was whispered about these. If of healthier inclinations, it was said, an heir would early and mysteriously die to make way for another more typical scion. There seemed to be an inner cult in the family, presided over by the head of the house, and sometimes closed except to a few members. Temperament rather than ancestry was evidently the basis of this cult, for it was entered by several who married into the family. Lady Margaret Trevor from Cornwall, wife of Godfrey, the second son of the fifth baron, became a favorite bane of children all over the countryside, and the daemon heroine of a particularly horrible old ballad not yet extinct near the Welsh border. Preserved in balladry, too, though not illustrating the same point, is the hideous tale of Lady Mary de la Poer, who shortly after her marriage to the Earl of Shrewsfield was killed by him and his mother, both of the slayers being absolved and blessed by the priest to whom they confessed what they dared not repeat to the world.

These myths and ballads, typical as they were of crude superstition, repelled me greatly. Their persistence, and their application to so long a line of my ancestors, were especially annoying; whilst the imputations of monstrous habits proved unpleasantly reminiscent of the one known scandal of my immediate forebears—the case of my cousin, young Randolph Delapore of Carfax, who went among the Negroes and became a voodoo priest after he returned from the Mexican War.

I was much less disturbed by the vaguer tales of wails and howlings in the barren, windswept valley beneath the limestone cliff; of the graveyard stenches after the spring rains; of the floundering, squealing white thing on which Sir John Clave's horse had trod one night in a lonely field; and of the servant who had gone mad at what he saw in the priory in the full light of day. These things were hackneyed spectral lore, and I was at that time a pronounced skeptic. The accounts of vanished peasants were less to be dismissed, though not especially significant in view of mediaeval custom. Prying curiosity meant death, and more than one severed head had been publicly shown on the bastions—now effaced—around Exham Priory.

A few of the tales were exceedingly picturesque, and made me wish I had learnt more of the comparative mythology in my youth. There was, for instance, the belief that a legion of batwinged devils kept witches' sabbath each night at the priory—a legion whose sustenance might explain the disproportionate abundance of coarse vegetables harvested in the vast gardens. And, most vivid of all, there was the dramatic epic of the rats—the scampering army of obscene vermin which had burst forth from the castle three months after the tragedy that doomed it to desertion—the lean, filthy, ravenous army which had swept all before it and devoured fowl, cats, dogs, hogs, sheep, and even two hapless human beings before its fury was spent. Around that unforgettable rodent army a whole separate cycle of myths revolves, for it scattered among the village homes and brought curses and horrors in its train.

Such was the lore that assailed me as I pushed to completion, with an elderly obstinacy, the work of restoring my ancestral home. It must not be imagined for a moment that these tales formed my principal psychological environment. On the other hand, I was constantly praised and encouraged by Capt. Norrys and the antiquarians who surrounded and aided me. When the task was done, over two years after its commencement, I viewed the great room, wainscotted walls, vaulted ceilings, mullioned windows, and broad staircases with a pride which fully compensated for the prodigious expense of the restoration.

Every attribute of the Middle Ages was cunningly reproduced, and the new parts blended perfectly with the original walls and foundations. The seat of my fathers was complete, and I looked forward to redeeming at last the local fame of the line which ended in me. I would reside here permanently, and prove that a de la Poer (for I had adopted again the original spelling of the name) need not be a fiend. My comfort was perhaps augmented by the fact that, although Exham Priory was mediaevally fitted, its interior was in truth wholly new and free from old vermin and old ghosts alike.

As I have said, I moved in on July 16, 1923. My household consisted of seven servants and nine cats, of which latter species I am particularly fond. My eldest cat, "Nigger-Man," was seven years old and had come with me from my home in Bolton, Massachusetts; the others I had accumulated whilst living with Capt. Norrys' family during the restoration of the priory.

For five days our routine proceeded with the utmost placidity, my time being spent mostly in the codification of old family data. I had now obtained some very circum-

stantial accounts of the final tragedy and flight of Walter
de la Poer, which I conceived to be the probable contents
of the hereditary paper lost in the fire at Carfax. It appeared
that my ancestor was accused with much reason of having
killed all the other members of his household, except four
servant confederates, in their sleep, about two weeks after
a shocking discovery which changed his whole demeanor,
but which, except by implication, he disclosed to no one
save perhaps the servants who assisted him and afterward
fled beyond reach.

This deliberate slaughter, which included a father, three
brothers, and two sisters, was largely condoned by the villagers, and so slackly treated by the law that its perpetra-
tor escaped honored, unharmed, and undisguised to Virginia;
the general whispered sentiment being that he had purged
the land of immemorial curse. What discovery had prompted
an act so terrible, I could scarcely even conjecture. Walter
de la Poer must have known for years the sinister tales about
his family, so that this material could have given him no
fresh impulse. Had he, then, witnessed some appalling ancient rite, or stumbled upon some frightful and revealing
symbol in the priory or its vicinity? He was reputed to have
been a shy, gentle youth in England. In Virginia he seemed
not so much hard or bitter as harassed and apprehensive.
He was spoken of in the diary of another gentleman ad-
venturer, Francis Harley of Bellview, as a man of unex-
ampled justice, honor, and delicacy.

On July 22 occurred the first incident which, though
lightly dismissed at the time, takes on a preternatural significance in relation to later events. It was so simple as to
be almost negligible, and could not possibly have been noticed under the circumstances; for it must be recalled that
since I was in a building practically fresh and new except
for the walls, and surrounded by a well-balanced staff of
servitors, apprehension would have been absurd despite the
locality.

What I afterward remembered is merely this—that my old black cat, whose moods I know so well, was undoubtedly alert and anxious to an extent wholly out of keeping with his natural character. He roved from room to room, restless and disturbed, and sniffed constantly about the walls which formed part of the Gothic structure. I realize how trite this sounds—like the inevitable dog in the ghost story, which always growls before his master sees the sheeted figure—yet I cannot consistently suppress it.

The following day a servant complained of restlessness among all the cats in the house. He came to me in my study, a lofty west room on the second story, with groined arches, black oak panelling, and a triple Gothic window overlooking the limestone cliff and desolate valley; and even as he spoke I saw the jetty form of Nigger-Man creeping along the west wall and scratching at the new panels which overlaid the ancient stone.

I told the man that there must be some singular odor or emanation from the old stonework, imperceptible to human senses, but affecting the delicate organs of cats even through the new woodwork. This I truly believed, and when the fellow suggested the presence of mice or rats, I mentioned that there had been no rats there for three hundred years, and that even the field mice of the surrounding country could hardly be found in these high walls, where they had never been known to stray. That afternoon I called on Capt. Norrys and he assured me that it would be quite incredible for field mice to infest the priory in such a sudden and unprecedent fashion.

That night, dispensing as usual with a valet, I retired in the west tower chamber which I had chosen as my own, reached from the study by a stone staircase and short gallery—the former partly ancient, the latter entirely restored. This room was circular, very high, and without wainscotting, being hung with arras which I had myself chosen in London.

Seeing that Nigger-Man was with me, I shut the heavy
Gothic door and retired by the light of the electric bulbs
which so cleverly counterfeited candles, finally switching
off the light and sinking on the carved and canopied four-
poster, with the venerable cat in his accustomed place across
my feet. I did not draw the curtains, but gazed out at the
narrow north window which I faced. There was a suspicion
of aurora in the sky, and the delicate traceries of the window were pleasantly silhouetted.

At some time I must have fallen quietly asleep, for I recall a distinct sense of leaving strange dreams, when the
cat started violently from his placid position. I saw him in
the faint auroral glow, head strained forward, forefeet on
my ankles, and hind feet stretched behind. He was looking
intensely at a point on the wall somewhat west of the window, a point which to my eye had nothing to mark it, but
toward which all my attention was now directed.

And as I watched, I knew that Nigger-Man was not vainly
excited. Whether the arras actually moved I cannot say. I
think it did, very slightly. But what I can swear to is that
behind it I heard a low, distinct scurrying as of rats or mice.
In a moment the cat had jumped bodily on the screening
tapestry, bringing the affected section to the floor with his
weight, and exposing a damp, ancient wall of stone; patched
here and there by the restorers, and devoid of any trace of
rodent prowlers.

Nigger-Man raced up and down the floor by this part of
the wall, clawing the fallen arras and seemingly trying at
times to insert a paw between the wall and the oaken floor.
He found nothing, and after a time returned wearily to his
place across my feet. I had not moved, but I did not sleep
again that night.

In the morning I questioned all the servants, and found
that none of them had noticed anything unusual, save that
the cook remembered the actions of a cat which had rested
on her windowsill. This cat had howled at some unknown

hour of the night, awaking the cook in time for her to see him dart purposefully out of the open door down the stairs. I drowsed away the noontime, and in the afternoon called again on Capt. Norrys, who became exceedingly interested in what I told him. The odd incidents—so slight yet so curious—appealed to his sense of the picturesque, and elicited from him a number of reminiscences of local ghostly lore. We were genuinely perplexed at the presence of rats, and Norrys lent me some traps and Paris green, which I had the servants place in strategic localities when I returned.

I retired early, being very sleepy, but was harassed by dreams of the most horrible sort. I seemed to be looking down from an immense height upon a twilit grotto, knee-deep with filth, where a white-bearded daemon swineherd drove about with his staff a flock of fungous, flabby beasts whose appearance filled me with unutterable loathing. Then, as the swineherd paused and nodded over his task, a mighty swarm of rats rained down on the stinking abyss and fell to devouring beasts and man alike.

From this terrific vision I was abruptly awaked by the motions of Nigger-Man, who had been sleeping as usual across my feet. This time I did not have to question the source of his snarls and hisses, and of the fear which made him sink his claws into my ankle, unconscious of their effect; for on every side of the chamber the walls were alive with nauseous sound—the verminous slithering of ravenous, gigantic rats. There was now no aurora to show the state of the arras—the fallen section of which had been replaced—but I was not too frightened to switch on the light.

As the bulbs leapt into radiance I saw a hideous shaking all over the tapestry, causing the somewhat peculiar designs to execute a singular dance of death. This motion disappeared almost at once, and the sound with it. Springing out of bed, I poked at the arras with the long handle of a warming-pan that rested near, and lifted one section to see what lay beneath. There was nothing but the patched stone wall, and even the cat had lost his tense realization of abnormal presences. When I examined the circular trap that had been placed in the room, I found all of the openings sprung, though no trace remained of what had been caught and had escaped.

Further sleep was out of the question, so, lighting a candle, I opened the door and went out in the gallery toward the stairs to my study, Nigger-Man following at my heels. Before we had reached the stone steps, however, the cat darted ahead of me and vanished down the ancient flight. As I descended the stairs myself, I became suddenly aware of sounds in the great room below; sounds of a nature which could not be mistaken.

The oak-panelled walls were alive with rats, scampering and milling, whilst Nigger-Man was racing about with the fury of a baffled hunter. Reaching the bottom, I switched on the light, which did not this time cause the noise to subside. The rats continued their riot, stampeding with such force and distinctness that I could finally assign to their motions a definite direction. These creatures, in numbers apparently inexhaustible, were engaged in one stupendous migration from inconceivable heights to some depth conceivably or inconceivably below.

I now heard steps in the corridor, and in another moment two servants pushed open the massive door. They were searching the house for some unknown source of disturbance which had thrown all the cats into a snarling panic and caused them to plunge precipitately down several flights of stairs and squat, yowling, before the closed door to the sub-cellar. I asked them if they had heard the rats, but they replied in the negative. And when I turned to call their attention to the sounds in the panels, I realized that the noise had ceased.

With the two men, I went down to the door of the sub-cellar, but found the cats already dispersed. Later I resolved to explore the crypt below, for the present I merely made a round of the traps. All were sprung, yet all were tenant-less. Satisfying myself that no one had heard the rats save the felines and me, I sat in my study till morning, thinking profoundly and recalling every scrap of legend I had un-earthed concerning the building I inhabited.

Absolutely nothing untoward was found, although we could not repress a thrill at the knowledge that this vault was built by Roman hands. Every low arch and massive pillar was Roman—not the debased Romanesque of the bungling Saxons, but the severe and harmonious classicism of the age of the Caesars; indeed, the walls abounded with inscriptions familiar to the antiquarians who had repeatedly explored the place—things like "P. GETAE. PROP . . . TEMP . . . DONA . . ." and "L. PRAEC . . . VS . . . PONTIFI . . . ATYS . . ."

The reference to Atys made me shiver, for I had read Catullus and knew something of the hideous rites of the Eastern god, whose worship was so mixed with that of Cy-bele. Norrys and I, by the light of lanterns, tried to inter-pret the odd and nearly effaced designs on certain irregularly rectangular blocks of stone generally held to be altars, but could make nothing of them. We remembered that one pat-tern, a sort of rayed sun, was held by students to imply a non-Roman origin, suggesting that these altars had merely been adopted by the Roman priests from some older and perhaps aboriginal temple on the same site. On one of these blocks were some brown stains which made me wonder. The largest, in the center of the room, had certain features on the upper surface which indicated its connection with fire—probably burnt offerings.

Such were the sights in that crypt before whose door the cats howled, and where Norrys and I now determined to pass the night. Couches were brought down by the servants, who were told not to mind any nocturnal actions of the cats, and Nigger-Man was admitted as much for help as for companionship. We decided to keep the great oak door—a modern replica with slits for ventilation—tightly closed; and,

with this attended to, we retired with lanterns still burning
to await whatever might occur.

The vault was very deep in the foundations of the priory, and undoubtedly far down on the face of the beetling
limestone cliff overlooking the waste valley. That it had
been the goal of the scuffling and unexplainable rats I could
not doubt, though why, I could not tell. As we lay there ex-
pectantly, I found my vigil occasionally mixed with half-
formed dreams from which the uneasy motions of the cat
across my feet would rouse me.

These dreams were not wholesome, but horribly like the
one I had had the night before. I saw again the twilit grotto,
and the swineherd with his unmentionable fungous beasts
wallowing in filth, and as I looked at these things they
seemed nearer and more distinct—so distinct that I could
almost observe their features. Then I did observe the flabby
features of one of them—and awaked with such a scream
that Nigger-Man started up, whilst Capt. Norrys, who had
not slept, laughed considerably. Norrys might have laughed
more—or perhaps less—had he known what it was that
made me scream. But I did not remember myself till later.
Ultimate horror often paralyses memory in a merciful way.

Norrys waked me when the phenomena began. Out of
the same frightful dream I was called by his gentle shaking and his urging to listen to the cats. Indeed, there was
much to listen to, for beyond the closed door at the head
of the stone steps was a veritable nightmare of feline yelling
and clawing, whilst Nigger-Man, unmindful of his kindred
outside, was running excitedly around the bare stone walls,
in which I heard the same babel of scurrying rats that had
troubled me the night before.

An acute terror now rose within me, for here were anom-
alies which nothing normal could well explain. These rats,
if not the creatures of a madness which I shared with the
cats alone, must be burrowing and sliding in Roman walls
I had thought to be of solid limestone blocks . . . unless per-

haps the action of water through more than seventeen centuries had eaten winding tunnels which rodent bodies had worn clear and ample. . . . But even so, the spectral horror was no less, for if these were living vermin why did not Norrys hear their disgusting commotion? Why did he urge me to watch Nigger-Man and listen to the cats outside, and why did he guess wildly and vaguely at what could have aroused them?

By the time I had managed to tell him, as rationally as I could, what I thought I was hearing, my ears gave me the last fading impression of the scurrying; which had retreated *still downward*, far underneath this deepest of sub-cellars till it seemed as if the whole cliff below were riddled with questing rats. Norrys was not as skeptical as I had anticipated, but instead seemed profoundly moved. He motioned to me to notice that the cats at the door had ceased their clamor, as if giving up the rats for lost; whilst Nigger-Man had a burst of renewed restlessness, and was clawing frantically around the bottom of the large stone altar in the center of the room, which was nearer Norrys' couch than mine.

My fear of the unknown was at this point very great. Something astounding had occurred, and I saw that Capt. Norrys, a younger, stouter, and presumably more naturally materialistic man, was affected fully as much as myself—perhaps because of his lifelong and intimate familiarity with local legend. We could for the moment do nothing but watch the old black cat as he pawed with decreasing fervor at the base of the altar, occasionally looking up and mewing to me in that persuasive manner which he used when he wished me to perform some favor for him.

Norrys now took a lantern close to the altar and examined the place where Nigger-Man was pawing; silently kneeling and scraping away the lichens of the centuries which joined the massive pre-Roman block to the tesselated floor. He did not find anything, and was about to abandon his efforts when I noticed a trivial circumstance which made

me shudder, even though it implied nothing more than I
had already imagined.

I told him of it, and we both looked at its almost imperceptible manifestation with the fixedness of fascinated
discovery and acknowledgment. It was only this—that the
flame of the lantern set down near the altar was slightly
but certainly flickering from a draught of air which it had
not before received, and which came indubitably from the
crevice between the floor and altar where Norrys was scraping away the lichens.

We spent the rest of the night in the brilliantly-lighted
study, nervously discussing what we should do next. The
discovery that some vault deeper than the deepest known
masonry of the Romans underlay this accursed pile; some
vault unsuspected by the curious antiquarians of three centuries; would have been sufficient to excite us without any
background of the sinister. As it was, the fascination became two-fold; and we paused in doubt whether to abandon our search and quit the priory forever in superstitious
caution, or to gratify our sense of adventure and brave whatever horrors might await us in the unknown depths.

By morning we had compromised, and decided to go to
London to gather a group of archaeologists and scientific
men fit to cope with the mystery. It should be mentioned
that before leaving the sub-cellar we had vainly tried to
move the central altar which we now recognized as the gate
to a new pit of nameless fear. What secret would open the
gate, wiser men than we would have to find.

During many days in London, Capt. Norrys and I presented our facts, conjectures, and legendary anecdotes to
five eminent authorities, all men who could be trusted to
respect any family disclosures which future explorations
might develop. We found most of them little disposed to
scoff, but, instead, intensely interested and sincerely sympathetic. It is hardly necessary to name them all, but I may
say that they included Sir William Brinton, whose excava-

tions in the Troad excited most of the world in their day. As we all took the train for Anchester I felt myself poised on the brink of frightful revelations, a sensation symbolized by the air of mourning among the many Americans at the unexpected death of the President on the other side of the world.

On the evening of August 7 we reached Exham Priory, where the servants assured me that nothing unusual had occurred. The cats, even old Nigger-Man, had been perfectly placid; and not a trap in the house had been sprung. We were to begin exploring on the following day, awaiting which I assigned well-appointed rooms to all my guests.

I myself retired in my own tower chamber, with Nigger-Man across my feet. Sleep came quickly, but hideous dreams assailed me. There was a vision of a Roman feast like that of Timalchio, with a horror in a covered platter. Then came that damnable, recurrent thing about the swineherd and his filthy drove in the twilit grotto. Yet when I awoke it was full daylight, with normal sounds in the house below. The rats, living or spectral, had not troubled me; and Nigger-Man was still quietly asleep. On going down, I found that the same tranquillity had prevailed elsewhere; a condition which one of the assembled savants—a fellow named Thornton, devoted to the psychic—rather absurdly laid to the fact that I had now been shown the thing which certain forces had wished to show me.

All was now ready, and at 11 A.M. our entire group of seven men, bearing powerful electric searchlights and implements of excavation, went down to the sub-cellar and bolted the door behind us. Nigger-Man was with us, for the investigators found no occasion to despise his excitability, and were indeed anxious that he be present in case of obscure rodent manifestations. We noted the Roman inscriptions and unknown altar designs only briefly, for three of the savants had already seen them, and all knew their characteristics. Prime attention was paid to the momentous cen-

tral altar, and within an hour Sir William Brinton had caused
it to tilt backward, balanced by some unknown species of
counterweight.

There now lay revealed such a horror as would have
overwhelmed us had we not been prepared. Through a nearly
square opening in the tiled floor, sprawling on a flight of
stone steps so prodigiously worn that it was little more than
an inclined plane at the center, was a ghastly array of human
or semi-human bones. Those which retained their colloca-
tion as skeletons showed attitudes of panic fear, and over
all were the marks of rodent gnawing. The skulls denoted
nothing short of utter idiocy, cretinism, or primitive semi-
apedom.

Above the hellishly littered steps arched a descending
passage seemingly chiseled from the solid rock, and con-
ducting a current of air. This current was not a sudden and
noxious rush as from a closed vault, but a cool breeze with
something of freshness in it. We did not pause long, but
shiveringly began to clear a passage down the steps. It was
then that Sir William, examining the hewn walls, made the
odd observation that the passage, according to the direction
of the strokes, must have been chiseled *from beneath.*

I must be very deliberate now, and choose my words.

After ploughing down a few steps amidst the gnawed
bones we saw that there was light ahead; not any mystic
phosphorescence, but a filtered daylight which could not
come except from unknown fissures in the cliff that overlooked the waste valley. That such fissures had escaped notice from outside was hardly remarkable, for not only is the
valley wholly uninhabited, but the cliff is so high and
beetling that only an aeronaut could study its face in detail.
A few steps more, and our breaths were literally snatched
from us by what we saw; so literally that Thornton, the psychic investigator, actually fainted in the arms of the dazed
man who stood behind him. Norrys, his plump face utterly
white and flabby, simply cried out inarticulately; whilst I

think that what I did was to gasp or hiss, and cover my eyes.

The man behind me—the only one of the party older than I—croaked the hackneyed "My God!" in the most cracked voice I ever heard. Of seven cultivated men, only Sir William Brinton retained his composure, a thing the more to his credit because he led the party and must have seen the sight first.

It was a twilit grotto of enormous height, stretching away farther than any eye could see; a subterraneous world of limitless mystery and horrible suggestion. There were buildings and other architectural remains—in one terrified glance I saw a weird pattern of tumuli, a savage circle of monoliths, a low-domed Roman ruin, a sprawling Saxon pile, and an early English edifice of wood—but all these were dwarfed by the ghoulish spectacle presented by the general surface of the ground. For yards about the steps extended an insane tangle of human bones, or bones at least as human as those on the steps. Like a foamy sea they stretched, some fallen apart, but others wholly or partly articulated as skeletons; these latter invariably in postures of daemoniac frenzy, either fighting off some menace or clutching other forms with cannibal intent.

When Dr. Trask, the anthropologist, stopped to classify the skulls, he found a degraded mixture which utterly baffled him. They were mostly lower than the Piltdown man in the scale of evolution, but in every case definitely human. Many were of higher grade, and a very few were the skulls of supremely and sensitively developed types. All the bones were gnawed, mostly by rats, but somewhat by others of the half-human drove. Mixed with them were many tiny bones of rats—fallen members of the lethal army which closed the ancient epic.

I wonder that any man among us lived and kept his sanity through that hideous day of discovery. Not Hoffman or Huysmans could conceive a scene more wildly incredible, more frenetically repellent, or more Gothically grotesque than the twilit grotto through which we seven staggered; each stumbling on revelation after revelation, and trying to keep for the nonce from thinking of the events which must have taken place there three hundred, or a thousand, or two thousand, or ten thousand years ago. It was the antechamber of hell, and poor Thornton fainted again when Trask told him that some of the skeleton things must have descended as quadrupeds through the last twenty or more generations.

Horror piled on horror as we began to interpret the architectural remains. The quadruped things—with their occasional recruits from the biped class—had been kept in stone pens, out of which they must have broken in their last delirium of hunger or rat-fear. There had been great herds of them, evidently fattened on the coarse vegetables whose remains could be found as a sort of poisonous ensilage at the bottom of huge stone bins older than Rome. I knew now why my ancestors had had such excessive gardens—would to heaven I could forget! The purpose of the herds I did not have to ask.

Sir William, standing with his searchlight in the Roman ruin, translated aloud the most shocking ritual I have ever known; and told of the diet of the antediluvian cult which the priest of Cybele found and mingled with their own. Norrys, used as he was to the trenches, could not walk straight when he came out of the English building. It was a butcher shop and kitchen—he had expected that—but it was too much to see familiar English implements in such a place, and to read familiar English *graffiti* there, some as recent as 1610. I could not go in that building—that building whose daemon activities were stopped only by the dagger of my ancestor Walter de la Poer.

What I did venture to enter was the low Saxon building whose oaken door had fallen, and there I found a terrible row of ten stone cells with rusty bars. Three had tenants, all skeletons of high grade, and on the bony forefinger of one I found a seal ring with my own coat-of-arms. Sir William found a vault with far older cells below the Roman chapel, but these cells were empty. Below them was a low crypt with cases of formally arranged bones, some of them bearing terrible parallel inscriptions carved in Latin, Greek, and the tongue of Phrygia.

Meanwhile, Dr. Trask had opened one of the prehistoric tumuli, and brought to light skulls which were slightly more human than a gorilla's, and which bore indescribably ideographic carvings. Through all this horror my cat stalked unperturbed. Once I saw him monstrously perched atop a mountain of bones, and wondered at the secrets that might lie behind his yellow eyes.

Having grasped to some slight degree the frightful revelations of this twilit area—an area so hideously foreshadowed by my recurrent dream—we turned to that apparently boundless depth of midnight cavern where no ray of light from the cliff could penetrate. We shall never know what sightless Stygian worlds yawn beyond the little distance we went, for it was decided that such secrets are not good for mankind. But there was plenty to engross us close at hand, for we had not gone far before the searchlights showed that accursed infinity of pits in which the rats had feasted, and whose sudden lack of replenishment had driven the ravenous rodent army first to turn on the living herds of starving things, and then to burst forth from the priory in that historic orgy of devastation which the peasants will never forget.

God! those carrion black pits of sawed, picked bones and opened skulls! Those nightmare chasms choked with the pithecanthropoid, Celtic, Roman, and English bones of countless unhallowed centuries! Some of them were full, and none can say how deep they had once been. Others were still bottomless to our searchlights, and peopled by unnameable fancies. What, I thought, of the hapless rats

that stumbled into such traps amidst the blackness of their
quests in this grisly Tartarus?

Once my foot slipped near a horribly yawning brink, and
I had a moment of ecstatic fear. I must have been musing
a long time, for I could not see any of the party but the
plump Capt. Norrys. Then there came a sound from inky,
boundless, farther distance that I thought I knew; and I saw
my old black cat dart past me like a winged Egyptian god,
straight into the illimitable gulf of the unknown. But I was
not far behind, for there was no doubt after another second.
It was the eldritch scurrying of those fiend-born rats, always questing for new horrors, and determined to lead me
on even unto those grinning caverns of earth's center where
Nyarlathotep, the mad faceless god, howls blindly in the
darkness to the piping of two amorphous idiot flute-players.

My searchlight expired, but still I ran. I heard voices,
and yowls, and echoes, but above all there gently rose that
impious, insidious scurrying; gently rising, rising, as a stiff
bloated corpse gently rises above an oily river that flows
under endless onyx bridges to a black, putrid sea.

Something bumped into me—something soft and plump.
It must have been the rats; the viscious, gelatinous, ravenous army that feast on the dead and the living. . . . Why
shouldn't rats eat a de la Poer as a de la Poer eats forbidden things? . . . The war ate my boy, damn them all . . . and
the Yanks ate Carfax with flames and burnt Grandsire Delapore and the secret . . . No, no, I tell you, I am *not* that
daemon swineherd in the twilit grotto! It was *not* Edward
Norrys' fat face on that flabby fungous thing! Who says I
am a de la Poer? He lived, but my boy died! . . . Shall a
Norrys hold the lands of a de la Poer? . . . It's voodoo, I
tell you . . . that spotted snake . . . Curse you, Thornton, I'll
teach you to faint at what my family do! . . . 'Sblood, thou
stinkard, I'll learn ye how to gust . . . wolde ye swynke me
thilke wys? . . . *Magna Mater! Magna Mater! . . . Atys . . .
Dia ad aghaids's ad aodaun . . . agus bas dunach ort!*

*Dhonas's dholas ort, agus leat-sa! . . . Ungl . . . ungl . . .
rrlh . . . chchch . . .*

That is what they say I said when they found me in the
blackness after three hours; found me crouching in the blackness over the plump, half-eaten body of Capt. Norrys, with
my own cat leaping and tearing at my throat. Now they
have blown up Exham Priory, taken my Nigger-Man away
from me, and shut me into this barred room at Hanwell
with fearful whispers about my heredity and experience.
Thornton is in the next room, but they prevent me from
talking to him. They are trying, too, to suppress most of
the facts concerning the priory. When I speak of poor Norrys they accuse me of a hideous thing, but they must know
that I did not do it. They must know it was the rats; the
slithering scurrying rats whose scampering will never let
me sleep; the daemon rats that race behind the padding in
this room and beckon me down to greater horrors than I
have ever known; the rats they can never hear; the rats, the
rats in the walls.

I have long been an admirer of Dennis Etchison's short stories; hypnotic deliriums which brilliantly evoke dread and the subconscious.

We both live in L.A., and Dennis' insights into the city's pathologies, particularly those of the film and television business, seethe with acuity; his is a scape of drowning psyches, bloodless calculation, of an industry town which dreams but rarely reflects.

In "The Dog Park," arguably one of Dennis' finest, most complex stories, he observes people exercising their dogs in a park that borders a deep, verdant canyon; serene, strangely ominous. The architectural houses beyond, stapled to steep, surrounding hillsides, are a privileged tranquility. Yet in Dennis' calm, assassinating hands, this setting becomes a crucible; a place of fates met.

The canyons, too, play their role; vast, Jungian ravines, throughout which balconied parties chatter and echo; voices, drifting poisonously.

And show business is never far away.

In "The Dog Park" Dennis has captured the desperate, tactical Morse code of Hollywood acolytes, their vacant dialogues subtitled with self-advancement, yet lacking affect; as if testimony in a courtroom of lost selves. As his characters await their dogs, their close-up, their moment, self-absorption is the only remaining intimacy.

Just beyond, L.A. glowers and seduces; a hip wasteland. Even in the lovely parks, where dogs play and owners mistakenly turn away for a moment, comforted by imagined civilization, the drift nets wait.

Throughout, the author provides no answers, though clearly he has worked in Hollywood and understands the creative and spiritual dissolution of its priorities. Yet, in measuring its anxieties and personal liquidations, he detects deeper meaning. In a town of esteem devoured, where surfaces become truth and talents are burned for temporary warmth, Dennis Etchison's "The Dog Park" responds, in the end, not with indictment but hope.

However lost.

—Richard Christian Matheson

THE DOG PARK
Dennis Etchison

Madding heard the dogs before he saw them.

They were snarling at each other through the hurricane fence, gums wet and incisors bared, as if about to snap the chain links that held them apart. A barrel-chested boxer reared and slobbered, driving a much smaller Australian kelpie away from the outside of the gate. Spittle flew and the links vibrated and rang.

A few seconds later their owners came running, barking commands and waving leashes like whips.

"Easy, boy," Madding said, reaching one hand out to the seat next to him. Then he remembered that he no longer had a dog of his own. There was nothing to worry about.

He set the brake, rolled the window up all the way, locked the car and walked across the lot to the park.

The boxer was far down the slope by now, pulled along by a man in a flowered shirt and pleated trousers. The Australian sheepdog still trembled by the fence. Its owner, a young woman, jerked a choke chain.

"Greta, sit!"

As Madding neared the gate, the dog growled and tried to stand.

She yanked the chain harder and slapped its hindquarters back into position.

"Hello, Greta," said Madding, lifting the steel latch. He smiled at the young woman. "You've got a brave little dog there."

"I don't know why she's acting this way," she said, embarrassed.

"Is this her first time?"

"Pardon?"

"At the Dog Park."

"Yes . . ."

"It takes some getting used to," he told her. "All the freedom. They're not sure how to behave."

"Did you have the same trouble?"

"Of course." He savored the memory, and at the same time wanted to put it out of his mind. "Everybody does. It's normal."

"I named her after Garbo—you know, the actress? I don't think she likes crowds." She looked around. "Where's your dog?"

"Down there, I hope." Madding opened the gate and let himself in, then held it wide for her.

She was squinting at him. "Excuse me," she said, "but you work at Tri-Mark, don't you?"

Madding shook his head. "I'm afraid not."

The kelpie dragged her down the slope with such force that she had to dig her feet into the grass to stop. The boxer was nowhere in sight.

"Greta, heel!"

"You can let her go," Madding said as he came down behind her. "The leash law is only till three o'clock."

"What time is it now?"

He checked his watch. "Almost five."

She bent over and unfastened the leash from the ring on the dog's collar. She was wearing white cotton shorts and a plain, loose-fitting top.

"Did I meet you in Joel Silver's office?" she said.

"I don't think so." He smiled again. "Well, you and Greta have fun."

He wandered off, tilting his face back and breathing deeply. The air was moving, scrubbed clean by the trees, rustling the shiny leaves as it circulated above the city, exchanging pollutants for fresh oxygen. It was easier to be on his own, but without a dog to pick the direction he was at loose ends. He felt the loss tugging at him like a cord that had not yet been broken.

The park was only a couple of acres, nestled between the high, winding turns of a mountain road on one side and a densely overgrown canyon on the other. This was the only park where dogs were allowed to run free, at least during certain hours, and in a few short months it had become an unofficial meeting place for people in the entertainment industry. Where once pitches had been delivered in detox clinics and the gourmet aisles of Westside supermarkets, now ambitious hustlers frequented the Dog Park to sharpen their networking skills. Here starlets connected with recently divorced producers, agents jockeyed for favor with young executives on the come, and actors and screenwriters exchanged tips about veterinarians, casting calls and pilots set to go to series in the fall. All it took was a dog, begged, borrowed or stolen, and the kind of desperate gregariousness that causes one to press business cards into the hands of absolute strangers.

He saw dozens of dogs, expensive breeds mingling shamelessly with common mutts, a microcosm of democracy at work. An English setter sniffed an unshorn French poodle, then gave up and joined the pack gathered around a honey-colored cocker spaniel. A pair of Great Dane puppies tumbled over each other golliwog-style, coming to rest at the feet of a tall, humorless German shepherd. An Afghan chased a Russian wolfhound. And there were the masters, posed against tree trunks, lounging at picnic tables, nervously cleaning up after their pets with long-handled scoopers while they waited to see who would enter the park next.

Madding played a game, trying to match up the animals with their owners. A man with a crewcut tossed a Frisbee, banking it against the setting sun like a translucent UFO before a bull terrier snatched it out of the air. Two fluffed Pekingese waddled across the path in front of Madding, trailing colorful leashes; when they neared the gorge at the edge of the park he started after them reflexively, then stopped as a short, piercing sound turned them and brought them back this way. A bodybuilder in a formfitting T-shirt glowered nearby, a silver whistle showing under his trimmed moustache.

Ahead, a Labrador, a chow and a schnauzer had a silkie cornered by a trash bin. Three people seated on a wooden bench glanced up, laughed, and returned to the curled script they were reading. Madding could not see the title, only that the cover was a bilious yellow-green.

"I know," said the young woman, drawing even with him, as her dog dashed off in an ever-widening circle. "It was at New Line. That was you, wasn't it?"

"I've never been to New Line," said Madding.

"Are you sure? The office on Robertson?"

"I'm sure."

"Oh." She was embarrassed once again, and tried to cover it with a self-conscious cheerfulness, the mark of a private person forced into playing the extrovert in order to survive. "You're not an actor, then?"

"Only a writer," said Madding.

She brightened. "I knew it!"

"Isn't everyone in this town?" he said. "The butcher, the baker, the kid who parks your car . . . My drycleaner says he's writing a script for Tim Burton."

"Really?" she said, quite seriously. "I'm writing a spec script."

Oh no, he thought. He wanted to sink down into the grass and disappear, among the ants and beetles, but the ground was damp from the sprinklers and her dog was circling, hemming him in.

"Sorry," he said.

"That's okay. I have a real job, too. I'm on staff at Fox Network."

"What show?" he asked, to be polite.

"*C.H.U.M.P.* The first episode is on next week. They've already ordered nine more, in case *Don't Worry, Be Happy* gets canceled."

"I've heard of it," he said.

"Have you? What have you heard?"

He racked his brain. "It's a cop series, right?"

"Canine-Human Unit, Metropolitan Police. You know, dogs that ride around in police cars, and the men and women they sacrifice themselves for? It has a lot of human interest, like *L.A. Law,* only it's told through the dog's eyes."

"*Look Who's Barking,*" he said.

"Sort of." She tilted her head to one side and thought for a moment. "I'm sorry," she said. "That was a joke, wasn't it?"

"Sort of."

"I get it." She went on. "But what I really want to write is Movies-of-the-Week. My agent says she'll put my script on Paul Nagle's desk, as soon as I have a first draft."

"What's it about?"

"It's called *A Little-Known Side of Elvis.* That's the working title. My agent says anything about Elvis will sell."

"Which side of Elvis is this one?"

"Well, for example, did you know about his relationship with dogs? Most people don't. *Hound Dog* wasn't just a song."

Her kelpie began to bark. A man with inflatable tennis shoes and a baseball cap worn backwards approached them, a clipboard in his hand.

"Hi!" he said, all teeth. "Would you take a minute to sign our petition?"

"No problem," said the young woman. "What's it for?"

"They're trying to close the park to outsiders, except on weekends."

She took his ballpoint pen and balanced the clipboard on her tanned forearm. "How come?"

"It's the residents. They say we take up too many parking places on Mulholland. They want to keep the canyon for themselves."

"Well," she said, "they better watch out, or we might

just start leaving our dogs here. Then they'll multiply and take over!"

She grinned, her capped front teeth shining in the sunlight like two chips of paint from a pearly-white Lexus.

"What residents?" asked Madding.

"The homeowners," said the man in the baseball cap, hooking a thumb over his shoulder.

Madding's eyes followed a line to the cliffs overlooking the park, where the cantilevered back-ends of several designer houses hung suspended above the gorge. The undersides of the decks, weathered and faded, were almost camouflaged by the weeds and chaparral.

"How about you?" The man took back the clipboard and held it out to Madding. "We need all the help we can get."

"I'm not a registered voter," said Madding.

"You're not?"

"I don't live here," he said. "I mean, I did, but I don't now. Not anymore."

"Are *you* registered?" the man asked her.

"Yes."

"In the business?"

"I work at Fox," she said.

"Oh, yeah? How's the new regime? I hear Lili put all the old-timers out to pasture."

"Not the studio," she said. "The network."

"Really? Do you know Kathryn Baker, by any chance?"

"I've seen her parking space. Why?"

"I used to be her dentist." The man took out his wallet. "Here, let me give you my card."

"That's all right," she said. "I already have someone."

"Well, hold onto it anyway. You never know. Do you have a card?"

She reached into a velcro pouch at her waist and handed him a card with a quill pen embossed on one corner.

The man read it. "*C.H.U.M.P.*—that's great! Do you have a dental adviser yet?"

"I don't think so."

"Could you find out?"

"I suppose."

He turned to Madding. "Are you an actor?"

"Writer," said Madding. "But not the kind you mean."

The man was puzzled. The young woman looked at him blankly. Madding felt the need to explain himself.

"I had a novel published, and somebody bought an option. I moved down here to write the screenplay."

"Title?" said the man.

"You've probably never heard of it," said Madding. "It was called *And Soon the Night.*"

"That's it!" she said. "I just finished reading it—I saw your picture on the back of the book!" She furrowed her brow, a slight dimple appearing on the perfectly smooth skin between her eyes, as she struggled to remember. "Don't tell me. Your name is . . ."

"David Madding," he said, holding out his hand.

"Hi!" she said. "I'm Stacey Chernak."

"Hi, yourself."

"Do you have a card?" the man said to him.

"I'm all out," said Madding. It wasn't exactly a lie. He had never bothered to have any printed.

"What's the start date?"

"There isn't one," said Madding. "They didn't renew the option."

"I see," said the man in the baseball cap, losing interest.

A daisy chain of small dogs ran by, a miniature collie chasing a longhaired daschund chasing a shivering chihuahua. The collie blurred as it went past, its long coat streaking like a flame.

"Well, I gotta get some more signatures before dark. Don't forget to call me," the man said to her. "I can advise on orthodontics, accident reconstruction, anything they want."

"How about animal dentistry?" she said.

"Hey, why not?"

"I'll give them your name."

"Great," he said to her. "Thanks!"

"Do you think that's his collie?" she said when he had gone.

Madding considered. "More likely the Irish setter."

They saw the man lean down to hook his fingers under the collar of a golden retriever. From the back, his baseball cap revealed the emblem of the New York Yankees. Not from around here, Madding thought. But then, who is?

"Close," she said, and laughed.

The man led his dog past a dirt mound, where there was a drinking fountain and a spigot that ran water into a trough for animals.

"Water," she said. "That's a good idea. Greta!"

The kelpie came bounding over, eager to escape the attentions of a randy pit bull. They led her to the mound. As Greta drank, Madding read the sign over the spigot.

CAUTION!
WATCH OUT FOR MOUNTAIN LIONS

"What do you think that means?" she said. "It isn't true, is it?"

Madding felt a tightness in his chest. "It could be. This is still wild country."

"Greta, stay with me . . ."

"Don't worry. They only come out at night, probably."

"Where's your dog?" she said.

"I wish I knew."

She tilted her head, uncertain whether or not he was making another joke.

"He ran away," Madding told her.

"When?"

"Last month. I used to bring him here all the time. One

day he didn't come when I called. It got dark, and they closed the park, but he never came back."

"Oh, I'm so sorry!"

"Yeah, me too."

"What was his name?"

"He didn't have one. I couldn't make up my mind, and then it was too late."

They walked on between the trees. She kept a close eye on Greta. Somewhere music was playing. The honey-colored cocker spaniel led the German shepherd, the Irish setter and a dalmatian to a redwood table. There the cocker's owner, a woman with brassy hair and a sagging green halter, poured white wine into plastic cups for several men.

"I didn't know," said Stacey.

"I missed him at first, but now I figure he's better off. Someplace where he can run free, all the time."

"I'm sorry about your dog," she said. "That's so sad. But what I meant was, I didn't know you were famous."

It was hard to believe that she knew the book. The odds against it were staggering, particularly considering the paltry royalties. He decided not to ask what she thought of it. That would be pressing his luck.

"Who's famous? I sold a novel. Big deal."

"Well, at least you're a real writer. I envy you."

"Why?"

"You have it made."

Sure I do, thought Madding. One decent review in the *Village Voice Literary Supplement*, and some reader at a production company makes an inquiry, and the next thing I know my agent makes a deal with all the money in the world at the top of the ladder. Only the ladder doesn't go far enough. And now I'm back to square one, the option money used up, with a screenplay written on spec that's not worth what it cost me to Xerox it, and I'm six months behind on the next novel. But I've got it made. Just ask the IRS.

The music grew louder as they walked. It seemed to be coming from somewhere overhead. Madding gazed up into the trees, where the late-afternoon rays sparkled through the leaves, gold coins edged in blackness. He thought he heard voices, too, and the clink of glasses. Was there a party? The entire expanse of the park was visible from here, but he could see no evidence of a large group anywhere. The sounds were diffused and unlocalized, as if played back through widely spaced, out-of-phase speakers.

"Where do you live?" she asked.

"What?"

"You said you don't live here anymore."

"In Calistoga."

"Where's that?"

"Up north."

"Oh."

He began to relax. He was glad to be finished with this town.

"I closed out my lease today," he told her. "Everything's packed. As soon as I hit the road, I'm out of here."

"Why did you come back to the park?"

A good question, he thought. He hadn't planned to stop by. It was a last-minute impulse.

"I'm not sure," he said. No, that wasn't true. He might as well admit it. "It sounds crazy, but I guess I wanted to look for my dog. I thought I'd give it one more chance. It doesn't feel right, leaving him."

"Do you think he's still here?"

He felt a tingling in the pit of his stomach. It was not a good feeling. *I shouldn't have come,* he thought. *Then I wouldn't have had to face it. It's dangerous here, too dangerous for there to be much hope.*

"At least I'll know," he said.

He heard a sudden intake of breath and turned to her. There were tears in her eyes, as clear as diamonds.

"It's like the end of your book," she said. "When the little girl is alone, and doesn't know what's going to happen next . . ."

My God, he thought, she did read it. He felt flattered, but kept his ego in check. She's not so tough. She has a heart, after all, under all the bravado. That's worth something—it's worth a lot. I hope she makes it, the Elvis script, whatever she really wants. She deserves it.

She composed herself and looked around, blinking, "What is that?"

"What's what?"

"Don't you hear it?" She raised her chin and moved her head from side to side, eyes closed.

She meant the music, the glasses, the sound of the party that wasn't there.

"I don't know."

Now there was the scraping of steel somewhere behind them, like a rough blade drawn through metal. He stopped and turned around quickly.

A couple of hundred yards away, at the top of the slope, a man in a uniform opened the gate to the park. Beyond the fence, a second man climbed out of an idling car with a red, white and blue shield on the door. He had a heavy chain in one hand.

"Come on," said Madding. "It's time to go."

"It can't be."

"The security guards are here. They close the park at six."

"Already?"

Madding was surprised, too. He wondered how long they had been walking. He saw the man with the crewcut searching for his frisbee in the grass, the bull terrier at his side. The group on the bench and the woman in the halter were collecting their things. The bodybuilder marched his two ribboned Pekingese to the slope. The Beverly Hills dentist whistled and stood waiting for his dog to come to him. Madding snapped to, as if waking up. It really was time.

The sun had dropped behind the hills and the grass under his feet was darkening. The car in the parking lot above continued to idle; the rumbling of the engine reverberated in the natural bowl of the park, as though close enough to bulldoze them out of the way. He heard a rhythm in the throbbing, and realized that it was music, after all.

They had wandered close to the edge, where the park ended and the gorge began. Over the gorge, the deck of one of the cantilevered houses beat like a drum.

"Where's Greta?" she said.

He saw the stark expression, the tendons outlined through the smooth skin of her throat.

"Here, girl! Over here . . . !"

She called out, expecting to see her dog. Then she clapped her hands together. The sound bounced back like the echo of a gunshot from the depths of the canyon. The dog did not come.

In the parking lot, the second security guard let a Dobermann out of the car. It was a sleek, black streak next to him as he carried the heavy chain to his partner, who was waiting for the park to empty before padlocking the gate.

Madding took her arm. Her skin was covered with gooseflesh. She drew away.

"I can't go," she said. "I have to find Greta."

He scanned the grassy slopes with her, avoiding the gorge until there was nowhere left to look. It was blacker than he remembered. Misshapen bushes and stunted shrubs filled the canyon below, extending all the way down to the formal boundaries of the city. He remembered standing here only a few weeks ago, in exactly the same position. He had told himself then that his dog could not have gone over the edge, but now he saw that there was nowhere else to go.

The breeze became a wind in the canyon and the black liquid eye of a swimming pool winked at him from far down the hillside. Above, the sound of the music stopped abruptly.

"You don't think she went down there, do you?" said
Stacey. There was a catch in her voice. "The mountain
lions . . ."

"They only come out at night."

"But it *is* night!"

They heard a high, broken keening.

"Listen!" she said. "That's Greta!"

"No, it's not. Dogs don't make that sound. It's—" He
stopped himself.

"*What?*"

"Coyotes."

He regretted saying it.

Now, without the music, the shuffling of footsteps on
the boards was clear and unmistakable. He glanced up.
Shadows appeared over the edge of the deck as a line of
heads gathered to look down. Ice cubes rattled and someone laughed. Then someone else made a shushing sound
and the silhouetted heads bobbed silently, listening and
watching.

Can they see us? he wondered.

Madding felt the presence of the Dobermann behind him,
at the top of the slope. How long would it take to close the
distance, once the guard set it loose to clear the park? Surely
they would call out a warning first. He waited for the voice,
as the seconds ticked by on his watch.

"I have to go get her," she said, starting for the gorge.

"No . . ."

"I can't just leave her."

"It's not safe," he said.

"But she's down there, I know it! Greta!"

There was a giggling from the deck.

They can hear us, too, he thought. Every sound, every
word magnified, like a Greek amphitheater. Or a Roman one.

Rover, Spot, Towser? No, Cubby. That's what I was going
to call you, if there had been time. I always liked the name.
Cubby.

He made a decision.

"Stay here," he said, pushing her aside.

"What are you doing?"

"I'm going over."

"You don't have to. It's my dog . . ."

"Mine, too."

Maybe they're both down there, he thought.

"I'll go with you," she said.

"No."

He stood there, thinking, It all comes down to this. There's no way to avoid it. There never was.

"But you don't know what's there . . . !"

"Go," he said to her, without turning around. "Get out of here while you can. There's still time."

Go home, he thought, wherever that is. You have a life ahead of you. It's not too late, if you go right now, without looking back.

"Wait . . . !"

He disappeared over the edge.

A moment later there was a new sound, something more than the breaking of branches and the thrashing. It was powerful and deep, followed immediately by a high, mournful yipping. Then there was only a silence, and the night.

From above the gorge, a series of quick, hard claps fell like rain.

It was the people on the deck.

They were applauding.

This is just the sort of Robert Bloch story I love. It's scary, creepy, offbeat, and the horror is of a realistic nature—meaning no supernatural elements. Just plain old twisted meanness. And yet, it's funny. Not in the "I just heard a good joke" kind of way, but in a deeper, more biting manner. Bloch makes you laugh, but makes you feel bad for laughing, while at the same time giving you a certain insight into human nature. Not always an insight you appreciate, but a truthful insight, nonetheless.

But you know what I love best about this story, about all of Robert Bloch's fiction, for that matter?

The simplicity with which he leads you into the tale, nails you to it, proceeds with a deceptively simple style, and won't let you go until the tale is told.

Wonderful.

"The Animal Fair," like so many of his stories, is caviar. Enjoy.

But I needn't suggest that. You won't be able to do otherwise.

—Joe R. Lansdale

THE ANIMAL FAIR
by Robert Bloch

It was dark when the truck dropped Dave off at the deserted freight depot. Dave had to squint to make out the lettering on the weather-faded sign. MEDLEY, OKLAHOMA—POP. 1,134.

The trucker said he could probably get another lift on the state highway up past the other end of town, so Dave hit the main drag. And it was a drag.

Nine o'clock of a hot summer evening, and Medley was closed for the night. Fred's Eats had locked up, the Jiffy SuperMart had shut down, even Phil's Phill-Up Gas stood

deserted. There were no cars parked on the dark street, not
even the usual cluster of kids on the corners.

Dave wondered about this, but not for long. In five minutes he covered the length of Main Street and emerged on
open fields at the far side, and that's when he saw the lights
and heard the music.

They had a carnival going in the little county fairgrounds
up ahead—canned music blasting from amplifiers, cars
crowding the parking lot, mobs milling across the midway.

Dave wasn't craving this kind of action, but he still had
eight cents in his jeans and he hadn't eaten anything since
breakfast. He turned down the sideroad leading to the fairgrounds.

As he figured, the carnival was a bummer. One of those
little mud shows, traveling by truck; a couple of beat-up
rides for the kids and a lot of come-ons for the local yokels.
Wheel o' Fortune, Pitch-a-Winner, Take a Chance on a Blanket, that kind of jive. By the time Dave got himself a burger
and coffee at one of the stands he knew the score. A big
fat zero.

But not for Medley, Oklahoma—Pop. 1,134. The whole
damn town was here tonight and probably every redneck
for miles around, shuffling and shoving himself to get
through to the far end of the midway.

And it was there, on the far end, that he saw the small
red tent with the tiny platform before it. Hanging limp and
listless in the still air, a sunbleached banner proclaimed the
wonders within.

CAPTAIN RYDER'S HOLLYWOOD JUNGLE SAFARI, the banner
read.

What a Hollywood Jungle Safari was, Dave didn't know.
And the wrinkled cloth posters lining the sides of the entrance weren't much help. A picture of a guy in an explorer's outfit, tangling with a big snake wrapped around
his neck—the same joker prying open the jaws of a crocodile—another drawing showing him wrestling a lion. The

last poster showed the guy standing next to a cage; inside the cage was a black, furry question mark, way over six feet high. The lettering underneath was black and furry too. WHAT IS IT? SEE THE MIGHTY MONARCH OF THE JUNGLE ALIVE ON THE INSIDE!

Dave didn't know what it was and he cared less. But he'd been bumping along those corduroy roads all day and he was wasted and the noise from the amplifiers here on the midway hurt his ears. At least there was some kind of a show going on inside, and when he saw the open space gaping between the canvas and the ground at the corner of the tent he stooped and slid under.

The tent was a canvas oven.

Dave could smell oil in the air; on hot summer nights in Oklahoma you can always smell it. And the crowd in here smelled worse. Bad enough that he was thumbing his way through and couldn't take a bath, but what was their excuse?

The crowd huddled around the base of a portable wooden stage at the rear of the tent, listening to a pitch from Captain Ryder. At least that's who Dave figured it was, even though the character with the phony safari hat and the dirty white riding breeches didn't look much like his pictures on the banners. He was handing out a spiel in one of those hoarse, gravelly voices that carries without a microphone— some hype about being a Hollywood stunt man and African explorer—and there wasn't a snake or a crocodile or a lion anywhere in sight.

The two-bit hamburger began churning up a storm in Dave's guts, and between the body heat and the smells he'd just about had it in here. He started to turn and push his way through the mob when the man up on the stage thumped the boards with his cane.

"And now friends, if you'll gather around a little closer—"

The crowd swept forward in unison, like the straws of

a giant broom, and Dave found himself pressed right up against the edge of the square-shaped canvas-covered pit beside the end of the platform. He couldn't get through now if he tried; all the rednecks were bunched together, waiting.

Dave waited, too, but he stopped listening to the voice on the platform. All that jive about Darkest Africa was a put-on. Maybe these clowns went for it, but Dave wasn't buying a word. He just hoped the old guy would hurry and get the show over with; all he wanted now was out of here.

Captain Ryder tapped the canvas covering of the pit with his cane and his harsh tones rose. The heat made Dave yawn loudly, but some of the phrases filtered through.

"—about to see here tonight the world's most ferocious monster—captured at deadly peril of life and limb—"

Dave shook his head. He knew what was in the pit. Some crummy animal picked up secondhand from a circus, maybe a scroungy hyena. And two to one it wasn't even alive, just stuffed. Big deal.

Captain Ryder lifted the canvas cover and pulled it back behind the pit. He flourished his cane.

"Behold—the lord of the jungle!"

The crowd pressed, pushed, peered over the rim of the pit.

The crowd gasped.

And Dave, pressing and peering with the rest, stared at the creature blinking up at him from the bottom of the pit.

It was a live, full-grown gorilla.

The monster squatted on a heap of straw, its huge fore-arms secured to steel stakes by lengths of heavy chain. It gaped upward at the rim of faces, moving its great gray head slowly from side to side, the yellow-fanged mouth open and the massive jaws set in a vacant grimace. Only the little rheumy, red-rimmed eyes held a hint of expression—enough to tell Dave, who had never seen a gorilla before, that this animal was sick.

The matted straw at the base of the pit was wet and stained; in one corner a battered tin plate rested untouched, its surface covered with a soggy slop of shredded carrots, okra and turnip greens floating in an oily scum beneath a cloud of buzzing blowflies. In the stifling heat of the tent the acrid odor arising from the pit was almost overpowering.

Dave felt his stomach muscles constrict. He tried to force his attention back to Captain Ryder. The old guy was stepping offstage now, moving behind the pit and reaching down into it with his cane.

"—nothing to be afraid of, folks, as you can see he's perfectly harmless, aren't you, Bobo?"

The gorilla whimpered, huddling back against the soiled straw to avoid the prodding cane. But the chains confined movement and the cane began to dig its tip into the beast's shaggy shoulders.

"And now Bobo's going to do a little dance for the folks—right?" The gorilla whimpered again, but the point of the cane jabbed deeply and the rasping voice firmed in command.

"Up, Bobo—up!"

The creature lumbered to its haunches. As the cane rose and fell about its shoulders, the bulky body began to sway. The crowd oohed and aahed and snickered.

"That's it! Dance for the people, Bobo—dance—"

A swarm of flies spiraled upward to swirl about the furry form shimmering in the heat. Dave saw the sick beast shuffle, moving to and fro, to and fro. Then his stomach was moving in responsive rhythm and he had to shut his eyes as he turned and fought his way blindly through the murmuring mob.

"Hey—watch where the hell ya goin', fella—"

Dave got out of the tent just in time.

Getting rid of the hamburger helped, and getting away from the carnival grounds helped too, but not enough. As Dave moved up the road between the open fields he felt the nausea return. Gulping the oily air made him dizzy and he knew he'd have to lie down for a minute. He dropped in the ditch beside the road, shielded behind a clump of weeds, and closed his eyes to stop the whirling sensation. Only for a minute—

The dizziness went away, but behind his closed eyes he could still see the gorilla, still see the expressionless face and the all-too-expressive eyes. Eyes peering up from the pile of dirty straw in the pit, eyes clouding with pain and hopeless resignation as the chains and the cane flicked across the hairy shoulders.

Ought to be a law, Dave thought. There must be some kind of law to stop it, treating a poor dumb animal like that. And the old guy, Captain Ryder—there ought to be a law for an animal like him, too.

Ah, to hell with it. Better shut it out of his mind now, get some rest. Another couple of minutes wouldn't hurt—

It was the thunder that finally woke him. The thunder jerked him into awareness, and then he felt the warm, heavy drops pelting his head and face.

Dave rose and the wind swept over him, whistling across the fields. He must have been asleep for hours, because everything was pitch-black, and when he glanced behind him the lights of the carnival were gone.

For an instant the sky turned silver and he could see the rain pour down. See it, hell—he could feel it, and then the thunder came again, giving him the message. This wasn't just a summer shower, it was a real storm. Another minute and he was going to be soaking wet. By the time he got up to the state highway he could drown, and there wouldn't be a lift there for him, either. Nobody traveled in this kind of weather.

Dave zipped up his jacket, pulled the collar around his

neck. It didn't help, and neither did walking up the road, but he might as well get going. The wind was at his back and that helped a little, but moving against the rain was like walking through a wall of water.

Another flicker of lightning, another rumble of thunder. And then the flickering and the rumbling merged and held steady; the light grew brighter and the sound rose over the hiss of wind and rain.

Dave glanced back over his shoulder and saw the source. The headlights and engine of a truck coming along the road from behind him. As it moved closer Dave realized it wasn't a truck; it was a camper, one of those two-decker jobs with a driver's cab up front.

Right now he didn't give a damn what it was as long as it stopped and picked him up. As the camper came alongside of him Dave stepped out, waving his arms.

The camper slowed, halted. The shadowy silhouette in the cab leaned over from behind the wheel and a hand pushed the window vent open on the passenger side.

"Want a lift, buddy?"

Dave nodded.

"Get in."

The door swung open and Dave climbed up into the cab. He slid across the seat and pulled the door shut behind him.

The camper started to move again.

"Shut the window," the driver said. "Rain's blowing in."

Dave closed it, then wished he hadn't. The air inside the cab was heavy with odors—not just perspiration, but something else. Dave recognized the smell even before the driver produced the bottle from his jacket pocket.

"Want a slug?"

Dave shook his head.

"Fresh corn likker. Tastes like hell, but it's better'n nothing."

"No, thanks."

"Suit yourself." The bottle tilted and gurgled. Lightning

flared across the roadway ahead, glinting across the glass of the windshield, the glass of the upturned bottle. In its momentary glare Dave caught a glimpse of the driver's face, and the flash of lightning brought a flash of recognition.

The driver was Captain Ryder.

Thunder growled, prowling the sky, and the heavy camper turned onto the slick, rain-swept surface of the state highway.

"—what's the matter, you deaf or something? I asked you where you're heading."

Dave came to with a start.

"Oklahoma City," he said.

"You hit the jackpot. That's where I'm going."

Some jackpot. Dave had been thinking about the old guy, remembering the gorilla in the pit. He hated this bastard's guts, and the idea of riding with him all the way to Oklahoma City made his stomach churn all over again. On the other hand it wouldn't help his stomach any if he got set down in a storm here in the middle of the prairie, so what the hell. One quick look at the rain made up his mind for him.

The camper lurched and Ryder fought the wheel.

"Boy—sure is a cutter!"

Dave nodded.

"Get these things often around here?"

"I wouldn't know," Dave said. "This is my first time through. I'm meeting a friend in Oklahoma City. We figure on driving out to Hollywood together—"

"Hollywood?" The hoarse voice deepened. "That goddamn place!"

"But don't you come from there?"

Ryder glanced up quickly and lightning flickered across his sudden frown. Seeing him this close, Dave realized he wasn't so old; something besides time had shaped that scowl, etched the bitter lines around eyes and mouth.

"Who told you that?" Ryder said.

"I was at the carnival tonight. I saw your show."

Ryder grunted and his eyes tracked the road ahead through the twin pendulums of the windshield wipers. "Pretty lousy, huh?"

Dave started to nod, then caught himself. No sense starting anything. "That gorilla of yours looked like it might be sick."

"Bobo? He's all right. Just the weather. We open up north, he'll be fine." Ryder nodded in the direction of the camper bulking behind him. "Haven't heard a peep out of him since we started."

"He's traveling with you?"

"Whaddya think, I ship him airmail?" A hand rose from the wheel, gesturing. "This camper's built special. I got the upstairs, he's down below. I keep the back open so's he gets some air, but no problem—I got it all barred. Take a look through that window behind you."

Dave turned and peered through the wire-meshed window at the rear of the cab. He could see the lighted interior of the camper's upper level, neatly and normally outfitted for occupancy. Shifting his gaze, he stared into the darkness below. Lashed securely to the side walls were the tent, the platform boards, the banners, and the rigging; the floor space between them was covered with straw, heaped into a sort of nest. Crouched against the barred opening at the far end was the black bulk of the gorilla, back turned as it faced the road to the rear, intent on the roaring rain. The camper went into a skid for a moment and the beast twitched, jerking its head around so that Dave caught a glimpse of its glazed eyes. It seemed to whimper softly, but because of the thunder Dave couldn't be sure.

"Snug as a bug," Ryder said. "And so are we." He had the bottle out again, deftly uncorking it with one hand.

"Sure you don't want a belt?"

"I'll pass," Dave said.

The bottle raised, then paused. "Hey, wait a minute."

Ryder was scowling at him again. "You're not on something else, are you, buddy?"

"Drugs?" Dave shook his head. "Not me."

"Good thing you're not." The bottle tilted, lowered again as Ryder corked it. "I hate that crap. Drugs. Drugs and hippies. Hollywood's full of both. You take my advice, you keep away from there. No place for a kid, not any more." He belched loudly, started to put the bottle back into his jacket pocket, then uncorked it again.

Watching him drink, Dave realized he was getting loaded. Best thing to do would be to keep him talking, take his mind off the bottle before he knocked the camper off the road.

"No kidding, were you really a Hollywood stunt man?" Dave said.

"Sure, one of the best. But that was back in the old days, before the place went to hell. Worked for all the majors—trick riding, fancy falls, doubling fight scenes, the works. You ask anybody who knows, they'll tell you old Cap Ryder was right up there with Yakima Canutt, maybe even better." The voice rasped on, harsh with pride. "Seven-fifty a day, that's what I drew. Seven hundred and fifty, every day I worked. And I worked a lot."

"I didn't know they paid that kind of dough," Dave told him.

"You got to remember one thing. I wasn't just taking falls in the long shots. When they hired Cap Ryder they knew they were getting some fancy talent. Not many stunt men can handle animals. You ever see any of those old jungle pictures on television—Tarzan movies, stuff like that? Well, in over half of 'em I'm the guy handling the cats. Lions, leopards, tigers, you name it."

"Sounds exciting."

"Sure, if you like hospitals. Wrestled a black panther once, like to rip my arm clean off in one shot they set up. Seven-fifty sounds like a lot of loot, but you should have seen what I laid out in medical bills. Not to mention what I paid for costumes and extras. Like the lion skins and the ape suit—"

"I don't get it." Dave frowned.

"Sometimes the way they set a shot for a close-up they need the star's face. So if it was a fight scene with a lion or whatever, that's where I came in handy—I doubled for the animal. Would you believe it, three grand I laid out for a lousy monkey suit alone! But it paid off. You should have seen the big pad I had up over Laurel Canyon. Four bedrooms, three-car garage, tennis court, swimming pool, sauna, everything you can think of. Melissa loved it—"

"Melissa?"

Ryder shook his head. "What'm I talking about? You don't want to hear any of that crud about the good old days. All water over the dam."

The mention of water evidently reminded him of something else, because Dave saw him reach for the bottle again. And this time, when he tilted it, it gurgled down to empty.

Ryder cranked the window down on his side and flung the bottle out into the rain.

"All gone," he muttered. "Finished. No more bottle. No more house. No more Melissa—"

"Who was she?" Dave said.

"You really want to know?" Ryder jerked his thumb toward the windshield. Dave followed the gesture, puzzled, until he raised his glance to the roof of the cab. There, fastened directly above the rear-view mirror, was a small picture frame. Staring out of it was the face of a girl; blonde hair, nice features, and with the kind of a smile you see in the pages of high school annuals.

"My niece," Ryder told him. "Sixteen. But I took her when she was only five, right after my sister died. Took her and raised her for eleven years. Raised her right, too. Let me tell you, that girl never lacked for anything. Whatever she wanted, whatever she needed, she got. The trips we took together—the good times we had—hell, I guess it sounds pretty silly, but you'd be surprised what a kick you can get out of seeing a kid have fun. And smart? President of the junior class at Brixley—that's the name of the private school I put her in, best in town, half the stars sent their own daughters there. And that's what she was to me, just like my own flesh-and-blood daughter. So go figure it. How it happened I'll never know." Ryder blinked at the road ahead, forcing his eyes into focus.

"How what happened?" Dave asked.

"The hippies. The goddamn sonsabitching hippies." The eyes were suddenly alert in the network of ugly wrinkles. "Don't ask me where she met the bastards, I thought I was guarding her from all that, but those lousy freaks are all over the place. She must of run into them through one of her friends at school—Christ knows, you see plenty of weirdos even in Bel Air. But you got to remember, she was just sixteen and how could she guess what she was getting into? I suppose at that age an older guy with a beard and a Fender guitar and a souped-up cycle looks pretty exciting.

"Anyhow they got to her. One night when I was away on location—maybe she invited them over to the house, maybe they just showed up and she asked them in. Four of 'em, all stoned out of their skulls. Dude, that was the oldest one's name—he was like the leader, and it was his idea from the start. She wouldn't smoke anything, but he hadn't really figured she would and he came prepared. Must have worked it so she served something cold to drink and he slipped the stuff into her glass. Enough to finish off a bull elephant, the coroner said."

"You mean it killed her—"

"Not right away. I wish to Christ it had." Ryder turned, his face working, and Dave had to strain to hear his voice mumbling through the rush of rain.

"According to the coroner she must have lived for at

least an hour. Long enough for them to take turns—Dude and the other three. Long enough after that for them to get the idea.

"They were in my den, and I had the place all fixed up like a kind of trophy room—animal skins all over the wall, native drums, voodoo masks, stuff I'd picked up on my trips. And here were these four freaks, spaced out, and the kid, blowing her mind. One of the bastards took down a drum and started beating on it. Another got hold of a mask and started hopping around like a witch doctor. And Dude— it was Dude all right, I know it for sure—he and the other creep pulled the lion skin off the wall and draped it over Melissa. Because this was a trip and they were playing Africa. Great White Hunter. Me Tarzan, You Jane.

"By this time Melissa couldn't even stand up any more. Dude got her down on her hands and knees and she just wobbled there. And then—that dirty rotten son of a bitch— he pulled down the drapery cords and tied the stinking lion skin over her head and shoulders. And he took a spear down from the wall, one of the Masai spears, and he was going to jab her in the ribs with it—

"That's what I saw when I came in. Dude, the big stud, standing over Melissa with that spear.

"He didn't stand long. One look at me and he must have known. I think he threw the spear before he ran, but I can't remember. I can't remember anything about the next couple of minutes. They said I broke one freak's collarbone, and the creep in the mask had a concussion from where his head hit the wall. The third one was almost dead by the time the squad arrived and pried my fingers loose from his neck. As it was, they were too late to save him.

"And they were too late for Melissa. She just lay there under that dirty lion skin—that's the part I do remember, the part I wish I could forget—"

"You killed a kid?" Dave said.

Ryder shook his head. "I killed an animal. That's what

I told them at the trial. When an animal goes vicious, you got a right. The judge said one to five, but I was out in a little over two years." He glanced at Dave. "Ever been inside?"

"No. How is it—rough?"

"You can say that again. Rough as a cob." Ryder's stomach rumbled. "I came in pretty feisty, so they put me down in solitary for a while and that didn't help. You sit there in the dark and you start thinking. Here am I, used to traveling all over the world, penned up in a little cage like an animal. And those animals—the ones who killed Melissa— they're running free. One was dead, of course, and the two others I tangled with had maybe learned their lesson. But the big one, the one who started it all, he was loose. Cops never did catch up with him, and they weren't about to waste any more time trying, now that the trial was over.

"I thought a lot about Dude. That was the big one's name, or did I tell you?" Ryder blinked at Dave, and he looked pretty smashed. But he was driving OK and he wouldn't fall asleep at the wheel as long as he kept talking, so Dave nodded.

"Mostly I thought about what I was going to do to Dude once I got out. Finding him would be tricky, but I knew I could do it—hell, I spent years in Africa, tracking animals. And I intended to hunt this one down."

"Then it's true about you being an explorer?" Dave asked.

"Animal-trapper," Ryder said. "Kenya, Uganda, Nigeria— this was before Hollywood, and I saw it all. Things these young punks today never dreamed of. Why, they were dancing and drumming and drugging over there before the first hippie crawled out from under his rock, and let me tell you, they know how to do this stuff for real.

"Like when this Dude tied the lion skin on Melissa, he was just freaked out, playing games. He should have seen what some of those witch doctors can do.

"First they steal themselves a girl, sometimes a young

boy, but let's say a girl because of Melissa. And they shut her up in a cave—a cave with a low ceiling, so she can't stand up, has to go on all fours. They put her on drugs right away, heavy doses, enough to keep her out for a long time. And when she wakes up her hands and feet have been operated on, so they can be fitted with claws. Lion claws, and they've sewed her into a lion skin. Not just put it over her— it's sewed on completely, and it can't be removed.

"You just think about what it's like. She's inside this lion skin, shut away in a cave, doped up, doesn't know where she is or what's going on. And they keep her that way. Feed her on nothing but raw meat. She's all alone in the dark, smelling that damn lion smell, nobody talking to her and nobody for her to talk to. Then pretty soon they come in and break some bones in her throat, her larynx, and all she can do is whine and growl. Whine and growl, and move around on all fours.

"You know what happens, boy? You know what happens to someone like that? They go crazy. And after a while they get to believing they really are a lion. The next step is for the witch doctor to take them out and train them to kill, but that's another story."

Dave glanced up quickly. "You're putting me on—"

"It's all there in the government reports. Maybe the jets come into Nairobi airport now, but back in the jungle things haven't changed. Like I say, some of these people know more about drugs than any hippie ever will. Especially a stupid animal like Dude."

"What happened after you got out?" Dave said. "Did you ever catch up with him?"

Ryder shook his head.

"But I thought you said you had it all planned—"

"Fella gets a lot of weird ideas in solitary. In a way it's pretty much like being shut up in one of those caves. Come to think of it, that's what first reminded me—"

"Of what?"

"Nothing," Ryder gestured hastily. "Forget it. That's what I did. When I got out I figured that was the best way. Forgive and forget."

"You didn't even try to find Dude?"

Ryder frowned. "I told you. I had other things to think about. Like being washed up in the business, losing the house, the furniture, everything. Also I had a drinking problem. But you don't want to hear about that. Anyway, I ended up with the carny and there's nothing more to tell."

Lightning streaked across the sky and thunder rolled in its wake. Dave turned his head, glancing back through the wire-meshed window. The gorilla was still hunched at the far end, peering through the bars into the night beyond. Dave stared at him for a long moment, not really wanting to stop, because then he knew he'd have to ask the question. But the longer he stared, the more he realized that he had no choice.

"What about him?" Dave asked.

"Who?" Ryder followed Dave's gaze. "Oh, you mean Bobo. I picked him up from a dealer I know."

"Must have been expensive."

"They don't come cheap. Not many left."

"Less than a hundred," Dave hesitated. "I read about it in the Sunday paper back home. Feature article on the national preserves. Said gorillas are government-protected, can't be sold."

"I was lucky," Ryder murmured. He leaned forward and Dave was immersed in the alcoholic reek. "I got connections, understand?"

"Right." Dave didn't want the words to come but he couldn't hold them back. "What I don't understand is this lousy carnival. With gorillas so scarce, you should be with a big show."

"That's my business," Ryder gave him a funny look.

"It's business I'm talking about." Dave took a deep

breath. "Like if you were so broke, where'd you get the money to buy an animal like this?"

Ryder scowled. "I already said, I sold off everything—the house, the furniture—"

"And your monkey suit?"

The fist came up so fast Dave didn't even see it. But it slammed into his forehead, knocking him back across the seat, against the unlocked side door.

Dave tried to make a grab for something but it was too late, he was falling. He hit the ditch on his back, and only the mud saved him.

Then the sky caught fire, thunder crashed, and the camper slid past him, disappearing into the dark tunnel of the night. But not before Dave caught one final glimpse of the gorilla, squatting behind the bars.

The gorilla, with its drug-dazed eyes, its masklike, motionless mouth, and its upraised arms revealing the pattern of heavy black stitches.

My first awareness of Ramsey Campbell came when I was eight or nine years old. At a magazine store in a North Carolina mall, I caught a glimpse of a paperback novel called *The Doll Who Ate His Mother*. I did not remove the book from the rack; nor, at the time, did I note the cover art or the author's name. Just that title was enough to scare me so badly that I wouldn't go into the public restroom by myself an hour later: I was sure some cannibalistic fetus would materialize in the toilet bowl and bite my butt.

At thirteen I was hardier, but he still managed to scare me. On the recommendation of Stephen King's great book index in *Danse Macabre*, I sought out Campbell's work. It changed the way I thought about description, style, and story structure more radically than anything since my discovery of Ray Bradbury. I'd never read anything like this. His prose was so crystalline, so hallucinatory; it seemed that he had reached into the substance of my nightmares and splashed them onto the page, a world where things swiveled and nodded and grew huge and soft and drifted toward you unbidden.

The collection *Dark Companions* was the first Campbell book I read, and "The Pattern" still stands out in my mind as one of his finest stories. It took a situation I'd already encountered numerous times in horror fiction—a nice family in peril—and turned it on its ear somehow. The last few paragraphs contain some of the most graphic, shocking imagery I'd ever encountered, yet the story was (and is) about more than blood and guts; it is about nothing less than the sheer inevitability of horror, and the conviction that your horrors will find you no matter how you try to run from them.

—Poppy Z. Brite

THE PATTERN
by Ramsey Campbell

Di seemed glad when he went outside. She was sitting on the settee, legs shoved beneath her, eyes squeezed

tight, looking for the end of her novel. She acknowledged
the sound of the door with a short nod, pinching her
mouth as if he'd been distracting her. He controlled his
resentment; he'd often felt the same way about her, while
painting.

He stood outside the cottage, gazing at the spread of
green. Scattered buttercups crystallized the yellow tinge of
the grass. At the center of the field a darker green rushed
up a thick tree, branching, multiplying; toward the edges of
the field, bushes were foaming explosions, blue-green, red-
edged green. Distant trees displayed an almost transparent
papery spray of green. Beyond them lay curves of hills,
toothed with tiny pines and a couple of random towers, all
silver as mist. As Tony gazed, sunlight spilled from behind
clouds to the sound of a huge soft wind in the trees. The
light filled the greens, intensifying them; they blazed.

Yes, he'd be able to paint here. For a while he had feared
he wouldn't. He'd imagined Di struggling to find her final
chapter, himself straining to paint, the two of them chafing
against each other in the little cottage. But good Lord, this
was only their second day here. They weren't giving themselves time. He began to pace, looking for the vantage point
of his painting.

There were patterns and harmonies everywhere. You only
had to find them, find the angle from which they were clear
to you. He had seen that one day, while painting the microcosm of patterns in a patch of verdure. Now he painted
nothing but glimpses of harmony, those moments when distant echoes of color or movement made sense of a whole
landscape; he painted only the harmonies, abstracted. Often
he felt they were glimpses of a total pattern that included
him, Di, his painting, her writing, life, the world: his being
there and seeing was part of the pattern. Though it was impossible to perceive the total pattern, the sense was there.
Perhaps that sense was the purpose of all real art.

Suddenly he halted. A May wind was passing through

the landscape. It unfurled through the tree in the field; in a
few moments the trees beyond the field responded. It rippled through the grass, and the lazy grounded swaying
echoed the leisurely unfolding of the clouds. All at once he
saw how the clouds elaborated the shapes of the trees and
bushes, subtracting color, lazily changing their shapes as
they drifted across the sky.

He had it now. The wind passed, but it didn't matter. He
could paint what he'd seen; he would see it again when the
breeze returned. He was already mixing colors in his mind,
feeling enjoyment begin: nobody could ever mass-produce
the colors he saw. He turned toward the cottage, to tiptoe
upstairs for his canvas and the rest without disturbing Di.

Behind him someone screamed.

In the distance, across the field. One scream: the hills
echoed curtly. Tony had to grab an upright of the cottage
porch to steady himself. Everything snapped sharp, the cottage garden, the uneven stone wall, the overgrown path beyond the wall, the fence and the wide empty flower-sprinkled
field. There was nobody in sight. The echoes of the cry had
stopped at once, except in Tony's head. The violence of the
cry reverberated there. Of what emotion? Terror, outrage,
disbelief, agony? All of them?

The door slammed open behind him. Di emerged, blinking red-eyed, like an angrily roused sleeper. "What's
wrong?" she demanded nervously. "Was that you?"

"I don't know what it was. Over there somewhere."

He was determined to be calm. The cry had unnerved
him; he didn't want her nervousness to reach him too—he
ignored it. "It might have been someone with their foot in
a trap," he said. "I'll see if I can see."

He backed the car off the end of the path, onto the road.
Di watched him over the stone wall, rather anxiously. He
didn't really expect to find the source of the cry; probably
its cause was past now. He was driving away from Di's

edginess, to give her a chance to calm down. He couldn't paint while he was aware of her nervousness.

He drove. Beside the road the field stretched placidly, easing the scream from his mind. Perhaps someone had just stumbled, had cried out with the shock. The landscape looked too peaceful for anything worse. But for a while he tried to remember the sound, some odd quality about it that nagged at him. It hadn't sounded quite like a cry; it had sounded as if— It was gone.

He drove past the far side of the field beyond the cottage. A path ran through the trees along the border; Ploughman's Path, a sign said. He parked and ventured up the path a few hundred yards. Patches of light flowed over the undergrowth, blurring and floating together, parting and dimming. The trees were full of the intricate trills and chirrups of birds. Tony called out a few times: "Anyone there? Anybody hurt?" But the leaves hushed him.

He drove farther uphill, toward the main road. He would return widely around the cottage, so that Di could be alone for a while. Sunlight and shadow glided softly over the Cotswold hills. Trees spread above the road, their trunks lagged with ivy. Distant foliage was a bank of green folds, elaborate as coral.

On the main road he found a pub, the Farmer's Rest. That would be good in the evenings. The London agent hadn't mentioned that; he'd said only that the cottage was isolated, peaceful. He'd shown them photographs, and though Tony had thought the man had never been near the cottage, Di had loved it at once. Perhaps it was what her book needed.

He glimpsed the cottage through a gap in the hills. Its mellow Cotswold stone seemed concentrated, a small warm amber block beyond the tiny tree-pinned field, a mile below. The green of the field looked simple now, among the fields where sheep and cattle strolled sporadically. He was sorry he'd come so far from it. He drove toward the turnoff that

would take him behind the cottage and eventually back to
its road.

Di ran to the garden wall as he drove onto the path.
"Where were you?" she said. "I was worried."

Oh, Christ, he thought, defeated. "Just looking. I didn't
find anything. Well, I found a pub on the main road."

She tutted at him, smiling wryly: just like him, she meant.
"Are you going to paint?"

She couldn't have made any progress on her book; she
would find it even more difficult now. "I don't think so,"
he said.

"Can't you work either? Oh, let's forget it for today. Let's
walk to the pub and get absolutely pissed."

At least the return journey would be downhill, he thought,
walking. A soft wind tugged at them whenever they passed
gaps; green light and shadow swarmed among branches.
The local beer was good, he found. Even Di liked it, though
she wasn't fond of beer. Among the Toby jugs and brack-
eted rifles, farmers discussed dwindling profits, the delivery of calves, the trapping of foxes, the swollen inflamed
eyes of myxomatosis. Tony considered asking one of them
about the scream, but now they were all intent on the dart-
board; they were a team, practicing somberly for a match.
"I know there's an ending that's right for the book," Di said.
"It's just finding it."

When they returned to the cottage, amber clouds floated
above the sunset. The horizon was the color of the stone.
The field lay quiet and chill. Di gazed at the cottage, her
hands light on the wall. After a while he thought of asking
why, but her feelings might be too delicate, too elusive. She
would tell him if she could.

They made love beneath the low dark beams. Afterward
he lay in her on their quilt, gazing out at the dimming field.
The tree was heavy with gathering darkness; a sheep bleated
sleepily. Tony felt peaceful, in harmony. But Di was moving beneath him. "Don't squash," she said. As she lay be-

side him he felt her going into herself, looking for her story. At the moment she didn't dare risk the lure of peace.

When he awoke, the room was gloomy. Di lay face up-turned, mouth slackly open. Outside the ground hissed with rain beneath a low gray sky; the walls of the room streamed with the shadows of water.

He felt dismally oppressed. He had hoped to paint today. Now he imagined himself and Di hemmed in by the rain, struggling with their balks beneath the low beams, wandering irritably about the small rooms, among the fat mock-leather furniture and stray electric fires. He knew Di hoped this book would make her more than just another children's novelist, but it couldn't while he was in the way.

Suddenly he glimpsed the landscape. All the field glowed sultry green. He saw how the dark sky and even the dark framing room were necessary to call forth the sullen glow. Perhaps he could paint that glimpse. After a while he kissed Di awake. She'd wanted to be awakened early.

After breakfast she reread *The Song of the Trees*. She turned over the last page of the penultimate chapter and stared at the blank table beneath. At last she pushed herself away from the table and began to pace shortly. Tony tried to keep out of her way. When his own work was frustrated she seemed merely an irritation; he was sure she must feel the same of him. "I'm going out for a walk," she called, opening the front door. He didn't offer to walk with her. He knew she was searching for her conclusion.

When the rain ceased he carried his painting materials outside. For a moment he wished he had music. But they couldn't have transported the stereo system, and their radio was decrepit. As he left the cottage he glanced back at Di's flowers, massed minutely in vases.

The gray sky hung down, trapping light in ragged flourishes of white cloud. Distant trees were smudges of mist; the greens of the field merged into a dark glow. On the near side of the fence the path unfurled innumerable leaves, oppressive in their dark intricacy, heavy with raindrops. Even the raindrops were relentlessly green. Metallic chimes and chirrs of birds surrounded him, as did a thick rich smell of earth.

Only the wall of the garden held back the green. The heavy jagged stones were a response to the landscape. He could paint that, the rough texture of stone, the amber stone spattered with darker ruggedness, opposing the overpowering lush green. But it wasn't what he'd hoped to paint, and it didn't seem likely to make him much money.

Di liked his paintings. At his first exhibition she'd sought him out to tell him so; that was how they'd met. Her first book was just beginning to earn royalties; she had been working on her second. Before they were married he'd begun to illustrate her work.

If exhibiting wasn't too lucrative, illustrating books was less so. He knew Di felt uneasy as the breadwinner; sometimes he felt frustrated that he couldn't earn them more—the inevitable castration anxiety. That was another reason why she wanted *The Song of the Trees* to sell well: to promote his work. She wanted his illustrations to be as important as the writing.

He liked what there was of the book. He felt his paintings could complement the prose; they'd discussed ways of setting out the pages. The story was about the last dryads of a forest, trapped among the remaining trees by a fire that had sprung from someone's cigarette. As they watched picnickers sitting on blackened stumps amid the ash, breaking branches from the surviving trees, leaving litter and matches among them, the dryads realized they must escape before the next fire. Though it was unheard of, they managed to relinquish the cool green peace of the trees and pass through the clinging dead ash to the greenery beyond. They coursed through the greenery, seeking welcoming trees. But the book was full of their tribulations: a huge grim oak-dryad who drove them away from the saplings he protected; willow-dryads who let them go deep into their forest, but only because they would distract the dark thick-voiced spirit of a swamp; glittering birch-drayds, too cold and aloof to bear; morose hawthorns, whose flowers farted at the dryads, in case they were animals come to chew the leaves.

He could tell Di loved writing the book—perhaps too much so, for she'd thought it would produce its own ending. But she had been balked for weeks. She wanted to write an ending that satisfied her totally; she was determined not to fake anything. He knew she hoped the book might appeal to adults too. "Maybe it needs peace," she'd said at last, and that had brought them to the cottage. Maybe she was right. This was only their third day, she had plenty of time.

As he mused, the sluggish sky parted. Sunlight spilled over an edge of cloud. At once the greens that had merged into green emerged again, separating: a dozen greens, two dozen. Dots of flowers brightened over the field, colors filled the raindrops piercingly. He saw the patterns at once: almost a mandala. The clouds were whiter now, fragmented by blue; the sky was rolling open from the horizon. He began to mix colors. Surely the dryads must have passed through such a landscape.

The patterns were emerging on his canvas when, beyond the field, someone screamed.

It wasn't Di. He was sure it wasn't a woman's voice. It was the voice he'd heard yesterday, but more outraged still; it sounded as if it were trying to utter something too dreadful for language. The hills swallowed its echoes at once, long before his heart stopped pounding loudly.

As he tried to breathe in calm, he realized what was odd about the scream. It had sounded almost as much like an echo as its reiteration in the hills: louder, but somehow lacking a source. It reminded him—yes, of the echo that sometimes precedes a loud sound-source on a record.

Just an acoustic effect. But that hardly explained the scream itself. Someone playing a joke? Someone trying to frighten the intruders at the cottage? The local simpleton? An animal in a trap, perhaps, for his memory of the scream contained little that sounded human. Someone was watching him.

He turned sharply. Beyond the nearby path, at the far side of the road, stood a clump of trees. The watcher was hiding among them; Tony could sense him there—he'd almost glimpsed him skulking hurriedly behind the trunks. He felt instinctively that the lurker was a man.

Was it the man who'd screamed? No, he hadn't had time to make his way round the edge of the field. Perhaps he had been drawn by the scream. Or perhaps he'd come to spy on the strangers. Tony stared at the trees, waiting for the man to betray his presence, but couldn't stare long; the trunks were vibrating restlessly, incessantly—heat-haze, of course, though it looked somehow odder. Oh, let the man spy if he wanted to. Maybe he'd venture closer to look at Tony's work, as people did. But when Tony rested from his next burst of painting, he could tell the man had gone.

Soon he saw Di hurrying anxiously down the road. Of course, she must have heard the scream. "I'm all right, love," he called.

"It was the same, wasn't it? Did you see what it was?"

"No. Maybe it's children. Playing a joke."

She wasn't reassured so easily. "It sounded like a man," she said. She gazed at his painting. "That *is* good," she said, and wandered into the cottage without mentioning her book. He knew she wasn't going in to write.

The scream had worried her more than she'd let him see. Her anxiety lingered even now she knew he was unharmed. Something else to hinder her book, he thought irritably. He couldn't paint now, but at least he knew what remained to be painted.

He sat at the kitchen table while she cooked a shepherd's

pie in the range. Inertia hung oppressively about them. "Do you want to go to the pub later?" he said.

"Maybe. I'll see."

He gazed ahead at the field in the window, the cooling tree; branches swayed a little behind the glass. In the kitchen something trembled—heat over the electric stove. Di was reaching for the teapot with one hand, lifting the kettle with the other; the steaming spout tilted above her bare leg. Tony stood up, mouth opening—but she'd put the kettle down. "It's all right," he answered her frown, as he scooped up spilled sugar from the table.

She stood at the range. "Maybe the pub might help us to relax," he said.

"I don't want to relax! That's no use!" She turned too quickly, and overbalanced toward the range. Her bare arm was going to rest on the metal that quivered with heat. She pushed herself back from the wall, barely in time. "You see what I mean?" she demanded.

"What's the matter? Clumsiness isn't like you."

"Stop watching me, then. You make me nervous."

"Hey, you can't just blame me." How would she have felt if she had been spied on earlier? There was more wrong with her than her book and her irrationally lingering worry about him, he was sure. Sometimes she had what seemed to be psychic glimpses. "Is it the cottage that's wrong?" he said.

"No, I like the cottage."

"The area, then? The field?"

She came to the table, to saw bread with a carving knife; the cottage lacked a bread knife. "I like it here. It's probably just me," she said, musing about something.

The kettle sizzled, parched. "Bloody clean simplicity," she said. She disliked electric stoves. She moved the kettle to a cold ring and turned back. The point of the carving knife thrust over the edge of the table. Her turn would impale her thigh on the blade.

Tony snatched the knife back. The blade and the wood of the table seemed to vibrate for a moment. He must have jarred the table. Di was staring rather abstractedly at the knife. "That's three," he said. "You'll be all right now."

During dinner she was abstracted. Once she said "I really like this cottage, you know. I really do." He didn't try to reach her. After dinner he said "Look, I'm sorry if I've been distracting you," but she shook her head, hardly listening. They didn't seem to be perceiving each other very well.

He was washing up when she said "My God." He glanced anxiously at her. She was staring up at the beams. "Of course. Of course," she said, reaching for her notebook. She pushed it away at once and hurried upstairs. Almost immediately he heard her begin typing.

He tried to paint, until darkness began to mix with his colors. He stood gazing as twilight collected in the field. The typewriter chattered. He felt rather unnecessary, out of place. He must buy some books in Camside tomorrow. He felt restless, a little resentful. "I'm going down to the pub for a while," he called. The typewriter's bell rang, rang again.

The pub was surrounded by jeeps, sports cars, floridly painted vans. Crowds of young people pressed close to the tables, on stools, on the floor; they shouted over each other, laughed, rolled cigarettes. One was passing around a sketchbook, but Tony didn't feel confident enough to introduce himself. A few of the older people doggedly practiced darts, the rest surrounded Tony at the bar. He chatted about the weather and the countryside, listened to prices of grain. He hoped he'd have a chance to ask about the scream.

He was slowing in the middle of his second pint when the barman said "One of the new ones, aren't you?"

"Yes, that's right." On an impulse he said loudly enough for the people around him to hear: "We're in the cottage across the field from Ploughman's Path."

The man didn't move hurriedly to serve someone else.

Nobody gasped, nobody backed away from Tony. Well, that was encouraging. "Are you liking it?" the barman said.

"Very much. There's just one odd thing." Now was his chance. "We keep hearing someone screaming across the field."

Even then the room didn't fall silent. But it was as if he'd broken a taboo; people withdrew slightly from him, some of them seemed resentful. Three women suddenly excused themselves from different groups at the bar, as if he were threatening to become offensive. "It'll be an animal caught in a trap," the barman said.

"I suppose so." He could see the man didn't believe it either.

The barman was staring at him. "Weren't you with a girl yesterday?"

"She's back at the cottage."

Everyone nearby looked at Tony. When he glanced at them, they looked away. "You want to be sure she's safe," the barman muttered, and hurried to fill flourished glasses. Tony gulped down his beer, cursing his imagination, and almost ran to the car.

Above the skimming patch of lit tarmac, moths ignited; a rabbit froze, then leaped. Discovered trees rushed out of the dark, to be snatched back at once by the night. The light bleached the leaves, the rushing tunnels of boles seemed subterraneously pale. The wide night was still. He could hear nothing but the hum of the car. Above the hills hung enormous dim clouds, gray as rocks.

He could see Di as he hurried up the path. Her head was silhouetted on the curtain; it leaned at an angle against the back of the settee. He fumbled high in the porch for the hidden key. Her eyes were closed, her mouth was loosely open. Her typescript lay at her feet.

She was blinking, smiling at him. He could see both needed effort; her eyes were red, she looked depressed— she always did when she finished a book. "See what you think of it," she said, handing him the pages. Beneath her attempt at a professional's impersonality he thought she was offering the chapter to him shyly as a young girl.

Emerging defeated from a patch of woodland, the dryads saw a cottage across a field. It stood in the still light, peaceful as the evening. They could feel the peace filling its timbers: not a green peace but a warmth, stillness, stability. As they drew nearer they saw an old couple within. The couple had worked hard for their peace; now they'd achieved it here. Tony knew they were himself and Di. One by one the dryads passed gratefully into the dark wood of the beams, the doors.

He felt oddly embarrassed. When he managed to look at her he could only say "Yes, it's good. You've done it."

"Good," she said. "I'm glad." She was smiling peacefully now.

As they climbed the stairs she said "If we have children they'll be able to help me too. They can criticize."

She hoped the book would let them afford children. "Yes, they will," he said.

The scream woke him. For a moment he thought he'd dreamed it, or had cried out in his sleep. But the last echo was caught in the hills. Faint as it was, he could feel its intolerable horror, its despair.

He lay blinking at the sunlight. The white-painted walls shone. Di hadn't awakened; he was glad. The scream throbbed in his brain. Today he must find out what it was.

After breakfast he told Di he was going into Camside. She was still depressed after completing the book; she looked drained. She didn't offer to accompany him. She stood at the garden wall, watching him blindly, dazzled by the sun. "Be careful driving," she called.

The clump of trees opposite the end of the path was quivering. Was somebody hiding behind the trunks? Tony frowned at her. "Do you feel—" but he didn't want to alarm her unnecessarily "—anything? Anything odd?"

"What sort of thing?" But he was wondering whether to tell her when she said "I like this place. Don't spoil it."

He went back to her. "What will you do while I'm out?"

"Just stay in the cottage. I want to read through the book. Why are you whispering?" He smiled at her, shaking his head. The sense of someone watching had faded, though the tree trunks still quivered.

Plushy white-and-silver layers of cloud sailed across the blue sky. He drove the fifteen miles to Camside, a slow roller-coaster ride between green quilts spread easily over the hills. Turned earth displayed each shoot on the nearer fields; trees met over the roads and parted again.

Camside was wholly the colors of rusty sand; similar stone framed the wide glass of the library. Mullioned windows multiplied reflections. Gardens and walls were thick with flowers. A small river coursed beneath a bridge; in the water, sunlight darted incessantly among pebbles. He parked outside a pub, The Wheatsheaf, and walked back. Next to the library stood an odd squat building of the amber stone, a square block full of small windows whose open casements were like griddles filled with panes; over its door a new plastic sign said *Camside Observer.* The newspaper's files might be useful. He went in.

A girl sat behind a low white Swedish desk; the crimson bell of her desk lamp clanged silently against the white walls, the amber windowsills. "Can I help you?"

"I hope so. I'm, I'm doing some research into an area near here, Ploughman's Path. Have you heard of it?"

"Oh, I don't know." She was glancing away, looking for help to a middle-aged man who had halted in a doorway behind her desk. "Mr. Poole?" she called.

"We've run a few stories about that place," the man told Tony. "You'll find them in our files, on microfilm. Next door, in the library."

"Oh, good. Thanks." But that might mean hours of searching. "Is there anyone here who knows the background?"

The man frowned, and saw Tony realize that meant yes. "The man who handled the last story is still on our staff," he said. "But he isn't here now."

"Will he be here later?"

"Yes, probably. No, I've no idea when." As Tony left he felt the man was simply trying to prevent his colleague from being pestered.

The library was a long room, spread with sunlight. Sunlight lay dazzling on the glossy tables, cleaved shade among the bookcases; a trolley overflowed with thrillers and romances. Ploughman's Path? Oh, yes—and the librarian showed him a card file that indexed local personalities, events, areas. She snapped up a card for him, as if it were a tarot's answer. Ploughman's Path: see Victor Hill, *Legendry and Customs of the Severn Valley*. "And there's something on microfilm," she said, but he was anxious to make sure the book was on the shelf.

It was. It was bound in op-art blues. He carried it to a table; its blues vibrated in the sunlight. The index told him the passage about Ploughman's Path covered six pages. He riffled hastily past photographs of standing stones, a trough in the binding full of breadcrumbs, a crushed jagged-legged fly. Ploughman's Path—

> Why the area bounding Ploughman's Path should be dogged by ill luck and tragedy is not known. Folk living in the cottage nearby have sometimes reported hearing screams produced by no visible agency. Despite the similarity of this to banshee legends, no such legend appears to have grown up locally. But Ploughman's Path, and the area bounding it farthest from the cottage (see map), has been so often visited by tragedy and misfortune that local folk dislike to even mention the name, which they fear will bring bad luck.

Farthest from the cottage. Tony relaxed. So long as the book said so, that was all right. And the last line told him why they'd behaved uneasily at the Farmer's Rest. He read on, his curiosity unmixed now with apprehension.

But good Lord, the area was unlucky. Rumors of Roman sacrifices were only its earliest horrors. As the history of the place became more accurately documented, the tragedies grew worse. A gallows set up within sight of the cottage, so that the couple living there must watch their seven-year-old daughter hanged for theft; it had taken her hours to die. An old woman accused of witchcraft by gossip, set on fire and left to burn alive on the path. A mute child who'd fallen down an old well: coping stones had fallen on him, breaking his limbs and hiding him from searchers—years later his skeleton had been found. A baby caught in an animal trap. God, Tony thought. No wonder he'd heard screams.

A student was using the microfilm reader. Tony went back to the *Observer* building. A pear-shaped red-faced man leaned against the wall, chatting to the receptionist; he wore a tweedy pork-pie hat, a blue shirt and waistcoat, tweed trousers. "Watch out, here's trouble," he said as Tony entered.

"Has he come in yet?" Tony asked the girl. "The man who knows about Ploughman's Path?"

"What's your interest?" the red-faced man demanded.

"I'm staying in the cottage near there. I've been hearing odd things. Cries."

"Have you now." The man pondered, frowning. "Well, you're looking at the man who knows," he decided to say, thumping his chest. "Roy Burley. Burly Roy, that's me. Don't you know me? Don't you read our paper? Time you did, then." He snatched the an *Observer* from a rack and stuffed it into Tony's hand.

"You want to know about the path, eh? It's all up here." He tapped his hat. "I'll tell you what, though, it's a hot day for talking. Do you fancy a drink? Tell old Puddle I'll be back soon," he told the girl.

He thumped on the door of The Wheatsheaf. "They'll open up. They know me here." At last a man reluctantly opened the door, glancing discouragingly at Tony. "It's all right, Bill, don't look so bloody glum," Roy Burley said. "He's a friend of mine."

A girl set out beer mats; her radio sang that everything was beautiful, in its own way. Roy Burley bought two pints and vainly tried to persuade Bill to join them. "Get that down you," he told Tony. "The only way to start work. You'd think they could do without me over the road, the way some of the buggers act. But they soon start screaming if they think my copy's going to be late. They'd like to see me out, some of them. Unfortunately for them, I've got friends. There I am," he said, poking a thick finger into the newspaper: "The Countryside This Week," by Countryman. "And there, and there." "Social Notes," by A. Guest. "Entertainments," by D. Plainman. "What's your line of business?" he demanded.

"I'm an artist, a painter."

"Ah, the painters always come down here. And the advertising people. I'll tell you, the other week we had a photographer—"

By the time it was his round Tony began to suspect he was just an excuse for beers. "You were going to tell me about the screams," he said when he returned to the table.

The man's eyes narrowed warily. "You've heard them. What do you think they are?"

"I was reading about the place earlier," Tony said, anxious to win his confidence. "I'm sure all those tragedies must have left an imprint somehow. A kind of recording. If there are ghosts, I think that's what they are."

"That's right," Roy Burley's eyes relaxed. "I've always thought that. There's a bit of science in that, it makes sense. Not like some of the things these spiritualists try to sell."

Tony opened his mouth to head him off from the next anecdote: too late. "We had one of them down here, trying to tell us about Ploughman's Path. A spiritualist or a medium, same thing. Came expecting us all to be yokels, I shouldn't wonder. The police weren't having any, so he tried it on us. Murder brings these mediums swarming like flies, so I've heard tell."

"What murder?" Tony said, confused.

"I thought you read about it." His eyes had narrowed again. "Oh, you read the book. No, it wouldn't be in there, too recent." He gulped beer; everything is beautiful, the radio sang. "Why, it was about the worst thing that ever happened at Ploughman's Path. I've seen pictures of what Jack the Ripper did, but this was worse. They talk about people being flayed alive, but—Christ. Put another in here, Bill."

He half emptied the refilled glass. "They never caught him. I'd have stopped him, I can tell you," he said in vague impotent fury. "The police didn't think he was a local man, because there wasn't any repetition. He left no clues, nobody saw him. At least, not what he looked like. There was a family picnicking in the field the day before the murder, they said they kept feeling there was someone watching. He must have been waiting to catch someone alone.

"I'll tell you the one clever suggestion this medium had. These picnickers heard the scream, what you called the recording. He thought maybe the screams were what attracted the maniac there."

Attracted him there. That reminded Tony of something, but the beer was heavy on his mind. "What else did the medium have to say?"

"Oh, all sorts of rubbish. You know, this mystical stuff. Seeing patterns everywhere, saying everything is a pattern."

"Yes?"

"Oh, yes," Roy Burley said irritably. "He didn't get that one past me, though. If everything's a pattern it has to include all the horror in the world, doesn't it? Things like this murder? That shut him up for a bit. Then he tried to say things like that may be necessary too, to make up the pattern. These people," he said with a gesture of disgust, "you can't talk to them."

Tony bought him another pint, restraining himself to a half. "Did he have any ideas about the screams?"

"God, I can't remember. Do you really want to hear that rubbish? You wouldn't have liked what he said, let me tell you. He didn't believe in your recording idea." He wiped his frothy lips sloppily. "He came here a couple of years after the murder," he reluctantly answered Tony's encouraging gaze. "He'd read about the tragedies. He held a three-day vigil at Ploughman's Path, or something. Wouldn't it be nice to have that much time to waste? He heard the screams, but—this is what I said you wouldn't like—he said he couldn't feel any trace of the tragedies at all."

"I don't understand."

"Well, you know these people are shupposed to be sen-shitive to sush things." When he'd finished laughing at himself he said "Oh, he had an explanation, he was full of them. He tried to tell the police and me that the real tragedy hadn't happened yet. He wanted us to believe he could see it in the future. Of course he couldn't say what or when. Do you know what he tried to make out? That there was something so awful in the future it was echoing back somehow, a sort of ghost in reverse. All the tragedies were just echoes, you see. He even made out the place was trying to make this final thing happen, so it could get rid of it at last. It had to make the worst thing possible happen, to purge itself. That was where the traces of the tragedies had gone— the psychic energy, he called it. The place had converted all that energy, to help it make the thing happen. Oh, he was a real comedian."

"But what about the screams?"

"Same kind of echo. Haven't you ever heard an echo on

a record before you hear the sound? He tried to say the screams were like that, coming back from the future. He was entertaining, I'll give him that. He had all sorts of charts, he'd worked out some kind of numerical pattern, the frequency of the tragedies or something. Didn't impress me. They're like statistics, those things, you can make them mean anything." His eyes had narrowed, gazing inward. "I ended up laughing at him. He went off very upset. Well, I had to get rid of him, I'd better things to do than listen to him. It wasn't my fault he was killed," he said angrily, "whatever some people may say."

"Why, how was he killed?"

"Oh, he went back to Ploughman's Path. If he was so upset he shouldn't have been driving. There were some children playing near the path. He must have meant to chase them away, but he lost control of the car, crashed at the end of the path. His legs were trapped and he caught fire. Of course he could have fitted that into his pattern," he mused. "I suppose he'd have said that was what the third scream meant."

Tony started. He fought back the shadows of beer, of the pub. "How do you mean, the third scream?"

"That was to do with his charts. He'd heard three screams in his vigil. He'd worked out that three screams meant it was time for a tragedy. He tried to show me, but I wasn't looking. What's the matter? Don't be going yet, it's my round. What's up, how many screams have you heard?"

"I don't know," Tony blurted. "Maybe I dreamt one." As he hurried out he saw Roy Burley picking up his abandoned beer, saying "Aren't you going to finish this?"

It was all right. There was nothing to worry about, he'd just better be getting back to the cottage. The key groped clumsily for the ignition. The rusty yellow of Camside rolled back, rushed by green. Tony felt as if he were floating in a stationary car, as the road wheeled by beneath him—as if he were sitting in the front stalls before a cinema screen, as the road poured through the screen, as the bank of a curve hurtled at him: look out! Nearly. He slowed. No need to take risks. But his mind was full of the memory of someone watching from the trees, perhaps drawn there by the screams.

Puffy clouds lazed above the hills. As the Farmer's Rest whipped by, Tony glimpsed the cottage and the field, laid out minutely below; the trees at Ploughman's Path were a tight band of green. He skidded into the side road, fighting the wheel; the road seemed absurdly narrow. Scents of blossoms billowed thickly at him. A few birds sang elaborately, otherwise the passing countryside was silent, deserted, weighed down by heat.

The trunks of the trees at the end of Ploughman's Path were twitching nervously, incessantly. He squeezed his eyes shut. Only heat-haze. Slow down. Nearly home now.

He slammed the car door, which sprang open. Never mind. He ran up the path and thrust the gate back, breaking its latch. The door of the cottage was ajar. He halted in the front room. The cottage seemed full of his harsh panting.

Di's typescript was scattered over the carpet. The dark chairs sat fatly; one lay on its side, its fake leather ripped. Beside it a small object glistened red. He picked it up, staining his fingers. Though it was thick with blood he recognized Di's wedding ring.

When he rushed out after searching the cottage he saw the trail at once. As he forced his way through the fence, sobbing dryly, barbed wire clawed at him. He ran across the field, stumbling and falling, toward Ploughman's Path. The discolored grass of the trail painted his trouser cuffs and hands red. The trees of Ploughman's Path shook violently, with terror or with eagerness. The trail touched their trunks, leading him beneath the foliage to what lay on the path.

It was huge. More than anything else it looked like a

tattered cutout silhouette of a woman's body. It gleamed red beneath the trees; its torso was perhaps three feet wide. On the width of the silhouette's head two eyes were arranged neatly.

The scream ripped the silence of the path, an outraged cry of horror beyond words. It startled him into stumbling forward. He felt numb and dull. His mind refused to grasp what he was seeing; it was like nothing he'd ever seen. There was most of the head, in the crotch of a tree. Other things dangled from branches.

His lips seemed glued together. Since reaching the path he had made no sound. He hadn't screamed, but he'd heard himself scream. At last he recognized that all the screams had been his voice.

He began to turn about rapidly, staring dull-eyed, seeking a direction in which he could look without being confronted with horror. There was none. He stood aimlessly, staring down near his feet, at a reddened gag.

As all the trees quivered like columns of water he heard movement behind him.

Though he had no will to live, it took him a long time to turn. He knew the pattern had reached its completion, and he was afraid. He had to close his eyes before he could turn, for he could still hear the scream he was about to utter.

To read the first several lines of Edgar Allan Poe's great, demonically inspired short tale is to be drawn at once into the vortex of his imagination. Once you begin, you can't back away.

This is the power of that species of art I call *fated, irresistible.* To distinguish it from the mediated and meditated and premeditated species of art that can rise as well to heights of greatness, but greatness of another kind, purposeful and willed. The *fated* art springs white-hot from its creator's often tormented imagination and need not be revised, or revised only minimally; the other sort of art can be revised, shaped, reshaped, calibrated, and reimagined at the creator's leisure. It may yield beauty and even terror, in time, but it will never have the uncanny power of the white-hot creation.

"The Tell-Tale Heart," more than any other tale of Poe's, is a *fated, irresistible* creation. When I first read it, as a child of perhaps ten, I wasn't sophisticated enough to grasp the writerly device of evoking a voice or persona. I suppose I knew that the author, "Edgar Allan Poe," could not possibly have committed the ghoulish murder he describes; yet, the voice is so convincing, the mounting anxiety and terror so real—maybe, in fact, he had? For children, particularly the more credulous and trusting children of a pre-television era, the printed word possessed unquestioned authority; it wasn't at all clear what the distinction was between "real" and "not-real," in the realm of adults who controlled such distinctions. In any case, I seem to have virtually memorized the first paragraph of this great Gothic tale, without knowing what I did. And over the years the madman's voice has come to me at odd, unexpected times, as if lurking close beneath the surface of my consciousness. *True!—nervous—very, very dreadfully nervous I had been and am; but why* will *you say that I am mad?* The voice didn't seem a particularly mad voice, rather more a lucid, appealing, somehow kindred voice.

Who can judge how early, untutored, impassioned readings of Edgar Allan Poe have permanently warped the psyches of the horror writers of America? All of us going about with Poe's madman voice shimmering, on the verge of becoming audible, in our heads.

*   *   *

"The Tell-Tale Heart" is surely the greatest of Edgar Allan Poe's *Tales of the Grotesque and Arabesque*, an extraordinary collection published in 1840 and containing such famous titles as "The Black Cat," "The Fall of the House of Usher," "The Pit and the Pendulum," and numerous others. Its immediate accomplishment is the brilliance of the narrator's voice, addressing us with astonishing verbal dexterity. His lack of motive for his act of murder ("It is impossible to say how first the idea entered my brain . . . I loved the old man") makes the tale one of terror and not simply cunning brutality. For the murderer, Poe knew instinctively, is as much a victim as the object of his deranged, malevolent desire. The "tell-tale heart"—its "hellish tattoo"—that "low, dull, quick sound such as a watch makes when enveloped in cotton"—is, of course, the narrator's heart, and has been so from the start.

—Joyce Carol Oates

THE TELL-TALE HEART
by Edgar Allan Poe

True!—nervous—very, very dreadfully nervous I had been and am; but why *will* you say that I am mad? The disease had sharpened my senses—not destroyed—not dulled them. Above all was the sense of hearing acute. I heard all things in the heaven and in the earth. I heard many things in hell. How, then, am I mad? Hearken! and observe how healthily—how calmly I can tell you the whole story.

It is impossible to say how first the idea entered my brain; but once conceived, it haunted me day and night. Object there was none. Passion there was none. I loved the old man. He had never wronged me. He had never given me insult. For his gold I had no desire. I think it was his eye! yes, it was this! One of his eyes resembled that of a vulture—a pale blue eye, with a film over it. Whenever it fell upon me, my blood ran cold; and so by degrees—very gradually—I made up my mind to take the life of the old man, and thus rid myself of the eye for ever.

Now this is the point. You fancy me mad. Madmen know nothing. But you should have seen *me*. You should have seen how wisely I proceeded—with what caution—with what foresight—with what dissimulation I went to work! I was never kinder to the old man than during the whole week before I killed him. And every night, about midnight, I turned the latch of his door and opened it—oh, so gently! And then, when I had made an opening sufficient for my head, I put in a dark lantern, all closed, closed, so that no light shone out, and then I thrust in my head. Oh, you would have laughed to see how cunningly I thrust it in! I moved it slowly—very, very slowly, so that I might not disturb the old man's sleep. It took me an hour to place my whole head within the opening so far that I could see him as he lay upon his bed. Ha!—would a madman have been so wise as this? And then, when my head was well in the room, I undid the lantern cautiously—oh, so cautiously—cautiously (for the hinges creaked)—I undid it just so much that a single thin ray fell upon the vulture eye. And this I did for seven long nights—every night just at midnight—but I found the eye always closed; and so it was impossible to do the work; for it was not the old man who vexed me, but his Evil Eye. And every morning, when the day broke, I went boldly into the chamber, and spoke courageously to him, calling him by name in a hearty tone, and inquiring how he had passed the night. So you see he would have been a very profound old man, indeed, to suspect that every night, just at twelve, I looked in upon him while he slept.

Upon the eighth night I was more than usually cautious in opening the door. A watch's minute hand moves more slowly than did mine. Never before that night had I *felt* the extent of my own powers—of my sagacity. I could scarcely contain my feelings of triumph. To think that there I was, opening the door, little by little, and he not even to dream of my secret deeds or thoughts. I fairly chuckled at the idea; and perhaps he heard me; for he moved on the bed suddenly, as if startled. Now you may think that I drew back—but no. His room was as black as pitch with the thick darkness (for the shutters were close fastened, through fear of robbers), and so I knew that he could not see the opening of the door, and I kept pushing it on steadily, steadily.

I had my head in, and was about to open the lantern, when my thumb slipped upon the tin fastening, and the old man sprang up in the bed, crying out—"Who's there?"

I kept quite still and said nothing. For a whole hour I did not move a muscle, and in the meantime I did not hear him lie down. He was still sitting up in the bed listening;—just as I have done, night after night, hearkening to the death watches in the wall.

Presently I heard a slight groan, and I knew it was the groan of mortal terror. It was not a groan of pain or of grief—oh, no!—it was the low stifled sound that arises from the bottom of the soul when overcharged with awe. I knew the sound well. Many a night, just at midnight, when all the world slept, it has welled up from my own bosom, deepening, with its dreadful echo, the terrors that distracted me. I say I knew it well. I knew what the old man felt, and pitied him, although I chuckled at heart. I knew that he had been lying awake ever since the first slight noise, when he had turned in the bed. His fears had been ever since growing upon him. He had been trying to fancy them causeless, but could not. He had been saying to himself—"It is nothing but the wind in the chimney—it is only a mouse crossing the floor," or "it is merely a cricket which has made a single chirp." Yes, he had been trying to comfort himself with these suppositions; but he had found all in vain. *All in vain;* because Death, in approaching him, had stalked with his black shadow before him, and enveloped the victim. And it was the mournful influence of the unperceived shadow that caused him to feel—although he neither saw nor heard—to *feel* the presence of my head within the room.

When I had waited a long time, very patiently, without hearing him lie down, I resolved to open a little—a very, very little crevice in the lantern. So I opened it—you cannot imagine how stealthily, stealthily—until, at length, a single dim ray, like the thread of the spider, shot from out the crevice and full upon the vulture eye.

It was open—wide, wide open—and I grew furious as I gazed upon it. I saw it with perfect distinctness—all a dull blue, with a hideous veil over it that chilled the very marrow in my bones; but I could see nothing else of the old man's face or person: for I had directed the ray as if by instinct, precisely upon the damned spot.

And now have I not told you that what you mistake for madness is but over-acuteness of the senses?—now, I say, there came to my ears a low, dull, quick sound, such as a watch makes when enveloped in cotton. I knew *that* sound well too. It was the beating of the old man's heart. It increased my fury, as the beating of a drum stimulates the soldier into courage.

But even yet I refrained and kept still. I scarcely breathed. I held the lantern motionless. I tried how steadily I could maintain the ray upon the eye. Meantime the hellish tattoo of the heart increased. It grew quicker and quicker, and louder and louder every instant. The old man's terror *must* have been extreme! It grew louder, I say, louder every moment!—do you mark me well? I have told you that I am nervous: so I am. And now at the dead hour of the night, amid the dreadful silence of that old house, so strange a noise as this excited me to uncontrollable terror. Yet, for some minutes longer I refrained and stood still. But the beating grew louder, louder! I thought the heart must burst. And now a new anxiety seized me—the sound would be heard by a neighbor! The old man's hour had come! With a loud yell, I threw open the lantern and leaped into the room. He shrieked once—once only. In an instant I dragged him to the floor, and pulled the heavy bed over him. I then smiled gaily, to find the deed so far done. But, for many minutes, the heart beat on with a muffled sound. This, however, did not vex me; it would not be heard through the wall. At length it ceased. The old man was dead. I removed the bed and examined the corpse. Yes, he was stone, stone dead. I placed my hand upon the heart and held it there many minutes. There was no pulsation. He was stone dead. His eye would trouble me no more.

If still you think me mad, you will think so no longer when I describe the wise precautions I took for the concealment of the body. The night waned, and I worked hastily, but in silence. First of all I dismembered the corpse. I cut off the head and the arms and the legs.

I then took up three planks from the flooring of the chamber, and deposited all between the scantlings. I then replaced the boards so cleverly, so cunningly, that no human eye—not even *his*—could have detected any thing wrong. There was nothing to wash out—no stain of any kind—no blood-spot whatever. I had been too wary for that. A tub had caught all—ha! ha!

When I had made an end to these labors, it was four o'clock—still dark as midnight. As the bell sounded the hour, there came a knocking at the street door. I went down to open it with a light heart—for what had I *now* to fear? There entered three men, who introduced themselves, with perfect suavity, as officers of the police. A shriek had been heard by a neighbor during the night; suspicion of foul play had been aroused; information had been lodged at the police office, and they (the officers) had been deputed to search the premises.

I smiled—for *what* had I to fear? I bade the gentlemen welcome. The shriek, I said, was my own in a dream. The old man, I mentioned, was absent in the country. I took my visitors all over the house. I bade them search—search *well*. I led them, at length, to *his* chamber. I showed them his treasures, secure, undisturbed. In the enthusiasm of my confidence, I brought chairs into the room, and desired them *here* to rest from their fatigues, while I myself, in the wild audacity of my perfect triumph, placed my own seat upon the very spot beneath which reposed the corpse of the victim.

The officers were satisfied. My *manner* had convinced them. I was singularly at ease. They sat, and while I answered cheerily, they chatted familiar things. But, ere long, I felt myself getting pale and wished them gone. My head ached, and I fancied a ringing in my ears; but still they sat and chatted. The ringing became more distinct:—it continued and became more distinct: I talked more freely to get rid of the feeling: but it continued and gained definitiveness—until, at length, I found that the noise was *not* within my ears.

No doubt I now grew *very* pale;—but I talked more fluently, and with a heightened voice. Yet the sound increased—and what could I do? It was *a low, dull, quick sound—much such a sound as a watch makes when enveloped in cotton*. I gasped for breath—and yet the officers heard it not. I talked more quickly—more vehemently; but the noise steadily increased. I arose and argued about trifles, in a high key and with violent gesticulations, but the noise steadily increased. Why *would* they not be gone? I paced the floor to and fro with heavy strides, as if excited to fury by the observation of the men—but the noise steadily increased. Oh God! what *could* I do? I foamed—I raved—I swore! I swung the chair upon which I had been sitting, and grated it upon the boards, but the noise arose over all and continually increased. It grew louder—louder—*louder!* And still the men chatted pleasantly, and smiled. Was it possible they heard not? Almighty God!—no, no! They heard!—they suspected!—they *knew!*—they were making a mockery of my horror!—this I thought, and this I think. But any thing was better than this agony! Any thing was more tolerable than this derision! I could bear those hypocritical smiles no longer! I felt that I must scream or die!—and now—again!—hark! louder! louder! louder! *louder!*—

"Villains!" I shrieked, "dissemble no more! I admit the deed!—tear up the planks!—here, here!—it is the beating of his hideous heart!"

Once you have tasted the best you are spoiled for life.

I first read "An Occurrence at Owl Creek Bridge"—one of the most famous short stories in American literature, though I didn't know it at the time—when I was ten or eleven years old.

Soon thereafter I discovered Ray Bradbury, whose overwhelmingly sensual prose inspired me to write stories of my own. Bradbury's influence was so great that I began by shamelessly imitating him. Eventually, however, I felt the need to try a more detached style—the influence of J. D. Salinger, perhaps, whose superb *Nine Stories* were told coolly, in the third-person objective. But I also found that I was inclined toward an unsparing, even cruel realism, an attitude not often found in the writers I consciously believed were my role models. Other stories I knew and loved, from Collier, Matheson, Bloch and Roald Dahl, contained a leavening tone of irony and moral justice, something that did not seem to have a place in my work.

Now I realize the power of first impressions.

Rereading Bierce after so many years, I am struck by certain qualities that all but lift off the page in bas-relief; the first time around, I could not recognize how remarkable they were. For example the opening paragraphs, so clean and filled with details carefully selected by a journalist's impartial eye, as stark and immediate as the photographs of Matthew Brady, and described in the third-person objective. The seamless transition to the protagonist's point of view does not occur until several hundred words into the story. As a principle of style, this is something I was taught not to do—to change horses once the race has started, as it were. Bierce breaks that rule, and so smoothly that the effect is invisible. Later there is another, even more radical transition—from past to present tense in the penultimate paragraph, and then back again, all the way to third-person objective for the unforgettable closing lines.

In 1891.

I can find no word or phrase in the story to hint that it was written in another century. Yet here is a model of modern writing and economical storytelling from a time before Hemingway and Salinger, and before any critic thought to coin the term *minimalism*. I had remembered it as much longer, containing the kind of psychological development and revelation as are found only in lengthier works. In the edition I have it takes up only eleven pages.

This is a lesson in the art of writing that I have yet to master, a tour de force undiminished by changing fashion, as startling as a rifle shot in the sun or the snap of a neck at the end of a rope. Many stories written since may be read as echo and variation, but none is quite as strong as the original.

I thought I had forgotten my early encounter with Bierce, the author of a series of stories about mysterious disappearances who himself sank below the borders of consciousness, into Mexico (to ride with Villa, it is said, or to change his name to B. Traven, as I would like to imagine), but it turns out that he has remained very much with me, after all. Bierce's daring, control and utter denial of sentimentality are combined here in a virtuoso performance that remains unsurpassed, a Zen slap in the face to those of us who write short fiction, a reminder of how far we have to go. I was both fortunate and cursed to begin my reading in this field at the top. For once you have tasted the real thing, a genuine masterpiece, you can never be truly satisfied with anything less.

—Dennis Etchison

AN OCCURRENCE AT OWL CREEK BRIDGE
by Ambrose Bierce

A man stood upon a railroad bridge in northern Alabama, looking down into the swift water twenty feet below. The man's hands were behind his back, the wrists bound with a cord. A rope closely encircled his neck. It was attached to a stout cross-timber above his head and the slack fell to the level of his knees. Some loose boards laid upon the sleepers supporting the metals of the railway supplied a footing for him and his executioners—two private soldiers of the Federal army, directed by a sergeant who in civil life may have been a deputy sheriff. At a short remove upon the same temporary platform was an officer in the uniform of his rank, armed. He was a captain. A sentinel at each end of the bridge stood with his rifle in the position known as "support," that is to say, vertical in front of the left shoulder, the hammer resting on the forearm thrown straight across the chest—a formal and unnatural position, enforcing an erect carriage of the body. It did not appear to be the duty of these two men to know what was occurring at the centre of the bridge; they merely blockaded the two ends of the foot planking that traversed it.

Beyond one of the sentinels nobody was in sight; the railroad ran straight away into a forest for a hundred yards, then, curving, was lost to view. Doubtless there was an outpost farther along. The other bank of the stream was open ground—a gentle activity topped with a stockade of vertical tree trunks, loop-holed for rifles, with a single embrasure through which protruded the muzzle of a brass cannon commanding the bridge. Midway of the slope between bridge and fort were the spectators—a single company of infantry in line, at "parade rest," the butts of the rifles on the ground, the barrels inclining slightly backward against the right shoulder, the hands crossed upon the stock. A lieutenant stood at the right of the line, the point of his sword upon the ground, his left hand resting upon his right. Excepting the group of four at the centre of the bridge, not a man moved. The company faced the bridge, staring stonily, motionless. The sentinels, facing the banks of the stream, might have been statues to adorn the bridge. The captain stood with folded arms, silent, observing, the work of his subordinates, but making no sign. Death is a dignitary who when he comes announced is to be received with formal manifestations of respect, even by those most familiar with him. In the code of military etiquette silence and fixity are forms of deference.

The man who was engaged in being hanged was apparently about thirty-five years of age. He was a civilian, if one might judge from his habit, which was that of a planter. His features were good—a straight nose, firm mouth, broad forehead, from which his long, dark hair was combed straight back, falling behind his ears to the collar of his well-fitting frock coat. He wore a mustache and pointed beard, but no whiskers; his eyes were large and dark gray, and had a kindly expression which one would hardly have expected in one whose neck was in the hemp. Evidently this was no vulgar assassin. The liberal military code makes provision for hanging many kinds of persons, and gentlemen are not excluded.

The preparations being complete, the two private soldiers stepped aside and each drew away the plank upon which he had been standing. The sergeant turned to the captain, saluted and placed himself immediately behind that officer, who in turn moved apart one pace. These movements left the condemned man and the sergeant standing on the two ends of the same plank, which spanned three of the cross-ties of the bridge. The end upon which the civilian stood almost, but not quite, reached a fourth. This plank had been held in place by the weight of the captain; it was now held by that of the sergeant. At a signal from the former the latter would step aside, the plank would tilt and the condemned man go down between two ties. The arrangement commended itself to his judgment as simple and effective. His face had not been covered nor his eyes bandaged. He looked a moment at his "unsteadfast footing," then let his gaze wander to the swirling water of the stream racing madly beneath his feet. A piece of dancing driftwood caught his attention and his eyes followed it down the current. How slowly it appeared to move! What a sluggish stream!

He closed his eyes in order to fix his last thoughts upon

his wife and children. The water, touched to gold by the early sun, the brooding mists under the banks at some distance down the stream, the fort, the soldiers, the piece of drift—all had distracted him. And now he became conscious of a new disturbance. Striking through the thought of his dear ones was a sound which he could neither ignore nor understand, a sharp, distinct, metallic percussion like the stroke of a blacksmith's hammer upon the anvil; it had the same ringing quality. He wondered what it was, and whether immeasurably distant or nearby—it seemed both. Its recurrence was regular, but as slow as the tolling of a death knell. He awaited each stroke with impatience and—he knew not why—apprehension. The intervals of silence grew progressively longer; the delays became maddening. With their greater infrequency the sounds increased in strength and sharpness. They hurt his ears like the thrust of a knife; he feared he would shriek. What he heard was the ticking of his watch.

He unclosed his eyes and saw again the water below him. "If I could free my hands," he thought, "I might throw off the noose and spring into the stream. By diving I could evade the bullets and, swimming vigorously, reach the bank, take to the woods and get away home. My home, thank God, is as yet outside their lines; my wife and little ones are still beyond the invader's farthest advance."

As these thoughts, which have here to be set down in words, were flashed into the doomed man's brain rather than evolved from it the captain nodded to the sergeant. The sergeant stepped aside.

2

Peyton Farquhar was a well-to-do planter, of an old and highly respected Alabama family. Being a slave owner and like other slave owners a politician he was naturally an original secessionist and ardently devoted to the Southern cause.

Circumstances of an imperious nature, which it is unnecessary to relate here, had prevented him from taking service with the gallant army that had fought the disastrous campaigns ending with the fall of Corinth, and he chafed under the inglorious restraint, longing for the release of his energies, the larger life of the soldier, the opportunity for distinction. That opportunity, he felt, would come, as it comes to all in war time. Meanwhile he did what he could. No service was too humble for him to perform in aid of the South, no adventure too perilous for him to undertake if consistent with the character of a civilian who was at heart a soldier, and who in good faith and without too much qualification assented to at least a part of the frankly villainous dictum that all is fair in love and war.

One evening while Farquhar and his wife were sitting on a rustic bench near the entrance to his grounds, a gray-clad soldier rode up to the gate and asked for a drink of water. Mrs. Farquhar was only too happy to serve him with her own white hands. While she was fetching the water her husband approached the dusty horseman and inquired eagerly for news from the front.

"The Yanks are repairing the railroads," said the man, "and are getting ready for another advance. They have reached the Owl Creek bridge, put it in order and built a stockade on the north bank. The commandant has issued an order, which is posted everywhere, declaring that any civilian caught interfering with the railroad, its bridges, tunnels or trains will be summarily hanged. I saw the order."

"How far is it to the Owl Creek bridge?" Farquhar asked.

"About thirty miles."

"Is there no force on this side of the creek?"

"Only a picket post half a mile out, on the railroad, and a single sentinel at this end of the bridge."

"Suppose a man—a civilian and student of hanging—should elude the picket post and perhaps get the better of the sentinel," said Farquhar, smiling, "what could he accomplish?"

The soldier reflected. "I was there a month ago," he replied. "I observed that the flood of last winter had lodged a great quantity of driftwood against the wooden pier at this end of the bridge. It is now dry and would burn like tow."

The lady had now brought the water, which the soldier drank. He thanked her ceremoniously, bowed to her husband and rode away. An hour later, after nightfall, he repassed the plantation, going northward in the direction from which he had come. He was a Federal scout.

3

As Peyton Farquhar fell straight downward through the bridge he lost consciousness and was as one already dead. From this state he was awakened—ages later, it seemed to him—by the pain of a sharp pressure upon his throat, followed by a sense of suffocation. Keen, poignant agonies seemed to shoot from his neck downward through every fibre of his body and limbs. These pains appeared to flash along well-defined lines of ramification and to beat with an inconceivably rapid periodicity. They seemed like streams of pulsating fire heating him to an intolerable temperature. As to his head, he was conscious of nothing but a feeling of fullness—of congestion. These sensations were unaccompanied by thought. The intellectual part of his nature was already effaced; he had power only to feel, and feeling was torment. He was conscious of motion. Encompassed in a luminous cloud, of which he was now merely the fiery heart, without material substance, he swung through unthinkable arcs of oscillation, like a vast pendulum. Then all at once, with terrible suddenness, the light about him shot upward with the noise of a loud splash; a frightful roaring was in his ears, and all was cold and dark. The power of thought was restored; he knew that the rope had broken and he had fallen into the stream. There was no additional strangulation; the noose about his neck was already suffocating him and kept the water from his lungs. To die of hanging at the bottom of a river!—the idea seemed to him ludicrous. He opened his eyes in the darkness and saw above him a gleam of light, but how distant, how inaccessible! He was still sinking, for the light became fainter and fainter until it was a mere glimmer. Then it began to grow and brighten, and he knew that he was rising toward the surface—knew it with reluctance, for he was now very comfortable. "To be hanged and drowned," he thought, "that is not so bad; but I do not wish to be shot. No; I will not be shot; that is not fair."

He was not conscious of an effort, but a sharp pain in his wrist apprised him that he was trying to free his hands. He gave the struggle his attention, as an idler might observe the feat of a juggler, without interest in the outcome. What splendid effort!—what magnificent, what superhuman strength! Ah, that was a fine endeavor! Bravo! The cord fell away; his arms parted and floated upward, the hands dimly seen on each side in the growing light. He watched them with a new interest as first one and then the other pounced upon the noose at his neck. They tore it away and thrust it fiercely aside, its undulations resembling those of a water-snake. "Put it back, put it back!" He thought he shouted these words to his hands, for the undoing of the noose had been succeeded by the direst pang that he had yet experienced. His neck ached horribly; his brain was on fire; his heart, which had been fluttering faintly, gave a great leap, trying to force itself out at his mouth. His whole body was racked and wrenched with an insupportable anguish! But his disobedient hands gave no heed to the command. They beat the water vigorously with quick, downward strokes, forcing him to the surface. He felt his head emerge; his eyes were blinded by the sunlight; his chest expanded convulsively, and with a supreme and crowning agony his lungs engulfed a great draught of air, which instantly he expelled in a shriek!

He was now in full possession of his physical senses. They were, indeed, preternaturally keen and alert. Something in the awful disturbance of his organic system had so exalted and refined them that they made record of things never before perceived. He felt the ripples upon his face and heard their separate sounds as they struck. He looked at the forest on the bank of the stream, saw the individual trees, the leaves and the veining of each leaf—saw the very insects upon them: the locusts, the brilliant-bodied flies, the gray spiders stretching their webs from twig to twig. He noted the prismatic colors in all the dewdrops upon a million blades of grass. The humming of the gnats that danced above the eddies of the stream, the beating of the dragon-flies' wings, the strokes of the water-spiders' legs, like oars which had lifted their boat—all these made audible music. A fish slid along beneath his eyes and he heard the rush of its body parting the water.

He had come to the surface facing down the stream; in a moment the visible world seemed to wheel slowly round, himself the pivotal point, and he saw the bridge, the fort, the soldiers upon the bridge, the captain, the sergeant, the two privates, his executioners. They were in silhouette against the blue sky. They shouted and gesticulated, pointing at him. The captain had drawn his pistol, but did not fire; the others were unarmed. Their movements were grotesque and horrible, their forms gigantic.

Suddenly he heard a sharp report and something struck the water smartly within a few inches of his head, spattering his face with spray. He heard a second report, and saw one of the sentinels with his rifle at his shoulder, a light cloud of blue smoke rising from the muzzle. The man in the water saw the eye of the man on the bridge gazing into his own through the sights of the rifle. He observed that it was a gray eye and remembered having read that gray eyes were keenest, and that all famous marksmen had them. Nevertheless, this one had missed.

A counter-swirl had caught Farquhar and turned him half round; he was again looking into the forest on the bank opposite the fort. The sound of a clear, high voice in a monotonous singsong now rang out behind him and came across the water with a distinctness that pierced and subdued all other sounds, even the beating of the ripples in his ears. Although no soldier, he had frequented camps enough to know the dread significance of that deliberate, drawling, aspirated chant; the lieutenant on shore was taking a part in the morning's work. How coldly and pitilessly—with what an even, calm intonation, presaging, and enforcing tranquillity in the men—with what accurately measured intervals fell those cruel words.

"Attention, company! . . . Shoulder arms! . . . Ready! . . . Aim! . . . Fire!"

Farquhar dived—dived as deeply as he could. The water roared in his ears like the voice of Niagara, yet he heard the dulled thunder of the volley and, rising again toward the surface, met shining bits of metal, singularly flattened, oscillating slowly downward. Some of them touched him on the face and hands, then fell away, continuing their descent. One lodged between his collar and neck; it was uncomfortably warm and he snatched it out.

As he rose to the surface, gasping for breath, he saw that he had been a long time under water; he was perceptibly farther down stream—nearer to safety. The soldiers had almost finished reloading; the metal ramrods flashed all at once in the sunshine as they were drawn from the barrels, turned in the air, and thrust into their sockets. The two sentinels fired again, independently and ineffectually.

The hunted man saw all this over his shoulder; he was now swimming vigorously with the current. His brain was

as energetic as his arms and legs; he thought with the ra-
pidity of lightning.

"The officer," he reasoned, "will not make that martinet's
error a second time. It is as easy to dodge a volley as a
single shot. He has probably already given the command to
fire at will. God help me, I cannot dodge them all!"

An appalling splash within two yards of him was followed by a loud, rushing sound, *diminuendo,* which seemed
to travel back through the air to the fort and died in an explosion which stirred the very river to its deeps! A rising
sheet of water curved over him, fell down upon him, blinded
him, strangled him! The cannon had taken a hand in the
game. As he shook his head free from the commotion of
the smitten water he heard the deflected shot humming
through the air ahead, and in an instant it was cracking and
smashing the branches in the forest beyond.

"They will not do that again," he thought; "the next time
they will use a charge of grape. I must keep my eye upon
the gun; the smoke will apprise me—the report arrives too
late; it lags behind the missile. That is a good gun."

Suddenly he felt himself whirled round and round—spin-
ning like a top. The water, the banks, the forests, the now
distant bridge, fort and men—all were commingled and
blurred. Objects were represented by their colors only; circular horizontal streaks of color—that was all he saw. He
had been caught in a vortex and was being whirled on with
a velocity of advance and gyration that made him giddy
and sick. In a few moments he was flung upon the gravel
at the foot of the left bank of the stream—the southern
bank—and behind a projecting point which concealed him
from his enemies. The sudden arrest of his motion, the abra-
sion of one of his hands on the gravel, restored him, and
he wept with delight. He dug his fingers into the sand, threw
it over himself in handfuls and audibly blessed it. It looked
like diamonds, rubies, emeralds; he could think of nothing
beautiful which it did not resemble. The trees upon the bank

were giant garden plants; he noted a definite order in their arrangement, inhaled the fragrance of their blooms. A strange, roseate light shone through the spaces among their trunks and the wind made in their branches the music of aeolian harps. He had no wish to perfect his escape—was content to remain in that enchanting spot until retaken.

A whiz and rattle of grapeshot among the branches high above his head roused him from his dream. The baffled cannoneer had fired him a random farewell. He sprang to his feet, rushed up the sloping bank, and plunged into the forest.

All that day he traveled, laying his course by the rounding sun. The forest seemed interminable; nowhere did he discover a break in it, not even a woodman's road. He had not known that he lived in so wild a region. There was something uncanny in the revelation.

By nightfall, he was fatigued, footsore, famishing. The thought of his wife and children urged him on. At last he found a road which led him in what he knew to be the right direction. It was as wide and straight as a city street, yet it seemed untraveled. No fields bordered it, no dwelling anywhere. Not so much as the barking of a dog suggested human habitation. The black bodies of the trees formed a straight wall on both sides, terminating on the horizon in a point, like a diagram in a lesson in perspective. Overhead, as he looked up through this rift in the wood, shone great golden stars looking unfamiliar and grouped in strange constellations. He was sure they were arranged in some order which had a secret and malign significance. The wood on either side was full of singular noises, among which—once, twice, and again—he distinctly heard whispers in an unknown tongue.

His neck was in pain and lifting his hand to it he found it horribly swollen. He knew that it had a circle of black where the rope had bruised it. His eyes felt congested; he could no longer close them. His tongue was swollen with

thirst; he relieved its fever by thrusting it forward from between his teeth into the cold air. How softly the turf had
carpeted the untraveled avenue—he could no longer feel the
roadway beneath his feet!

Doubtless, despite his suffering, he had fallen asleep
while walking, for now he sees another scene—perhaps he
has merely recovered from a delirium. He stands at the gate
of his own home. All is as he left it, and all bright and
beautiful in the morning sunshine. He must have traveled
the entire night. As he pushes open the gate and passes up
the wide white walk, he sees a flutter of female garments;
his wife, looking fresh and cool and sweet, steps down from
the veranda to meet him. At the bottom of the steps she
stands waiting, with a smile of ineffable joy, an attitude of
matchless grace and dignity. Ah, how beautiful she is! He
springs forward with extended arms. As he is about to clasp
her he feels a stunning blow upon the back of the neck; a
blinding white light blazes all about him with a sound like
the shock of a cannon—then all is darkness and silence!

Peyton Farquhar was dead; his body, with a broken neck,
swung gently from side to side beneath the timbers of the
Owl Creek bridge.

Sight unseen, *tabula rasa* as regards the passion, quality or intensity of weirdness passim the selections made by my co-anthologees in this volume, I am willing to bet at least five bucks that "The Human Chair" is the most bizarre story on the table of contents. I am willing to put my money where my story-judgment is.

This story is, by a skosh, my favoritest of the four top faves I always name when people ask me, "what is your favorite horror story?" It commands my adoration because . . .

But wait. A moment's pause.

Let us play a little game, just the two of us, you and I. I will say something, and you repeat it. Here we go:

Edogawa Rampo.

Not bad. Let's try that again. Like this: Ed-O-Gah-Wah Ram-Po. Edogawa Rampo. Say it again. Edogawa Rampo. Now say it faster. Edogawa Rampo. Faster, go faster, say it faster, and slur it a little.

Edogawa Rampo, Edagarapo, Edgarawanpo, Edgarawanpoe.

Edgar Allan Poe.

The pseudonym is a homonym. In Japanese, the pronunciation of the sainted Poe's name becomes:

Edogawa Rampo. The pen name of Taro Hirai (1894– 1965), who is universally acknowledged as "the father of the Japanese mystery." That isn't *my* judgment, it was the encomium written by the late Ellery Queen in "their" classic history of the mystery story *Queen's Quorum* (1951, revised 1969). The Messrs. "Queen" placed Rampo in the period between Agatha Christie and Edgar Wallace when they listed the world's most famous creators of short mystery stories. That Queen—certainly one of the finest of the top half-dozen authors of, and students of the history of, mystery fiction—was enormously inveigled by Rampo and his *oeuvre* blazes in every word of his subsequent introduction to the 1971 anthology *Ellery Queen's Japanese Golden Dozen*:

"Edogawa Rampo's name has a familiar sound to Western ears; if one says the name aloud, and keeps repeating it, the name becomes a verbal translation of the Japanese pronunciation of Edgar Allan Poe . . . . Then, in

1923, Edogawa Rampo founded a native Japanese school. The first original Japanese mystery story was his 'Nisen Doka' ('The Two-Sen Copper Coin'), which appeared in *Shin-seinen* (New Youth), the only mystery magazine published in all Japan at that time. The detective tie with China, if not with the West, was broken forever. . . . The period from 1923 to its end just before World War II, the period of the modern Japanese detective story, Rampo's period, is called the Tantei era. Tantei means 'to solve a puzzle,' and the emphasis in this period was on the qualities that distinguished The Golden Age of the Detective Story in the West, between 1920 and 1940 . . ."

As a full-service author, here not merely to tickle your risibilities, but to broaden your knowledge, I have slathered all that background data into what would otherwise be merely another gibbering rave for a favorite piece of reading matter, because I think it is a crying shame that Rampo is probably unknown to most of you reading this anthology. Tsk-tsk.

It is, of course, just one more manifestation of our provincial American attitude toward international literature. If it has to be translated, if it ain't in English (and occasionally French), if it ain't upfront in the mass market racks of Borders, or as a pop-up on Amazon.com, it has about as much weight and corporeality as a Dixie Cup full of ectoplasm.

Well, at close of day, that is neither here nor there. It just *is*. But that doesn't mean I'm going to miss this plangent moment, to hype Rampo to the skies, in aid of explaining *why,* of all the great horror fiction that has compelled my attention since childhood, the story I've selected here is the top-line, best-in-show, absolute creepy best horror yarn I've ever read.

The title, in Japanese, is "Ningen isu." It was written in 1925, but it didn't appear in English till 1956. I encountered it in 1962 in a Crest paperback anthology of detective stories edited by the estimable (though now, sadly, mostly forgotten) novelist David Alexander. It was the fourteenth Mystery Writers of American anthology *Tales For A Rainy Night,* as smart and offbeat a gathering of little-known fictions as I've ever encountered. And there, amid Borges and Miriam Allen de Ford and Anthony Boucher and

Stanley Ellin, there lying all unassuming and innocent seeming, was this . . . this . . . poisonous mushroom. This construct of cold shark eyes and curare, a confection as deadly as the darkest desires to which we are prone, and to which we will never admit.

I read this story late at night, in a treehouse surrounded by wind and darkness and the ominous fingernails on slate of tree branches that raked the sides of that tiny eyrie. I tell you this sans hyperbole: it scared the living crap out of me.

There is only one book of Edogawa Rampo's stories in English. It was published by Tuttle, many years ago, and they kept it in print for decades . . . then let it go away. It is called *Japanese Tales of Mystery and Imagination*, thus demonstrating Rampo's admiration for Poe. It is a book *more* than worthy of your time browsing the stacks of used bookstores, or your ass-asleep time surfing the antiquarian book.coms of the Web. Nine stories with titles like "The Hell of Mirrors" and "The Traveler With the Pasted Rag Picture." They will unhinge you.

This was a *great* writer, *sui generis.* That you do not know his brilliance, till now, is a shame. But that you now come to "The Human Chair" all innocent and unwary, despite my cautions, makes you an object of envy. *You* are about to have that cathartic *frisson* of terror and awakening that once I knew on a cold night beneath the bone-scraping branches.

I envy you. And I can't wait to see your face when you read the last page.

—Harlan Ellison

THE HUMAN CHAIR
by Edogawa Rampo

Oshiko saw her husband off to his work at the Foreign Office at a little past ten o'clock. Then, now that her time was once again her very own, she shut herself up in the study she shared with her husband to resume work on the story she was to submit for the special summer issue of *K*—magazine.

She was a versatile writer with high literary talent and a smooth-flowing style. Even her husband's popularity as a diplomat was overshadowed by hers as an authoress.

Daily she was overwhelmed with letters from readers praising her works. In fact, this very morning, as soon as she sat down before her desk, she immediately proceeded to glance through the numerous letters which the morning mail had brought. Without exception, in content they all followed the same pattern, but prompted by her deep feminine sense of consideration, she always read through each piece of correspondence addressed to her, whether monotonous or interesting.

Taking the short and simple letters first, she quickly noted their contents. Finally she came to one which was a bulky, manuscript-like sheaf of pages. Although she had not received any advance notice that a manuscript was to be sent her, still it was not uncommon for her to receive the efforts of amateur writers seeking her valuable criticism. In most cases these were long-winded, pointless, and yawn-provoking attempts at writing. Nevertheless, she now opened the envelope in her hand and took out the numerous, closely written sheets.

As she had anticipated, it was a manuscript, carefully bound. But somehow, for some unknown reason, there was neither a title nor a by-line. The manuscript began abruptly:

"Dear Madam: . . ."

Momentarily she reflected. Maybe, after all, it was just a letter. Unconsciously her eyes hurried on to read two or three lines, and then gradually she became absorbed in a strangely gruesome narrative. Her curiosity aroused to the bursting point and spurred on by some unknown magnetic force, she continued to read:

Dear Madam: I do hope you will forgive this presumptuous letter from a complete stranger. What I am about to write, Madam, may shock you no end. However, I am determined to lay bare before you a confession—my own— and to describe in detail the terrible crime I have committed.

For many months I have hidden myself away from the light of civilization, hidden, as it were, like the devil himself. In this whole wide world no one knows of my deeds. However, quite recently a queer change took place in my conscious mind, and I just couldn't bear to keep my secret any longer. I simply had to confess!

All that I have written so far must certainly have awakened only perplexity in your mind. However, I beseech you to bear with me and kindly read my communication to the bitter end, because if you do, you will fully understand the strange workings of my mind and the reason why it is to you in particular that I make this confession.

I am really at a loss as to where to begin, for the facts which I am setting forth are all so grotesquely out of the ordinary. Frankly, words fail me, for human words seem utterly inadequate to sketch all the details. But, nevertheless, I will try to lay bare the events in chronological order, just as they happened.

First let me explain that I am ugly beyond description. Please bear this fact in mind; otherwise I fear that if and when you do grant my ultimate request and *do* see me, you may be shocked and horrified at the sight of my face— after so many months of unsanitary living. However, I implore you to believe me when I state that, despite the extreme ugliness of my face, within my heart there has always burned a pure and overwhelming passion!

Next, let me explain that I am a humble workman by trade. Had I been born in a well-to-do family, I might have found the power, with money, to ease the torture of my soul brought on by my ugliness. Or perhaps, if I had been endowed by nature with artistic talents, I might again have been able to forget my bestial countenance and seek consolation in music or poetry. But, unblessed with any such talents, and being the unfortunate creature that I am, I had no trade to turn to except that of a humble cabinet-maker. Eventually my specialty became that of making assorted types of chairs.

In this particular line I was fairly successful, to such a degree in fact that I gained the reputation of being able to satisfy any kind of order, no matter how complicated. For this reason, in woodworking circles I came to enjoy the special privilege of accepting only orders for luxury chairs, with complicated requests for unique carvings, new designs for the back-rest and arm-supports, fancy padding for the cushions and seat—all work of a nature which called for skilled hands and patient trial and study, work which an amateur craftsman could hardly undertake.

The reward for all my pains, however, lay in the sheer delight of creating. You may even consider me a braggart when you hear this, but it all seemed to me to be the same type of thrill which a true artist feels upon creating a masterpiece.

As soon as a chair was completed, it was my usual custom to sit on it to see how it felt, and despite the dismal life of one of my humble profession, at such moments I experienced an indescribable thrill. Giving my mind free rein, I used to imagine the types of people who would eventually curl up in the chair, certainly people of nobility, living in palatial residences, with exquisite, priceless paintings hanging on the walls, glittering crystal chandeliers hanging from the ceilings, expensive rugs on the floor, etc.; and one particular chair, which I imagined standing before a mahogany table, gave me the vision of fragrant Western flowers scenting the air with sweet perfume. Enwrapped in these strange visions, I came to feel that I, too, belonged to such settings, and I derived no end of pleasure from imagining myself to be an influential figure in society.

Foolish thoughts such as these kept coming to me in

rapid succession. Imagine, Madam, the pathetic figure I made, sitting comfortably in a luxurious chair of my own making and pretending that I was holding hands with the girl of my dreams. As was always the case, however, the noisy chattering of the uncouth women of the neighborhood and the hysterical shrieking, babbling, and wailing of their children quickly dispelled all my beautiful dreams; again grim reality reared its ugly head before my eyes.

Once back to earth I again found myself a miserable creature, a helpless crawling worm! And as for my beloved, that angelic woman, she too vanished like a mist. I cursed myself for my folly! Why, even the dirty women tending babies in the streets did not so much as bother to glance in my direction. Every time I completed a new chair I was haunted by feelings of utter despair. And with the passing of the months, my long-accumulated misery was enough to choke me.

One day I was charged with the task of making a huge, leather-covered armchair, of a type I had never before conceived, for a foreign hotel located in Yokohama. Actually, this particular type of chair was to have been imported from abroad, but through the persuasion of my employer, who admired my skill as a chair-maker, I received the order.

In order to live up to my reputation as a super-craftsman, I began to devote myself seriously to my new assignment. Steadily I became so engrossed in my labors that at times I even skipped food and sleep. Really, it would be no exaggeration to state that the job became my very life, every fiber of the wood I used seemingly linked to my heart and soul.

At last when the chair was completed, I experienced a satisfaction hitherto unknown, for I honestly believed I had achieved a piece of work which immeasurably surpassed all my other creations. As before, I rested the weight of my body on the four legs that supported the chair, first dragging it to a sunny spot on the porch of my workshop. What

comfort! What supreme luxury! Not too hard or too soft,
the springs seemed to match the cushion with uncanny precision. And as for the leather, what an alluring touch it possessed! This chair not only supported the person who sat
in it, but it also seemed to embrace and to hug. Still further, I also noted the perfect reclining angle of the back-
support, the delicate puffy swelling of the arm-rests, the
perfect symmetry of each of the component parts. Surely,
no product could have expressed with greater eloquence the
definition of the word "comfort."

I let my body sink deeply into the chair and, caressing
the two arm-rests with my hands, gasped with genuine s
atisfaction and pleasure.

Again my imagination began to play its usual tricks raising strange fancies in my mind. The scene which I imagined now rose before my eyes so vividly that, for a moment,
I asked myself if I were not slowly going insane. While in
this mental condition, a weird idea suddenly leaped to my
mind. Assuredly, it was the whispering of the devil himself. Although it was a sinister idea, it attracted me with a
powerful magnetism which I found impossible to resist.

At first, no doubt, the idea found its seed in my secret
yearning to keep the chair for myself. Realizing, however,
that this was totally out of the question, I next longed to
accompany the chair wherever it went. Slowly but steadily,
as I continued to nurse this fantastic notion, my mind fell
into the grip of an almost terrifying temptation. Imagine,
Madam, I really and actually made up my mind to carry
out that awful scheme to the end, come what may!

Quickly I took the armchair apart, and then put it together again to suit my weird purposes. As it was a large
armchair, with the seat covered right down to the level of
the floor, and furthermore, as the back rest and arm-supports
were all large in dimensions, I soon contrived to make the
cavity inside large enough to accommodate a man without
any danger of exposure. Of course, my work was hampered

by the large amount of wooden framework and the springs inside, but with my usual skill as a craftsman I remodeled the chair so that the knees could be placed below the seat, the torso and the head inside the back-rest. Seated thus in the cavity, one could remain perfectly concealed.

As this type of craftsmanship came as second nature to me, I also added a few finishing touches, such as improved acoustics to catch outside noises and of course a peep-hole cut out in the leather but absolutely unnoticeable. Furthermore, I also provided storage space for supplies, wherein I placed a few boxes of hardtack and a water bottle. For another of nature's needs I also inserted a large rubber bag, and by the time I finished fitting the interior of the chair with these and other unique facilities, it had become quite a habitable place, but not for longer than two or three days at a stretch.

Completing my weird task, I stripped down to my waist and buried myself inside the chair. Just imagine the strange feeling I experienced, Madam! Really, I felt that I had buried myself in a lonely grave. Upon careful reflection I realized that it was indeed a grave. As soon as I entered the chair I was swallowed up by complete darkness, and to everyone else in the world I no longer existed!

Presently a messenger arrived from the dealer's to take delivery of the armchair, bringing with him a large handcart. My apprentice, the only person with whom I lived, was utterly unaware of what had happened. I saw him talking to the messenger.

While my chair was being loaded onto the handcart, one of the cart-pullers exclaimed: "Good God! This chair certainly is heavy! It must weigh a ton!"

When I heard this, my heart leaped to my mouth. However, as the chair itself was obviously an extraordinarily heavy one, no suspicions were aroused, and before long I could feel the vibration of the rattling handcart being pulled along the streets. Of course, I worried incessantly, but at length, that same afternoon, the armchair in which I was concealed was placed with a thud on the floor of a room in the hotel. Later I discovered that it was not an ordinary room, but the lobby.

Now as you may already have guessed long ago, my key motive in this mad venture was to leave my hole in the chair when the coast was clear, loiter around the hotel, and start stealing. Who would dream that a man was concealed inside a chair? Like a fleeting shadow I could ransack every room at will, and by the time any alarm was sounded, I would be safe and sound inside my sanctuary, holding my breath and observing the ridiculous antics of the people outside looking for me.

Possibly you have heard of the hermit crab that is often found on coastal rocks. Shaped like a large spider, this crab crawls about stealthily and, as soon as it hears footsteps, quickly retreats into an empty shell, from which hiding place, with gruesome, hairy front legs partly exposed, it looks furtively about. I was just like this freak monster-crab. But instead of a shell, I had a better shield—a chair which would conceal me far more effectively.

As you can imagine, my plan was so unique and original, so utterly unexpected, that no one was ever the wiser. Consequently, my adventure was a complete success. On the third day after my arrival at the hotel I discovered that I had already taken in quite a haul.

Imagine the thrill and excitement of being able to rob to my heart's content, not to mention the fun derived from observing the people rushing hither and thither only a few inches away under my very nose, shouting: "The thief went this way!" and: "He went that way!" Unfortunately, I do not have the time to describe all my experiences in detail. Rather, allow me to proceed with my narrative and tell you of a far greater source of weird joy which I managed to discover—in fact, what I am about to relate now is the key point of this letter.

First, however, I must request you to turn your thoughts back to the moment when my chair—and I—were both placed in the lobby of the hotel. As soon as the chair was put on the floor all the various members of the staff took turns testing out the seat. After the novelty wore off they all left the room, and then silence reigned, absolute and complete. However, I could not find the courage to leave my sanctum, for I began to imagine a thousand dangers. For what seemed like ages I kept my ears alerted for the slightest sound. After a while I heard heavy footsteps drawing near, evidently from the direction of the corridor. The next moment the unknown feet must have started to tread on heavy carpet, for the walking sound died out completely.

Some time later the sound of a man panting, all out of breath, assailed my ears. Before I could anticipate what the next development would be, a large, heavy body like that of a European fell on my knees and seemed to bounce two or three times before settling down. With just a thin layer of leather between the seat of his trousers and my knees, I could almost feel the warmth of his body. As for his broad, muscular shoulders, they rested flatly against my chest, while his two heavy arms were deposited squarely on mine. I could imagine this individual puffing away at his cigar, for the strong aroma came floating to my nostrils.

Just imagine yourself in my queer position, Madam, and reflect for a brief moment on the utterly unnatural state of affairs. As for myself, however, I was utterly frightened, so much so that I crouched in my dark hideout as if petrified, cold sweat running down my armpits.

Beginning with this individual, several people "sat on my knees" that day, as if they had patiently awaited their turn. No one, however, suspected even for a fleeting moment that the soft "cushion" on which they were sitting was actually human flesh with blood circulating in its veins—confined in a strange world of darkness.

What was it about this mystic hole that fascinated me

so? I somehow felt like an animal living in a totally new world. And as for the people who lived in the world outside, I could distinguish them only as people who made weird noises, breathed heavily, talked, rustled their clothes, and possessed soft, round bodies.

Gradually I could begin to distinguish the sitters just by the sense of touch rather than of sight. Those who were fat felt like large jellyfish, while those who were especially thin made me feel that I was supporting a skeleton. Other distinguishing factors consisted of the curve of the spine, the breadth of the shoulder blades, the length of the arms, and the thickness of their thighs as well as the contour of their bottoms. It may seem strange, but I speak nothing but the truth when I say that, although all people may seem alike, there are countless distinguishing traits among all men which can be "seen" merely by the feel of their bodies. In fact, there are just as many differences as in the case of fingerprints or facial contours. This theory, of course, also applies to female bodies.

Usually women are classified in two large categories— the plain and the beautiful. However, in my dark, confined world inside the chair, facial merits or demerits were of secondary importance, being overshadowed by the more meaningful qualities found in the feel of flesh, the sound of the voice, body odor. (Madam, I do hope you will not be offended by the boldness with which I sometimes speak.)

And so, to continue with my narration, there was one girl—the first who ever sat on me—who kindled in my heart a passionate love. Judging solely by her voice, she was European. At the moment, although there was no one else present in the room, her heart must have been filled with happiness, because she was singing with a sweet voice when she came tripping into the room.

Soon I heard her standing immediately in front of my chair, and without giving any warning she suddenly burst into laughter. The very next moment I could hear her flapping her arms like a fish struggling in a net, and then she sat down—on me! For a period of about thirty minutes she continued to sing, moving her body and feet in tempo with her melody.

For me this was quite an unexpected development, for I had always held aloof from all members of the opposite sex because of my ugly face. Now I realized that I was present in the same room with a European girl whom I had never seen, my skin virtually touching hers through a thin layer of leather.

Unaware of my presence, she continued to act with unreserved freedom, doing as she pleased. Inside the chair, I could visualize myself hugging her, kissing her snowy white neck—if only I could remove that layer of leather. . . .

Following this somewhat unhallowed but nevertheless enjoyable experience, I forgot all about my original intentions of committing robbery. Instead, I seemed to be plunging headlong into a new whirlpool of maddening pleasure.

Long I pondered: "Maybe I was destined to enjoy this type of existence." Gradually the truth seemed to dawn on me. For those who were as ugly and as shunned as myself, it was assuredly wiser to enjoy life inside a chair. For in this strange, dark world I could hear and touch all desirable creatures.

Love in a chair! This may seem altogether too fantastic. Only one who has actually experienced it will be able to vouch for the thrills and the joys it provides. Of course, it is a strange sort of love, limited to the senses of touch, hearing, and smell, a love burning in a world of darkness.

Believe it or not, many of the events that take place in this world are beyond full understanding. In the beginning I had intended only to perpetrate a series of robberies, and then flee. Now, however, I became so attached to my "quarters" that I adjusted them more and more to permanent living.

In my nocturnal prowling I always took the greatest of

precautions, watching each step I took, hardly making a sound. Hence there was little danger of being detected. When I recall, however, that I spent several months inside the chair without being discovered even once, it indeed surprises even me.

For the better part of each day I remained inside the chair, sitting like a contortionist with my arms folded and knees bent. As a consequence, I felt as if my whole body was paralyzed. Furthermore, as I could never stand up straight, my muscles became taut and inflexible, and gradually I began to crawl instead of walk to the washroom. What a madman I was! Even in the face of all these sufferings I could not persuade myself to abandon my folly and leave that weird world of sensual pleasure.

In the hotel, although there were several guests who stayed for a month or even two, making the place their home, there was always a constant inflow of new guests, and an equal exodus of the old. As a result I could never manage to enjoy a permanent love. Even now, as I bring back to mind all my "love affairs," I can recall nothing but the touch of warm flesh.

Some of the women possessed the firm bodies of ponies; others seemed to have the slimy bodies of snakes; and still others had bodies composed of nothing but fat, giving them the bounce of a rubber ball. There were also the unusual exceptions who seemed to have bodies made only of sheer muscle, like artistic Greek statues. But notwithstanding the species or types, one and all had a special magnetic allure quite distinctive from the others, and I was perpetually shifting the object of my passions.

At one time, for example, an internationally famous dancer came to Japan and happened to stay at this same hotel. Although she sat in my chair only on one single occasion, the contact of her smooth, soft flesh against my own afforded me a hitherto unknown thrill. So divine was the touch of her body that I felt inspired to a state of positive exaltation. On this occasion, instead of my carnal instincts being aroused, I simply felt like a gifted artist being caressed by the magic wand of a fairy.

Strange, eerie episodes followed in rapid succession. However, as space prohibits, I shall refrain from giving a detailed description of each and every case. Instead, I shall continue to outline the general course of events.

One day, several months following my arrival at the hotel, there suddenly occurred an unexpected change in the shape of my destiny. For some reason the foreign proprietor of the hotel was forced to leave for his homeland, and as a result the management was transferred to Japanese hands.

Originating from this change in proprietorship, a new policy was adopted, calling for a drastic retrenchment in expenditures, abolishment of luxurious fittings, and other steps to increase profits through economy. One of the first results of this new policy was that the management put all the extravagant furnishings of the hotel up for auction. Included in the list of items for sale was my chair.

When I learned of this new development, I immediately felt the greatest of disappointments. Soon, however, a voice inside me advised that I should return to the natural world outside—and spend the tidy sum I had acquired by stealing. I of course realized that I would no longer have to return to my humble life as a craftsman, for actually I was comparatively wealthy. The thought of my new role in society seemed to overcome my disappointment in having to leave the hotel. Also, when I reflected deeply on all the pleasures which I had derived there, I was forced to admit that, although my "love affairs" had been many, they had all been with foreign women and that somehow something had always been lacking.

I then realized fully and deeply that as a Japanese I really craved a lover of my own kind. While I was turning these thoughts over in my mind, my chair—with me still in it— was sent to a furniture store to be sold at auction. Maybe this time, I told myself, the chair will be purchased by a Japanese home. With my fingers crossed, I decided to be patient and to continue with my existence in the chair a while longer.

Although I suffered for two or three days in my chair while it stood in front of the furniture store, eventually it came up for sale and was promptly purchased. This, fortunately, was because of the excellent workmanship which had gone into its making, and although it was no longer new, it still had a "dignified bearing."

The purchaser was a high-ranking official who lived in Tokyo. When I was being transferred from the furniture store to the man's palatial residence, the bouncing and vibrating of the vehicle almost killed me. I gritted my teeth and bore up bravely, however, comforted by the thought that at last I had been bought by a Japanese.

Inside his house I was placed in a spacious Western-style study. One thing about the room which gave me the greatest of satisfactions was the fact that my chair was meant more for the use of his young and attractive wife than for his own.

Within a month I had come to be with the wife constantly, united with her as one, so to speak. With the exception of the dining and sleeping hours, her soft body was always seated on my knees for the simple reason that she was engaged in a deep-thinking task.

You have no idea how much I loved this lady! She was the first Japanese woman with whom I had ever come into such close contact, and moreover she possessed a wonderfully appealing body. She seemed the answer to all my prayers! Compared with this, all my other "affairs" with the various women in the hotel seemed like childish flirtations, nothing more.

Proof of the mad love which I now cherished for this intellectual lady was found in the fact that I longed to hold her every moment of the time. When she was away, even for a fleeting moment, I waited for her return like a love-crazed Romeo yearning for his Juliet. Such feelings I had never hitherto experienced.

Gradually I came to want to convey my feelings to her . . . somehow. I tried vainly to carry out my purpose, but always encountered a blank wall, for I was absolutely helpless. Oh how I longed to have her reciprocate my love! Yes, you may consider this the confession of a madman, for I *was* mad—madly in love with her!

But how could I signal to her? If I revealed myself, the shock of the discovery would immediately prompt her to call her husband and the servants. And that, of course, would be fatal to me, for exposure would not only mean disgrace, but severe punishment for the crimes I had committed.

I therefore decided on another course of action, namely, to add in every way to her comfort and thus awaken in her a natural love for—the chair! As she was a true artist, I somehow felt confident that her natural love of beauty would guide her in the direction I desired. And as for myself, I was willing to find pure contentment in the love even for a material object, for I could find solace in the belief that her delicate feelings of love for even a mere chair were powerful enough to penetrate to the creature that dwelt inside . . . which was myself!

In every way I endeavored to make her more comfortable every time she placed her weight on my chair. Whenever she became tired from sitting long in one position on my humble person, I would slowly move my knees and embrace her more warmly, making her more snug. And when she dozed off to sleep I would move my knees, ever so softly, to rock her into a deeper slumber.

Somehow, possibly by a miracle (or was it just my imagination?), this lady now seemed to love my chair deeply, for every time she sat down she acted like a baby falling into a mother's embrace, or a girl surrendering herself into the arms of her lover. And when she moved herself about in the chair, I felt that she was feeling an almost amorous joy. In this way the fire of my love and passion rose into a leaping flame that could never be extinguished, and I finally reached a stage where I simply had to make a strange, bold plea.

Ultimately I began to feel that if she would just look at me, even for a brief passing moment, I could die with the deepest contentment.

No doubt, Madam, by this time, you must certainly have guessed who the object of my mad passion is. To put it explicitly, she happens to be none other than yourself, Madam! Ever since your husband brought the chair from that furniture store I have been suffering excruciating pains because of my mad love and longing for you. I am but a worm . . . a loathsome creature.

I have but one request. Could you meet me once, just once? I will ask nothing further of you. I of course do not deserve your sympathy, for I have always been nothing but a villain, unworthy even to touch the soles of your feet. But if you will grant me this one request, just out of compassion, my gratitude will be eternal.

Last night I stole out of your residence to write this confession because, even leaving aside the danger, I did not possess the courage to meet you suddenly face to face, without any warning or preparation.

While you are reading this letter, I will be roaming around your house with bated breath. If you will agree to my request, please place your handkerchief on the pot of flowers that stands outside your window. At this signal I will open your front door and enter as a humble visitor. . . .

Thus ended the letter.

Even before Yoshiko had read many pages, some premonition of evil had caused her to become deadly pale. Rising unconsciously, she had fled from the study, from *that chair* upon which she had been seated, and had sought sanctuary in one of the Japanese rooms of her house.

For a moment it had been her intention to stop reading and tear up the eerie message; but somehow, she had read on, with the closely-written sheets laid on a low desk.

Now that she had finished, her premonition was proved correct. That chair on which she had sat from day to day . . . had it really contained a man? If true, what a horrible experience she had unknowingly undergone! A sudden chill came over her, as if ice water had been poured down her back, and the shivers that followed seemed never to stop.

Like one in a trance, she gazed into space. Should she examine the chair? But how could she possibly steel herself for such a horrible ordeal? Even though the chair might now be empty, what about the filthy remains, such as the food and other necessary items which he must have used?

"Madam, a letter for you."

With a start, she looked up and found her maid standing at the doorway with an envelope in her hand.

In a daze, Yoshiko took the envelope and stifled a scream. Horror of horrors! It was another message from the same man! Again her name was written in that same familiar scrawl.

For a long while she hesitated, wondering whether she should open it. At last she mustered up enough courage to break the seal and shakingly took out the pages. The second communication was short and curt, and it contained another breath-taking surprise:

Forgive my boldness in addressing another message to you. To begin with, I merely happen to be one of your ardent admirers. The manuscript which I submitted to you under separate cover was based on pure imagination and my knowledge that you had recently bought *that chair.* It is a sample of my own humble attempts at fictional writing. If you would kindly comment on it, I shall know no greater satisfaction.

For personal reasons I submitted my MS prior to writing this letter of explanation, and I assume you have already read it. How did you find it? If, Madam, you have found it amusing or entertaining in some degree, I shall feel that my literary efforts have not been wasted.

Although I purposely refrained from telling you in the MS, I intend to give my story the title of "The Human Chair."

With all my deepest respects and sincere wishes, I remain,

Cordially yours,

. . . .

ABOUT THE AUTHORS

Robert Bloch (1917–1994) is best remembered as the writer of the book *Psycho,* the basis for Alfred Hitchcock's famous film of the same name. However, this is not to slight his vast, excellent body of work in fiction and film. He got his start writing stories for pulp magazines such as *Weird Tales, Fantastic Adventures,* and *Unknown.* Later in his career he wrote the novels *American Gothic, Firebug,* and *Fear and Trembling,* among many others. He was a prolific scriptwriter in Hollywood, writing *Straight-Jacket, The Night Walker,* and *Asylum.* He also edited several anthologies, including *Psycho-paths* and *Monsters in Our Midst.*

Philip K. Dick (1928–1982) wrote novels and stories which examined "reality" in all of its myriad forms, letting his protagonists, along with his readers, try to sort out what was real and what wasn't. His novel *The Man in the High Castle* won the Hugo Award in 1962, and he also received the John W. Campbell Memorial Award. His work has also inspired films, most notable the Ridley Scott-directed *Blade Runner.*

Richard Matheson (1926–   ) is one of the most respected writers of the past forty years. His novel *I Am Legend* is considered one of the seminal vampire novels, a classic tale of the last man on an Earth populated entirely by the undead. His books *The Shrinking Man* and *Hell House* also broke new ground in the horror field. His work has been adapted for television as well, most notably as several episodes of the original *Twilight Zone* series, and also made into several recent motion pictures, including *What Dreams May Come* and *Stir of Echoes*.

M. R. James (1862–1936) was the most-lauded author of the nineteenth-century ghost story in his time, and his reputation continues decades after his death. A scholar of classical languages and medieval and Biblical legend, he enjoyed a successful career as the director of the Fitzwilliam Museum in Cambridge and as Provost at King's College from 1905–1918 as well as Vice-Chancellor at Cambridge from 1913–1915. He was awarded various honorary degrees during his career and received the Order of Merit in 1930. It is his supernatural fiction, however, that is what he will be remembered for, stories that didn't rely on overt horror or description, but rather the gently lurking terror that crept up on the usually unsuspecting protagonist, until he came face-to-face with what he most feared.

Arthur Machen (1863–1947) held several jobs during his career as a writer, including positions as a clerk for a publishing company and an actor with the Benson Shakespearean Repertory Company. He was also a regular contributor to the *Evening News*. Primarily known for his flamboyant short stories, including his masterpiece, "The Great God Pan," his work explored the nebulous ground between sheer physical horror and psychological terror. Notable novels include *The Hill of Dreams* and *The Three Imposters*.

Robert Aickman (1914–1981) wrote fantasy and horror for much of the latter half of his life. Before turning to writing, he worked for a literary agency, was the drama and film critic for various newspapers, and served as chairman for various opera and ballet companies. Known for his oblique, subtle ghost stories, he practiced the art of misdirection and illusion to sometimes impractical lengths in his fiction. Other stories of his appear in *The Dark Descent* and *Shudder Again*. He also edited the first eight volumes of the *Fontana Books of Great Ghost Stories*.

Nathaniel Hawthorne (1804–1864) is held in high regard as one of America's pioneering and influential authors. Examining the frailty and ambiguity of the human heart in such stories as "The Birthmark," "Dr. Heidigger's Experiment," and "Rappacini's Daughter," he also used man's ever-increasing reliance on the scientific method to illustrate the dangers that tinkering with nature might bring. His work created a literary framework for many authors afterward.

Dennis Etchison's (1943–) penetrating explorations of the power of loss and loneliness and its toll on the human psyche fill his three collections of fiction. He has also written several novels of contemporary urban horror, including *Darkside, The Shadow Man,* and *California Gothic.* He has also written the novelizations for several films, including *Halloween* and *The Fog.* He is a distinctive editor, whose collections *Meta-Horror* and *Cutting Edge* and his acclaimed *Masters of Darkness* series showcased some of the finest horror fiction of the past fifty years.

There can be no doubt that Ramsey Campbell (1946–) has earned his rarefied standing as the most inventive and stylistic horror writer of the past thirty years. Born in Liverpool, England, he attended St. Edward's College, and from there worked as an Inland Revenue clerical officer, librarian, and film reviewer before beginning his writing career. His work has been unanimously praised by audiences, fellow authors, and critics, and has garnered him four British Fantasy Awards, two World Fantasy Awards, and the Stoker Award for best single-author collection. He lives with his family in Merseyside, England.

Edgar Allan Poe (1809–1849) has been called the founder of the American mystery story. Indeed, the annual awards given out by the Mystery Writers of America for excellence in mystery and suspense fiction bear his name. After being dismissed from West Point military academy, he enlisted in the United States Army under an assumed name, and advanced to the rank of sergeant-major. Afterward, he turned to writing and editing, founding *The Penn* magazine and serving as editor of the *Southern Literary Messenger* and *Graham's Magazine*. His short stories "The Murders in the Rue Morgue" and "The Purloined Letter" still rival anything being written today for their inventiveness and attention to detail.

Ambrose Bierce (1842–1914) was second only to Edgar Allan Poe in terms of literary achievement, and is often considered his successor in writing tales of supernatural terror. But he was far more accomplished in life than Poe, serving on the Union side during the Civil War, and advancing to the rank of major. He also was a famous columnist for several major city newspapers, including the San Francisco *Examiner* and the New York *Journal*. Later in life he was a Washington correspondent for *Cosmopolitan*. He traveled to Mexico in the early part of the twentieth century and joined Pancho Villa's forces, in whose service he was presumably killed in action during the battle of Ojinaga in January, 1914.

Edogawa Rampo (1894–1965) was the pseudonym of Taro Hirai, the man widely credited with creating the modern Japanese mystery story. His seminal story, "The Two-Sen Copper Coin" is recognized as the first short Japanese mystery fiction. Influenced by the works of Edgar Allan Poe (his pseudonym is a play on Poe's name) he first wrote tales of horror and fantasy, then novel-length thrillers. He was also a staunch advocate of the mystery in all of its forms, especially by Western authors.

From time immemorial, they have stalked the night . . .

TALES OF THE UNDEAD

☐ **CELEBRITY VAMPIRES**   UE2667—$4.99
   Martin H. Greenberg, editor
From a Catskill song and dance team, to an act of kindness by Marilyn
Monroe, to a mysterious admirer of Tallulah Bankhead, here are 20 origi-
nal tales about those who thirst to drink the rich, dark wine of fame.

☐ **DRACULA: PRINCE OF DARKNESS**   UE2531—$4.99
   Martin H. Greenberg, editor
A blood-draining collection of all-original Dracula stories. From Dracula's
traditional stalking grounds to the heart of modern-day cities, the Prince
of Darkness casts his spell over his prey in a private blood drive from
which there is no escape!

☐ **THE TIME OF THE VAMPIRES**   UE2693—$5.50
   P.N. Elrod & Martin H. Greenberg, editors
Creatures of legend—or something all too real? From a vampire blessed
by Christ to the truth about the notorious Oscar Wilde to a tale of vampir-
ism and the Bow Street Runners, here are 18 original tales of vampires
from Tanya Huff, P.N. Elrod, Lois Tilton, and others.

☐ **VAMPIRE DETECTIVES**   UE2626—$4.99
   Martin H. Greenberg, editor
From newly-made vampire detective Victory Nelson who must defend To-
ronto against one of her own, to a cop on the trail of an international serial
killer with a bloodlust that just won't quit, here are blood-chilling new tales
of vampires who stalk the night in search of crimes to commit or criminals
to be stopped.

Buy them at your local bookstore or use this convenient coupon for ordering.

PENGUIN USA   P.O. Box 999—Dep. #17109, Bergenfield, New Jersey 07621

Please send me the DAW BOOKS I have checked above, for which I am enclosing
$_____ (please add $2.00 to cover postage and handling). Send check or money
order (no cash or C.O.D.'s) or charge by Mastercard or VISA (with a $15.00 minimum). Prices and
numbers are subject to change without notice.

Card #_____ Exp. Date _____
Signature_____
Name_____
Address_____
City _____ State _____ Zip Code _____

For faster service when ordering by credit card call 1-800-253-6476

Allow a minimum of 4-6 weeks for delivery. This offer is subject to change without notice.